ANDREW

MORE

THAN

BLOOD

'A friend loves at all times, and a brother is born for a time of adversity.'

(Proverbs 17:17)

One

'Before you know it'

Orange flames burned bright on the dark horizon, roaring from gas towers erected from the Teesside chemical plant on the coast.

Bomber watched the flaring gas from the passenger seat of the Toyota Hilux, listening to the music that played low on the cab's radio, fighting against the continuous drum of heavy rain against the roof.

'Where the hell is he?' Bomber said, checking his watch. 'It's after two and I've got shit I could be doing.'

'Like what? Wrapping presents?' Quinn said in the driver's seat. He pushed his brown rimmed glasses back up the bridge of his crooked nose. 'You work for Michael, and Michael wants you here.'

'You might not have a life beyond the brothel and Michael, but I do.'

'I have a fucking life.'

'Yeah? You chase up that Catherine yet? Get your money back?'

'Not yet, no. But I will.' Quinn saw a pair of approaching headlights and climbed out into the moonlit countryside car park. 'Here is,' he said, the vapour from his breath visible in the cold air. He ran a hand through his short brown hair, using the rain to help finger-comb it into a side parting.

Bomber also climbed out and pulled on a pair of black leather gloves. The pair were dressed in dark trousers and thick, dark coats, each with their collars turned up to fight off the night's wet chill. Quinn was in his mid-forties and heavily built with a six foot seven frame. Bomber was almost ten years younger, standing five foot eleven. His hair was dark and cropped short to his head with thick sideboards running down either side of his face. The pair walked to the rear of the Hilux and Quinn dropped the rear tailgate and lifted the blacked-out window of the fixed cab. He then reached in and grabbed hold of a man's ankle.

Michael circled them once and crawled to a stop, his headlights illuminating the rear of the pickup.

Dressed only in a pair of navy-blue chequered boxer-shorts and black socks, the skinny male laid there shivering, bruised and silent, a red gimp ball strapped to his mouth, his hands duct taped behind his back. The man kicked and struggled as Quinn pulled him into the rain, a look of fear visible in his bruising eyes.

5

Michael allowed his door to swing open before opening up his dark umbrella and stepping out into the rain. He was a well-dressed man in his late thirties, dressed in a dark charcoal suit with a white shirt and long dark coat. As always, he was well groomed with a shaved receding hairline. He lit a cigarette with his silver petrol lighter and watched Quinn pull the semi-naked male from the back of the Hilux. The man landed hard on the loose gravel, pushing a muffled moan up passed the red ball in his mouth.

Quinn reached down and grabbed him by his mop of brown hair, pulling him to his knees. 'Get the fuck up,' he said.

The man grunted in protest, feeling the stinging rain cascade down over his skinny chest and the cold wet stones bite into his knees. On his left shoulder was a tattoo, clean and clear in the rain: Paratrooper wings.

'William, William, William. What am I going to do with you?' Michael said, raising his voice to be heard over the sound of rain beating off his umbrella.

Will tried to speak, but the ball in his mouth allowed only muffles and moans to be heard. A sharp pain flashed across his face as Bomber threw a fast right, bruising his left eye.

'When Mr Maloney is speaking to you, you fucking listen,' Bomber said. Quinn reached down and pulled Will back to his knees, realigning his head to face his boss.

Michael crouched down to Will's eye level and took a deep drag on his cigarette. The red cinders glowed brighter, reflecting the fiery depths of his cruelty. He grabbed hold of Will's bony cheeks and pulled his face close to his. 'I don't appreciate being made a fool of, especially by a skinny little maggot like you,' he said. 'The only reason you're not lying face down in the fucking river is because I still require the gear inspecting.'

Tears spilled from Will's eyes.

'So, you're gonna get on the phone. You're gonna give your brother a ring. And he's gonna do the fucking job for you. Otherwise, things are gonna get very uncomfortable for you. Nod if you understand.'

Will nodded his head, his eyes wide, vapour from his breath expelling from his nostrils.

Michael pushed his face back, releasing his grip on his cheeks, and allowed him to fall back onto the wet ground. 'I want him here by Saturday.' He stood up straight and turned to Quinn and Bomber. 'Let the prick walk home.'

Quinn nodded.

Michael turned back to his car. Behind him he could hear Quinn and Bomber removing the duct tape and gimp ball from Will and throwing him back his clothes. He hated being played for a fool, and Will had done just that.

'There won't be a second time,' he said to himself.

*

Nausea hit Shaw the instant he regained consciousness. In the background he could hear banging. He opened his eyes, resurrecting the throbbing in his head. The banging sounded again, only this time louder. He peeled his face off the living room sofa and sat upright, holding his head in his hands, trying to gain some control of the throbbing. The television was still turned on and tuned into the national weather, where an attractive woman with dark bobbed hair talked about the mixture of rain, sleet and snow that was due to hit the North East of England and Scotland over Christmas and the New Year. A plate cemented with microwave Chinese food and a half-filled glass of whiskey sat at his feet. The curtains were closed, limiting the light in the room to that of the television set. Three more bangs sounded, testing the front door's hinges and locks.

'I'm coming,' he said.

The impatient visitor banged three more times.

'I'm fucking coming!' He knocked over a quarter bottle of whiskey at the side of the sofa and cursed, using the arm of the chair as support to pick it up.

Dressed only in a pair of navy-blue briefs and carrying a three day growth of facial hair, Shaw made his way down the passage to the front door. Standing six foot, Shaw held a strong frame and wide shoulders. A full sleeve tattoo covered his right arm and shoulder and a half sleeve covered his left bicep and shoulder. His body was mapped with scars, from gunshot wounds to fist fights; his most prominent ones being a series of stretching scars that webbed out across his left cheek, reaching as far back as his ear, and a gruesome scar that cut through his right calf, from his knee to his ankle.

He unlocked the front door and opened it. Behind it was a bulldog looking man with a shaved head and fat round cheeks. Shaw slammed the door on him; only for the man to wedge it open with his foot.

'Oh no ye don't, Ryan-lad,' the man said, emphasising the 'oh' in a broad Glaswegian accent.

In no fit state to battle with the Scotsman, Shaw released the pressure on the door. 'What the fuck do you want, Boyd?'

'Now, now, Ryan. That drunken temper of yers is what got ye 'ere

7

in the first place. Remember?' Boyd's blue Rangers T-shirt was tight against his body, exposing every curve and crease in his fat, broad torso. His black tracksuit bottoms were dotted with cream paint and his once white trainers were stained black with age. His pale face was red and flustered with perforations of sweat seeping through his brow. 'Still getting blootered, I see,' he added, noticing the quarter bottle of whiskey in Shaw's hand and the hungover state in which he held it.

'What do you want?'

Boyd waved a brown A4 paper envelope in front of him. 'Well I didn't come all the way te fucken Dagenham te catch up on oul times. Amy's been waiting months for ye te sign these fucken papers.' He offered them to him, but Shaw showed no sign of accepting them. 'Just sign 'em, would ye.' He threw the envelope past Shaw's head and into the flat behind him. 'I'll be back tomorrow te collect 'em. And if they're not signed, I promise ye, regardless of history, I'll not be so polite. Oh, byraway, Merry Christmas.'

Shaw slammed the door on him and walked back to his couch, stepping on the brown paper envelope. He made his way back into the stale, thick air of the living room and sat on the couch. All the painful, unforgivable memories of how he'd treated his wife before his time in prison came flooding back to him, letting loose an ache of self-hatred in his heart.

He'd met his wife, Amy, eleven years ago, almost to the day, on an icy December afternoon in Arbroath. He'd been shopping on Christmas leave when an old lady had fallen on the high street. Other than himself, the only other person to attend to her was her. He remembered her celestial beauty: Long dark hair, wide hazel eyes with a slender, toned figure, all wrapped up in smooth tanned skin. Even after the ambulance had arrived and taken the old lady away, they had stayed together, walking, talking and shopping. She had even helped him choose his mother's gift.

He removed his silver watch from his wrist and held it, caressing its smooth glass face in hope that a warm memory would halt his pain. Amy had bought him the watch for his twenty-sixth birthday, the first birthday they'd spent together. It was the only thing he had left from his life with Amy, after losing his wedding ring on operations, and leaving everything else to her and his son, Douglas. The second-hand ticked round, reminding him that time waited for no man.

'They should have left me in the dirt to rot,' he said out loud. He bent forward and picked up the glass of whiskey at his feet from the night

8

before and swallowed it in one. The whiskey was rough on his throat and did nothing to help his headache, but the alcohol did ease his mind and halt any coming tears.

He placed his watch on the TV unit and headed for the bathroom. He'd had hundreds of cold showers over the past twenty-five months, but this had been his first since leaving prison five weeks ago. He'd rang Amy last night in hope that she would allow him to apologise for all the heartache he'd caused her. He'd also asked to speak with his four-year-old son, to wish him a Merry Christmas, and for him to tell him that he'd always be here for him, no matter what. Amy had refused both. The only conversation he'd received was an argument.

He finished his shower, dried and pulled on a pair of old clothes. An old friend from the Regiment had stuck his neck out and arranged work for him. Not the kind of work he was used to, but work nonetheless. He grabbed his rucksack and headed for the front door.

*

The smell of oil and metal was thick in the factory air, and the deafening sound of roaring machinery drowned out all but the loudest of noises. Shaw was only a third of his way through his twelve-hour nightshift and already he was feeling tired and drained. With a last minute sprint from home, he'd managed to make it to the required platform just in time to catch the tube. The train journey had been busy with commuters and had taken its usual forty-five minutes to complete, stopping only once for a line change.

The shop floor's fifteen-minute break was due to be called and Shaw seriously needed a hit of caffeine. His hangover had faded compared to when he'd first opened his eyes, but his lack of sleep and the constant roar from the machinery was getting the better of him. As expected, his line manager appeared, dressed in his usual clean, tight fitted red coveralls, bright white hard hat and his crystal, unscratched goggles. Lee Allen was a heavily over weight man in his late forties who suffered from diabetes and a bad case of psoriasis. He held up his right hand and gave Shaw the peace sign, followed by a snapping action. *Two minutes till break.* Shaw acknowledged with a thumbs up and the production line came to a grinding halt minutes later, allowing the eighteen workers to take their allocated fifteen-minute break. The majority of the line would be running for the smoking shelter outside, but what Shaw required was in the vending machine in the canteen. The cool air licked his clammy skin as he exited the workshop floor. He removed his hard hat and goggles and released a sigh of relief, pulling the heavy ear defenders off his hot sweaty ears, and ran a hand through his damp hair in a futile effort to ease the throbbing.

'Grabbing a coffee?' a work colleague said from the machine next to his.

Shaw nodded. 'Need to get some change first. I'll see you in there.' The conversation between him and his brother-in-law had been replaying itself over and over in his head, his words repeating themselves like a scratched disc. *Just sign the divorce papers.* That and the brown paper envelope on his floor back in his flat were the only things on his mind. He knew his marriage was over, her respect for him had died the second he'd struck that first police officer, but Boyd's visit had made it all the more real. He'd always hoped she would have forgiven him and, maybe one day, taken him back. But deep down he knew that was never to be. He'd fucked it up, just like he'd fucked up everything else.

He entered the changing room and approached his locker. On his right was a young Central European man speaking foreign into his mobile phone. Judging by his body language and a few key Slavic phrases Shaw was familiar with, he could tell he was getting highly frustrated over a conversation involving money. He removed the padlock from his grey locker and opened it with a loud creek, not bothering the young Pole's obvious argument. He slid a few coins of the top shelve and checked his mobile phone: Twelve missed calls, one voice mail message and four text alerts, all from his younger brother, William.

17:58. VOICE MAIL MESSAGE.

18:13. RYAN PLZZ RING ME WEN U GET THIS!! VERY IMPORTANT.

19:01. ANS UR FUKIN FONE MAN. ITS AN EMERGENCY.

20:12. CUM ON M8 WAT THE FUK U DOIN. RING ME. WILL.

He phoned the voice mailing service and placed a finger in his free ear to block out the Pole's loud rant.

'Ryan, it's Will. Give us ring back, mate when get this. Got myself into a bit of bother and really need your help. Cheers.'

Shaw dialled his number. It had been almost six months since Will had contacted him. The last time they'd spoken he'd been in prison.

'About fucking time,' Will said the instant he answered. 'Where have you been?'

'I'm good thanks, yeah. It's great to be out of prison. How are you?'

'What you doing tomorrow?'

'Working, why?'

'I need you to come to Sunderland.'

'No can do, mate. I'm on nights till Monday. Besides, I'm on probation. Why? What's happened?'

'You have to. If you don't…' Will's voice trailed off into nothing. 'I'm in big fucking trouble, Ryan, and I need your help.'

'What have you done?'

'It's a long story.'

'Then brief me.'

'Has our mam mentioned the girl I met from Sunderland?'

'The one off the internet?' Shaw said. 'What about her?'

Will inhaled, as if preparing himself for a confession. 'Well she introduced me to her cousin and we all started to hang out a little.'

'And?'

Will paused. 'And now I kinda owe him, and don't really know how to pay him back.'

'Right,' Shaw said, taking a seat on one of the fixed wooden benches. 'Well I've got no money to give you. I barely make enough to feed myself.'

'It's not money he wants.'

'Will, just go back home. Fuck him off,' he said, avoiding the subject of him getting involved.

'It's not as easy as that.'

'Of course it is. You just leave.'

Will released a sigh of guilt. 'They know where our mam lives.'

'And why should that be an issue?' Shaw paused, taking Will's silence as an indication of caution. 'Is our mam in any danger?'

Will said nothing.

'Will?' Shaw could feel his bad day was about to get even worse. His head throbbed and his eyes ached, and now there was this.

'I think so, yeah.'

'Are you fucking kidding me?' Shaw stood up from the bench and started pacing the room. The Polish man ended his call and left. 'How?'

Will remained silent.

'Will, how's our mam in danger?'

'If I don't get him what he wants, he said he'd hurt her. And me.'

'Who did? The cousin?'

'Yes.'

Shaw pulled the phone away from his ear and interlocked his

11

fingers behind his head. He stared at a health and safety notice pinned to the locker-room wall and filled his lungs, trying to get a grasp of what his brother was telling him. 'And is he in a position to hurt her?' Shaw said, placing the phone back to his ear.

'What do you mean?'

'Would he hurt her? Or is he full of shit?'

'Yes he'd hurt her.'

Shaw sighed. 'So what is it he wants exactly?'

'You're an expert on automatic weapons and the like, aren't you?' Will asked him, knowing fine well he was.

'What? This is a fucking windup, isn't it?' he said. 'I'm not getting wrapped up in any of that shit. I'm on fucking probation.'

'You are though, aren't you?'

'I know how to use them, Will, but that's all. I'm no fucking expert.' An unnerving knot formed in his stomach as he waited for Will to respond.

'I know you did more than that when you were in the Marines, Ryan. Come on, I was in the Army too, you know.'

Will explained the trouble he was in; how he'd talked openly about his days in the Parachute Regiment and all the action he'd apparently seen, including a handful of impressive skills which he claimed to possess, one of which being firearms.

'And now he's found out you're full of shit?' Shaw said.

'I didn't think he'd actually want me to inspect any, though, did I?'

Shaw remained silent, still trying to get his head around it all.

'All I need is for you to come to Sunderland and check a few over. That's all. It should only take you a couple of hours. No one will even know you're gone.'

'And what about mam?'

'If you do the inspection, she'll be okay,' Will said. 'Besides, it's not as if we can take her anywhere. There is no one we can take her to and I don't have the money to put her up anywhere.'

Shaw sat back down and rubbed his aching forehead with his free hand. 'And if I do this inspection, your debt will be paid?'

'Yeah. Everyone will be okay. And you'll be back at work before you know it.'

A break in Will's voice told him otherwise.

'I can't believe you've gone and done this,' Shaw said. 'If I miss any kind of appointment, they'll send me straight back to prison.'

'I wouldn't ask if it wasn't serious.'

'You haven't left me with much of a choice, have you?'

'I'm sorry, Ryan.'

'I'm sure you are. I'll ring you in the morning once I've finished work.' He thought about leaving now and getting up north as soon as he could but decided against it. After all, what would it achieve? He wasn't required until tomorrow and he still had his own life to try and put back together once the inspection had been done. Shaw hung up and rushed back onto the shop floor, his body still craving the caffeine he'd promised it. The machines were already up and running by the time he got back, with their operators waiting impatiently for the progress to restart.

Two

'It'll happen tomorrow. Probably'

'We are at our terminated station, sir,' the ticket collector said, waking Shaw from his sleep.

As soon as he'd arrived home from work, Shaw had started to pack, packing only one change of clothing and a toothbrush, not intending on staying in Sunderland any longer than two nights. He'd grabbed a shower and dressed himself in his brown leather boots, blue denim jeans, grey T-shirt and khaki-green surplus style jacket. Not forgetting his watch. He'd rung Victoria Lane, his probation officer, around 08:00 and told her he'd been feeling rotten, and that a couple of days off work maybe required, whilst also asking for permission to miss their next two appointments due to his illness. Because of the progress in his therapy and his cooperation since leaving prison, Victoria had agreed under the strict condition that if he was to leave his house for anywhere but the local shop, he had to inform her. He'd arrived at Kings Cross station an hour later and purchased his ticket to Newcastle. For the journey he'd bought himself a baguette, a bottle of water and a newspaper. Within minutes of getting comfortable in his seat, Shaw's eyes had grown heavy and closed, dropping him into a deep sleep.

He stepped off the train, recalling the last time he'd visited Sunderland. He'd been a coffin bearer for a friend who'd died in a car crash six years ago. Other than that, he was totally unfamiliar with the city, although he'd heard plenty about it from a young Bootneck he'd served with called Dinger. He recalled how much of a Black Cats fan Dinger was, and how he'd worn the city's football badge on one of his skinny white arms; showing it off every chance he got. He wiped the thought of Dinger from his mind and focused on his brother's problems. He swigged down the last of his water and threw the empty bottle into the waste bin. Newcastle station was alive with activity, packed with busy, disregarding people. Shaw's keen intuition, a perception heightened through intense military experiences, picked out the flustered, irritated Caucasian man in his cheap suit blazer that was a little too large for him, the elderly Middle Eastern man who mumbled words of prayer at a younger, recently shaved man, and the short African woman who stood staring at a blank departures and arrivals screen, her bright traditional brocade dress also a little too large, each of them showing a trait common with suicide bombers. Shaw disregarded them and walked out through the main doors.

14

His brother stood resting against the driver's door of his maroon Saxo, sucking on a cigarette. Will had lost weight since Shaw had seen him last, and his once short, brown hair was now longer and cut into a typical indie-boy fashion. The ground was wet, and mounds of filthy slush lay frozen in the dark corners of the surrounding buildings.

'You still smoking?' Shaw said.

Will's eyes smiled behind his sunglasses as he flicked away his cigarette butt. 'Well, we don't all have your willpower, do we?'

Shaw threw his hold-all onto the back seat and climbed in the front. 'Thought you'd got rid of this piece of shit?' he said, applying his seatbelt.

Will laughed. 'Nothing wrong with her.' He gunned the ignition and sparked the one litre engine to life, turning down the dance music that erupted from the speakers.

'What happened to your eye?' Shaw said, noticing the yellowing bruise behind the right lens of Will's glasses.

'Had a bit of an accident,' he said, removing his glasses.

'Let me guess. Walked into a door?'

Will said nothing and pushed the gearstick into first.

'So tell me about this cousin,' Shaw said, waiting until Will had started to move.

'He's called Michael Maloney. He's about your age.' Will looked left and right before pulling out into the flowing traffic. 'He owns a club in the town called Vanilla.'

'What about his social standing?'

'He gets a few hard hitters in his club every now and again who he sits and drinks with.'

'So, he's not someone who'll rollover if I break his arm?'

Will laughed. 'Unlikely. Besides, Quinn and Bomber would see that didn't happen.'

'And they are?'

Will turned on the windscreen wipers to fight off the incoming snow. 'They're his muscle. Quinn's his main pit-bull. I think him, and Michael go way back. He's the big dozy looking one out of the two. You can't miss him. Bomber on the other hand's more civilised, but don't mistake that for being soft.' Will subconsciously touched his bruised eye.

Shaw rubbed his forehead, feeling the lack of sleep getting the better of him. 'And the deal's for real?'

'As far as I'm aware.'

'So how did shagging some lass off the internet turn into this? I mean, you only met her a few weeks ago, for Christ's sake.'

'I'm not quite sure. She took me to her cousin's club to meet him one night. Told him I was an Ex-Para.'

'So how long had you been seeing her before see introduced the pair of you?'

'Two nights, maybe. I figured she was just showing off. But now…'

'But now you think you were baited?' Shaw paused. 'If I do this inspection, will that honestly be the end of it?'

'What do you mean if? If you don't do the inspection, Ryan they'll fucking kill me. Then they'll kill mam.'

A silence stretched between them before Shaw spoke. 'So, how's it gonna work?'

'What do you mean?'

'When and where are we doing it?'

'Kimberly's going to sort something with him today. So we'll probably see him tomorrow at some point.'

A knot of muscle flexed in Shaw's jaw. 'You said it would only take a couple of hours.'

'And the inspection probably will.'

'Will, I've got to get back. If anyone finds out I'm even up here, let alone the reason why, I'm back inside.'

'Yeah, I know,' he said. 'It'll happen tomorrow. Probably.'

'That's one too many probablys for my liking.' Shaw looked out of his window, frustrated with his brother's disregard for other people. 'You're unbelievable. Do you know that?' He looked back at him. 'And how is it they even know where our mam lives? We've never taken our shit home. Not even girls.'

'What do you want me to say? I fucked up.'

'Yes, you did.' Shaw turned back to the window and looked out at the Angel of the North standing tall and proud in the swirling snow, its wings outstretched. 'So why did you say you would inspect the guns if you knew you couldn't?'

'I thought he was full shit. You know what these gangster wannabes are like.'

Shaw looked at him. 'Actually no, I don't.' The traffic started to slow as road signs came into view, warning of road works ahead. Amber flashing lights pierced the snow, guiding the traffic towards their required lanes. 'What were you getting in return?' he said out of the blue.

'What? Nothing?'

'Come off it. You must have been getting something. You wouldn't have gone along with it for nothing. What was it? Money? Drink?' Shaw paused. 'Drugs?' Will's guilty silence was all he needed. 'Drugs. You're taking fucking drugs again?'

'You can't say anything, all the shit you poured down your neck.'

'My situation was fucking different. Besides, drink never got me kicked out of the Marines.'

'No. But kicking fuck out of three coppers and half the camp guard whilst drunk did, though,' Will said, manoeuvring the Saxo into the required lane. 'Look, you only have to inspect them, that's all.'

'That's all.' Shaw laughed, shaking his head. 'I don't know if I've said it enough or not, mate, but I've only just come out of the fucking nick. One wrong turn and I'm back inside for another twenty-four months. And that's without adding the extra years I'll get for handling illegal firearms.

'So where are we going now?' he asked him, breaking the uncomfortable atmosphere that had formed inside the car.

'I was gonna take us for a pint.'

'Will, I'm fucked. I've been up for nearly twenty-four hours and I'd rather have a clear head in the morning.'

'Come on, only a few, maybe a game off pool or something. We've not seen each other in ages.'

'And who's fault's that? It's not as if you didn't know where I was.'

Will wound down the driver's window and lit up another cigarette, momentarily filling the cab with smoke. 'Come on, I know just the place.'

A little while later, Will pulled into a side street in the heart of Sunderland's city centre. Expensive looking buildings lined either side of the street, all of them painted white with three stories to their structure, each one appearing to be occupied by a solicitor, a letting agent or a quirky coffee shop. The road was dark and cobbled, thick with slushy puddles from the morning's snowfall.

'We're here,' Will said, clipping the curb as he parked.

Shaw opened his eyes and climbed out into the light snow, burying his head into his shoulders.

'Down here.' Will skipped down several stone steps, leading him into a basement style bar. The place was split into two main rooms and surprisingly spacious for a basement. The first room had an enormous sixty inch flat screen television mounted on the wall, surrounded by cheap looking leather sofas. The second room was much larger, containing fourteen American style pool tables, the main drinking bar and a traditional looking jukebox that was playing a song by The Doors. Images of Marilyn Monroe, Julia Roberts from 'Pretty Woman' and John F Kennedy decorated the walls of the venue, including the odd state side number plate and numerous NFL tops. Only three of the fourteen tables were in use, their large illuminated Budweiser lamps hanging low above them. Shaw counted six men on the first table, two middle aged men on the second and two young women on the last.

'Two pints of Carling please, sweetheart,' Will said to the barmaid.

The barmaid was a chubby girl with long mousey-brown hair and a round pretty face. 'Coming up.'

Shaw scanned the bar, taking in every feature. It was a bar typical of his brother, fake and over the top. 'So what should I expect when I meet him tomorrow?' he said, leaning against the bar.

'Truthfully, I'm not sure. He'll probably want to meet you at his club. Thinks it makes him look important; sat behind his large oak desk like some fucking Bond villain.'

'I take it this Quinn and Bomber will be present tomorrow?'

The barmaid returned, carrying two pints of lager.

Will paid her and turned back to Shaw. 'Oh aye.' He watched one of the women playing pool take a shot. 'They're always somewhere close by. Fancy a game of pool?' Before Shaw could reply, Will was asking the barmaid for some balls.

'What have you told them about me?' Shaw said, dreading the answer.

'Nothing. All they know is that you were a sergeant in the Marines. You get the balls. I'll grab the drinks.' The pair headed over to a table and the recently illuminated lamp hanging above it.

Feeling no more relaxed about tomorrow, Shaw racked up the balls and watched as Will broke. 'You can't have forgotten that much in nine years, about guns I mean.'

'Let's be honest. I didn't know that much to begin with. Plus it's been nearly a decade since I played with one. I don't even think I could strip one now, let alone inspect it.'

Shaw held the cue beneath his chin. 'So how come he knows where mam lives?'

18

Will had been waiting for him to ask the question again. 'The Saxo packed in last week and I needed a lift home.'

'Will,' he said, disappointed. 'You know the craic about taking shit home, especially after Dad died.'

'I didn't think.'

Shaw picked up his pint and took a mouthful. 'What does he drive?'

'What's that got to do with it?'

'What's he drive?' Shaw repeated.

'A Nissan GT-R, but that's not why I accepted the lift.'

'Of course it's not,' he said.

Will looked up at him and took another shot.

Three

'The less he knew, the less he was involved'

Shaw's throat was dry. His tongue was swollen and stuck to the roof of his mouth, a feeling he'd grown accustomed to before his time in prison. He opened his mouth and yawned, arching his back off the sofa to stretch out his stiffened joints. A young woman in her mid-twenties, wearing a white cotton thong and thick cream woollen socks, pulled up high above her knees, walked in front of him. Her glossy jet-black hair tumbled forwards over her sun kissed shoulders and onto her round breasts as she bent forward over the coffee table.

'Morning,' Shaw said.

The female stood up straight and turned to face him, as if she'd always been aware of his presence. His eyes followed the contours of her body beneath her surgically enhanced breasts, towards the triangle of the white cotton thong that dipped between her smooth thighs. Her stomach was flat and firm with a diamanté stud piercing her naval. She stood in front of him, parading herself for her one man audience. Her deep green eyes washed over his physique and tattoos and focused on the scars webbing the left side of his face, an air of judgment behind them, before she turned and walked back the way she'd came.

Shaw sat upright and adjusted the single man duvet, making sure it was still covering the lower portion of his body.

'Feeling rough?' a familiar male voice said, interrupting his train of thought, a random thought he hadn't had for almost a year.

Shaw looked over his left shoulder at Will. 'No, just tired, and a little stiff,' he said.

Will made his way into the kitchen. 'Fancy a cuppa?' he said with a raised voice.

'Coffee please.' Shaw pulled on the denim jeans he'd worn the day before. 'Milk with two,' he added, following his brother barefoot and topless into the kitchen. The cream coloured floor tiles were cold against the soles of his feet and a moist chill nipped at his naked shoulders from an open window.

Will placed two mugs on the bench in front of him and dropped a spoon full of coffee into each.

'That was never your lass parading around the flat with fuck all on, was it?'

Will poured boiling water into the two mugs, simultaneously stirring with his free hand. 'Yep,' he said with a smug grin, stirring in his two sugars and milk. 'Gorgeous, isn't she?'

'What did she see in you?' he said with a smile.

'What's that supposed to mean?' Will handed Shaw his steaming mug. 'She liked my Para pictures, actually. Thought I was well hot.'

A door opened in the corridor across from the living room, interrupting their conversation. Kimberly's long, glossy black hair with a cut in fringe was tied up behind her head, complimenting her sharp attractive features. Shaw regarded her with appraising eyes. She now wore a pair of blood-red high heeled shoes, tight navy-blue jeans and an equally tight dark grey turtle-neck sweater.

'We'll be heading to the club in the next half hour,' she said to Will in a soft Mackem accent. 'I'm popping out first, though, so make sure that front room's tidy,' she added, closing the door behind her.

Shaw looked at his watch, 09:46. 'So that's where we're doing this, at the club?' He put the mug to his lips and took a mouthful.

Will took a sip of his. 'Yeah. We'll follow her in the Saxo.'

Shaw placed the steaming mug back on the kitchen worktop. 'Am I okay for a shower?'

'Yeah, of course,' Will said.

*

Will's windscreen wipers struggled to keep off the thrashing rain and sleet, limiting his view. Shaw's stomach was doing summersaults, alive with apprehension. He hated feeling wide open and vulnerable, and Will had managed to do just that. He thought again about the young driver he'd once called Dinger, remembering his straight, blond, almost white hair, and his child-like feminine face.

'We're nearly there,' Will said, again breaking Shaw's train of thought. He pulled up behind Kimberly's red MR2 and Shaw watched her climb out and run to the shelter of some roofed wooden steps, using her tiny black handbag for protection against the rain. They'd parked up outside what appeared to be the rear entrance to the club. Chrome kegs and empty yellow crates lined the walls, along with red wheelie bins and black bin bags filled with rubbish. A black pickup truck, the type with white writing on its extra-large tyres, was also parked in the small compound, taking up the majority of the space. The pair of them climbed out into the rain and Will jogged to the shelter of the canopy, not wanting to ruin his hair, and smiled up at a CCTV camera that watched the base of the steps. Shaw followed, not as bothered by the rain as his brother or Kimberly, stopping half way up behind his brother whilst Kimberly spoke to the doorman at the top. After a small exchange of words, the heavily built doorman stepped aside, allowing them access. He stared at Shaw, long and hard, as if challenging him to do something. His hair was shaved tight to his head and his skin was sunbed-tanned. He wore a smartly pressed blue shirt with black trousers and shoes.

Inside the club the lighting was low, casting an ambient glow throughout the building. A pleasant smell filled the air, whilst the song 'Gold Digger' by Kanye West played through the club's speakers. The walls were painted in a pastel red paint and lined with mirrors, creating the illusion of a bigger venue. Domed CCTV cameras were placed strategically throughout the white coloured ceiling, watching every move the clientele made.

A male with dark cropped hair and thick sideboards approached the three of them as they entered the main room, his eyes locking onto Shaw's.

'Michael's waiting in his office,' Bomber said to Kimberly.

She thanked him and led the way. To their right, a beautiful platinum haired dancer rehearsed her routine on the stage, sliding head first down a chrome pole, her legs open horizontally above her. Shaw noted the way her eyes shadowed the four of them as they walked through the club and through a door labelled 'Private'. The windowless corridor behind was short and well lit with two doors either side. Both were varnished a deep brown with the right-hand one labelled 'Manager's Office'. Kimberly knocked and entered.

'Wait here,' Bomber told Will. He looked at Shaw. 'After you.'

The office was compact and cold. The same dark red pastel paint coloured the walls and the carpet was dark grey. A flat screen TV and a four-drawer metal filing cabinet lined the left wall with a simple drink's unit in the corner. A two-seat leather sofa sat against the right wall with three black and white photographs mounted above it. The first was of the man he assumed to be Michael holding a younger, fair haired lad in a friendly headlock in the stands of a football stadium. The second was of him sitting on the bonnet of a classic Porsche 911. And the third was of Michael again, this time posing in shorts and boxing gloves, his fists up in front of him in an orthodox pose. But the most dominating piece of furniture was a large oak desk situated directly opposite the door. Sat behind it was the same man from the photographs, only older. Kimberly rested her buttocks on the corner of his desk, her legs crossed in front of her.

'So you're Sergeant Shaw?' Michael said, looking him up and down. 'I've heard a lot about you.'

Shaw couldn't see his legs, but he assumed he was wearing dark trousers to match his pressed white shirt and black tie.

'Help yourself to a drink.' Michael nodded his head towards the drink's cabinet.

Shaw glanced at the cabinet and wanted one. 'I'm good, thanks,' he said.

'Please yourself. Do you know who I am?'

'I have a fair idea.'

'Then I take it you know why you're here?'

Shaw held his focus on Michael's eyes. 'Yeah.'

'Excellent. Then I don't have to explain myself.' Michael stood up and walked from behind his desk. 'Follow me.'

'Before I go anywhere, I want your word that no harm will come to either Will or our mam if I do this.'

Michael stopped at the door to his office and turned to face him. 'I give you my word that they will come to harm if you don't. How's that?'

They collected Will outside and made their way back through the club and down a tight back staircase into a brightly lit corridor. Michael opened a door at the end and stepped through into a dimly lit, cold room. A large male wearing a crisp clean shirt and trousers welcomed them in. He stood at least five inches taller than Shaw and looked down at him as he pushed a pair of brown rimmed glasses back up the bridge of his nose. Shaw could smell the cheap aftershave on him as he brushed passed, followed by the overpowering smell of cold damp plaster and stale beer. The walls of the room were unpainted and grey, lined with chrome kegs and stacked with yellow crates that were filled with various bottles of different colours. An old desk painted white, similar to the ones used in primary schools with the hinged lids, sat in the centre of the room, along with a lone wooden chair.

Shaw sized up the room, mentally noting all the exits, who was in the room with him, and where they were all situated. The only exit from the badly lit, windowless room was the door from which he'd just entered. Bomber positioned himself to the left of the table, resting his back against the wall and folding his arms in front of him. He was wearing dark trousers, shoes and a white shirt with the sleeves rolled up, exposing tanned, hairy forearms. To the right of the room, resting against one of the several chrome kegs was another man standing equal height to Shaw. He had short dark hair and prominent sticky-out ears. Shaw's heart pounded faster in his

23

chest, now realising his own stupidity. The door closed behind him, limiting the light within the room to the single bulb hanging above the desk. Shaw looked behind him, only to confirm his suspicions. The big man wearing the glasses had closed the door and positioned himself in front of it, adopting a similar pose to Bomber

'Take a seat,' Michael said.

'I'll stand thanks,' Shaw said, sweat secreting from his brow, despite the cold temperature of the room.

'That wasn't an offer. Sit the fuck down.'

Shaw's eyes scanned the room, searching for a reaction in his hired muscle, but found only empty stares looking back at him. He also noticed there were no CCTV cameras in this room, although the rest of the club was kitted out like the 'Big Brother house'. Figuring it was in his best interest, he pulled the wooden chair out from beneath the table and sat down. Kimberly walked past him on his right, her blood-red heels striking the silence within the room like a hammer through glass, coming to a rest at the far end of the room behind her cousin, as if getting front row seats for the entertainment.

'Michael,' Will said from over Shaw's right shoulder.

Michael's eyes stared at him with the same disgusted look Kimberly had given Shaw that same morning. 'What?'

'Nothing,' Will replied, fear getting the best of him.

'Nothing? Thought as much.'

Will looked down and took a single step back.

The shifting shadows within the room caused by the solitary swinging bulb only increased Shaw's feeling of dread. His eyes followed Michael as he made his way over to Sticky-out Ears and held out his right hand. Ears reached back under his blazer and unsheathed an eight inch blade. Shaw recognised it immediately. It was a kukri blade, famously used by the Ghurkhas in the British Army, thicker towards the tip of the blade and bent forward close to the hilt. The room fell uncomfortably silent and the atmosphere grew thick and intense. Sweat seeped through the skin on his back, dampening his T-shirt. Michael held the kukri blade in his hands, passing it from right to left and back again, as if testing its weight and balance.

'Do knives frighten you, Shaw?' Michael said, pacing from left to right.

'Not particularly.'

'Didn't think so. Not a guy who's taken a few bullets, eh.'

Shaw massaged his right hand, as if suddenly aware of the constant ache that ran the full length of his arm.

A thick hand passed by Shaw's face from behind and the joint from a thick forearm and a bicep was pulled tight into his throat. An equally firm hand was pressed on the back of his head, immediately forcing his eyes to bulge and his mouth to open, cutting off his blood flow. His right hand searched for the attacker's face behind him but found only air. He attempted to stand but the man was too strong and had caught him off guard. Quinn's sleeper-hold was tight and secure, draining him of his energy and consciousness. Shaw's fighting spirit soon dwindled, and his flailing arms descended to the desk top. In the distance he could make out Will trying to talk his way out of the mess he'd gotten them into. Just when things were beginning to go cloudy and unconsciousness was creeping in, the hold loosened. The forearm and bicep slipped away and instead slipped up under his right arm and behind his head, placing him in a half-nelson hold. Before he could even take breath, Quinn smashed his face off the wooden desk, sending a blinding pain up through his brow. Shaw coughed, feeling incapacitated and exposed. Thick saliva ran from his mouth and was smeared over his face as Quinn held his head firmly against the desk top. Unexpectedly, Shaw's eyes flinched shut as the desk top splintered, fragmenting white painted wood only inches from his face. The kukri blade pierced the wood deep enough to allow it to stand upright.

'If going to the police even crosses your mind after leaving here or you refuse to do anything that I ask of you, so help me God, I'll bury that useless prick there.' Michael glanced at Will. 'And as soon as I've put him in the ground, I'll get my boys in Boro to turn the lights out in Canterbury Grove, permanently.'

Will stepped forward again, hoping to find the courage to say something, but Michael's cold, angry gaze forced him back.

Michael pulled the kukri blade from the desk and handed it back to Ears.

The door behind Shaw opened, spilling fresh light and a welcoming feeling of relief into the room. A physically fit looking woman dressed in grey jogging pants and a black zip-up hoody swaggered into his line of sight. She approached Michael from Shaw's right and kissed him before handing him a rucksack.

'Who's this?' she said in an unmistakable Northern Irish accent.

'This is Ryan Shaw, he'll be inspecting the hardware,' Michael said.

'I thought Will was doing that for ya?'

'My new friend here wants to do it for me. Don't you?'

'Fuck you!' Shaw said, his face pressed against the desk top, his eyes transfixed on Michael's.

Michael laughed and pulled an item from the rucksack and placed it on the desk for Shaw to see. 'What can you tell me about this?'

It was an Ingram Mac-10, one of the deadliest and widely used submachine-guns on the market, capable of unleashing over one thousand rounds per minute at a range of one hundred metres, making it very effective in close quarters. That combined with its light weight made it just as difficult to control as it was deadly.

Shaw looked up at the Ulster girl in disbelief; now realising she was the woman he'd seen sliding down the pole earlier. Her platinum hair was cut short and pixie and her figure appeared athletic and slender. A look of concerned anticipation was evident behind her captivating blue eyes, as if dreading the result he was going to come up with.

'It's a Mac-10,' he said, accepting it was in everyone's best interest to do as he was told, for now.

Michael's eyes locked on Will's. 'Well at least you know what it is.' He looked back to Shaw. 'I want you to inspect it, make sure it's not a piece of shit.' He gave Quinn a nod.

The pressure on Shaw's head momentarily increased before it was released. His face was pushed harder into the desk top, giving his attacker that extra second to pull back. Shaw sat upright and rubbed his throat, turning to give Quinn a steely look, who returned it with an amused smile.

Shaw looked back at the weapon and then to Michael. 'Don't suppose you've got any gloves?' he said, concerned about his fingerprints.

'No.'

'Didn't think so.' He reached forward and took the Mac-10 and started stripping it to sequence. Once you'd learnt how to strip one automatic weapon, the sequence was similar for them all. He activated the magazine release catch and pulled free the cheap plastic magazine before pulling back on the working parts to reveal an empty chamber, thick with carbon. 'I'll need a small screwdriver,' he said, firing off the dry action.

'Sherman.' The pitch in Michael's voice reminded Shaw of a kid at Christmas. Ears rolled his eyes, unimpressed with the request.

'And it needs to be thin and flat,' Shaw emphasised, still feeling tender around his throat.

Within minutes Sherman returned, bringing with him a temporary river of fresh light from the corridor outside. He pictured Quinn standing behind him with his arms folded, his eyes glaring two holes into the back of his head, constantly pushing his glasses back up his crooked nose.

A small red handled screwdriver was placed on the table next to his left hand. Shaw picked up the screwdriver and used it to remove the front two-piece locking pin, allowing him to split the Mac-10 into two. It felt good handling a firearm again, it had been a long time and Shaw hadn't realised how much he'd missed until now. He continued with the inspection, sliding the cocking handle to the rear to remove the bolt and recoil spring assembly from the top receiver. He then removed its extractor pin, taking care not to lose the small extractor spring, and checked the firing pin.

He turned to Sherman on his right. 'Keep a tight hold of that,' he said, indicating the bolt and recoil spring assembly. 'And use your thighs to keep pressure applied to the springs.'

With the springs compressed, Shaw carefully muscled the pin free and removed the guide rod that ran the length of the spring, the spring itself, and the weapon's ejector and examined them closely. He then turned to the lower receiver, the portion of the Mac-10 containing the trigger mechanism and magazine housing.

'I take it you're aware it's been converted?' he said, noticing deliberate damage.

'What do you mean, converted?' Michael said.

'The upper contact lobe of the trip's been hacksawed off. And not by a pro either, going by the messy work,' he said, looking at the Ulster girl.

'And what does that mean?' Kimberly said, not understanding what he was talking about.

'It means the weapon's been illegally modified to fire fully automatic.'

'Doesn't it fire fully automatic anyway?' Michael said.

'No.'

Michael exhaled. 'So is it a piece of shit?'

'I wouldn't say that, no. Depends what you're buying it for.'

'I want it to fire a lot of bullets very quickly.'

'Well it'll do that.' He looked at the magazine on the desk. 'It'd empty that in about two seconds now.'

'So it will fire?'

'It must work to some degree, it's covered in carbon. But I couldn't say for certain until I'd test fired it myself.'

'And how many did you say we were getting?' Kimberly asked Michael, who in turn looked at Quinn.

'There's two more of these, a shotgun, two AK's, two Glock 19's, a Sig and a revolver,' Quinn said. 'Plus, the body armour and assault vests.'

Shaw took each piece of the firearm in exactly the reverse order and reassembled it, deliberately leaving off the magazine. He cocked the weapon and pulled the trigger, allowing the working parts to go forward, repeating the action with the safety catch applied. Shaw was curious to know why Michael was purchasing that much firepower. The three converted submachine-guns alone were crazy enough, let alone adding two AK's and a shotgun to the menu. But he knew better than to ask questions like that. The less he knew, the less he was involved. This act alone could see him straight back to his en-suite room and three square meals a day. He looked up at Miss Northern Ireland and saw a nervous, uneasy look in her eyes.

'Apart from it being filthy and totally illegal, I guess it's okay,' he said. 'But again, I couldn't say for sure until I'd fired it.'

Michael took back the Mac-10. 'Well you won't be firing it.'

Shaw couldn't have cared less if he was going to fire it or not, he was more concerned that the weapon had been fired before and was now covered in his fingerprints.

'Is that it then?' Kimberly said, stepping forward out of the shadows.

'For now. I'll let you know the rest of the details once Quinn and I have got them sorted.' Michael turned back to Will and Shaw who was standing up from the chair. 'Don't yous two be going too far,' he said with a smile.

*

Light snow floated down from the sky like powder, disintegrating the instant it made contact with the wet ground.

'I'd listen to him if I were you,' Kimberly said with a smug tone, leading the way back down the wooden steps towards her MR2.

'Is that right?' Shaw said.

She nodded. 'Yeah.'

'Well I don't seem to have much of a fucking option now, do I?' he said, laying his eyes on Will.

Kimberly stopped at her car and smiled. 'No, I guess you don't.'

'Where you going?' Will asked her, reaching for her hand.

'Got things to do,' she said, 'I'll call you when I'm free.' She edged forward and buried her tongue into his mouth, all the while keeping her eyes locked on Shaw, as if proving some point.

Will and Shaw watched her MR2 speed off up the back street and turn into the main traffic.

'You should lay off Kim, it's not her fault, you know,' Will said, looking at Shaw across the roof of the Saxo.

'You know what, Will, you're right. It's not her fault, it's fucking yours.'

'What? I didn't know that was going to happen.'

'Maybe not, but you knew what you we're getting me into,' he said. 'For fuck sake, Will, I'm fighting like hell to just speak with Douglas, let alone see him.' He dragged his hands through his hair. 'And now you go and throw all this shit at me. This is gonna send me straight back to fucking prison.'

'Well I'm sorry. I didn't know what else to do.'

He climbed into the passenger seat, refraining from saying anymore. 'Drop me of at a cheap hotel or something.'

'Don't be daft. You can stay at the flat.'

'I don't want to stay at the flat. Drop me off at a B and B. I want a quiet room and a fresh head for tomorrow.'

Four

'The real deal'

The Saxo rocked from side to side, its windows steamed up with condensation. Kimberly's body went ridged as she pushed her palms against the ceiling of the small car, faking her orgasm. A popular dance tune erupted from her handbag on the front passenger seat, followed by a deep vibrating. It rang several times and stopped.

'Did you want to answer that?' Will said, his hands gripping her naked hips.

Kimberly fingered her thick, black hair behind her ears and climbed off him onto the backseat beside him. 'What do you think?' she said, pulling up her tight jeans.

Will snapped off his condom and pulled up his jeans. 'What you doing later?'

Before Kimberly could answer, the popular tune started again, followed by the vibrating. 'Reach me my handbag,' she said.

Will reached forward into the front of the car and grabbed it. 'Thought we could do something if you were free.'

She opened her handbag and answered her phone, reading Michael's name on the screen. 'Yeah?' She rested the phone between her head and shoulder and pulled down her tight grey sweater, rectifying her appearance. 'Yeah, Will's with me now, why?'

Will leaned over the folded forward passenger seat and opened the passenger door and climbed out. He scanned the cold underground car park, making sure no one had been watching. Even at twenty-five past twelve in the afternoon, the car park was dark and empty. The only sound to reach them was from the passing traffic outside.

'Yeah okay, I'll tell him,' she said. 'He'll be there in about fifteen minutes.'

'Who was that?'

'Michael.'

'What did he want?'

Headlights from another vehicle beamed down the ramp in the darkness ahead and a dark coloured saloon appeared from the corner, coming to a steady stop some distance away. Voices could be heard as the passengers of the vehicle went about their business.

Kimberly put her phone back in her handbag and clipped it shut.

30

'He wants to see you.'

'What about?'

'I don't know, Will. But I told him you'd be there in about fifteen minutes. And you know what he's like if he's kept waiting.' She stretched her legs and climbed out the passenger door into the car park, adjusting her clothing further.

'You not coming?'

'No, I've got stuff to do.' She approached her MR2 parked in the bay opposite and opened her driver's door.

'Okay. Will I see you later?'

She climbed behind her wheel and flipped down the vanity mirror to fix her makeup and hair. 'Maybe,' she said, gunning the ignition, filling the car park with the sound of chart music.

'Bye then,' he said in a pathetic tone. He closed her driver's door and watched her speed away, leaving him with only his used condom for company. The thought of seeing Michael again unnerved him, especially after what had happened earlier. He straightened the two front seats in his Saxo and climbed behind the wheel, lighting a cigarette. It was only a week ago that him and Michael had been, what he had thought to be, close friends. Michael had taken him out, shown him things, spent money on him, bought him drinks, got him drugs, and shown him how to have a good time. But most of all he'd never judged him. Michael had become the brother Will thought he'd always wanted. They would spend hours talking and laughing about the years he'd served in The Parachute Regiment. Only all of Will's stories had been fabricated. Will remembered how disappointed and humiliated he was with himself for being kicked out the British Army for having class A drugs detected in his urine. '*Services no longer required*' is how the Colonel of 3 Para had phrased it. He remembered the shame radiating from his family because of his discharge. But if they'd known about the severe bullying and the degrading initiations he'd had to endeavour, then maybe they'd have understood his actions. He mentally slapped himself and pulled away, releasing a small spin from his tyres.

*

He pulled into the back compound of the nightclub and parked in-between Michael's GT-R and Bomber's black Alfa Romeo, which hadn't been there when they'd visited earlier. He waved up at the CCTV camera watching the front steps and buzzed the buzzer. Moments later the steel door opened.

'Wait here,' the same overly tanned doorman said.

Soon after, Bomber appeared. 'Oi, this way.'

31

Will had hoped he'd be greeted by Bomber and not Quinn. Michael always preferred Bomber if he was available, due to him being the most civilised out of the two. 'Don't suppose you know why he wants to see me, do ya?'

'No,' Bomber said, walking back the way he'd come.

The club was now quiet. No music played and no girls rehearsed. Will followed Bomber, wiping his clammy palms on the legs of his jeans. Bomber knocked on the Manager's office door twice and entered, shutting Will out in the corridor. Seconds later the door re-opened.

'Howay in,' Bomber said, closing the door behind them.

Michael sat reclined in his brown leather chair behind his oak desk. In his hand was a half-filled glass.

'Relax, Will. Christ, you look like you're about to shit.' He twisted from right to left on the chair's pivot. 'Sit down.'

Will sat and glanced at Bomber, willing his knees to stop trembling.

'Help yourself to a drink.'

Will paused. 'Yeah, okay. Cheers.' He stood and walked over to the drinks unit. Gin, whiskey, vodka, slices of lime and several small pieces of ice in a glass container were all at hand on a tray. 'You know I got here as fast as I could,' he said, finding the calm talking Michael equally as nerving as the shouting, threatening one. He poured himself a small glass of gin and added two cubes of ice to take the edge off.

'I'm sure you did.' Michael watched him sit back down, the fear evident in his body language. 'Your brother's not going to be a problem, is he?' he said. 'I don't need any more problems, Will. You, don't need any more problems.'

Will took a sip from his glass. 'No, Ryan's good. He's the real deal.'

'That's not what I asked, is it?' Michael sat upright in his chair and pulled himself under the desk. 'Can he be controlled, Will? Because if he can't, it spells trouble for you.'

'Honestly, Ryan's okay. He won't be a problem, I'll speak to him. He knows the score.'

'I really hope so, Will, for both your sakes. Because if for any reason this deal goes sour because of Ryan, the only nicety you'll get from me is I'll make sure you're buried next to your dear mother.'

Will said nothing. Michael meant every word spoken and Will knew it. He took another nervous sip of his drink and glanced back at

Bomber who was stood at the door.

'On a brighter note, I am impressed with his knowledge on the topic. All I need now is to be happy with his attitude. Make sure he comes down here tonight.' Michael twisted his glass between his fingers, swirling the contents within. 'So we can socialise a bit. Get to know each other a little better.'

A knock sounded on the door behind Bomber, stealing everyone's attention. Bomber stepped to the side as the platinum haired Ulster girl appeared from behind it.

'Ye nearly finished, Michael,' she said. 'Oh sorry, didn't realise ye were busy.' She had changed out of her grey sweat pants and hoody and was now dressed in loose fitted jeans and a tight white T-shirt with a designer print across its chest.

'Give me a few minutes, Mel. Grab a quick drink and wait at the bar, okay?' Michael said.

She mouthed the word okay and gave Will a smile before closing the door.

Michael had been sleeping with Melanie for over six weeks now, even though she'd been working at the club a lot longer. Will remembered how Kimberly had taken an instant disliking to her the second she found out he was sleeping with her. Wanting to know why she was all of a sudden sniffing around her cousin like some lost puppy, and why Michael had been so keen to involve her in his business. It hadn't taken her long, she ticked all Michael's boxes: athletic, attractive, glamorous, and more importantly, she looked good on his arm. Somehow, she'd managed to get in on the act, grabbing Michael's full attention. Ultimately, Melanie was a nice girl. She'd always been friendly and polite to Will, even when she didn't have to. Sometimes he wondered why she was even involved with Michael at all.

'Well, as you can see, I'm very busy,' Michael said.

'Yeah, got some shit to do myself.' Will stood up and replaced the empty glass on the tray after knocking back the remainder of his drink. 'I'll see you tonight then.'

Bomber opened the door and ushered Will through it. Mel sat on a bar stool with her legs crossed, waiting patiently for Michael to finish, her foot wiggling as if listening to an imaginary tune.

'See you tonight, Mel,' Will said.

Mel looked up, broken from her thoughts, and smiled.

Five

'My treat'

The metallic taste of blood and sand was almost as overpowering as the pain in his torso and left hand. Shaw raised his head and shoulders from the dirt, choking on the blood that spilled from his broken nose into his thick, dark beard. The sky, thick with dust and smoke, rained earth and stones down on top of him. The ground was hard and cold. Ringing dominated his hearing. He rolled onto his left side and saw the overturned wreckage of a destroyed Jackal in the ditch beside him, its underbelly black and dented, its remaining front wheel spinning. Two thirds of the way along the Jackal protruded Bobby's torso, crushed beneath the automatic grenade launcher mounted on the back. Bobby's filthy bearded face looked up to the sky, untouched by the violence; his young, gentle eyes open and staring; his body, like the vehicle above him, was bent and mangled.

Shaw touched his face and scrambled back against a compound wall, identifying the pain in his dislocated left thumb. He looked out into the distance, passed the wreckage, attempting to clear the fog that filled his mind, trying to figure out where he was and what had happened. He could see a raised track leading away through a compound, the sun rising slowly in the east, spilling warm rays of light that sliced through the climbing icy mists of the surrounding poppy fields.

A voice beside him cried out, barely audible above the ringing in his ears.

He looked back at the Jackal. Through the endless dust and rolling smoke he made out his driver's child-like face, blackened and bloodied, hanging upside down in the driver's seat.

'Sarge,' Dinger cried, tears running down his face, paving paths through the dirt around his eyes.

Shaw dragged himself towards him, the fog lifting from his thoughts. He could now hear the sound of heavy gunfire coming from further up the track.

'I see you,' he said. 'Can you—' His words were snatched from him by a round hitting him in the right leg below the knee. A second slipped between the plates in his body armour and punched into his right side. A dozen more thundered past him, snapping and biting at the air and ground around him. He groaned in pain and snatched the Browning pistol from the holster strapped to his chest. To his right, a slender bearded man, skin dark from the sun, wrapped in cloth and rags stood less than thirty metres away, his AK47 pointing right at him. He aimed the pistol in his direction and fired seven times, stopping only when the chamber jammed. A cloud of compressed sand splashed up from the compound wall, centimetres to the right of the insurgent's face, just before his right shoulder snapped back followed by his chest and head, misting up a haze of red behind him. The insurgent crumpled to the ground.

He applied pressure to his right side and took a moment to catch his breath. 'Get out,' he said through broken breath and blood stained teeth.

Dinger tugged on his seatbelt. 'I can't, Sarge,' he said. 'It's jammed.'

Shaw unsheathed his knife from his waist and threw it towards him. Without waiting to see where it landed, he laid his head back in the dirt and clutched at the bullet wound in his right side. He shook away the need to close his eyes and inspected his weapon. He fought back the top slide, smearing his own blood along its dark metallic surface, and shook free the jammed round. He heard a male voice call his name, followed by more automatic gunfire.

But before he could reply, Dinger screamed. 'R-P-G!'

He looked back along the compound wall in the direction of the dead insurgent and saw another, younger than one he'd previously killed, standing a further fifty metres away. On his shoulder was an RPG-7. He cursed and rolled onto his stomach, pinning his hands to his ears, his eyes clenched tight. He pressed his body as deep as it would go into the dirt and held his breath; every one of his muscles rigid with fear.

The rocket screamed above him, missing him by only feet, and exploded on impact with the compound wall several metres behind them. Chunks of wall, sand, dirt and small stones showered him and the front of the overturned Jackal. A second explosion, louder than the first, exploded, sending a bright orange fireball high into the air, enveloped in thick black smoke.

Fire raged out from a destroyed compound generator through the new hole in the wall, consuming everything in its path. Its diesel fuelled flames ignited the material on his back and helmet, whilst also igniting the daysacks strapped to the front of the Jackal.

Shaw scrambled back from the heat and rolled onto his back, extinguishing the flames. He glanced back towards the insurgent, who had retreated back behind the cover of the compound wall and looked at the five water cans strapped to the side of the Jackal. All but one leaked water. He prayed the five jerry cans on the other side were in better condition.

'Sarge,' Dinger cried again, reaching for the blade that now lay beneath him, out of his reach.

Shaw lumbered through the dirt towards him, his lower right trouser leg and boot deep red in colour; his waist, shirt and body armour saturated with sticky blood.

'Don't leave me, Sarge,' Dinger said, his voice wavering through fear and panic.

He reached for the knife and stopped. The knife lay partially submerged in a puddle, surrounded by a large damp stain in the dirt. He looked up past Dinger at the Commander's seat and swallowed. There he saw the tinted glisten of diesel running along the front frame and dripping onto the ground beneath his driver. The Commander's seat was painted with thick wet sand, sand wet with diesel. He switched his gaze to the burning debris around them and the burning daysacks strapped to the front of the vehicle.

'Please don't leave me,' Dinger repeated. 'Sarge, please don't let me die.'

'No one's leaving anybody,' he said.

A dampened roar of heavy gunfire burst forth over them, sending fifty or more glowing tracer rounds into the direction of the insurgents. To his relief, a second troop Jackal had manage to fight its way to them to give support.

His heart beat so hard he could feel it against the inside of his Kevlar chest plate. He grabbed the blade and reached up with his right hand, biting back the pain in his side, and started to cut at Dinger's seatbelt.

Fletch, his Junior Callsign's commander, called out for him and slid down the bank into the ditch at the rear of the Jackal.

'I'm here,' Shaw yelled, breathing out a sigh of relief. 'Bobby's dead and Dinger's trapped.'

But just as Fletch appeared, the three of them took incoming fire from the same position as before. Fletch turned on the spot and fell back against the rear of the Jackal, injured. He returned fire, showering the enemy area accompanied by the sound of the GPMG mounted on the supporting Jackal. Dinger flinched back, narrowly avoiding any rounds, and watched as a burning daysack fell from the front of the vehicle.

Dinger snatched out for Shaw and grabbed his body armour. 'Get me out of here,' he cried. 'I want to go home.'

'Keep still.'

'I don't want to die. Please don't let me die.'

Then, in the blink of an eye, the diesel beneath Dinger ignited, engulfing Dinger with orange flame and black smoke.

Shaw jerked back from the heat, breaking Dinger's grip. He felt it burn the front of his face, singeing away the hairs on his beard to nothing but spiky bristles. Dinger thrashed his limbs uncontrollably, screaming in agony.

'No!' Shaw yelled, flinching back from the heat and the pain in his gut. He dug deep and raised himself up to the flames. He fought off Dinger's thrashing limbs and attempted to cut him free, determined not to see him die.

Several rounds pinged off the Jackal's armour beside him and whizzed past his head. He glimpsed to the right, just in time to feel a 7.62 round hit him in the right shoulder, spinning him to face the enemy front on.

Dinger screamed out.

Two more rounds punched into Shaw's chest plate, with a single round slipping beneath his body armour and puncturing the skin left of his naval.

.   *

Shaw sat bolt upright in the bed, thick with sweat. His eyes scanned the room of the B and B, trying to steady his breathing and calm his heart rate, focusing on what was real. He ran a hand down his tired face, trying to accept the dream he hadn't experienced for almost twelve months.

His phone suddenly rang, jolting his already fragile nerves. He picked it up and focused on its display. Withheld. He answered the call and ran his free hand through his damp hair.

'Where the fuck are ye?' a distinctive Glaswegian accent bellowed down the line.

'Boyd?'

'Aye it's Boyd, now where the fuck are ye?'

'I'm in Sunderland.'

'Sunderland? Ye taking the fucken piss outta me?'

'Not at all. She'll just have to wait for those papers. Like I said I'm in Sunderland. If you leave me your number, though, I'll get back to you once I'm back in London.'

'I fucken warned ye, Ryan. I told ye what would happen.'

'That you did, Boyd. See you around.'

'Oh, ye fucken will, ye—'

Shaw disconnected and lay back down, looking up at the ceiling, his phone still in his hand.

He had phoned his mother the instant he'd booked into the B and B, concerned for her safety after what Michael had said. But she was fine and oblivious to their situation, more concerned about whether her two sons would be home for Christmas or not. Which is how he wanted it kept.

His phone rang again, again startling him. He read Will's name on its display and answered it. 'What?'

'What you doing?' Will asked him.

'I'm sleeping.'

'Sleeping? Fuck that. Get yourself ready. Michael wants us at his club.'

Shaw sat out of bed, his feet firmly on the floor, his head in his left hand. 'He wants us at his club? I stopped taking orders the day I was discharged from the Marines.'

'Yeah, I know, but what can we do? What you going to do all night anyway, sit in your room and wank your cock off? Be ready for nine.' Before Shaw had time to decline, Will hung up, leaving the line dead.

*

Several hours later, Will and Shaw made their way to the front of the queue, bypassing the scantily dressed women and drunken men who protested at the brothers' VIP treatment. The familiar doorman removed the red rope blocking their entrance and allowed them to pass.

'Michael's waiting upstairs,' the doorman said.

The music in the club was loud and repetitive, bordering on deafening. People danced like tranced-out zombies, arms flailing and bodies jumping to the heavy beat of the base-filled music. Professional dancers gyrated provocatively in their booths, entertaining and driving on the crowds beneath them. Green, red and blue lasers flooded the dance floors, penetrating the self-produced smoke that hung thin in the air, whilst the crowds packed themselves side by side in order to worship the DJ like some ancient, forgotten god.

The spiralling grand stairs to the strip club above could be accessed via a doorway at the rear of the nightclub. Standing guard at the doorway was another large male, dressed in a black shirt and trousers. He stood in the entrance, watching a small group of young, scantily dressed girls sitting on the stairs, attending to one of their very drunk friends. He acknowledged Will with a nod and allowed them to ascend the staircase.

Will pushed open the double doors, mimicking a scene from a Clint Eastwood western. 'Now isn't this worth coming all this way for?' he said, nodding towards the flexible naked redhead spinning around the pole. The same pole the Ulster girl had been rehearsing on.

An alluring blonde dressed in a tight purple micro-dress with attached garters approached them. 'Hiya, Will,' she said. 'You here to see Michael?'

'Yeah,' Will said, unable to hide his growing smile.

'He's over here. You can follow me.'

Michael sat at one of his tables, his right arm outstretched around Melanie; an empty defeated look in her eyes. Across the room, sitting at the bar, Shaw noticed Bomber watching them.

'Michael,' Will said, as if asking for permission to speak before nodding at Melanie. 'Mel.'

Melanie smiled.

'Take a seat,' Michael said. 'Drink?' He gestured to the silver ice bucket in front and the opened champagne bottle within it.

Shaw pulled back one of the chairs and sat down. 'I'll have a whiskey. Irish if you've got it,' he said, bringing a subconscious smile to Melanie's lips.

Before Will could take his seat, Michael indicated for him to go to the bar and retrieve the order. 'So what do you think?' he asked Shaw, placing his right hand on Melanie's smooth thigh.

'Of what?'

Michael threw his eyes around the room. 'My club.'

Shaw leaned forward on the table, his eyes unnerving. 'Let's get something straight,' he said. 'I'm not here to grade your club or socialise with you. And I'm definitely not here to enjoy your fucking company. I'm here because Will needs me here. And as soon as this inspection's done, we're leaving.'

'Is that right?'

'You may frighten Will with your confident demeanour,' Shaw's eyes travelled down to Michael's shoes and back up again, 'your fancy suits, flash cars and club full of girls, but one things for dam sure, you don't frighten me. And the first sign I get that you've physically threatened my mam with anything, I'll put you in the fucking ground.'

There was a small silence between them, neither of them wanting to surrender eye contact. Michael could see Shaw wasn't afraid of him. Even

39

earlier in the club's cellar there had been no fear, only concern.

'Maybe I came across a little heavy this morning,' Michael said. 'But you know how it is. I can't allow you the opportunity to make a fool out of me. Not like I did with Will.'

Shaw looked across at Will standing at the bar.

'I want us to get along, Ryan. I was impressed with how you handled the weapon. You seem to know your stuff.' He took a mouthful of champagne. 'Look, why don't you have one of my girls dance for you? Help you unwind.'

'I'm fine, thanks.'

'You sure, Ryan? They're all very good, especially Bianca.'

Shaw glanced back at Will, needing his whiskey. 'I said I'm fine.'

'One of my girls must appeal to you,' Michael persisted. 'Or is it boys you prefer?'

Shaw met Melanie's gaze, a break of a smile cracking his lips. 'And I can have any girl?'

Michael nodded. 'Any girl. On me. My treat.'

Shaw turned in his chair and scanned the club floor, looking at the half naked girls. He counted five in total: the hot redhead with the fake large breasts that was finishing her routine on the pole, the petite blonde girl who'd escorted them over to Michael earlier, and three other attractive girls, all dressed in the bare minimum. But he'd already decided which one he wanted.

'Okay,' he said, turning back to face Michael. 'I'll have her.'

Melanie looked at Michael for a response. 'Oh, not tonight, sweetheart. Maybe another time.'

Shaw looked at Michael, awaiting his reaction.

'No,' Michael said, staring back at Shaw, 'no, you go and show our new friend here the best five minutes he'll ever have.'

'But—' Melanie said.

'But nothing.'

Melanie stood up and straightened her little dress. She picked up her champagne glass and took Shaw's hand. 'This way,' she said, leading him through the club to one of the several gently lit private booths. She pulled back the thick, red curtain revealing a small, circular room, lined on one side by a red cushioned seat.

Shaw sat down and placed his hands on his lap. 'You don't have to do this, you know. I just wanted to piss him off.'

'No touching now,' she teased.

Shaw's heart raced as Melanie bent towards him. She placed her manicured hands on his knees and pushed them open.

He grabbed her wrists and looked in her eyes. 'I said you don't have to do this.'

'Ya I do.' She looked up at the ceiling behind him. Shaw twisted round and followed her eyes, seeing the small enclosed CCTV camera looking down at them.

The music was slow and seductive allowing her to gyrate in time to the rhythm. He looked down his torso and watched her run her hands up his thighs and over his flat stomach and back again, before meeting her hypnotic gaze. She straightened her back and leaned forward onto him, pressing her small breasts against his face. She could feel his warm breath on her chest as she slid down him onto her knees, her dress riding up above her hips. He felt himself stirring almost immediately, swallowed by her irresistible scent. It had been a long time since he'd been this close to a woman, especially a woman as attractive as Melanie. She crept back up him, brushing her breasts against his growing erection. She placed her hands on the back rest behind Shaw's head and placed her left knee on the cushion beside his right thigh.

He pressed himself back against the seat, now aware of her closeness. 'Where are the guns coming from, Mel?' he said, losing himself in her erotic movements. 'Have you got anything to do with them?'

She slid her right knee up beside him and knelt up in front of him. She gyrated her hips and ran her delicate hands up her smooth thighs to her breasts, flashing him a glimpse of her tiny, baby-blue thong.

'Who's supplying them, Mel?' he said again.

She slid back down him, stopping in a squatted position between his knees.

'I need to know what I'm getting myself into.'

She pivoted and reversed onto him, sitting her firm buttocks on his lap. She straightened her right leg out in front of her and slowly opened it out to the side, running her fingernails along the inside of her thigh. She hushed him as she pulled her thin halter neck strap up over her head and peeled the top portion of her dress down over her ribs, fully exposing her soft, round breasts. She squeezed them provocatively, her pink nipples growing hard and erect between her fingers.

'Nothing for you te worry about,' she said.

'But I am worried, you being from the province, and all.'

She kept her body close to his as she turned to face him and

41

squeezed his growing erection. 'Sure, ya don't feel that worried.' She smiled.

Her figure was better than he had ever imagined: smooth unblemished skin, round pert breasts, strong flat stomach, and this irresistible scent as inviting as freshly picked strawberries. She reached behind him and took her glass, leaning her nipples close to his face as she filled her mouth with the bubbly champagne, taking care not to swallow. She teasingly reached down to kiss him, causing Shaw's lips to pout, mirroring hers. Her penetrating blue eyes were as tranquil as the clear liquid that trickled from between her full red lips. As if hypnotised, Shaw opened his mouth catching the falling warm liquid, allowing its bubbles to flow over his tongue and down his throat. He watched her step back from between his knees and her baby-blue dress fall to her strapped black stiletto heels. She turned and sat back on his lap, draping herself across his chest.

'Answer me this, then,' he said. 'Are you helping to supply them?'

'No,' she whispered in his ear, spreading her flexible legs wide in front of her. 'They've got nothing te do with me.'

'So where are they coming from?'

Before another word could be spoken, the curtain opened, breaking the intimate atmosphere between them.

'That's enough,' Michael said, entering the booth. 'Get dressed.'

Melanie sat upright on Shaw's lap and closed her legs before crouching down to collect her clothes.

Shaw looked up at Michael and grinned. 'I don't think she was finished.'

'She was finished,' he said, following Melanie out of the booth.

A glass of Irish whiskey sat waiting on the table as Shaw returned. 'Where's Will?' he said.

Michael sat at the table, looking as angry as Shaw had hoped. 'I've sent the useless prick home. The mere sight of him annoys me.' He crossed his legs and took another mouthful of his champagne. 'Now sit down.'

Reluctantly, Shaw did as he was told.

'You on the other hand are doing a job for me tomorrow.'

'I don't think so. I'm here to check your damn guns, nothing else.'

'I need a package collecting,' Michael continued, as if oblivious to Shaw's reply.

'I'm not your postman. Get your fucking ape to do it.'

Michael finished the contents of his glass and poured himself another. 'He'll be going, too.'

Shaw rubbed his eyes and exhaled, feeling Michael's imaginary bindings grip tighter around his wrists. 'What's the package?' He swallowed his whiskey in one, wishing it was the bottle he was drinking from.

'That's none of your concern. You're just to collect it.'

'And the inspection? I thought that was happening tomorrow?'

'First things first, Ryan. Quinn will ring you tomorrow morning with the details. He has your number.' Michael turned his head towards the bar and watched Melanie order another bottle of champagne. 'You decide, Ryan, easy way or the hard way. It's your choice. But whichever way you choose, you'll be doing exactly what I tell you to.'

Shaw slammed the empty glass down on the table. 'Is there anything else you want me to do? Walk your dog? Wash your car?'

Michael smiled. 'No, you can go. Just make sure your phones turned on. Don't want you missing any important calls.'

Ryan stood up and headed for the exit, eyeballing the doorman as he left.

Six

'Dressed like a cunt'

The taxi indicated and pulled out of the flow of morning traffic and into the bus stop, allowing Melanie to climb in the back out of the cold. She closed the door and pulled on the seatbelt. The taxi pulled away and turned left at the first corner. It drove for a further ten minutes before turning into a retail park and parking up.

'Were they of any use?' she said.

DCI Slater twisted in the driver's seat to face her, wedging his left arm around the front passenger chair.

'The pictures I mean,' she added.

'Very,' he said. 'What was he like, this Shaw?'

Whilst Melanie had been standing at the bar ordering Michael's second bottle of champagne last night, she had quickly taken a series of photographs of Shaw on her mobile phone, and sent them to her handler, DCI Slater.

She shrugged. 'I don't know. Pissed off, I guess.'

'Pissed off how?'

'Well, sure, they had him in a headlock when I walked in, and he was telling Michael te fuck off, so he was.'

'So you're saying he was there under duress?'

'It appeared so, sure.'

'And he's only inspecting the guns, nothing else?'

'As far as I'm aware. Who is he, like?'

'No one for you to worry about,' he said.

'Well he's obviously ex-military. He referred te Norn Iron as the province. If he's someone dangerous, I need te know.'

He found her strong Ulster accent as irresistible as he did her looks. 'For starters, Mel, you don't need to know anything. And secondly, if you do decide to back out, you know what will happen.' He paused, allowing his threat to sink in. 'He has a history involving firearms, that's all you need to know.'

Melanie looked out the window at the parked cars and people going about their business, wishing she was a part of it.

'Look, Mel, you're doing a great job. Without you this whole operation would fall apart. How long have you been working at the club now? Seven months?'

44

'Six,' she said.

'Okay and you've been working for me, for what, three weeks? We're running out of time. As you know, Michael's already got the tester.'

'I know!' she said, her voice wavering with emotion. 'I know. I'm fucken trying, aren't I? The only people he trusts are Kimberly, Bomber and Quinn.' Melanie fought back the coming break in her voice. 'I'm no good at this.'

'I appreciate it's not easy for you, and I am aware of the lack of training you've been given in this field.'

She locked her blue eyes on Slater's. 'Lack of?' She laughed. 'I haven't had any! I'm not a peeler. I'm a dancer.'

'Just hang in there,' he continued, ignoring her outburst. 'You've always got immediate back up if required. We just need to know when and where, and we'll do the rest. Then you can go back to doing whatever it is you do.'

'I don't know what else te do,' she said, emotion getting the better of her voice.

'Drugs and sex usually work, Mel,' he said with a sickening seriousness.

Melanie couldn't believe what she was hearing. 'Ya've already forced me te act like a whore and have me sleep with a man I didn't want te, now ya want me te be a drug user te?'

'Don't be so fucking melodramatic, Mel. Just do what's required and then everything can go back to normal.'

Melanie found it impossible to hide her feelings on that comment. 'Is there anything else?' she said, wanting out of the taxi.

'No, you can go.'

Melanie unclipped her seatbelt and opened the door but was stopped by Slater's hand on her arm.

'You're doing a great job, Melanie, don't tell yourself otherwise.'

She forced a smile and stepped out of the taxi, closing the door behind her, and took shelter from the rain beneath the canopy overlooking the shop's entrances. She recalled how hard she'd studied dance at The Division of Performing Arts at Bedfordshire University, how happy she'd felt being around all her closest friends and studying what she loved, how happy and proud her parents had been on attending her graduation nine years ago, especially her dedicated Republican father who'd introduced her to dancing at the fragile age of seven. By the time she was fourteen, he'd already watched her perform in numerous ballets and collect many awards.

45

She remembered the fear and sadness that accompanied her move to England, leaving her home and family in Northern Ireland to pursue her dream. And like always, the shame soon followed, wriggling through her, reminding her of all the unpaid debts that had rolled in, and the heartbreak from all the auditions she'd failed, before she'd finally swallowed her pride and danced in a club. She remembered the mind-numbing fear of removing her clothing for the first time in front of strangers, the shame in exposing herself for money.

Slater had approached her one night in Michael's club and requested a private dance, paying the usual fee for her company. During the dance, Slater had asked her if she did private functions or parties, requiring a dancer on a night she was conveniently available. Needing the extra money and going against all her principles of meeting in private locations, Melanie had agreed. She had arrived the following night at a hotel in Newcastle and made her way up to the pre-arranged room. The corridor had been empty that night except for the maid's trolley filled with toilet rolls and hotel compliments. Her knock on the door had been light and timid. Slater had answered almost immediately, his tired, coffee stained smile, shallow and deceitful. Her only comforting thought that night, was that Chloe Banks, a friend from the club, had dropped her off and was waiting in the car park for her to finish, knowing exactly which room she was in. A room Melanie had found to be empty.

'Don't worry. I'm not going to hurt you,' he'd said. As if it would have calmed the sickening nerves that had erupted within her. 'I'm actually going to arrest you,' he'd added, showing her his police warrant card and badge.

'Arrest me for what?' she'd said.

He'd wiggled a small bag of white powder in front of him. 'Possession of class A drugs and prostitution.' DCI Slater had fabricated a charge that night and arrested her, informing her he would have all the charges dropped if she complied with his investigation against Michael, forcing her to indulge in a sexual relationship with him to obtain information. Not wanting to shame her father's name any further, she'd agreed.

*

The red embers glowed bright at the end of Michael's cigarette, filling his lungs with much needed nicotine. He pulled the cigarette from between his lips and glanced at the dashboard clock, 10:06, thinking about the other two meets he had scheduled later in the day.

The concrete walls of the A19 flyover were lined with litter and decorated with thick, bright graffiti. A distinctive one reading: 'CHERYL WOZ FUCKED ERE BY DAVA, BREZO AND MILLY'. The people he was due to meet had decided on the location, and Michael was in no position to argue about their decision. Now that Michael had found the right man to inspect the potential hardware, he now needed the funds to purchase them and, unfortunately, these were his only source.

A luxurious Range Rover drove into view and made its way through the hammering rain, bumping and dipping in the many pot holes that covered the ground. Michael exhaled a line of smoke through his open window and climbed out, flicking his half smoked cigarette. The black SUV broke through the wall of water at the freeway's edge and stopped short of Michael's GT-R. A large, curly haired male sat upright behind the steering wheel. The two middle-aged men known as the Mallinson Brothers exited the Range Rover's rear seats, dressed in dark suits and matching ties, their ginger hair shaved short to their heads. The right-hand brother, Billy Mallinson, was a heavily built man from many years of lifting weights in his youth, but now bordering on sixty, his body wasn't as toned as it had once been. The left-hand brother, Tony, the younger of the two, was of equal size, standing an impressive six foot four. The pair of them approached the front of the vehicle, an air of confidence surrounding them.

'Who the fuck do you think you are?' Billy said, deep and threatening.

'Sorry?' Michael said, genuinely confused.

'Sorry?' Billy echoed. 'You fucking will be. When me and me brother come to meet someone, we don't expect to be greeted by some fucker dressed as a cunt!'

Michael looked down at himself: trendy white trainers, blue jeans and a black jacket, all designer.

'If Tony and me can make the fucking effort to come smart for some little tosser, then that little tosser should also be wearing something fucking smart. Otherwise, that little tosser dressed like a cunt, makes me and Tony feel like a pair of cunts. Don't you agree?'

Fear rose up within Michael, causing his hands to shake and his knees to tremble. 'Yes, Billy.'

'Billy? Are we fucking mates?'

'No, Mr Mallinson, we're not,' Michael corrected. 'Sorry.'

The two brothers stared at him, as if calculating his execution.

'If this happens again, Michael,' Tony said, breaking his silence, 'the next suit you'll be wearing will be the one you get fucking buried in. Is that understood?'

'Completely,' Michael said.

'Good. Now what's this proposal?'

Michael looked him in the eyes, seeing a cold seriousness and a history of violence behind them. 'How would you like to make a bit of money?'

'And how the fuck are you going to do that?' Tony said.

'You selling your club?' Billy mocked.

The last thing Michael wanted was any more people getting involved in his affairs, but the money he needed was theirs. 'I've got a bit of guaranteed business coming my way. But I'm a little short on funds,' he said, choosing his words carefully. He had no doubt they would try and muscle in on his plans the first chance they got. Plus he knew they were close acquaintances of a man called Nolan Weathers, a powerful North Eastern man doing time for manslaughter. The last thing he needed was him getting word of his plans, even if he was banged up in prison for the next ten years.

'The only business you're any good for is cheap whores and low-class dancers,' Billy said, raising his voice to be heard over a passing lorry above them.

'What's the business?' Tony said, showing interest.

'Cars.'

'Cars? We've already got people selling cars,' Billy said. 'We don't need anymore.'

'These are high performance cars. Three of.'

'What, like Ferraris?'

'Lamborghini Aventadors. All three of them.'

'How much do you need?' Tony said.

Michael cleared his throat. 'Ten grand.'

Billy laughed. 'You expect us to believe you can get hold of three Lambos for ten grand?'

'No of course not,' Michael said. 'I'm providing the rest. I'm short by ten grand, is all, and I didn't want to pass up on the opportunity.'

'You mean you want to be able to carry the weight of our name?' Tony said.

Michael's eyes shifted between the pair of them. He didn't need their name, and there were no cars for sale. All he needed was their money. 'Yes.'

'And what will we get out of it?'

48

'One hundred per cent interest.'

'Another ten grand?' Billy said. 'On the sale of three Lambos? I don't think so. If you want our name, we want fifty per cent of the profits.'

Michael was afraid of this happening. The last thing he wanted was two over the hill thugs muscling in and possibly ruining his chance of making some real money. 'Fifteen per cent. That's still thirty grand,' he said.

'Make it fifty grand and you've got yourself a deal,' Tony said.

Fifty grand out of the money he was planning to make seemed like a fair price. 'Okay.'

'When do you want the money?' Tony said.

'You screw us over, and I'll make sure they're finding pieces of you for the next two decades,' Billy said, his brow frowning into a threatening crease.

Tony looked at his brother, wondering if he ever relaxed. 'When do you want this money for?' he repeated.

'As soon as possible,' Michael said.

'Right, okay. We'll send Paul to your club tonight. Make sure he feels welcome.'

'We'll be in touch,' Billy said.

Michael watched the two brothers climb back in their SUV and reverse back out into the rain, driving away as calmly as they'd arrived. He dug his hands through his pockets and pulled out his cigarettes and petrol lighter. He stuck one between his lips and lit it. 'Well that went well,' he said, searching his jacket pockets for his iPhone. His eyes squinted from the rising smoke as he pressed the relevant numbers on its keypad.

'Yeah,' Quinn answered.

Michael climbed behind the wheel of his GT-R. 'When's the earliest you can arrange this gun deal?'

Quinn finished screwing the false number plate onto the back of the white Transit van and stood up. 'If I ring him now, tomorrow.'

'Good. Get it sorted. I want it as quick as you can.'

'I'll speak with him as soon as I get off the phone with you.' Once Michael had hung up, Quinn scrolled through his phone and made a call, confirming the order.

*

Michael raced along the A1 towards Gateshead, spraying filthy surface water high into the air behind him, the Angel of the North standing proud on his right. His second meeting of the day was arranged for 12:30 in the Metro Centre's yellow car park. A simple exchange: money for drugs.

As arranged, the sellers were parked and waiting. Around them men and women pushed trolleys back into their collection shelters, screaming at their children to stop running in front of cars.

Michael reversed back into the space beside the white BMW coupe and lowered his window. Its occupants consisted of two males aged between thirty and thirty-five: a medium built black man with a shaved head and trimmed pencil line beard, and a large fat, white bald man who sat behind him in the rear seats.

'Who the fuck's this?' Michael said in a heated, un-approving tone.

'He's cool, man. He's with me,' the black man answered.

'I don't give a fuck who he's with. I don't fucking know him.'

The fat man leaned forward. 'If there's a problem, Jammin.'

Michael restarted his engine. 'Forget it.'

'Hey, Michael, calm down. Everything's cool.' Jammin raised his hand to calm the situation. 'He's cool. I've known him for years.'

Michael killed the engine and climbed out, carrying a small black carrier bag. He made his way around to the BMW's passenger door, sucking on a cigarette, and climbed in, smoke streaming from his nostrils.

Jammin raised his hand in protest. 'Whoa, Michael, no smoking in the beamer, man.'

Michael took one last drag on his cigarette and flicked into the now drizzling rain. 'I never want to see this fat cunt again,' he said.

'Yeah, okay.'

Michael sat in the passenger seat and handed the carrier bag to Jammin. 'Five grand.'

'Cool. Dooley, pass him the bag.'

The fat white man reached forward, handing Michael a bag of similar appearance. Michael placed the bag on his lap and opened it, checking its contents.

'What, you don't trust me?' Jammin said, raising the pitch in his voice,

'No,' he said, seeing the small plastic container packed with 80grams of dirty white powder. 'And if this shit isn't decent gear, I know where you live.'

Jammin tutted. 'Shit, man, relax. Nolan's brown's always good. Have I ever let you down before?'

'His brown's always good shit,' Dooley echoed from the back seat.

Michael looked back at him. 'You wanna keep that fucking mouth for eating, son, not talking.' He opened the car door and stepped into the drizzling rain, taking his heroin with him. 'I don't wanna see this fat cunt again,' he said, slamming the car door.

Seven

'Welcome'

'Pull over here,' Quinn said.

Shaw indicated and brought the white Transit van to a gradual halt, parking in the flooded gutter of the cul-de-sac. The semi-detached houses surrounding them were all well-presented and expensive in appearance, with groomed front lawns and cobbled driveways. He killed the engine and looked at Quinn beside him and watched him pull on a pair of black leather gloves.

Quinn had done exactly what Michael had said and rang him earlier that morning, waking him from a night of restless sleep, and instructed him to make his way to the club for pick up.

'Here,' the man in the back said, handing Quinn a black balaclava. Picco had already been sat in the back of the van when Quinn had collected him and thrown him the keys. He was of equal height and weight to Quinn, but instead of greasy hair and glasses, Picco wore a shaved head and thick brow.

'What's that for?' Shaw said, switching his gaze from the balaclava to Picco.

Picco mimicked Quinn and pulled his down on his head in a beanie hat fashion. 'Michael said he was ending their meeting around one. So, they should be here within the next ten to fifteen,' he said to Quinn, searching through a dark hockey style sports bag beside him.

'What's going on, Quinn?' Shaw said.

Quinn ignored him and removed his glasses. He placed them in a black leather snap case and put that in his pocket. 'Let's go,' he said. He grabbed a black holdall from his footwell and climbed out.

Shaw twisted in his seat and peered over his shoulder into the back. 'I think I should stay here,' he said, seeing a baseball bat and shovel in the hockey bag. Picco slid open the side door with an audible creek and stepped out beside Quinn, pulling the hockey bag with him.

Quinn grabbed the bat and leaned forward through the open passenger door. 'Get out that fucking van now, or I'll ram this down your fucking throat.'

Shaw clenched the steering wheel, turning his knuckles white. His door creaked open, breaking the atmosphere between them.

'Do you want Bomber to fuck up your brother?' Picco said, leaning his head through the doorway, saliva gathering in the corners of his mouth. 'Then get out of the van.'

Shaw pulled the keys from the ignition and climbed out. Quinn placed the bat back in the hockey bag and reached into his holdall, pulling out a tin of black spray paint. He pulled the balaclava down over his face and approached the rear gate of number twelve. He unlatched it and fired a burst of black spray paint up at a CCTV camera monitoring the rear garden's entrance. Shaw heard a whistle from the rear of the house and Picco pushed him towards it.

'After you,' Picco said.

Green plastic swings swung gently in the back garden, alongside a red plastic slide that sat gathering rainwater near a child's playhouse. The patio doors and windows to the house were all PVC double-glazed and locked down tight. Several items of wet clothing, including lady's underwear, T-shirts and children's white socks hung from the home's washing line. Black paint dripped from the lens of a second camera positioned above the doors. On the opposite side of the far garden wall midday traffic could be heard. Shaw looked up at a red alarm box mounted high on the wall.

Picco dropped the hockey bag at the patio door and reached in for the shovel. 'I wouldn't worry about that,' he said, jamming the shovel head into the lip between the two PVC doors. He pushed and pulled on its shaft, using the handle as leverage to break the doors multipoint lock. A loud snap sounded followed by several minor cracks, causing the smooth white patio doors to swing open, inviting the three of them into the kitchen. On the black and white floor tiles was a dark wiry foot mat, ironically reading: 'Welcome'.

No alarm sounded, surprising Shaw that such a nice house, irrespective of its area, wouldn't have its alarm set. He recalled how he'd broken down dozens of doors during his time served, involved in 'Hard Knock' operations, going door to door around the world, searching houses and clearing buildings.

Expensive kitchen utensils lined the immaculate black worktops of the modern kitchen. Shiny large pans hung from the ceiling and a collection of razor-sharp knives clung magnetically to the far wall in uniformed sequence of size.

Picco pulled his balaclava down over his face. 'I'll check upstairs,' he said, leaving the hockey bag with Quinn.

The wide passageway was plainly decorated with oak wooden flooring and magnolia walls. Numerous framed photographs of a cute baby girl hung from them along with a dozen or so Christmas cards draped over string. Shaw followed Quinn into the living room, his eye catching a black and white photograph of the family: Mam, Dad and daughter of toddler age. The living room was spacious and minimalist in presentation. A cream armchair sat in the corner directly opposite the entrance, a large corner sofa of the same design sat against the opposite wall, left of the door, and a large flat screen entertainment system sat below the bay window. Right of the bay window was a Christmas tree standing more than eight feet tall.

'All clear up here,' Picco said from the landing.

Quinn dropped the two bags beside the sofa and pulled out the baseball bat.

'What are we doing here, Quinn?' Shaw said, scanning the room nervously.

Quinn moved the vertical blinds at the bay window with the tip of his bat and stared out at the driveway. 'They'll be here shortly.'

'Who will?'

Quinn stayed quiet.

'Quinn, what the fuck are we doing here? I didn't come here for this.'

Quinn faced him. 'You came for whatever I deem fit. Now shut your mouth.' He turned back to the window. 'Right, they're here.' He pointed his bat to the front centre of the room in front of the flat screen TV. 'Stand there.'

'Are you for real? They'll see my face.'

'Stand there!' Quinn said, his chest heaving with built up fury.

Shaw sighed with disbelief. Sweat seeped through his skin and trickled down his back. His face was visible and there was no backup plan or information on who was coming in. He didn't even know how many of them there were. Then he realised, it wasn't fear that had stricken him, but worry, a worry that the cute little girl in photograph would be with them, a worry that the actions that were about to take place would send him straight back to prison with no chance of him seeing his own little boy again.

Quinn took up position behind the door to the room and stood his bat up against the wall. 'And it's the nigga we want,' he said.

*

The Rhythm and Base boomed from the speakers of the BMW, so loud Jammin missed what his friend had said. 'What was that?' he said, reducing the volume.

Dooley finished sending a text and put his phone in his pocket. 'I said I hate this weather.'

'Tell me about it; just wish the snow would lay. All Abbey's gone on about is wanting to build a fuckin' snowman.'

Dooley grinned and glanced at the bag at his feet. Five grand in used notes laid rolled up in the black carrier bag.

'Why is it some drivers feel the need to huddle together when it's raining?' Jammin complained, negotiating the flooded roads. 'You get your motor fixed yet?'

'Not yet. Trev's gonna take a look at it for me tomorrow.'

'Trevor Harrison? That guy's off the rails. You don't want him messing with your car.'

'Yeah, but he's cheap. And he does know what he's doing.'

'Back when he wasn't fucked up on smack, maybe. The guy would sell his mother's liver for the feel of a needle now. Him and his stinking mate, Smithy.'

'Yeah, but he's cheap,' Dooley repeated with a smile. 'Will your lass be in when we get there?'

'No, she's at her mam's. Don't want her knowing I'm dealing for Nolan again. She'd kick off if she knew.'

'I can't see how. The money she spends today came from what you sold yesterday,' Dooley said.

Jammin tilted his head in acknowledgement.

The local shops were busy; full of youths with their hoods pulled up over their heads and their tracksuit bottoms tucked into their socks, young girls with their bleached blonde hair and large hooped earrings, middle aged women with greasy hair pulled back tight into pony tails and half smoked cigarettes hanging from their bottom lip. Toddlers sat in their prams covered in sausage roll, whilst all the local unemployed males hung around the local bookies or stood outside the local unwelcoming pub, smoking and drinking.

Jammin pulled into a space beside a bus stop. 'Two seconds, mate,' he said. 'I won't be long.' He climbed out and ran into an off license. Dooley seized the opportunity and climbed out, searching for his cigarettes.

A young boy dressed in a white tracksuit and matching baseball cap stepped forward from his mates. ''Ere, you, giza' tab.'

Dooley placed a cigarette between his lips. 'Does your mother know you smoke?'

'No, but your mam does,' the boy said, flicking him the middle finger. 'Ye fat cunt.'

Within seconds of lighting up, Jammin emerged from the store carrying a bottle of red wine. Dooley took several more drags on the cigarette and flicked it towards the young boy and his crew.

*

The BMW splashed through the flooded portion of the cul-de-sac, mounting the driveway with a bump. Jammin exited the vehicle and glanced at the white van parked outside his house, Dooley also climbed out, grabbing the carrier bag at his feet.

'You want a drink?' Jammin said, entering his house.

'Aye, anything but water,' Dooley said, heading for the living room. 'Your Xbox still in 'ere?'

'Yeah, the controller should be near the TV, unless she's moved it again.' Jammin's voice echoed within the confines of the kitchen walls. 'She's always cleaning and moving stuff. Besides, I'm not even too sure there's any batteries in it.'

Dooley opened the door and stopped beneath the doorframe, feeling his phone vibrate in his pocket. He pulled it free and entered, seeing a suggestive picture and an alluring text. So engrossed was Dooley, he failed to notice the six-foot male standing in front of him.

Eight

'Pink and blue'

Shaw stood silent, not even a breath leaving his lips. He watched the large white man enter the living room, his eyes glued to his phone. The man was dressed in a white zip-up hoody, baggy blue jeans and white trainers. Shaw's eyes darted to Quinn who held his position behind the door.

Dooley continued slowly towards him, oblivious to his presence. He took four slow steps, smiled, and looked up. The sight of the stranger froze him solid, but only for a moment.

'Who are you?' he said.

Shaw said nothing. His eyes darted to Quinn and back again.

Dooley had known Jammin long enough to know this man didn't belong in his house, and that Jammin would have mentioned him if he did. Within seconds, Dooley's chubby face creased into a face of aggression. His shoulders hunched and his limbs tensed. His hands balled into large hard fists and his face flushed with blood. He lunged forward, cocking back his right shoulder, telegraphing his attack.

Shaw stepped back with his right foot, shifting his weight to his rear leg. He snapped across a sharp left hook at a perfect right angle, twisting at the hip and pivoting on the toes. The impact shuddered up through Shaw's arm into the muscles of his shoulder and back. Dooley's jaw dislocated, and his arms fell by his side, unconscious before his face hit the floor.

Jammin burst into the room, holding a glass of fizzy liquid in each hand. 'What the hell was that?'

Quinn kicked the door, catching Jammin by surprise, and grabbed him from behind. His arms wrapped around his neck and held him tight, enforcing his trademark sleeper hold. Jammin dropped the glasses and kicked out in panic, but Quinn held him strong, lifting him off the ground to add gravity to his embrace. Picco appeared in the doorway and threw a crippling body shot to Jammin's stomach, weakening him further.

Shaw crouched down to Dooley and assessed his state of health. Even though his jaw was broken and he was unconscious, Shaw was relieved to see he was still breathing. He knew punches weren't like what they were in the movies. Hit a guy properly in the real world and there's a good chance he'll never get back up.

57

Quinn threw Jammin head first into the cream armchair, sliding it back over a foot on the smooth wooden floor, stopping only when it struck the wall. Jammin turned in the seat, saliva drooling from his open mouth. Before Jammin could get comfortable, Quinn was on him again. He cocked back his right fist and smashed it into Jammin's left eye.

'You fucking listening?' Quinn said, clamping Jammin's wrists to the chair's arms.

'Just take the money,' Jammin said.

'I'm fuckin gonna.' Quinn pushed his masked face close to Jammin's, 'but I want everything. I want your stash.'

Jammin's eyes widened. 'There is no st—'

His words were cut short by Quinn's fist smashing into the bridge of his nose, more for speed than power. His nose broke instantly, spilling thick red blood down the back of his throat and over the lower portion of his face and trendy yellow T-shirt. Tears and blood filled his eyes, blurring his vision. Quinn paused for a moment and stared into his blood-filled eyes.

Jammin choked on the blood. 'Look, just walk away,' he pleaded more than offered, knowing his girlfriend would be home any minute.

Quinn turned from him and reached into his holdall and pulled out an eight inch yellow screwdriver. Without warning or emotion, Quinn drove it deep into Jammin's right hand. The sharp point felt little resistance as it penetrated his flesh and nailed him to the arm of the chair. He screamed, reaching for the screwdriver with his good hand, only for Quinn to hold it down.

Shaw gasped in shock and took a step forward, as if to prevent what was happening, only to be stopped by Picco's gaze.

Jammin fell silent, watching his hand shake and his blood seep into the chair.

Quinn leant forward again, putting his masked mouth to Jammin's right ear. 'If you don't give me what I want, when I've finished fucking you up, I'm gonna sit on that sofa and wait for your cute little girl to come home, and then I'm gonna fuck her and her mam up, too.'

Quinn's words broke what little fight Jammin had in him. 'Upstairs… in the attic… under the magazines… in a suitcase,' he said, struggling to get his words out from behind the long strands of clotted blood and the breath-taking pain in his hand.

'Go check,' Quinn said, his empty gaze never leaving Jammin. Picco looked at Shaw.

Shaw negotiated the stairs two at a time, grateful to have escaped the violent atmosphere of the living room. Once he was on the landing, he scanned the ceiling for the attics hatch, finding it above the master bedroom's entrance. He climbed up onto the pine coloured banister railing, balancing himself against the door frame of the bedroom and reached up, pushing open the wooden lid. The hatch lifted easily, revealing a blanket of cold darkness within. Cold air seeped down from the gap as particles of dust fell from its broken seal. He jumped up and pulled himself inside and entered the darkness. The attic appeared small considering the grand size of the house and, to Shaw's surprise, it was un-converted. Only half of the attic floor was boarded and safe to walk on, whilst the remainder exposed the dirty woollen installation running between the joists. He pulled out his mobile phone and used the illuminated screen to light up the darkness, throwing gloomy deep shadows around the attic's dirty contents. Numerous cardboard boxes were stacked in neat rows, ranging from shoebox size to household removal size, each one consisting of old books, VHS tapes, old ornaments, or photo album looking binders. A weights bench lay flat across the open joists, whilst several black bags filled a corner. An old scalextric box, taped up at the corners, caught his eye, sparking an old memory of him and his brother playing with theirs when they were children. Finally, the phones artificial light spilled across a large collection of lad's magazines, dating as far back as twelve years. Underneath, as Jammin had stated, was a suitcase. He kicked off the magazines, pushing them to one side, and placed his mobile phone between his teeth. He aimed the light at the brown plastic suitcase and unclipped the two rusty weak clasps, struggling with the left one. Inside were five transparent bags, each packed with a fine, dirty white powder, equal in size to a bag of sugar. Stuffed beside them were four smaller bags filled with pink and blue tablets. Underneath the bags were A4 brown paper envelopes. But what caught his eye more than anything was the matte black semi-automatic pistol that sat on top of it all. He reached in and picked it up. He released the magazine from its housing and pulled back on the top slide, checking its chamber. A brass 9mm round ejected into the suitcase and rolled down between the bags. The weapon was a Glock 17 with a standard seventeen round capacity magazine fitted; a weapon popular with American and British law enforcement. He rehoused the magazine along with the ejected round and fired off the action, rending the gun safe. He then tucked in the back of his jeans and resealed the suitcase.

He lowered the suitcase down through the attic hatch and dropped it the remaining seven feet to the landing below. Shaw then followed. He placed his body weight against the wall and doorframe, giving his hands the freedom to replace the wooden cover before finally dropping back down to the landing, rubbing away any scuff marks left by his boots. The consequences of his fingerprints being discovered if the police got involved turned his stomach with worry.

'Can't believe I'm doing this,' he said. He picked up the suitcase and hurried down the stairs, not wanting to be in the house any longer than was necessary. Jammin sat in the chair, thick blood oozing from his broken nose; his right hand impaled to the chair arm. His right leg twitched uncontrollably. His breathing was rapid and shallow, and his brow appeared moist and clammy. 'He's going into shock,' he said, recognising the tell-tale signs.

Quinn turned and faced him, his eyes burning behind the balaclava. 'So?'

Picco took the suitcase from him and threw it onto the cream corner sofa, marking it with the dirt from the attic. He unclipped the clasps and opened it. 'That's it,' he said, satisfied.

'And the money?' Quinn asked.

Picco shook his head.

Quinn turned back to Jammin, who was now breathing deeper and faster. 'Where's the money?'

Jammin said nothing, unable to speak due to the increased rate of breath.

Quinn pointed the bat at him. 'Where's the fucking money?'

'He's hyperventilating! He's gone into shock,' Shaw said. 'He needs a fucking ambulance.'

As if deaf to Shaw's words, Quinn swung the bat high above Jammin's limp body and crashed it down hard against his left shoulder. The audible snap of his collarbone breaking filled the silence, followed by Jammin's gurgled scream.

'I won't ask you again,' Quinn said.

Shaw grabbed Quinn by the arm and pulled him back from the unconscious black man. 'That's enough. You'll fucking kill him.'

Quinn met Shaw's gaze, his eyes deadpan. 'Let's go.'

Picco closed the suitcase and fastened its clasps, lifting it from the sofa. Shaw looked at Jammin, wanting to ring an ambulance, wanting to attend to his wounds, knowing that if he didn't, the chances of his survival were unlikely. But he couldn't, he couldn't take the risk. Instead, he reached down and picked up the black carrier bag containing Michael's five grand. Out the corner of his eye, he noticed Quinn reaching into his holdall.

Quinn pulled free a double-barrelled sawn-off shotgun and fired both barrels, point blank, into Jammin's chest. His body bounced where it was sat as his torso exploded, the twelve gauge shells shredding through his blood stained T-shirt and into his ribcage. Blood back-splashed over Quinn, spitting his balaclava and top with speckles of red. The shot echoed around the room, amplified by the wooden floor and lack of contents, deafening everyone within.

Shaw jumped upright and cupped his ears, attempting to stop the ringing. 'What the fuck have you done?'

'Grab the gear,' Quinn said.

Nine

'Consequences'

The cold polymer of the Glock 17 now tucked into the waist of his jeans was uncomfortable against the flesh of his lower back, but then Shaw hadn't carried such a weapon in such a fashion for a long time. He turned the key, gunning the engine, and pulled away.

'What did we get?' Quinn said, wiping the spotted blood from his face.

'About five K of Brown, a few bags of Eddies and a couple of envelopes of trips,' Picco said. 'Plus Michael's five grand.'

Shaw remained silent and focused on driving towards Sunderland's city centre. Quinn's actions replayed over and over in his head: the sound of the gunshot reverberating around the room like a caged lion, the sight of the man's chest exploding, and the knowledge that, not only were his fingerprints all over the attic hatch, but also the man lying unconscious on the floor had seen his face.

'Take a right at this roundabout,' Quinn said, 'we're heading across the bridge.'

Shaw indicated and manoeuvred the white van into the relevant lane, stopping at the roundabout's traffic lights. He'd been driving the van for almost twenty minutes, although he wasn't quite sure of the exact time of departure, stopping only once to change the registration plates. The lights turned green and Shaw pulled away, crossing the Queen Alexandra Bridge that spanned the River Wear.

'Turn right again at the next roundabout,' Quinn said.

'We're not going to the club?' Shaw said.

Quinn pushed his brown rimmed glasses up the bridge of his nose. 'No.'

Shaw continued to follow Quinn's directions, leading him up a heavily pedestrianised road lined with cars and shops, popular with takeaways and fast food outlets. Street bins over flowed with empty white cartons and pizza boxes. Pigeons swooped like a squadron of fearless fighter jets spreading the trash far up the road and along the gutters, searching for any leftover scraps.

'After the zebra crossing, we're going left,' Quinn said.

The street was narrow with cars parked all the way along one side, giving the narrow street even less room to manoeuvre. The terrace houses that lined the street were all small and similar in appearance, each one built identically to the other, with a single step leading up to their plain front doors.

'Just here,' Quinn said, pointing to the house on the corner. Parked out front, Shaw recognised Kimberly's red MR2 and Will's maroon Saxo. He found a space close to the house and parallel parked, swivelling the van effortlessly into the space. Without saying a word, Picco and Quinn exited, taking everything with them.

Kimberly appeared at the door wearing a dangerously short tartan miniskirt. 'What took you so long?'

'Where's Michael?' Quinn said, ignoring Kimberly's question.

'He'll be here later. Said he had some things that needed sorting.'

Shaw slammed the driver's door and approached the house. Kimberly looked him up and down and turned back inside. He watched her hips sway from side to side and the muscles in her calves tense with every step. He paused at the entrance, seeing Will appear from what looked to be the living room at the end of the passage. In his hands he carried a large white tub of liquid and a concerned smile on his face. Shaw stood aside and allowed him to step out onto the street.

'How'd it go?' Will said.

Shaw grabbed him by the scruff of his bright green tracksuit jacket and slammed him into the side of the Saxo. The tub fell into the gutter. 'What the fuck have you got me into?'

'I'm sorry, Ryan.'

'You're sorry?'

'You wouldn't have helped me otherwise.'

Shaw pushed his knuckles into Will's chin, fighting back the urge to punch him. 'Do you know what you've done? You've fucking buried me.'

'They were going to kill me,' Will said, his bottom lip quivering with shame.

'Better you than me,' he said. 'I have a little boy. You…' Shaw allowed his sentence to trail off as he forced his knuckles into his brother's chin, determined to cause him harm. 'Did you know what was going to happen today?'

'No.'

'Tell the truth, Will.'

'I knew you were going with Quinn to tax someone, but that's all I knew. Honestly, Ryan, that's all I knew.'

'You fucking arsehole. Why didn't you warn me?'

'You wouldn't have gone.'

Shaw could see the tears surfacing in his brother's eyes.

'Please don't leave me, Ryan. I'm a fucking dead man if you go.'

The pair were interrupted by the impressive sound of a powerful engine pulling into the narrow street.

Will turned to see Michael's GT-R crawling towards them. 'I better get on with this,' he said, looking down to the large tub of bleach lying in the gutter. 'Just don't say anything yet, please.'

Shaw let him go and watched Michael park the sports car a few doors down in the only space available. He knew he should leave. Every muscle and gut feeling told him to. The thought of going back to prison and never seeing his little boy again crippled him, yet the thought of abandoning his brother hurt him even more. Will wasn't strong enough to see this through on his own, and he definitely wasn't strong enough to go to prison. He remembered how much Will had cried when they'd both been caught smashing a rival school's windows when they were children. He would sacrifice his life for his brother if he had to, Shaw knew that, but if it came to him losing his future for Will, he would never forgive him.

Michael smiled. 'Enjoy today?'

Shaw didn't answer, still thinking about earlier and the consequences that would soon follow.

Michael entered the house, releasing a lung full of smoke from his cigarette. 'Howay in, have a cuppa.'

Shaw glanced down at his brother who was now in the process of bleaching the inside of the van.

'I'm sorry,' Will mouthed.

The air in the house was thick and sweet, as if far too much air freshener had been sprayed and not enough fresh air had been allowed to circulate. The passageway was narrow with an open doorway at the end where the living room was. There was a closed door to his right, and beside that was a staircase. Shaw glanced up as he passed, seeing a pretty dark haired girl of maybe fourteen years peering around the corner. The living room was small and confined, sizing around fourteen feet by twelve. An old three seat sofa and armchair of different designs sat upon a threadbare, red floral carpet, surrounded by yellowing walls and a yellow ceiling from years of nicotine abuse. Sat on the sofa with her legs crossed was Kimberly. Sat to her left was Bomber. The suitcase lay open on a coffee table in front of them. Picco stood resting against the doorway of the kitchen, his arms folded across his chest. In the kitchen, Shaw could hear Quinn clanging

64

cutlery.

Michael weaved his way around the coffee table towards Kimberly and Bomber. 'Come on, shift up,' he said, sitting in-between the pair of them. 'Did you get my money?'

'Only the five grand,' Picco said.

'Do you think it was wise to tax one of Nolan's dealers?' Kimberly said, adjusting her skirt to hide what it could of her modesty.

'Nolan doesn't know it was us who shafted him, and he never will,' he assured her, placing his right hand on her knee.

Shaw wondered if Michael knew what had happened at the house today, or if he even cared. Maybe he'd even ordered it.

'Help yourself if you want a coffee,' Michael said, looking through his new merchandise. Shaw didn't reply, instead he focused on not staring at Kimberly's thighs. He tried to look away but found his eyes returning every time. The slender shape and firmness of her flesh was highly complimented by the black nylon wrapping.

'Where's the toilet?' he said.

'Top of the stairs, on the left,' Michael said, counting his pills. 'Make sure it's the only room you go in.'

He attacked the stairs two at a time and identified the room he was after. Once inside, he leaned on the browning sink, allowing it to support his weight, and stared hard into the moulding cracked mirror. He could feel his foundations crumbling beneath him, his life falling further into ruin. A guilt gnawed at him, but not from today, a guilt from before, a buried guilt from years ago. His mind flashed back to the dream he'd had yesterday, the nightmare he'd thought he'd learned to accept. He turned the tap and filled his hands, splashing his face with icy cold water. He hated not being in control. Not being in control scared him; filled him with a fear few people would understand. And the only way he could see out of the situation was to see it through to the end, wherever that may be.

He dried his hands on his jeans and left, noticing one of the bedroom doors was ajar. He crept forward and knocked the door open with his boot. The scent of lavender was overpowering, as if trying to mask the odour of something far worse. He pushed the door open fully and entered, spilling light from the landing into the dark room. The curtains were pulled closed, hiding the room from the world outside. Female's clothes were spread across the floor and the unmade double bed. A single lamp sat upon an open chest of draws, exposing its contents. A cereal bowl filled with condoms of random flavours and colours sat on the bedside cabinet next to

65

an open tube of lubricant and an overflowing ashtray.

'What are you doing in Sara's room?' An accented female voice said from the landing outside.

*

Michael closed the suitcase and refastened its clasps. 'That should convince the buyers,' he said. 'Plus, the Mallinsons are dropping their money off at the club tonight.' He looked at Quinn. 'And the guns will be sorted for tomorrow, right?'

'Aye. I spoke to him earlier. He's getting the gear ready as we speak.'

'Will that bitch be joining us?' Kimberly said.

Michael smiled. 'I'm not sure, why? Don't you like her?'

'No I don't, and I don't trust her either. There's something iffy about her.'

'Well I like her,' he said, taking a mouthful of his tea.

'You mean you like the way she fucks?'

Michael grinned.

'That's the van done,' Will said, entering the living room.

'It better have been cleaned properly,' Quinn said.

'It has. Front and back.'

'It better had.' Quinn pushed his glasses back up his nose and took a mouthful of tea.

'Where's your brother?' Bomber asked Will.

'He's still upstairs, probably snooping through the rooms,' Kimberly said.

Michael turned his gaze to Will. 'You better get a fucking grip of your brother. Quinn, go bring him down here.'

*

Shaw exited the room and focused on the two remaining doors, seeing the one on the left was open. 'I was looking for a towel,' he said, seeing the voice had come from the pretty dark-haired girl, her long wavy hair hanging loose in front of her pale face. 'Where's Sara now?' he said in his friendliest voice, keeping his volume low.

'She is out working.' Her accent was East Slavic; Russian maybe.

'How old are you?'

'I am one six years old.'

'Sixteen? Are you sure?' he said, certain she was younger.

'What happened to your face?' she said, not acknowledging his question.

'I was in an accident.'

The girl retreated back inside her room and closed the door, abruptly ending their conversation.

'Michael told you to leave all the other rooms alone,' Quinn said, standing three quarters of the way up the stairs.

Shaw turned and faced him. His empty, unkind eyes were shielded from view behind his cold glasses, and his greasy hair was a mess from the balaclava worn earlier.

'I was talking to the girl. And Michael said not to go into the rooms. And as you can see, I'm stood on the landing.'

'I know why Michael has you hanging around, but as soon as that weapon deal's done, I'm gonna introduce myself to you properly.'

'I look forward to it,' Shaw said, deadpan.

'Ryan,' Will yelled from downstairs. 'Michael wants a word.'

'Another time, eh.' Shaw pushed passed him and made his way down the stairs, re-entering the living room. 'What?'

Michael smiled. 'The inspection's happening tomorrow. Make sure you're at the club for twelve. No later, do you hear me?'

'Tomorrow?' Shaw echoed.

'Yes, tomorrow. Is there a problem?'

'Yeah, tomorrow's no good.'

'What?' Michael said, looking at Will. 'What do you mean it's no good?'

Will took Shaw by the shoulder and turned him to face him. 'Ryan,' he said, his eyes pleading with his.

'Be ready for twelve,' Michael repeated. 'Now get out.'

Shaw gave Will a steely look and left. Will said his goodbyes and followed. He opened the doors to his Saxo and allowed Shaw to climb into the passenger seat.

'A couple of hours is what you said.' Shaw kept his eyes pinned out the passenger window, refusing to look at Will or the house. 'They'll never even know you're gone is what you said.'

'I know. I'm—'

'Don't you fucking dare say you're sorry.'

Will pulled away, turning down the dance music that inappropriately blasted from the speakers. 'I don't know what else to say.'

Shaw gripped his forehead and massaged his temples with his forefinger and thumb, his gaze transfixed on the rain drops running along the glass. 'Don't say anything. I don't want to hear it.' He thought about

67

how he was going to get around the problem. He was due to meet with his counsellor tomorrow afternoon. Failure to keep that appointment was a sure ticket back into prison, regardless of how much of a rapport he'd built with his probation officer.

Will turned left out of the narrow street and stopped at a busy cross junction of traffic lights. 'What happened exactly?'

Shaw looked at him. 'You screwed me is what happened.'

Will said nothing.

'Quinn killed a man.'

'Killed him? Will echoed, genuinely taken back. 'Are you sure?'

'Am I sure? Yes I'm fucking sure. I think the shotgun blast to the chest was the biggest clue. And for what? A suitcase full of shit?'

'Ryan, I'm sorry.'

'You're sorry? Well, that's okay then, nothing for me to worry about, seeing as though my prints are all over the attic hatch and the dead guy's fat friend couldn't have got a better look at me.'

'Shit, Ryan. I didn't know. Honestly.'

'Fine. You didn't know.' Shaw believed him, how could he not, they were brothers after all. 'Pull in here.' Shaw pointed to a pub car park. 'I need a drink.'

Will pulled in and stopped. The pub was a white Edwardian build with large bay windows either side of its double doors. The first floor and attic looked large enough to function as a hotel. Outside the main doors were several picnic tables and two large heated canopies. Beneath the right-hand canopy was a middle-aged woman dressed in a dark grey trouser suit, smoke exhaling from between her thin lips.

'Are you sure self-medication is the answer?' Will said.

'It's either this or I break your nose.' Shaw waited for Will to climb out before he pulled the Glock 17 from the back of his jeans and slipped it beneath the passenger seat.

Once inside, Will ordered two lagers. 'What are we gonna do?' he said, resting against the bar.

'About what?'

'About the fat friend. The prints may go unnoticed but the filth are gonna speak to him, and he's gonna talk.'

'What would you like me to do? Visit him in the hospital and shut him up?'

'I don't know. I just want it to all go away. Wish I'd never replied to Kim's fucking message.

The barman returned with the drinks and Will paid him.

'Yeah well, you did, and now we're here. Both of us.' Shaw took a mouthful of his drink.

'I honestly didn't know that was going to happen today.'

'So you've said.'

The pair sat in silence for a few more seconds before Will spoke again. 'Why is tomorrow no good for you?'

'How many times do I have to say it to you? I'm on fucking probation. I have appointments I have to keep. People I have to see. If I don't, I go back inside.'

'So what happens now? If you don't inspect the gear they'll…' Will paused. 'Couldn't one of your old friends pay Michael a visit or something, shake him up a little; scare him off?'

Shaw held his gaze on the condensation running down the side of his glass. 'What friends? All but Pikey turned their backs on me the day I was booted. And he's done enough for me already. Besides, he's out of the country.'

'Are you going to do this inspection?'

Shaw looked at him. He could see the desperation in his brother's eyes, the fear of what his answer may be. 'I'll give my probation officer a ring. See if she can, somehow, sort me another day.'

'She?'

'Yeah, she,' Shaw said.

'Is she hot?'

'Hot? What are you, an American high schooler?'

Will laughed. 'Well, is she?'

Shaw's phone started to ring in his pocket. He pulled it out and read his counsellor's name on its screen. 'Shit,' he said. He wasn't ready to speak to him yet. 'What's he want?'

Will jutted his chin towards Shaw's phone. 'Who is it?'

Shaw ignored it slipped his phone back in his pocket. 'You know, there's a dead man slumped in his armchair, just waiting for his wife and daughter to come home and find him, and you're asking me about how hot my probation officer is.'

Will went quiet.

'And to top it off. It'll be me going down for it.'

'It won't come to that. You'll carry out the inspection tomorrow and then we'll go home. Forget this all happened.'

'And then everything will be peachy? Just carry on as if nothing had even taken place?'

'Yes,' Will said.

'Quinn killed that black lad today for nothing. He'd already given him everything he wanted. He hadn't even seen Quinn's face. Yet he still killed him. Whatever Michael's after, he's prepared to have people killed for it. Why do you think he had me tag along today with my face on show for the world to see? He didn't need me there. Why do you think he had me inspect that fired weapon without any gloves? There's something else going on here. I felt it the second Kimberly looked at me.'

Ten

'Half a bernie'

Bomber laughed at Michael's joke, even though he didn't find it particularly funny. He knew how to play the game. Keeping the boss happy was half the job. He'd known Michael for more than four years now, first coming across him in a club in Soho, selling drugs with Quinn as background muscle. Michael was only a street level player back then, working the street corners and pushing prostitutes for the local big shot. It had taken Michael years of 'yes sir, no sir' to get enough money together to open his own club up North, and when he moved, Bomber had moved back with him.

Quinn laughed also, filling the living room with a hearty roar. 'They're both cunts, Michael, not just Will.'

Bomber wondered if his colleague had even understood the humour behind Michael's comment. 'Ryan's not like Will,' he said. 'He's motivated. Controlling him may prove difficult.

'He just needs his fucking skull kicking in, is all. The guy's a fanny,' Quinn said. He turned to Picco. 'You saw him in the house, he was fucking useless. Cunt just stood there.'

Picco disagreed. 'That's not what I saw.'

'And what did you see?' Quinn said.

'No, Bomber's right. People like him are unpredictable,' Michael concurred. 'Besides, he doesn't seem to be too frightened of you, big lad.'

'Well he fucking should be,' Quinn said, rising to Michael's taunt, 'because as soon as this deal's done, I'm putting him in the ground.'

Michael laughed light-heartedly. 'I am a little concerned he won't play ball tomorrow, though, especially after the way he reacted today.'

'Well if he doesn't, I'll just kill him,' Quinn said, not really thinking long term.

'Not as easy as that, though, is it, Leroy? We still need the hardware inspecting, and he doesn't seem to scare easily.'

'Why don't we take Will?' Kimberly suggested. 'After all, we did include him to use him. So let's use him.'

'And I know just the place to hold him, too,' Quinn said, smiling with pride.

Michael slapped his thighs and stood up with a groan. 'Okay, make it happen,' he said. He bent forward and picked up the suitcase.

Bomber stood up too. 'We're leaving now?'

Michael nodded and looked at Quinn slouching in the armchair. 'Make sure this contact of yours delivers tomorrow. I'm trusting your judgment on this,' he said with a cringe. He didn't want to rely on Quinn's judgement, but it was his contact that had the hardware he needed.

'It's happening, relax,' Quinn said.

'Relax!' He dropped the suitcase and stood at Quinn's feet, looking down at him. 'Do you think I want to rely on you? Because I don't. I'm placing all my trust on you because I have too. So don't fuck it up.'

'I won't,' Quinn said, his shoulders sloped like a told off schoolboy.

'I hope not, Leroy. I really do, because if this all goes shitty, it's not just me that will be getting buried. Is that understood? These aren't just some idiots off a street corner. These Turks'll cut us up.'

'I know.'

'Then start acting like it.' Michael relaxed his stiffened posture and picked up the suitcase. 'Now make sure it's sorted.' He turned to Bomber. 'Come on,' he said, heading for the door.

*

The block of flats towered eighteen stories into the air. Dozens of windows were wide open, leaving the nets behind them to be sucked out into wet air and flutter wildly, mimicking haunting spirits. The occasional balcony housed random pieces of colourful clothing in the hope they would dry beneath the cover of the balcony above.

Michael pulled the rear-view mirror towards him and appraised his appearance. Dressed in a dark grey suit and white shirt, Michael already knew he looked good, but he asked anyway.

'Sharp,' Bomber said. 'You need me to come up?'

'No, you'll have to wait down here and watch the car. Kids are little bastards round here,' he said, feeling the nerves of the coming meeting.

He exited the car, taking the carrier bag containing the heroin, and walked towards the Newcastle block of flats. Heavy CCTV units caged in wire mesh monitored the front entrance. Graffiti decorated the entrances walls, and McDonald wrappers and fizzy pop cans spilled from the overflowing trash bin. He approached the lift and pressed the call button with a biro from his inside pocket, avoiding the dried-on phlegm that covered it. Moments later, the spray painted chrome doors slid open, revealing a girl, no older than thirteen, dressed in bright leggings, red trainers and a blue puffer jacket. In front of her was a buggy with a screaming girl sat in it, her face bright red and eyes squeezed tight in protest.

He allowed her to leave the lift first and entered, choosing the fourteenth floor. The doors closed with a judder and the lift began to climb. When the doors opened, he was again welcomed by screaming. A couple stood yelling at each other in the corridor and, from what Michael could make out, a heavily overweight woman was accusing her man of sleeping with her sister.

The woman's greasy black hair was tied up into a ponytail, exposing the filth that floated on the sweat that ran between the folds of fat in her neck.

'What the fuck you looking at?' she said.

Michael turned without answering and made his way down the corridor, away from the explosive argument, stopping at the required flat, four doors down. Only the tarnished brass door number decorated the peeling red paint of the door. He checked his watch, 15:28, suddenly aware of his increased heart rate and his need to urinate. He knew there was a possibility, that if he didn't impress the tenants inside, he could enter the flat and never walk out. He knocked three times.

'Who is it?' a deep foreign voice said from behind the door.

'It's Michael,' he said, glancing left and right.

The door opened, pulling the length of a brass chain. 'You're late,' said a thick black moustache on a heavy set, unshaven face.

'No. I'm not.' He checked his watch again. 'I'm right on time.'

'You're late,' the large, swirly skinned male repeated, closing the door to remove the chain.

Apart from an old black leather sofa, a nineteen inch flat screen TV, which was sat upon a grey poly-prop chair, and a cheap looking chemistry set sitting on the windowsill, the room was empty.

The heavy-set Turk closed the door behind him and locked it, reapplying the chain.

'Michael Maloney.' The man known as Abdullah Paytak, a major player in a Turkish gang based in Tottenham, appeared from the kitchen. The middle-aged Turk stood the same height as him and was dressed casually in jeans and a dark jacket.

'Thank you for agreeing to see me,' Michael said, attempting to hide his nerves.

'It's no big deal. I was on my way through to Manchester anyway,' he said in a deceivingly gritty Cockney accent.

'Yeah I know, but I know you're busy, so I—'

'So what? You think you can actually deliver on this?' Abdullah interrupted, closing in on Michael.

Michael could smell cigarettes on his clothing and alcohol on his breath. His face was weathered and unshaven. 'I know I can,' he said, standing tall and upright.

Abdullah circled him. He placed his hand on his shoulder and looked him up and down as if sizing him for a coffin. 'What does Nolan have to say about you selling drugs on his patch?'

'I'll be seeing Nolan later.'

'You mean you haven't cleared this with him already?'

'What do you think?' Michael said, feeling the knot in his stomach grow tighter. 'Why do you think you're getting it so cheap?'

'You don't talk to me until you've cleared it with Nolan.'

'Now hang on, you're a hard man to get hold of. I had to snatch the opportunity to talk to you when I could.'

'You don't speak to me until you've spoken with Nolan,' Abdullah repeated. 'Nolan could make it very difficult for me up here.'

'Look, I'm selling you ten kilos of uncut brown here, and all I'm asking for is a five hundred grand. You could double that. Triple it even.' Before Abdullah could interrupt, Michael continued. 'Like we arranged, I've brought you a sample to test. If you don't like it, we'll call the whole thing off.'

Abdullah lit up a cigarette. 'If I don't like it, I'll hack your fucking head off.'

Michael swallowed. 'I'm sure it won't come to that.'

Abdullah waved over the heavy-set male from the front door who took the carrier bag from Michael and placed it on the windowsill next to the chemistry set. He pulled out the plastic tub and used the handle end of a tea spoon to add the heroin to liquid he'd poured into one of the beakers. Gradually, the liquid turned a light blue in colour as he swirled the beaker, holding it up to the window for inspection. Michael watched him, barely breathing, praying it would react correctly. He pulled out a cigarette of his own and put it in his mouth, his fingers fumbling with his petrol lighter. The man turned to Abdullah and spoke in a language Michael couldn't comprehend.

'Okay, I'll buy your gear,' Abdullah said. 'Nolan doesn't own me, but he does own the freeways of the North East. It would be bad for business if anyone found out I was dealing with you without his consent.'

Michael nodded, releasing an unaware held breath and a long stream of smoke along with it. 'No one will hear it from me.'

'Seems we've got a deal. I'll give you half a bernie for it, plus I get

74

to keep this sample.'

Knowing a bernie was slang for a million, Michael shook his hand.

'Good, are you happy with how this is all going to work?' Abdullah said. 'I'll arrange a time and a place, and we'll carry out a one for one.' He closed in on him, entering his private space. 'What currency do you want it in?'

'Sterling.'

Abdullah picked off an unseen piece of fluff from Michael's shoulder and discarded it. 'How soon can you get the gear?'

'How soon can you get the money?'

Abdullah smiled. 'How soon can you get the gear?'

'I can be ready Thursday.'

'Thursday? I'll be in touch with a time and location.'

The heavy-set Turk stood from the windowsill and showed Michael to the door.

'Oh and, Michael,' Abdullah added, stopping Michael before he could leave. 'I don't have to warn you, do I?'

'No,' Michael said before the Turk could close the door behind him.

*

Melanie's taxi ride back to her flat had been quick and uneventful. No words had been spoken between her and her driver and the stereo had been switched down low. She paid her fare and climbed out. Her ground floor flat was a small attractive new build in what some people would class as a less glamorous area of Gateshead. The new brickwork and PVC double-glazed windows appeared stylish and modern, and the recently laid turf in the front lawn was already in need of a cut. Parked next to the small patch of grass was her blue Toyota Yaris. Lying motionless on the windowsill with his face pressed up against the inside of the glass was Trigger, her beloved tabby cat, soaking up what little sun escaped through the clouds. Inside, the flat was as it always was; not a mess, but not showroom tidy either. Lived in was how she liked to describe it. A few items of clean clothing were strung over one of the two leather sofas and a mug and plate lay forgotten beside the other. The laminated flooring throughout the flat created the appearance of space within the living room and helped capture the light coming through the single window. She flicked on her forty inch flat screen TV and walked into the bathroom, followed closely by Trigger.

Hot, thick steam clouded up the bathroom mirror like a distant memory. The refreshing warm water cascaded down over her naked body, spraying her face and breasts. Her mind focused on the soothing aromas coming from the inexpensive body wash, trying to forget the incidents of the day when she heard the faint tone of a distant ring. She killed the shower and pulled the curtain too, hearing the ring of the landline telephone. She stepped out the bathtub and ran naked to the bedroom, leaving foamy footprints with every step. She picked up the receiver, water dripping onto the un-made bed sheets.

'Hello,' she said, running her free hand through her wet hair.

'Could I speak to Melanie MacDermott please?' a male voice said.

'Speaking.'

'Melanie, it's Slater. Can you talk?'

'Yeah why, what's up?'

'When was the last time you saw Shaw?'

'Yesterday. Why?'

'What about Michael?'

'Not since this morning. Why? What's happened?'

Slater looked at the photographs of Jammin's dead body pinned to the homicide board in his office. 'Nothing important,' he said. 'Something's come up, is all.'

Melanie sat herself down on the bed, wetting her sheets further. 'Has something happened?'

'Nothing for you to worry about,' he said.

Trigger made an appearance in the bedroom and approached Melanie, smearing his scent over her naked wet feet.

'If something's happened, then I want te know about it,' she said.

Slater had just ended a call to his colleague who was in the hospital, speaking to the dead man's friend, Kevin Dooley. Dooley had made a statement claiming he'd seen nothing, but dirt on Jammin's sofa had led them to his attic, where Shaw's fingerprints had been found. 'Nothing's happened,' he reassured her. 'I just needed to know if you'd seen either of them, is all.'

'Then no, I haven't. And I won't see Michael till tonight.'

'Okay.'

'Well if there's nothing else, I have te go get ready for work, sure.'

'Yeah of course. And, Mel, if you can, find out what Michael's been up to today.'

The thought of going back to work sickened her. 'I'll try.' She hung up and returned to the bathroom. She wiped a single line through the steamed-up mirror and looked at her naked reflection, wishing for it to be all over. 'Keep it together, girl.'

She sprayed the final burst of hairspray around her head and pulled on her designer zip-up hoody. She picked up her rucksack containing her night's outfit and headed into the front room, just in time to witness her iPhone vibrate across the pine coffee table. She picked it up and read the received text message.

'LEAVING MINE NOW HON. WILL BE AT YOURS IN 10. CB xx'

She put the phone in her pocket and lifted Trigger to eye level. A tradition she'd carried out every night since meeting Slater; every night since he'd forced her to be his informant; every night since she'd feared her shift at work.

'Wish me luck,' she said, staring into his dark eyes.

Trigger meowed in response, turning his head to see out into the front garden

'Aye, I know,' she said, placing him down on the windowsill. 'As soon as all this is over, we'll move te Norn Iron. Ya'd prefer it there, anyhow.' She peered through her front room window with her cat, her ghostly reflection visible in the glass, and watched the rain waterlog the gardens and flood the drains and gutters. At ten past seven in the evening, the sky was black and the moon was out.

A car pulled up outside her front lawn and sounded its horn. She collected her umbrella from beneath the sink, grabbed her rucksack, and exited the house. The rain beat off her umbrella, wetting her tan coloured suede boots and grey jogging bottoms as she ran towards the silver Micra parked at the end of her drive. Outdated chart music played from the car stereo at a volume that was loud yet comfortable. Chloe Banks smiled infectiously in the driver's seat, her chest length black hair was thick and wavy over her slender, spray tanned shoulders, and her eyes were dark with makeup. She had worked as a stripper at the club for little over a year, taking off her clothes three times a week, and earning up to two hundred and fifty pounds a night. She'd befriended Melanie almost immediately, due to her having a close friend from Northern Ireland, back from her days in university when she studied law, which Melanie found both equally ironic and surprising.

'Weather's proper shocking,' Chloe said, stating the obvious. 'Just wish it would snow and get it over and done with.'

Melanie gave her umbrella a quick shake and closed the car door.

'It's been a lousy winter, so it has.'

Chloe reversed her Micra, manoeuvring it to face out of the cul–de-sac, and pulled away.

Eleven

'Easy prey'

The pub was busy and loud with chatter and laughter. Dozens of people queued at the bar, shouting orders nonstop at the bar staff. A table behind Shaw erupted into a burst of laughter and high pitched heckles. Eight women, ranging from their early twenties to late forties, sat on high stools, indulging in several bottles of wine and mixed spirits. Judging by their dark coloured suits and the identity badges that swung from the necks of three of them, Shaw guessed that they'd came straight from work. He watched them in the mirror behind the bar, studying their characteristics and mannerisms, one in particular catching his eye. She had long brown hair like Amy and wore a tight fitted white blouse and dark pencil skirt. Her bare legs were crossed beneath the table, ending at the tips with one of her simple black heeled shoes hanging from her toes.

'Same again?' Will said, breaking Shaw's train of thought.

'What?'

'Do you want another one?' Will's words slurred from the intake of alcohol.

Shaw turned without answering and made his way past the large Christmas tree to the main doors. If he didn't call his probation officer soon, it would be too late.

'I'll get you another one.'

Outside, a middle aged man took shelter from the cold rain in the doorway. 'I need to quit,' he said, vapour escaping his mouth and nose. 'Can't be doing this every time I need a tab.'

Shaw said nothing.

The stranger's smile soon dispersed, turning into an uncomfortable look of concern as he focused on the scars that cut through the left side of Shaw's face. He flicked away the remainder of his cigarette and went back inside.

Shaw stood for a moment, watching the rain spit across the parked cars. He pulled out his phone and activated the screen. The main doors behind him opened, releasing the volume of customers inside. Beside him stopped one of the suited women from the table in the mirror. She placed a cigarette between her lips and searched through her handbag, murmuring under her breath. Finally, she stopped and looked up at Shaw.

'Haven't got the time, have ya?' she said.

Shaw glanced at his watch. 'Twenty past seven.'

'Thanks,' she said, pulling a lighter out her bag.

Shaw looked at his phone and read the on-screen notification of one missed call and one left voicemail message. He placed the phone to his ear and listened.

'Hi, Mr Shaw, it's Graham Johnson. I'm really sorry, but I won't be able to make our appointment tomorrow. Something's come up, but I'll be in touch with Victoria to arrange another one as soon as possible,' his counsellor said.

Shaw strained to hear his voice as a seven seated white taxi pulled up in the car park opposite him, allowing four young males to climb out into the drizzle. Already heavily influenced by alcohol, they laughed and carried on as they approached Shaw and the main door, making obscene comments towards the middle-aged woman finishing her cigarette.

'So don't worry, you'll not fall behind or get forgotten about.'

Shaw cursed and disconnected. During his nineteen months of therapy, Graham had never cancelled an appointment. But his biggest clue to something being wrong was Graham calling him Mr Shaw. Shaw hated being called that. It was either Shaw or Ryan. And Graham, being his counsellor, knew that. He cursed again and looked up into the black sky, suddenly appreciative of the rain that struck his face. He was going back to prison. He slid his phone back in his pocket and headed back into the pub.

Will stood at the bar, nursing two pints of lager. 'Everything sorted?' he said.

'What kind of a stupid question is that? Is everything sorted? No it's not sorted. Not by a fucking long shot.' He could feel an anger swelling in his chest and burning through his limbs. He took a mouthful of his drink and swallowed, hoping his anger would be swallowed along with it. But it didn't. Instead it ate at him, strengthened by the poignant guilt that had gripped him since entering Sunderland.

'Okay,' Will said, feeling as though he may have just been told off.

Standing at the bar, beside Will, were the four males from the taxi. They were all in their early twenties and averaging medium to thin build. The loudest of the four had light-blond, pretty-boy hair. The other three had brown hair, two with it shaved short and one with it shoulder length. They cursed with volume, talking openly about their sexual achievements at the weekend, involving a girl from Newcastle, and how two of them had spit-roasted a drunken university student.

Shaw grabbed the barman's attention. 'Get me a double whiskey,' he said, needing to calm the rage within him.

'Any in particular?' the barman said.

'Your strongest.'

The barman returned with the drink and the price.

'He's getting it,' he said, pointing at Will and downing it in one.

Will pulled out his wallet, not expecting the charge, and paid the barman. 'Everything okay?'

'No, Will, it's not. My life's crumbling beneath my very feet. My brother's an idiot… and those fuckers,' he said, pointing at the four men behind Will, 'are giving me a fucking headache.'

Will slid his wallet back into his back pocket and knocked the guy behind him. 'Sorry, mate,' he said, turning to face him.

'Sorry?' the blond pretty-boy said, looking Will up and down, calculating his ability to win the challenge. 'Sorry? You've just spilt my fucking drink all over me.'

'I'm sorry,' Will said. 'It was an accident.'

Will was thin and there were four of them. Easy prey. 'If you don't pay for the drink you've just spilt all over me, you'll be sorry.'

'Alright, calm yourself. Hardly any of it spilt.'

Shaw stepped forward, pushing Will aside. 'If he buys you a drink, I'll make sure it's the last one you have tonight.'

'You what?' Pretty-Boy said, stepping towards Shaw, his chest inflating like a peacock.

Shaw stood his ground. Blood shunted from his digestive track and was re-directed to his muscles and limbs. His pupils dilated. His senses sharpened. His fists clenched. Shaw was ready. He didn't have a wisecrack remark or a phrase to frighten his opponent into submission. He didn't want him to submit. He wanted to smash his face in. 'Come on then,' he said through gritted teeth.

'Just leave it, Gaz. It's not worth it,' Shoulder-Length said, put off by Shaw's aggressive confidence and facial scarring.

Shaw's eyes burned holes into Pretty-Boy's, welcoming his growing rage. 'Yeah, Gaz, go and fuck off.'

Pretty-Boy thought twice and re-joined his friends who had settled elsewhere in the pub.

Will placed his hand on his brother's shoulder. 'Come on. We'll finish these off then head to mine. Sleep it off and sort it out in the morning. Things always appear better in the morning.'

'I doubt it.' Shaw sighed and ran a hand down his face. 'I'm going for a piss,' he said, staggering towards the gents. The toilets stunk of urine and graffiti decorated the magnolia walls. A giant 'SAFC' was scraped into one wall along with 'MILLER IS A GRASS' branded in thick permanent marker on another. There was a single chrome urinal manning the whole length of the side wall, with two private cubicles opposite. He rested his forehead against the cold wall and emptied his bladder, firing his urine at one of the many yellow tablets that lay in the metallic trough. A mixture of emotions pumped around him, blurred and confused by the intake of alcohol.

The door to the toilets burst open behind him and crashed off the wall. He turned his head to see what the excitement was, only to have an ache flash from the bridge of his nose to the back of his head, filling his taste buds with warm iron.

*

Chloe laid her naked back against the cold wooden flooring of the stage and separated her legs into a one-hundred-and-eighty-degree box-split, pointing her blood-red heels in opposite directions.

Michael watched her like a hawk, mesmerised by her strong flexibility. 'I've invited Chloe to join us tonight,' he said to Melanie, who stood resting against the bar beside him.

'What do ya mean,' she said, 'join us?'

'She'll be coming to mine tonight, with you.' His tone was final, as if she didn't have any say in the matter. He took a mouthful of his Jack Daniels and coke and headed off towards his office, leaving Melanie alone at the bar.

Chloe finished her routine and collected her discarded clothing. Melanie could see she was attractive, but not in a way that would sexually arouse her. She was no lesbian and had never been confused or curious in that department.

'God, I hope not,' she said.

'Hope what?' Bomber said, startling her.

'Oh, wha' bout cha,' she said with a forced smile. 'I didn't see ya there.'

'I guess not. You okay? You look like there's something on your mind.'

'No, no. I'm fine. Still get a little nervous before dancing, would ya believe.'

Bomber appraised her up and down, admiring her black seamed stockings that were attached to the garter straps leading up beneath her fitted pinstripe waistcoat, and the black, square rimmed glasses that finished

82

off the sexy secretary look.

Melanie leaned back against the bar, aware of his eyes, and pushed her humble cleavage forward. 'What's the craic with this Shaw? Is Will really that wick?' she said, hoping she'd learn something new.

Bomber's eyes did exactly what Melanie had hoped and glanced down at her breasts. 'Will's useless.'

'Right. And that's the only reason Michael has Shaw around, te do Will's job?'

Bomber's eyes turned cold. 'What other reason could there be?'

'I don't know, just a few things have changed these last couple of days, is all,' she said, back peddling from the conversation. 'New faces and such. Like those guys over there.' Melanie nodded towards three men who were being escorted to a corner booth by one of the girls. Every one of them wore a smart dark suit and swaggered like a premiership footballer. The youngest of the three carried a black leather holdall. 'They're clearly not just here for the tits.'

'I don't know what you mean.'

Melanie stood up straight, feeling the cold gravity in his words. 'I'm just saying. Michael doesn't really tell me anything.' Thankfully, the DJ started her song, 'Beauty' by Mötley Crüe.

'I think that's your cue,' he said.

Melanie left the bar and approached the stage, happy to be leaving the conversation behind her, and span around the chrome pole, holding it firmly in both hands. She box-split her legs and raised her buttocks up to her hands, her arms and legs perfectly straight, mimicking the rotors of a helicopter.

*

'Can I get any of you something to drink?' Jennifer asked the three men.

'Three bottles of cider if you've got it, love,' the youngest of the three said. 'And don't you be going and being a stranger to us tonight, ya hear,' he added with a wink.

The blonde dancer smiled and walked away. 'Creep.'

Michael approached the table, calculating his every move, sizing up his three unwanted, but equally needed guests. 'Gentlemen.'

The youngest of the three men looked up at his host. 'Mikey Maloney,' he said.

'Paul.' Michael offered him his hand. He didn't know Paul Mallinson directly, only knowing what he'd heard from others; that he was spoilt and childish, playing in a sea with fish he couldn't keep up with. But

83

he was the Mallinson's only nephew and they treated him like he was their own. Everywhere he went, he was chaperoned by at least one of his heavies, protecting him from all the people who wanted to hurt his uncles.

Paul stood up and firmly shook Michael's hand, as if trying to prove his superior masculinity. 'Looking good, Mikey. You been hitting the gym?' he said with a mocking grin. 'Things seem to be going well for you here.' He glanced around the club and sat down. 'Even your hair looks like it's stopped receding.'

Michael hated being called Mikey. 'Things aren't too bad, but let's cut the shit. You've come here to do business. So let's—'

'I'm also here to have a good time, Mikey,' Paul interrupted. He leaned forward on the sofa and stared at him with beady eyes. 'And it's important that I have a good time.'

'What I was going to say, Paul, was that we get the business end out of the way. Then it's just girls, drink and tits. On the house of course.'

As if on cue, Jennifer reappeared with the tray of drinks, placing it on the table in front of them. 'Will that be everything?' she asked Michael.

'Yeah, Jen, cheers, sweetheart.'

*

Melanie gyrated on her knees and removed her glasses. She slowly undid each of the three white buttons of her waistcoat, revealing her matching waist-high garter belt and petrified nipples. She kept her eyes on the table of premiership footballers and gripped the pole over her right shoulder with both hands, arching her back up onto her eight-inch stiletto heels. She box-split her legs, her movements slow and controlled, and pulled her lower body up above her head, gripping the pole with her feet, but observing the meeting whilst performing her routine was proving difficult. She hung upside down and watched Michael receive the leather holdall. He looked inside and smiled before meeting the man's gaze to shake his hand. She relaxed her shoulders and allowed her waistcoat to fall to the stage beneath her as Michael called two young girls over to the table, two girls she hadn't seen in the club before.

*

The CCTV monitors mounted on the office wall to Michael's left continually buzzed, flicking in series throughout the different cameras positioned around the club. He placed the bag on his desk and flicked the main monitor to show only his three guests and the two prostitutes that now accompanied them. Three gentle knocks rapped on his office door. 'Yeah?'

Bomber entered. 'How'd it go?'

'Fine. The little prick's being entertained by Olga and Sara.'

Bomber sat on the leather sofa. 'Melanie was acting funny earlier, asking questions about Shaw.'

'Like what?'

'Like if there was any other reason we'd got him involved. Plus, she seemed pretty interested in our new friends.'

Michael poured himself a drink. 'Was she now? What did you tell her?'

'The truth, that Will's fucking useless. I didn't comment on them three.' He nodded at the monitor.

Michael sat back in his brown leather chair, taking slow sips from his Jack Daniels. 'She's probably just concerned. After all, it's not as if it's sweets we're sorting out.'

'Maybe. What we gonna do about the Mallinsons? The last thing we need are their grubby hands in our business.'

'I know.' Michael swirled the drink in his glass, watching the three men on his monitor. 'We'll wait until we have the guns before deciding anything final,' he said.

Twelve

'Not today you're not'

The punch connected hard with Shaw's nose, breaking it instantly. Urine ran down his leg, his eyes blinded with pain and tears, but his legs stayed strong and kept him vertical. He stumbled back, dazed and confused, his mind clouded by the alcohol, unable to prevent the two hands from gripping his T-shirt and throwing him of balance. His back crashed against the wall-mounted hand dryer behind him, activating the loud rush of air. A second punch landed firmly against his jaw, knocking him to the ground. He instinctively brought his hands and knees up, tucking in his elbows to deflect as many of the kicks and stamps as possible. Thick blood spilled down over his T-shirt and across his face from his broken nose, bubbling through his nasal cavity, forcing him to inhale through his mouth.

*

Richard finished the contents of his pint glass and placed it on the table in front. 'I'm telling ya, Sunderland football club was formed in 1879.'

'No, mate, it wasn't. It was 1890,' his close friend argued.

Richard tutted. 'Google it whilst I go for a piss.' He stood up and guided himself to the gents. He pulled open the first door, hearing the sound of disorder coming from inside. He pushed open the second, being careful not to disturb its occupants. Inside he saw four males kicking and stamping on another, his face and T-shirt saturated with thick crimson. Richard stepped back from the door and retreated back to the bar. 'You better call the police,' he told the barman. 'There's someone getting their head kicked in in the bogs.'

'What?' Will said. Before the short ginger haired male could answer, Will left his pint and ran to his brother's aid.

*

Shaw glanced up between his forearms, hoping to gain a better understanding of what was happening. The four men that surrounded him were instantly recognisable as the four from the taxi, the same four men from the bar.

'Still think you're a fucking hard man, d'ya?' one of them said.

Un-phased by his broken nose, Shaw dropped out of his defence, palming away a half-hearted kick, and tracked Skinhead One's right ankle with his left hand, striking his ankle with his right. Skinhead One dropped instantly to the wet tiles allowing Shaw to climb to his knees and kneel on his ankle. He brushed off another attack and snapped Skinhead One's ankle beneath him before lunging forward into Shoulder-Length's knees, wrapping his hands around the back of his calves. Due to his limited movement, Shoulder-Length fell, his arms wind-milling in desperation. Shaw crawled up his legs, blood spilling from his broken nose, and punched him twice in his testicles. Skinhead Two pulled him off him and slipped his arm around his throat, pulling him into a tight rear-naked choke hold. He gripped Skinhead Two's forearm and kicked out in retaliation, striking Pretty-Boy in the left thigh. He then jumped and kicked off the toilet wall, throwing himself and Skinhead Two back into the urine filled trough behind them. Skinhead Two slipped on the wet tiles and fell onto his back. He gasped into Shaw's hair as his head struck the base of the chrome urinal with Shaw landing heavily on top.

The sudden rush of violence filled Shaw's every muscle, travelling through his every nerve, filling him with a rage he not only welcomed, but enjoyed. He pulled forward from Skinhead Two's constricting grasp and stabbed a piercing elbow to his lower abdomen, following it through with a brutal rear head-butt.

'Get the fuck off him,' Pretty-Boy screamed, lunging in for an attack.

Shaw twisted his body to face him and parried away two blows, catching his right fist on the third. He simultaneously kicked forward with his right foot and locked his leg out beneath Pretty-Boy's right arm on his stomach, forcing him to lean towards him, his arm out stretched. He looked into Pretty-Boy's eyes and heel kicked down on his outstretched arm with his free leg, following it with a vicious stamp to his face. Pretty-Boy dropped to his knees, unable to prevent Shaw from stamping into his face again.

Will burst in. 'Ryan!'

Undistracted, Shaw stamped again, dislocating Pretty-Boy's jaw and breaking his wrist.

'Ryan! You'll break his fucking neck.'

Skinhead One lay groaning on his side, his right ankle broken. Shoulder-Length lay seething beside him, clutching his groin. Skinhead Two lay unconscious on his back, blood oozing from his collapsed nose. Shaw looked up to see his brother standing in the doorway. His adrenaline slowed, his body relaxed, and the ache in his face became evident. He released his hold on Pretty-Boy's broken wrist, leaving him unconscious in a puddle of urine.

Will stepped over Skinhead One and grabbed Shaw by the arm.

'We need to get out of here,' he said. 'The police are on their way.' Shaw obeyed and followed his brother, his vision blurring with every second. The bar was now quiet. People parted like the red sea, standing from their chairs to avoid the bleeding, beaten male. Will led him past the Christmas tree and out through the double doors into the car park outside. 'Get in,' he said, unlocking the passenger door of his car. 'We need to get you to a hospital.'

Shaw climbed in and rested his head back against the head rest. 'No hospital.'

Will started the car and pulled away, knowing his ability to handle the vehicle had been reduced by the unlawful quantity of alcohol he'd consumed. 'Ryan, your nose is all over your face.'

'I said no hospital. Just take me to yours.' He stabilised the bridge of his nose between the forefingers of his two hands and muscled the dislodged bone back into place; the loud crack reverberating through his skull.

Will cringed at the sound, trying his best to concentrate on the traffic ahead as a wailing police van screamed past them, its blue lights flashing. 'What the hell happened?' he said, occasionally glancing at his brother's face.

'Nothing.'

'Doesn't look like nothing.'

Even though Shaw's face hurt like hell and his eyes were already bruising, he felt surprisingly relieved, as if a raging tension had been allowed to escape. 'Stop talking and take me to yours,' he said.

*

'Go get yourself cleaned up. I'll put the kettle on,' Will said, unlocking Kimberly's front door.

Shaw followed behind, pulling his ripped T-shirt up over his head. 'Fuck the kettle. Get me a proper drink,' he said. 'No ice.' He entered the bathroom and pulled the cord, illuminating the small room, revealing his blood-soaked reflection in the mirror. He turned on the taps and filled the sink with cold, milky water, and gently swilled his face.

Will returned with a half-filled glass of whiskey and placed it on the bath ledge. 'I still think you should see a doctor.'

Shaw took the glass and emptied it in one. 'I'm fine. Just keep these coming,' he said, handing Will back the empty glass.

'Maybe you should rest, then. Get some ice on that.'

'Maybe you should fuck off and go get me that bottle.'

Will retrieved the cheap bottle of whiskey and slammed it on the bath. 'This isn't the answer, you know.'

Shaw looked at Will's reflection in the mirror. 'What the fuck would you know?'

'I've said I was sorry.'

Shaw said nothing.

'I can only apologise so many times, Ryan. I'm sorry. I shouldn't have got you involved.'

Shaw turned to face him and closed the gap between them, his nose centimetres from Will's. 'If you say you're sorry to me one more time, I'm gonna make you wish our parents had never met.'

Will looked back at him, silent and filled with regret.

'Now fuck off out.' Shaw pushed him back out the bathroom and slammed the door shut. He lifted the bottle of whiskey and screwed off its lid, pouring himself another generous measure. He held the glass and turned back to the mirror. He was a mess. His eyes were swelling and turning blue, watery blood trickled along the scars that mapped the left side of his face, and his chin and chest were painted with thick clotted blood.

He thought back to a group session he'd had in prison, when they'd all sat in a circle and identified their emotions and given them names. Naming them made them easier control, made them easier to overcome. He touched his left cheek; the scars a constant trigger to the self-loathing emotion that intruded his thoughts, a feeling he could never shake, a feeling, deep down, he didn't want to. He needed to be reminded of what he'd let happen that day. He needed to be punished. He raised the glass and swallowed his second whiskey.

Once his face and chest were clean, the laceration to the bridge of his nose proved to be less severe than the spilt blood had first indicated. He exited the bathroom carrying the bottle of whiskey in one hand and another filled glass in the other.

Will stood in the lounge, waiting for him to appear. 'Do you wanna hit me?' he said. 'Is that it?'

Shaw stood topless, looking at his brother, the brother he'd bailed out so many times he'd lost count. 'Don't,' he said, placing the whiskey bottle on a cabinet beside him.

Will approached him. 'Do it then. Hit me. Hit your—'

Shaw threw a short solid punch to Will's stomach, dropping him to his knees. 'Just leave me alone, Will.' He picked up the bottle and walked past him into the living room.

Will remained on all fours, struggling to control his breathing.

'Fine,' he spurted through broken breath, 'I'll leave you to it. Drink yourself into oblivion, again. See if I care.'

Shaw sat on the sofa and emptied another glass of whiskey.

Once Will was back to his feet, he grabbed his door key and left, slamming the door behind him.

*

Will pulled out his mobile phone and thumbed the ground floor button in the lift. He needed something to take away his anger, help him calm his rage, never mind his brother's. The phone rang and rang until it was finally answered by Kimberly's answering service, telling him to leave a message after the tone. He hung up and re-dialled, only this time she answered.

'You at the club, babe?' he said, hearing loud, muffled music in the background.

'What?' she said, one finger in her ear, struggling to hear him over the music.

'Where are you?'

'I'm at the club. Why?'

'You think Michael would mind if I came over?'

'Of course not,' she said, knowing Michael would be more than pleased to know he was on his way. 'Come on over. It just so happens I've got a little bag of white happiness, too,' she added, knowing he could never turn away free coke.

Will hung up and phoned a taxi, already feeling better with himself.

*

Even though the time was nearing midnight and the air had turned so cold the ground was freezing over, the queue for the club was still running the full length of the building. Will did what he had done dozens of times in the past and jumped the queue, entering through the VIP entrance.

The doorman pulled the red rope from the brass stand and allowed him access. 'She's up in the VIP lounge,' he said, recognising Will.

The club inside was how Will had expected it to be: dark, loud and packed with people. The entrance to the club's VIP suite was situated to the rear of the main dance floor, leading up a black metal framed spiral staircase to a generously sized balcony lounge that was frosted in dark vibrant colours and mirrored panels.

90

*

Kimberly and her two friends were the only people in the VIP suite. They sat around one of the glass tables in the private booths, fining out thin lines of cocaine with their debit cards. Kelly, an attractive dark haired girl to Kimberly's right, pulled out a rolled up ten pound note and snorted her third line of cocaine. Whilst Spence, the man on Kimberly's left, sat close enough to stroke the inside of her bare thigh.

A doorman approached as Kimberly snorted her fourth line. 'He's here,' he said.

Kimberly looked up, sweeping the hair from her face and tucking it behind her ear. 'Have him escorted out the back. I'll get Bomber to meet you there.'

'You want us to rough him up?'

'Do whatever it is you need to.' She waited for the doorman to leave before turning to kiss Spence.

*

Will weaved his way across the dance floor, tilting and turning his body to avoid dancing limbs. The smoke machine above him blasted out a stream of scented smoke, allowing the laser lighting to strobe through it. To his right, one of the club's doormen appeared from the crowd.

'Come with me,' the doorman said, taking Will by the arm.

Will looked at his bicep in disapproval. 'What for?

'We want a word.'

'About what?' Will tried to pull his arm away but failed.

The doorman pulled harder. The people surrounding them moved, allowing the doorman room to do his job.

'Get the fuck off me. I'm not going anywhere with you.'

A second doorman appeared behind him, grabbing him by the throat. 'Fucking move,' he said. The pair of them dragged him from the dance floor and crashed him through a black side door.

'Get off me. I'm here to see Kimberly,' Will said, hearing the door close behind him.

The second doorman lifted him from the carpet, preventing him from getting a foot hold. 'Not today you're not.' The pair of them carried him down the corridor, kicking and protesting, and threw him through the rear fire exit doors onto the frozen, hard gravel outside.

He pulled himself up onto his hands and knees. 'What have I done?' he said, his voice a pathetic whimper.

Doorman two replied with a boot to his gut. Will rolled onto his side, feeling the cold from the ground seep into his body. Another boot followed, kicking any of the remaining air from his lungs, followed closely by another to his back.

'Please,' he said. 'I'm sorry.'

'Throw him in the boot,' a familiar Geordie voice said.

The two doormen hooked their arms under each of his armpits and lifted him from the ground, his feet limp beneath him. The last thing Will saw was Bomber slam the boot shut above him.

*

The freshly laid lines of cocaine seemed to almost glow on the glass surface. Chloe's naked body was still moist from the nights dancing. Her thick dark hair clung to her face and the top of her back as she ran her fingers through it, sweeping it back from her shimmering face. She knelt beside the coffee table and picked up the trimmed-down straw, using it to make one of the thin white lines disappear up her nose. Her reflection stared back at her in the balcony doors, smiling, happy, and naked. Her firm, large breasts glistened in the dimmed light from the lamp, her pink nipples hard with excitement. She rolled onto her back, feeling the effects of the cocaine and the soft carpet press against her flesh, and slid her hand down between her thighs, stirring a teased pleasure within her.

Michael's erection throbbed against his stomach as he watched Chloe roll onto her hands and knees and approach him, her face flushed with sexual desire. He reached down and entwined her hair around his fist and pulled her up onto the sofa, insisting she engulf his stiffness. His second hand reached up behind Melanie's head and pulled her into him, gripping her short platinum hair to increase the passion of his kiss. His lips pressed against hers, his eyes open, his lust forcing his tongue to the back of her throat.

*

Michael re-entered the bedroom carrying a glass of water to see Chloe draped naked across the bed sheets, her dark hair spread out around her as if frozen in a timeless wind. 'You okay?' he asked, seeing Melanie lying beside her, staring at the ceiling.

Melanie remained silent, unmoving.

'Here, drink this.'

Melanie sat up, stiff and slow.

He handed her the glass of water, placing it to her lips. 'You're still high. You'll come down shortly.'

She sipped the water and looked at him, her eyes wide and dilated.

'What time is it?'

Michael glanced at the clock. It had been three hours since they'd first started on the cocaine. 'It's just after two-thirty,' he said. 'Tonight was your first time, wasn't it?' He took back the glass. 'The coke I mean.'

'Ya.'

He looked over her shoulder at Chloe lying peacefully and took hold of Melanie's hand. 'Come with me,' he said, leading her naked through his apartment and out onto the balcony, overlooking the harbour and mouth of the Wear.

The cold, frosty air sent shivers across her naked flesh, hardening her nipples and transforming her once smooth skin to that of rippled goose pimples. She looked up at the dark sky, taking in every twinkle of the million stars above her. 'Why ya buying those guns?' she said boldly, not really knowing why.

He looked at her. 'Because I'm gonna use them to rob someone.'

She froze, momentarily speechless, not really expecting an answer. 'Of what?'

Michael leant forward, resting his elbows on the wet wood finish of the balcony. 'Five hundred grand,' he said, matter-of-fact.

Her head snapped round towards him. 'Are ya serious? Half a million?'

Michael's face creased into a smile. 'Very.'

Melanie couldn't believe what she'd just heard. She tried her hardest to fight off the effects of the cocaine and take in everything Michael was telling her. 'How ya gonna do that?'

Michael remained silent, looking out at the sea.

Melanie held her tongue, finding it difficult to judge the right moment to ask certain questions. Not sure if it was the cocaine doing the talking or her. 'When ya getting them?' she said after a prolonged silence. 'The guns I mean.'

'Why? You wanna come?'

Melanie couldn't think of anything she'd rather do less. 'Sure,' she said with a nod. 'As long as I'm not in the way.'

'You won't.' Michael met her nervous gaze, a gaze he found irresistible. 'We're getting them later today,' he told her.

'Teday?' she gasped, immediately thinking about informing Slater. This was her ticket out. 'Where?' The word spluttered out, involuntary, causing Michael's eyes to glaze with suspicion.

'Where?' His face was firm, his body language cold and closed.

Her heart thundered in her chest at the realisation of her mistake. Fear washed through her, so wild she thought she may faint. 'I just don't want te be wearing heels if we're gonna be stood in a field, is all,' she said, wanting to cry, wanting to go home.

'In a field?' He laughed. 'No, we're meeting them at someplace called White Chapel Cottage at two o'clock,' he said, falling for her innocence. 'Quinn knows how to get there.'

'Why you's out there?' a drowsy voice said behind them.

Melanie turned to see Chloe wrapped in one of Michael's bed sheets, her hair wild and untamed.

'Cooling off,' Michael said, walking naked passed her, back into the warmth of the apartment.

Once inside, Melanie laid her head down on her pillow and reminded herself one more time of the time and location of the handover, before drifting silently to sleep.

Thirteen

'Smoke on the water'

Quinn parked his Hilux outside a house in a less glamorous part of the city, well known for its high crime rate and drug dealings and killed the engine and headlights. A gang of ten youths had gathered at the end of the street outside the local off license. Each one of them, including the two girls with their extra-large hooped earrings, had their tracksuit bottoms tucked into their socks. And more than half of them had their hoods pulled up over their heads. But Quinn wasn't here to carry out the neighbourhood watch. He sat next to Sherman, watching the house. The front garden was wild and un-kept with a long abandoned rusty white car sitting in the middle of it, its wheels removed, and windows smashed.

'Who lives here?' Sherman said.

Quinn kept his gaze pinned on the house across the street. 'An old girlfriend.'

*

The music was loud, and the curtains were pulled tight. The only source of light in the filthy bedroom came from the TV, now showing vintage porn from the seventies. Ray's head fell back and his left arm dropped out by his side. The used needle that had punctured his arm fell to the cigarette burnt carpet, followed closely by his torso. In the distance he thought he could hear a baby crying. But it was too distant, too far away. Then the sound faded altogether, blending with the deafening beat of his heart. The heroin whisked him away, effortlessly carrying him to places unreachable by normal means.

Catherine tried to ignore her seven-week old daughter who continued to scream in the room next door, loud enough to be heard above the Deep Purple track that blasted from the down stairs hi-fi. She reached down beside Ray's skinny naked body and picked up the warm sticky syringe.

'Ray!' she yelled. 'Ray. You thieving shit. Where's the rest of it?' She threw the blackened needle at his limp body and cursed him as she searched the room, hungrily looking for her next fix. Her head pounded with frustration and the need for her hit. Anger swelled in her, knowing that Ray was high on her heroin. She stomped along the landing and released it on the only person she could. 'What!' she screamed at a volume equal to her daughter. 'What! What the fuck are you crying for, you little bitch?' She reached into the filthy cot and snatched her defenceless baby, holding her fragile body at arm's length.

'Oi,' a male voice yelled from downstairs. 'Shut that little witch up! For fuck sake.'

Catherine turned to the landing behind her. 'Fuck off, Tommo!'

Tommo stood topless at the base of the stairs, his grimy jeans hanging from his bony hips. His greasy, long dark hair clung to his thin, unshaven face and a badly rolled up spliff hung from his scabbing lips. 'Sick to the back teeth of that screaming little bitch,' he said to himself.

Three loud knocks boomed from the front door.

'If this is that complaining cunt from next door again, I'll cut his throat.' He took a deep drag on his spliff and approached the door.

*

Quinn pushed open the letter box and peered inside. The song 'Smoke on the water' could be heard playing, and a thick, foul odour could be smelt. The outside of the terrace house was old looking and in need of repair. The windows were black with dirt and the brown discoloured curtains were pulled tight. He stood straight and knocked three more times on the flaking red door, growing impatient. He knew there were people inside. Even with the loud music he could hear the distressed screams of a baby upstairs. Finally, the front door opened, revealing a gaunt looking man in his early thirties with long, dark, greasy hair.

'Who the fuck are you?' the man said. 'And what the fuck do you want?'

Quinn stared at the topless male, taking in his weak, thin torso, and allowed a hammer to slip down from his right sleeve.

'Are you fucking deaf? What the fuck do you want?' Tommo repeated, seemingly unafraid of Quinn's imposing frame.

Quinn took a deep breath and smashed the head of the hammer into the man's forehead. The man stumbled back into the badly lit passage and fell onto his back, blood seeping down the side of his face into the filthy carpet. The hi-fi continued to play the Deep Purple track, filling the house with an atmosphere of the early 70's. Blood seeped through the man's fingers as he groaned, attempting to roll onto his hands and knees. Quinn followed him in and crashed the hammer down again, splitting open the back of his skull. The half-naked man fell onto his face, motionless, blood pooling beneath his face. Quinn grabbed his wrist and dragged him into the living room.

Catherine dropped her screaming child back into her cot and

96

headed back out onto the landing. 'Tommo,' she yelled, looking down over the banister. But who she saw wasn't Tommo.

'My little Catherine,' Quinn said with a crocked smile, the same crocked smile that had beaten her so many times in the past, forcing her to carry out sexual acts on other men for money.

Her heart sank. Her legs fell beneath her as if weakened by Quinn's presence. Her back fell against the landing wall and her bruised knees rose up to her chest, watching Quinn's head appear through the wooden railings of the banister. She buried her face into her knees, allowing the tears to roll down her cheeks. A small part of her hoped that Quinn would show her mercy, but the larger part knew that was not to be. She recalled the evening, three months ago, that she ran from Michael's brothel, taking the house takings with her.

Quinn made his way onto the landing and crouched down beside her. 'Don't cry, Catherine,' he said, stroking her long dark hair.

'It wasn't my idea, Leroy. I swear,' she begged through red, teary eyes.

'I know. I know you would never steal from me, Cat. Just tell me who it was, and I promise everything will be okay.'

'It was Ray,' she said with a sniff. 'He made me do it.'

'Ray?'

She nodded and aimed her gaze into the master bedroom to her left.

Quinn followed her eyes. 'He's in there?'

Catherine nodded, mucus mixed with the tears stringing from her face.

'Introduce me, I wanna meet him.'

She stood up with a helping hand from Quinn and led the way towards the room. Her initial fear started to subside. She stopped crying and began sniffing. 'He's off his face, mind, Leroy.'

'Is he now?' he said, having to raise his voice to be heard above the screaming child. He hesitated, allowing her to enter first. From the inside pocket of his coat, Quinn pulled out a polyethylene plastic bag and pulled it down over her head, pulling it tight around her face.

Catherine's hands snatched up at the suffocating bag and clawed at the plastic. Her arms flailed, and her legs kicked out, but Quinn had it pulled tight, his arms locked out at the elbows. He'd never suffocated anybody before, and now he wondered why. It was so easy, effortless in fact. He avoided her wild hands with ease, keeping the plastic bag firmly in place until her flailing had stopped. He left the bag around her face and walked into the bedroom, finding Ray lying naked on his back, a thin black leather belt wrapped loosely around his weak bicep. Scattered around him were burnt sheets of tinfoil and ashtrays filled high with cigarette ends.

'So, you're Ray.' He crouched down beside him and pinched his nose and covered his mouth. Once Ray's body had finished juddering, he made his way back downstairs. 'Grab his arms,' he said, nodding at Tommo's dead body.

Sherman did as he was told and reached down and grabbed the half-naked man's wrists

'We'll take him upstairs and put him with the other two,' Quinn said.

Sherman went first, trying his best to avoid the dead man's dripping blood. 'What made you choose this house?' he said, fighting with the volume of the bawling baby.

Quinn paused for a moment, as if deciding on his answer. 'Go and shut that fucking baby up,' he said, dropping the dead man's body beside Ray's, choosing to ignore his question altogether.

Sherman took the hint and left the room. He hushed the wailing child as he entered her bedroom, placing his index finger to his lips. The baby was filthy and reeked of putrid urine. Black faeces were visible down the child's bare legs, escaping from the full, rotten nappy. He grabbed a towel off the bathroom floor and wrapped it around her, holding her at arm's length. 'What we doing with this one?' he said, entering the master bedroom.

'I don't know. Fill the bath and put it in it.'

'You mean drown her?'

'Yes, drown her,' he answered without hesitation. 'Unless you want it.'

'I don't want her, but I'm not fucking drowning her either.'

'Well do what you want with it then, but it's not staying in here, crying and covered in fucking shit.'

'I'll drop her somewhere where she'll be found later.'

'Whatever,' Quinn said, not caring what he did with the baby. He pulled the grubby duvet off the double bed and laid it on the floor. 'Help me wrap these up.'

Sherman placed the child on the bed and did as Quinn requested.

Fourteen

'Always has been'

Melanie had awoken only hours after she'd fallen asleep, or so she had thought. Chunks of the night were still hazy, clouded by the effects of the cocaine. She blushed recalling the intimate orgasms she'd shared with Chloe, the shame of how good it felt adding to her embarrassment. 'Stop it,' she told herself, digging for the memory of Michael's conversation. White Chapel Cottage at two o'clock was what he'd said, she was sure of it.

The taxi which she'd called earlier chauffeured her home. The sun was hanging high in the air, promising a dry, if not cold day.

She pulled out her iPhone and called Slater. 'It's Mel,' she said. 'I've got some news.'

'Please tell me it's about the exchange.'

'It is.' She flushed with a sense of achievement.

'Where are you now?'

'I've just got home.'

Slater sighed with relief. 'A taxi will collect you at eleven o'clock.' Slater hung up.

Once home, Melanie showered and applied minimal makeup before dressing in a white blouse and jumper, and stonewashed skinny jeans. As Slater had said, a taxi pulled up outside her flat and beeped its horn. She picked up her leather jacket and left her flat. In the driver's seat sat DCI Slater, wearing a casual T-shirt and jeans. She placed her feet in the rear passenger footwell and closed the door, feeling the pull of the taxi as Slater pulled forward. She studied his reflection in the rear-view mirror. The slacking flesh beneath his eyes and the strong scent of coffee in the cab told her Slater hadn't been sleeping well either. They sat silent until the taxi had left the estate.

'You said you had something for me.' Slater's voice was desperate and forward, a gleam of hope evident behind his sharp eyes.

'Aye,' she said. 'The gun deal's happening today at a place called White Chapel Cottage at te o'clock.'

'And you didn't think that was urgent enough to tell me over the phone?' he said, his eyes shifting between the road and her reflection.

'Ya told me never te report anything over the phone,' she said, feeling her sense of achievement diminish.

He glanced at his watch, calculating the hours he had to arrange

99

everything. 'No, you're right,' he said. 'Well done. I'll inform HQ as soon as I've dropped you off, give them time to get themselves ready and in position. Did he mention anything on why he's purchasing the guns?'

'Says he's stealing five hundred grand from someone.'

His eyes darted to her reflection. 'Did he say who?'

'No, I didn't want te pry te much. He was getting funny about the questions I was asking, anyway.'

Slater sighed and glanced out his driver's window. 'But it's not Michael's style,' he said, thinking out loud.

'What's not?'

'All this: the guns, the stealing. Michael's a business man. Always has been.'

'Oh, and a group of men brought an important bag inte the club last night,' Melanie added.

'Containing what?'

'I'm not sure, but Michael looked really pleased with himself when he took it. He shipped it off pretty sharpish te his office, like.'

'Money?'

'Could be.' She shrugged, not knowing what else to say. 'Funny ya suggest money. I'm actually beginning te think he hasn't got any.'

'What makes you say that?'

'Some of the things he says and the way he goes on. Sure, he hasn't paid the girls for nearly a month now, keeps making excuses, so he does.'

'The men who brought the bag, have you've seen them before?'

Melanie shook her head. 'No. Never.'

'Would you be able to identify them if you saw them again?'

Melanie nodded.

'Well, if what you say is true, and he is having money problems, that could make him desperate. And the last thing we want is a desperate man getting hold of automatic weapons.' Slater felt the knot of muscle tighten in his stomach, for this was his OP, and he would be held accountable for any casualties, friend or foe, or worse yet, innocents. 'Do you know where Shaw's staying?'

'As far as I know he was staying with his brother at Kimberly's place, but I don't know about now. Te tell the truth, I haven't seen either of them since Saturday. Why?'

Slater found himself hearing her striking Northern Irish words, but not listening to them. Instead he focused on her full soft lips and perfect white teeth, her high cheek bones and piercing blue eyes, the way her platinum hair was poker straight and combed back from her face. 'Why?' he repeated back to her, finally catching her words.

'Yeah.'

He paused for thought. 'We just need to keep tabs on him, is all,' he said. 'He's a valuable piece in our investigation.'

'Well surely ya should have him lifted then.'

'We can't risk it, not yet. If we don't catch Michael red handed, nothing will stick, and he won't buy the guns without Shaw inspecting them first.'

Melanie looked out her window, wishing she was somewhere else, Warrenpoint with her friend's maybe.

'How are you coping?' Slater said, recognising the tell-tale signs of stress.

'How do ya think I'm coping?'

'Look at it this way, Mel. This time Thursday morning, it'll all be over.'

'Aye, if I'm not dead.'

Slater eased off on the accelerator and changed down a gear. 'It'll never come to that. I promise you.'

'I hope not,' she said, feeling a lump of dread pulse within her. 'Let me out 'ere, I can make me own way back.' The taxi stopped, and she climbed out, closing the door behind her.

Fifteen

'Change of plan'

Shaw took upon himself to make his own morning coffee, figuring Will must have already left in a sulk. His body ached, and his head thumped. His knuckles were swollen and bloody, and his breathing had become difficult through his nose, forcing him to inhale more through his mouth. A thin white adhesive strip was pulled tight across the bridge of his nose, covering the break in his skin. His eyes were swollen and bruised, and his bottom lip had swollen on the inside of his mouth, pressing against his bottom teeth. His phone rang in his coat pocket. He made his way back into the living room and grabbed it, answering it as he returned to the kitchen, not checking its display.

'Hello,' he said.

'Where the fuck are ye?' a rough Glaswegian accent said.

'Boyd? Jesus, man, I could do without all your shit right now.'

'Is that right? Well just thought ye should know, I'm in Sunderland, and if I come across ye, I'll be breaking yer fucken legs.'

'You actually came to Sunderland?'

'Aye, I have,' his brother-in-law said, killing the line.

'That's all I need,' he said, stirring his coffee.

His phone rang again, startling him. He cursed and picked it up. 'Boyd, I get the fucking message.'

'Who's Boyd?' a different voice said.

'Who's this?'

'It's Michael. Just thought I'd ring to make sure you weren't thinking about skipping your appointment.'

'No, I'll be there,' Shaw said, feeling the anger instantly re-breed inside him. He was going back to prison now, no matter what.

'Glad to hear it. Be at the club at twelve-thirty.'

After hanging up, Shaw grabbed some essentials from his brother's drawers: a fresh T-shirt, a pair of training pants, socks, and wash kit. He grabbed a bin liner from the kitchen and stuffed the clothes he'd been wearing into it. He scrubbed his boots, leather and soul, and pulled them on. He also picked up Will's car keys from the passageway unit, figuring he must have left with Kimberly, and left, dropping his bag of old clothes in a neighbour's wheelie bin.

*

He parked up outside the B and B and reached under the passenger seat, retrieving the Glock 17. He lifted his T-shirt and tucked it in the front of his training pants, pulling his T-shirt down over it. He picked a carrier bag up off the passenger seat containing some newly purchased clothes and entered the B and B. He was welcomed warmly by Mrs Henry, the sixty-two-year-old owner. During the nineteen years she'd ran the B and B, she'd seen many faces come and go, but something told Shaw his face would be hard to forget.

'Hello, son,' she said, greeting him as he entered. 'Would you like a cup of tea? Just made a fresh pot.'

'No thank you, Mrs Henry, I'll not be stopping long.'

'Oh, my goodness, what in the devil has happened to your face?' she said, approaching him for a closer look. 'Oh, you've got two nasty black eyes there and a cut on your nose.'

'I'm fine, Mrs Henry. Walked into a bloody door would you believe?'

'You need to be more careful, Ryan.'

'I'm fine, honestly.'

'*Late yesterday afternoon, the body of a man was found shot dead in his living room by his three year old daughter. The victim was found nailed to an armchair and violently beaten before being shot at close range in the chest. Officers say this is one of the most violent, bloody murders in the history of Sunderland,*' read the balding male newsreader on BBC Look North.

Shaw watched the outdated television set, trying his hardest to listen to the details being given.

'*The murder took place in Sulgrave, Washington at around one-thirty yesterday afternoon,*' the newsreader continued. '*The reason for the murder is as yet unknown, no names have been given.*'

'Horrible ordeal that isn't it? And found by his daughter three days before Christmas, too, poor little beggar. Hope she's okay. Can scar a girl for life, that can.'

Shaw nodded and made his excuses before heading up to his rented room on the top floor. A fresh bottle of water sat on the bedside cabinet, alongside a complimentary chocolate biscuit. The holdall containing his belongings was where he'd left it and appeared untouched, not that there was anything of importance within it. He closed the door behind him and threw the bag containing his new clothes onto the bed and pulled the Glock 17 from the front of his pants. He pulled the duvet back from the bottom of the bed and sat down on the edge. He extracted the weapon's magazine and pulled back on the top slide, double checking the firearm was fully unloaded. He thought about his mother's safety as he thumbed out thirteen 9mm rounds onto the bed sheet; four less than its capacity and hid the Glock in his holdall. Will being Will had managed to get her involved without her even knowing it, and he couldn't make any real decisions until that worry had gone. He chose to ignore it for now, though, accepting there was nothing he could do about it, just yet. It would have to wait. He straightened the duvet, covering the empty magazine and rounds and headed into the bathroom, taking his newly acquired wash kit with him.

He considered shaving along with his shower, hoping it would make him feel a little better, but abandoned the idea. The shower alone had worked well enough. The scars on the left side of his face, clearer now he was washed clean, were a constant reminder of the mistakes he'd made and the family he'd lost. He remembered how he'd once smashed every mirror in the house after getting drunk, how he'd caused Douglas to wake up screaming, and how Amy had had to deal with it all, trying to understand her husband's pain. But even true love can only take so much. Even true love has its limits.

He slipped on his silver watch, displaying the time 12:06, and clipped shut its fasteners. But before Shaw could dress fully, several things needed to happen. He searched through his holdall and pulled out his Swiss Army penknife. He opened the blade and cut a hole in the right pocket of his new jeans. He then re-bombed the magazine with the thirteen rounds and pulled on his recently purchased clothes, consisting of a black T-shirt, dark zip-up hoody and dark trainers. Once he was fully dressed, wearing his brother's socks and briefs, Shaw placed the penknife in the right pocket of his hoody and tucked the Glock's magazine down the front of his briefs, positioning it to the right of his testicles.

*

Detective Holt flinched in pain as steaming gravy from his chicken and mushroom pot noodle splashed his lower lip, causing him to drop the remaining fork full onto his lap.

'Fucking thing,' he said, rubbing at his mouth. 'Anything yet?'

'No, not yet,' Detective Gardener said, looking through the telescopic lens of her camera, growing tired through boredom. She hated stakeout duty, especially with Holt, who only ever wanted to eat, sleep or read the paper, anything except his job. How he'd ever even made it into CID baffled her.

The view of Michael's club from the flat window was adequate, enabling Gardener to see the entrance to the yard and the majority of the back road. The pair of them had been sat in the rented flat above the kebab shop since 06:00 that morning, taking it in two hour turns at the window. The pair had been sharing the shifts in the flat with their colleagues, Hodgson and Counden, since Wednesday when the submachine-gun had been reportedly brought in for inspection. Their hi-tech surveillance equipment consisted of a camera that was set up on a tripod in a position to make best use of the view available, and a pair of standard issue binoculars. The front of the building was being monitored continually using the cities own CCTV system.

Gardener observed the road, occasionally looking over towards the back of the club for any sign of Michael and his crew, expecting them to be arriving shortly. There hadn't been anyone all morning, which wasn't unusual, as people didn't start coming until noon.

'Oi,' she said, throwing a pencil at Holt. 'It looks like we have someone, right on time.'

He jumped up and peered over Gardener's shoulder, looking down the back road towards the male figure approaching. 'Who is it?' he said, picking up the binoculars.

She looked through the cameras optical zoom. 'Looks like Shaw.'

He peered through the binoculars, confirming the sighting. 'Yeah, that's him.' He replaced the binoculars and picked up his mobile phone. 'Slater, it's Holt. Shaw's arrived. It's starting.'

'Roger that,' Slater said, sitting upright in the unmarked police car. 'Let me know when they're leaving.'

*

The walk from the B and B to the club had taken Shaw only fifteen minutes, even with the quick detour to the local shop's skip, allowing him to discard his boots. He'd hated having to throw out his clothes, his khaki surplus jacket had been his only decent jacket, and his brown leather boots had been, what he would have called, expensive. But he knew better than to keep anything that could place him at the scene of a crime, let alone a murder. He sat himself down on one of the wooden steps leading up to the rear entrance of the strip club and waited for the others to arrive. It wasn't long before Quinn's pickup turned into the yard and stopped just short of the wheelie bins, loud rock music bellowing from its dark cab.

He stood and approached the descending driver's window. 'What time we leaving?' he said, trying to control the frustration in his voice.

'What the fuck happened to you?' Quinn said, not hiding his

amusement. He turned to Bomber who was sat in the passenger seat. 'Have you seen his face?' He laughed.

Shaw visualised grabbing Quinn by his greasy hair, pulling out his bladed penknife and punching it into his jugular. It would be fast, clean and easy. But all that was academic, Shaw's hands were all but tied. The impressive panther-like growl behind him told Shaw Michael was approaching. He turned to see him park parallel to Quinn's Hilux.

'What happened to you?' Michael also asked, climbing out and looking over the roof of his car.

Shaw remained silent.

Michael smiled and turned to Quinn. 'I'll follow you.'

'Aye, it's not far,' Quinn said.

Shaw opened the back door to Quinn's pickup and climbed inside, clipping in the seatbelt.

'Was Melanie in that car?' Bomber asked.

'Yeah, why?' Shaw replied.

'What-the-hell's he brung her for?'

'Who cares? It's his call,' Quinn said, gunning the engine. 'Just as long as she doesn't get in my way.'

*

'Slater, it's Holt. They're on the move. Quinn, Bomber and Shaw in the pickup. Michael and Melanie in the GT-R.'

'No Kimberly?' Slater confirmed.

'Correct. No Kimberly.'

'Roger that.' Slater placed his polystyrene cup of hot coffee in the car's cup holder. 'You and Gardener sit tight. Keep eyes on the club. If Kimberly or Will turn up, let me know.'

'Will do.' Holt hung up.

*

Iron Maiden blasted from Quinn's speakers, filling the cab with the sound of thrashing guitar solos and beating drums. Shaw was familiar with rock music, growing up with the likes of The Who, Led Zepplin and Van Halen, but he'd always been more of a Beatles man.

'Does this have to be so loud?' Bomber said, obviously feeling the same way as Shaw.

'Can't hear you,' Quinn mused, smiling at his colleague.

Bomber leaned forward and killed the power on the stereo, blanketing the cab with a welcomed sheet of silence. 'Can you hear me now?' he said, spreading a smile of his own.

106

'Don't you ever touch my fucking stereo!' Quinn reached forward to turn it back on, only to be stopped by a quieter, tamer version of the same song. He reached into his pocket, adjusting himself in his seat, and pulled out his mobile phone. 'Yeah?' he said, answering the call.

'Change of plan,' the voice on the phone said, 'meeting won't be happening at the cottage.'

'You can't change the location mid-flow!'

'I can change whatever I like, they're my fucking guns. Instead, head towards an abandoned church east of Fishburn.'

'Michael won't be pleased.'

'Fuck Michael. We're not meeting at the cottage. If he wants these things, he'll be there.'

'Okay, I'll let him know.' Quinn cancelled the call, not looking forward to Michael's response. 'Fucking Argentinians,' he said.

Shaw leaned forward in his seat. 'What's the problem?'

Quinn ignored him and dialled Michael. 'There's been a change of plan.'

'What do you mean a change of plan?' Michael said; one hand on the steering wheel, the other holding the phone to his ear.

'Doc's changed the location. He's not happy with the cottage anymore. Don't know why.'

'So where does he want to meet now?'

'A church not far from here.'

*

Melanie watched Michael and listened. The fear rose up inside her, congealing in the pits of her stomach. If the location of the deal changed, she'd have no back up. 'What we changing location for?' she said, once Michael had hung up.

'What?' he snapped at her, his mind focused on other things.

'Why we changing location?'

'I don't know.'

'It just seems a little weird, is all.' She had to let Slater know. If they discovered she was wearing a digital recording device pinned to the left breast of her leather jacket, she'd be dead for sure.

*

Shaw could feel the tension in the cab. 'I thought these were friends of yours?'

Quinn met his gaze in the rear-view mirror. 'When I want your opinion on something, I'll ask for it.'

'Well how well do you know these people?' Shaw persisted, pressing on Quinn's patience. 'I'd rather not get arrested by some undercover copper, or worse yet, executed by some greedy low-life.'

'Well enough. Now shut the fuck up! Your job's to inspect the guns, nothing else.'

Shaw laughed in disbelief and sat back in his seat.

Bomber remained as silent as he always did during times like these, peering out at the countryside, calculating in his head how to keep himself alive.

'You've never been to this church before, have you?' Shaw said, feeling less comfortable about the situation.

'Shut the fuck up.'

'Have you even done business with these before?'

'If you don't shut your fucking mouth, I'll shut it for you.' Quinn reached forward and turned up the stereo, drowning out Shaw's voice.

Sixteen

'Murder of crows'

The country lane appeared more of a track than a road. Quinn's pickup tackled the bumps and dips with ease, barely using its 4x4 capability. The overhanging trees either side of the road loomed low above them, as if selfishly hiding them from the daylight above. Puddles of frozen mud filled the holes, unable to melt in the perpetual shade. Up ahead, where the looming trees finally broke, Shaw could make out an open wooden gate resting against a stone wall in waist high grass. A head of the gate was a rundown church, its windows smashed, and roof starved of materials. A murder of crows circled its deteriorating spire like vultures circling a battlefield. Outside the church, beside an ancient looking graveyard, were two parked vehicles, a rusty, blue Transit van and a muddy black Vectra. Leaning up against the blue van were two swirly coloured men of average build, dressed in jeans and steel cap toed working boots. One rested against the side door that was already slid open, whilst the other man, wearing a Manchester United football top, crouched down on the wet, weed filled path, resting his back against the rear passenger wheel. To Shaw's astonishment, in his hands was an AK47. Another swirly skinned male appeared from within the van, stepping out through the open side door, revealing himself as Quinn pulled up in front of them. Dressed in raggy thread bare jeans, black boots and a black leather jacket, he looked as though he should have arrived on the back of a Harley Davison than in a van, with his shoulder length, greasy hair and greying beard finishing off the look.

'You're late,' the biker said in a raised tone, the hint of an Italian accent present.

Quinn climbed out and shut the door, leaving his driver's window down. 'You're lucky we're here at all, trying to find this place.'

The biker laughed, exposing his teeth.

Bomber opened his passenger door and stepped out onto the path.

'Is the AK really necessary?' Quinn said, looking at the two men resting against the van.

'Until I'm happy about your boss, it is.'

Shaw also exited the vehicle, noticing a walkie-talkie on the belt of the man resting against the van. A clear indication that there were more than just the three men stood in front of them. He immediately entered a state of increased alertness and scanned the surrounding area: the area around the church, the smashed windows, the roof top, the spire, and the wood line in the distance for any visible signs of activity.

Mr Man United cradling the AK47 stood up, feeling the pressure of Shaw's wondering eyes. 'Éste lleva la cara del diablo,' he said, causing the other two Argentinians to laugh. *'This one wears the face of the devil.'*

Michael's GT-R pulled up alongside Quinn's Hilux, the growling engine turning into a purr as its revs dropped. The biker turned to the sports car and looked at its occupants.

'And this must be your boss?' Doc said. 'Is she a nice ride?' he added, raising his voice so Michael could hear him.

'Zero to sixty in less than three and half seconds,' Michael said proudly, shutting the driver's door.

Doc grinned, exposing thick wrinkles around his eyes. 'I wasn't talking about the motor.' Michael's eyes turned cold, causing Doc's grin to grow even wider. He ran a hand through his greasy, grey hair, expressing his lack of concern. 'Let's get down to business. I have somewhere else I need to be.'

Melanie climbed from Michael's car, placing her black ankle boot on the broken, wet path.

'What's more important than making money?' Michael said.

'El cumpleaños de mi nieto,' Doc said. 'My grandson's birthday. And I never miss my grandson's birthday.'

Whilst everyone else bickered like children, Shaw's concerns raced at a 100mph. Where were the extra men located? And where was the gear? There was nothing in the back of the van, which meant the gear had to be elsewhere, that's if there was any gear at all.

Doc considered Melanie up and down. 'Speaking of money, where is it?' He placed his hands on his hips, purposely revealing the pistol grip of a chrome revolver tucked into the waist of his jeans.

Michael glanced down at the weapon and swallowed. 'Not until I'm happy with the guns. If the gear's as good as you've told Quinn, there won't be a problem.'

'I guess that's fair,' Doc said. 'Follow me.' He turned and headed towards the church.

Quinn stepped forward, wanting to be the first to follow the hairy Argentinian into the church, as if proving himself worthy to Michael.

Doc raised his hand. 'Whoa big fella, where the fuck do you think you're going?'

'In there.'

Doc shook his head. 'I don't think so. You can wait out here with Ramiro and Dante.'

'It's fine. You wait here with Mel and Bomber. This shouldn't take too long,' Michael said, nudging Shaw forward.

Doc looked Melanie up and down once again, nourishing his eyes on her skin-tight denim jeans and black leather jacket. 'You're not leaving pretty Mel out in the cold, are ya?'

She didn't want to venture anywhere with the three men, and she certainly didn't want to enter that church, but that was why she was here. She needed to be involved. She looked at Michael and forced a mischievous smile.

'You're not seriously considering following him in there, are you?' Shaw asked Michael. The inside of the church would be the perfect killing zone for the Argentinians, plenty of concealed high ground and dark corners. And Quinn and Bomber would be easy pickings for a concealed sniper or a prepared AK47.

'Yes, now get a move on,' Michael said, not hiding his frustration.

'Well surely you're not letting her come?'

'Let's just get it over and done with. I don't want to be spending all day here.'

'Before we go anywhere, you can put your arms out to the side,' Doc said. He looked at Shaw. 'You first, scarface.' Shaw held his arms out straight, adopting a T shape, as Doc padded him down. He started with his ankles and made his way up his legs. Shaw tried to relax, fixing his gaze on the church in front.

Mr Man United approached Melanie, his mouth salivating, his eyes hungry. 'Arms up,' he said. Melanie looked at Michael and raised her arms, mimicking Shaw.

'Ella es mía,' Doc said. *She's mine.* He bypassed Shaw's groin and went straight for his waist and torso, not even searching his arms or wrists. Shaw breathed out, alleviated; the sharp corners of the Glock magazine digging into his testicles. Mr Man United tutted, stopped what he was doing, and frisked Michael instead. Doc approached Melanie and smiled. He crouched down in front of her, his eyes never leaving hers, and ringed her ankle with both his hands. He ran his hands up her leg, increasing the pressure the higher he got. His right hand turned up, applying pressure to her crotch, whilst his left-hand circled round and squeezed her right buttock.

'Is that really necessary?' Shaw said, seeing the frightened, disgusted look on Melanie's face.

Doc looked across at him and smiled, repeating the process with her left leg.

'Que está limpio,' Mr Man United said, stepping back from Michael. *He's clean.* But Doc wasn't interested. He stood up straight, close to Melanie, and slipped his hands beneath her leather jacket. He caressed her firm slender back and gripped her buttocks. He then weaved his hands round to her stomach and groped her up beneath her sweater, cupping her breasts.

'You'll do,' he said, their noses almost touching. He stepped back and turned to Michael. 'Follow me.'

Bomber watched the four of them head into the church. 'I've got a bad feeling about this,' he said.

The Argentinian holding the walkie-talkie sat back in the door space of the Transit van and spoke into his handheld, speaking in a language neither of them understood.

*

'Where the hell are they?' Slater said, thinking more out loud than asking a direct question. 'I knew I needed a tail from the club.' He checked the clock on his dashboard. It had turned 13:30 five minutes ago, and there had been no sign of either party. 'They're not coming, are they? She's fucking screwed us.'

'You don't know that,' Inspector Joss of The Specialist Firearms Command said. 'Anything could have happened. Let's just hope she has lied and that they haven't sussed her out.'

Slater picked up the radio. 'Do we have anything on the receiver yet?'

'No, sir,' a male voice said, 'she must be out of range still.'

Slater didn't want to hear all this. 'If we'd had a tail on them from the beginning, we wouldn't be having this problem.'

Joss had seen situations like this many times during his thirty years' service. 'Let's just hope she's okay.'

The pair of them had been sat on location at the cottage for over three hours, watching the area from the comfort of their unmarked Land Rover. The team consisted of an armed response unit waiting in a barn a mile away. Snipers had eyes on the target location, and there was a police chopper on call if the need arose. A command base had been set up within the vicinity in the back of a fitted out lorry, which relayed everything they had back to Slater and Joss.

Slater kept looking at the clock, watching the time slip away. 'They're not coming, are they?'

'We'll give it another forty to sixty minutes, Ian, and then we'll have to call it in.'

*

The weather bleached heavy door to the rundown church pushed open with mild difficulty, grinding over the rough surface of the ground. The smell of moist wood and fungus filled the church, and shafts of light beamed through the broken stained-glass windows, penetrating the dusty air like fingers from heaven. The sound of flapping wings erupted above them, startled by their entrance. The ground and furniture was spotted with white splats, similar to that of bird faeces, and the mosaicked walls were decorated with the artistic talent of the local graffiti artists. The four of them made their way down the vandalised isle towards an old deteriorating alter. Leaves brushed past their feet as a gust of wind followed in behind them.

Shaw's hands were clammy to touch and sweat trickled down his back. It wasn't fear that raged within him, but the lack of control he had over the coming situation. His only comfort was the thirteen rounds he had stuffed in his underwear. He slipped his hands into his pockets and looked up at the rafters, fingering the magazine out from his briefs and into his pocket. He gripped it in the palm of his hand and switched his hands to his hoody's pockets, placing the magazine in the right. He now hoped Quinn had been correct with the makes of guns on the list.

'Down here,' Doc said, making his way through a stone arched doorway and down a set of stone steps. At the bottom he was welcomed by another heavy set, wooden door, similar in appearance to every other heavy door in the church. He banged loudly three times against it. 'Abrir.' *Open up.*

Melanie fought off the urge to cry, petrified in case someone grew suspicious of her actions and discovered the audio recorder pinned to her jacket. Her knees trembled with fear. A fear magnified by the sound of locks being pulled free on the other side of the door. The door creaked open, revealing a young thin man. A Mac-10 submachine-gun, much like the one Shaw had inspected in Michael's club, was strapped over his shoulder.

Shaw followed Doc inside, leaning his hand against the top of the doorframe as not to bang his head as he entered. He scanned the room, sweeping from left to right, taking in as much information as possible. A strange feeling of déjà vu overwhelmed him. The room was of generous

113

size, approximately five metres by twelve and filled with junk. Two more men were present within the confined subterranean room, both dressed in similar attire, dirty blue jeans and T-shirts, both armed and ready for trouble. The one closest to them, standing at the door, held the Mac-10 submachine-gun with an extended magazine, whilst the other positioned in the far left-hand corner, carelessly wielded another AK47. Even through his damaged nose, the smell of foist, urine and tobacco smoke was present. Shafts of head height light pierced the dusty air from small slit windows on his right. The ceiling was low to his head with its cobwebbed beams on show, and dark shadows filled the corners, cast by two battery powered lamps that supplied the majority of the light within the basement. Dusty old shelving units lined the left-hand wall, filled with the abandoned junk of the church, the decomposing remains of a rat lay beneath them. A long wooden bench was fitted to the right-hand wall under the filthy, thin windows. Everything appeared to be covered in a thin to thick sheet of dust, including the spider webs that decorated the ceiling and walls, giving him the impression they didn't use this basement very often.

Mr AK looked at Michael's suit and laughed. 'Me siento un poco mal vestido.' *I suddenly feel a little underdressed.*

Mr Mac-10 laughed.

'Is there really any need for these guns?' Michael asked Doc, looking at Mr Mac-10 behind him. 'You already know we're unarmed.'

'I think so. After all, you're just a friend of Quinn, and that means nothing to me.'

'Fine,' Michael said. 'What have you got for me?'

'Exactly what we agreed: two assault rifles, two submachine-guns, and four handguns, plus the shotgun. Now where's my money?' Doc said with an audible change in his tone.

'And the body armour and vests?'

Doc looked behind him where several sets of black body armour rested against the concrete wall. 'Managed to get hold of five, plus the six viper assault vests you asked for. Now, where's the money?'

'I wanna see the rest of the merchandise first, I'm not stupid,' Michael said, standing tall, but unable to hide the perspiration on his brow.

Mr Mac-10 closed the door behind them, resurrecting a memory of Shaw's prison cell. He watched how Mr Mac-10's fingers gripped the pistol grip of the weapon, how his itchy index finger stroked the trigger with a look of impatient excitement. Shaw knew that if that weapon was to go off, it would buck like a pissed off mule, spitting 9mm rounds into everyone

114

in front of it.

Doc nodded in agreement and instructed Mr AK to help him with the bag. The pair of them placed a large khaki bag on the table in the middle of the room and Doc unzipped it, exposing its contents for inspection. 'Take a look. I know you won't be disappointed.'

Shaw walked over and peered in, pulling out an AKMS-F, a modernised version of the AK47 with fold away stock.

'Doesn't say much, does he?' Doc said to Michael, looking at Shaw.

'I didn't bring him for his ability to socialise.'

'Can I take one of the lamps?' Shaw asked.

'Knock yourself out,' Doc said with a grin.

Shaw picked one up and carried it over to the long bench fitted to the wall beneath the small windows. With Mr AK's help, Shaw placed the bag under the bench, choosing the folding stocked AKMS-F first. He reached into his hoody pocket, fingered the loaded magazine up his sleeve, and pulled out the Swiss Army penknife and started the inspection, stripping them to sequence.

Doc stared at Melanie, making her uncomfortable. 'You're from Ireland?'

'Norn Iron,' she corrected, her voice wavering.

He smiled. 'I thought so, cause my cock's-a-Dublin, looking at you,' he said with a laugh, Mr Mac-10 and Mr AK joining him. 'I like her, Michael. Leave her here for me to play with and you can have the guns for free.'

A look of worry flashed across Melanie's face, causing Doc to laugh out loud again.

'I'm fucking around, sweetheart. As if I'd pass on twenty grand for a piece of pussy, no matter how fucking tasty it looked.'

Shaw finished the second rifle, a Type 56, China's version of the AK47 in less than twenty minutes, not wanting to spend too much time on them knowing the Ingram Mac-10's would take longer. AK's, along with all their copies, were simply made with fewer working parts than the Mac-10's, which was one of the main reasons they were so reliable; fewer mechanisms to jam.

'They're good,' he said, placing the two assault rifles to the side and reaching in for his first Mac-10. Out the corner of his eye, he noticed several dozen holes, five pence piece in size, peppered into the solid stone wall to his right, with a dozen or so similar holes in the bench top and wooden door behind Michael. The voice in his head bellowed the words, causing his heart to almost miss a beat. Bullet holes. He then noticed the thick dust that covered the majority of the room appeared to have been brushed away, leaving a clear sign of disturbance.

Michael stabbed a cigarette between his lips, oblivious to Shaw's findings.

'Is one of them for me?' Doc said, reaching out before Michael could refuse.

He allowed him to take one and replaced the packet back in his suit jacket. 'What about ammo?'

Doc nodded, running a hand through his greasy hair and lighting his cigarette. 'Like I said, exactly what we'd agreed.' Passive smoke rose to the ceiling and swirled in the air amongst them

'They're both good,' Shaw said, placing the two Mac-10s alongside the assault rifles he'd already done. His mind raced through the actions that maybe required for the situation he'd found himself in. Mr Mac-10 rested against the wall to his right, watching him go about his inspection. Mr AK sat on an old red crate beside his bearded colleague, tapping an annoying rhythm onto the body of his AK47, whilst Doc held the back rest of a grey polypropylene school chair, his revolver tucked in his jeans.

'How many more has he got left to look at?' Doc questioned. 'He's taking all day.' He sat back in his chair and pulled the chrome, four inch hand canon from the front of his jeans, lifting his feet onto an empty shelf.

Michael looked at his watch, 14:34. 'You nearly done yet?' he asked Shaw, feeling the pressure.

Shaw looked back at him. 'Do you want to do it?'

'Just get a move on.'

The last of the guns to be inspected after the Mossberg 590 shotgun were the four handguns. A smile spread across Shaw's face as he picked out the first of two Glock 19's and inspected it. A stainless steel Sig Sauer P226 came second, followed by a heavy black .357 FN Barracuda revolver.

Melanie slid her hand into her jacket pocket and stroked her mobile phone, yearning to call Slater and inform him of their location. She knew he'd have no idea where they were, and that she was all alone with these men. But she couldn't risk it, too frightened to even activate it in case it made a sound. She stood and watched in silence, trembling, longing for it to be over.

Finally, Shaw pulled out the second Glock 19 and stripped it, systematically going through every check, rebuilding it as he finished. He pulled back on its working parts and purposefully knocked his penknife off the counter with his elbow. As Mr Mac-10 bent forward to pick it up, Shaw slipped the loaded magazine down from his sleeve and punched it into the Glock's housing. He fired off the dead action and cocked it again, loading a 9mm round into its chamber. He placed it on the counter within arm's reach, concerned Doc would notice the seventeen round magazine protruding from the bottom of the Glock 19's fifteen round pistol grip.

'Apart from actually test firing them, they've passed every inspection I can think of?' he said. It had taken him over an hour to finish the checks on all nine of the guns.

'There you go,' Doc said, 'there all good. Just like I knew they would be. Now where's my money?'

Michael pulled out his iPhone and pressed redial, bringing up Quinn's name.

'You won't get any reception down here.' Doc threw him a walkie-talkie. 'Use that. Tell him to pass the money to Dante. He can bring it down.'

Michael caught the handheld radio, not liking the way Doc was speaking to him in front of Mel. 'Who will I be speaking to?'

'Ramiro.'

Michael spoke into the radio.

'Sí,' the Argentinian answered.

'Put Quinn on.'

A moment later a crackle was heard, followed by Quinn's voice. 'Quinn.'

'Hand over the cash. Their gear's good. Me and Ryan will bring it up and put it in your truck.'

'Okay.'

Shaw turned to face the room and watched Doc, trying to get a feel for his body language. 'Why don't we carry these outside and we can give you your money upstairs in the daylight. That way you'll not count it wrong.'

'I'd prefer we did the exchange down here,' Doc said, his eyes full of betrayal.

A short while later three bangs were heard at the door, followed by a male voice. 'Es Dante.'

Doc nodded at Mr Mac-10, indicating for him to open the door.

'Póngalo sobre la mesa,' he said. *Put it on the table.* Dante carried the holdall past them and did as Doc had instructed. Shaw could see the excitement in Doc's eyes, the satisfaction of a deal done.

'Make sure all the gear's in the bag,' Michael said to Shaw before turning to Doc. 'There you go. Twenty grand.'

'So, I see,' Doc said, thumbing through the holdall's contents. 'But there's been a slight complication.'

Michael frowned. 'What kind of complication?'

'You can't take the guns.' Doc smiled, exhaling smoke through his nostrils. 'I've promised them to someone else. Double booked them you could say.'

'What do you mean, I can't take the guns? I've just fucking paid you!'

'He means he's screwing you,' Shaw interrupted, feeling the tension squeeze at his temples. He watched Mr Mac-10 manoeuvre himself in front of Michael, lining himself up with Melanie.

Doc picked up his handheld radio. 'Your friend isn't as dumb as he looks.'

Melanie's mind went blank, her body frozen. She stared at Doc, too afraid to look away. Almost knowing that she was about to die.

Doc spoke into the handset. 'El trato está hecho. Mátalos.' To Melanie and Michael, the words were meaningless. To Shaw, one phrase stuck out: Mátalos. *Kill them.*

*

Mr Man United stepped forward from the van and took the holdall filled with fifties and twenties from Quinn and handed it to his colleague, who then headed into the church.

'What's with all the hardware?' Quinn said, noticing the square-like shape of the Ingram Mac-10 slung over Dante's shoulder.

Mr Man United raised Quinn an eyebrow.

'The guns. You'd think you were planning on taking back the Falkland Islands.'

The Argentinean laughed, finding Quinn's comment genuinely funny. 'Perro sucio,' he said. *Filthy dog.*

'What did you say?' Quinn said. 'Say that in fucking English. I dare ya.'

'Leroy, leave it,' Bomber said, standing at the Hilux's passenger door.

'You.' Mr Man United addressed Bomber, breaking a prolonged

118

silence. 'Come around here and stand next to him.'

'Fuck off'

A crackling sound came over the radio, followed by a message spoken in Spanish.

Mr Man United pointed his assault rifle at Bomber. 'Come stand next to him. Now!'

'Fuck off.'

Gunfire erupted from the church, short and sharp. Mr Man United hesitated, not expecting to hear the gunfire so soon, giving Bomber the seconds he required. He snatched Quinn's sawn–off shotgun from the passenger chair and fired both barrels through the glass in the driver's side window, shredding the Argentinean's Manchester United T-shirt. The blast threw him off his feet, slamming him against the side of the blue Transit van.

Quinn reached down and took the Argentinian's AK47 and fired three shots into his chest. 'Stay with the truck,' he said, turning towards the church.

Seventeen

'The heavy smell of cordite'

Instinct rather than reaction took control of Shaw. His right hand snatched the loaded Glock off the worktop and flashed it up in front of him. He gripped it firmly in both hands, ceased his breathing and controlled his limbs. He locked his sights onto the target he feared most, Mr Mac-10 standing directly opposite, and snapped off two shots in rapid succession. The first opened up his left eye socket, deafening everyone in the confined room. The second punched a clean hole in his forehead. His head snapped back, exploding behind him, painting the shelving with grey matter and splashing Melanie's face with speckles of blood. Less than a second later, he snapped to the right with choreographed precision and emptied two more rounds into the face of Mr AK who sat stunned on the crate, his weapon still laid across his lap. His dead body fell to the right, motionless, brain matter leaking around him.

Michael dropped to the filthy floor of the basement, taking cover behind anything he could find. He pulled Melanie down with him and covered his ears.

Next was Doc, who was now stood to his feet, his Smith and Wesson 500, the most powerful hand canon on the market, aimed in Shaw's direction. He fired the weapon, holding it in only one hand. The aimless round thundered past Shaw's head, snapping at mid-air before punching into the stone wall behind him. Shaw flinched from the wall's debris and returned two shots, cracking open his hairy jaw and punching a second between his eyes. The fourth man in the room, whom Shaw had thought to be unarmed, lifted a weapon up in his direction and let rip. The flare from the Mac-10's muzzle flashed as he fired the submachine-gun from the hip. The uncontrolled automatic fire caught Shaw off guard, blasting holes into the brickwork to his left, shattering the grimy windows, allowing more daylight to fill the confined room. The battery powered lamp to Shaw's left also exploded, sending shards of plastic in all directions, transforming light into dark. Shaw dropped to his right knee, avoiding the fully automatic fire, and fired again. Five rounds punched into the man. Two rounds ripped into his chest, pushing him back, causing his firing arm to drop. The Mac-10 continued to spit out rounds, digging them deep into the surrounding room and the ground at his feet. Shaw's third round bit into his throat, spilling bright red blood, before the fourth and fifth punched into his face,

120

dropping him dead. Shaw stood, fuelled on adrenalin, and turned the gun on Michael.

Michael stood to his feet and raised his hands in the air. 'What? You gonna shoot me now, then Melanie?'

'Just you.' Shaw kept the smoking gun on him. He knew he still had two rounds in the pistol: one in the clip and one in the chamber, more than enough.

The door to the basement slammed open and Quinn burst in, an AK47 in hand. 'What the hell,' he said, choking on the heavy smell of cordite. He scanned his eyes from left to right, taking in Shaw's stance, Michael's pose of submission, and the four dead bodies lying on the ground. 'Drop the gun, dickhead.'

Shaw's mind, refusing to be beaten, calculated the actions required. Step forward, snatch the barrel of Quinn's rifle and empty the last two rounds into him. Take his AK47 and pivot to the right, emptying the clip into Michael.

'Stop it. Please!' Melanie screamed, standing to her feet. 'Please.' Her dirty face was lined with mascara and speckled with blood, her jacket and jeans painted with filth.

Shaw could see she was a stupid girl, caught up in something she had no business being in. She didn't deserve to die today, but if he carried out his actions, he couldn't guarantee she wouldn't be caught in the fire. 'How do I know you're not just gonna kill me now?' he said.

'I'm not a murderer, Ryan. I'm a business man,' Michael said.

'No, but he is.' He nodded to Quinn.

Michael knew first hand Shaw had the skill to take them both out. 'Look, no one's going to kill you.'

'Please.' Melanie sobbed, tears rolling down her cheeks, 'both of ya, put down the guns.'

Shaw raised his hands up in front of him and relaxed his grip on his pistol, allowing it to swing loosely on his trigger finger. Quinn took the pistol from him and stuffed it in the waist band of his trousers.

Michael turned to the dead bodies. 'Didn't fuck about, did ya.' He was amazed at the speed and accuracy in which Shaw had dispersed with the problem. He had been incredible, as if it had been second nature to him, all happening within the blink of an eye. He kicked Doc's dead body and picked up the handheld radio and asked for Bomber.

'Michael?' Bomber said over the radio.

'Get yourself down here. Give us a hand with this lot.'

121

'What's going on?'

'I'll explain later, just get down here. We haven't got much time.' Michael smiled, more than happy with the final outcome. Not only was he still alive, but he now owned more artillery than he'd ordered. Plus, he was twenty grand up.

They gathered what was available and loaded it into the back of Quinn's Hilux, confiscating four assault rifles, four Mac-10's, five handguns, a shotgun, and dozens of boxes of various ammunition and magazines.

Melanie sat in Michael's car, unable to do anything apart from stare at her mobile phone and cry. She sat silent, staring at her shaking hands, diluted mascara running down her cheeks. She couldn't believe what she had just witnessed, what she had just heard. Her ears still rang from the gun shots and every time she closed her eyes, the image of the man's head exploding in front of her filled her mind. Her stomach muscles contracted, followed by an involuntary deep breath, pushing up its contents. She opened the car door just in time to feel the vomit break past her lips and splash on the frozen path.

Once Quinn's Hilux was packed, Shaw and Bomber carried Mr Man United's dead body down into the basement and dumped him beside his colleagues.

'There, that's it. I'm done, finished,' Shaw said, trying to ignore the voice in his head telling him otherwise.

Bomber didn't comment.

The pair made their way back up the stairs and out into the church grounds.

'What we doing about those bodies?' Bomber said to anybody who was listening. 'We just gonna leave them down in the church?'

Before anyone could answer, Shaw spoke. 'Burn them.'

'What, so the fire brigade can attend and find them? Are you completely thick?' Quinn said, turning to Michael. 'We don't even need this prick anymore.'

Shaw became aware of his vulnerability, realising his presence was no longer a requirement. 'They're gonna get found at some point,' he said. 'At least this way our fingerprints and DNA won't be all over the place.'

'Why don't you let me put his body down there with the rest of them?' Quinn suggested to Michael.

Michael looked at him with steely eyes, as if reminding him of who was in charge. 'No, Shaw's right, burn them.'

A look of disappointment washed over Quinn's face. 'Well go on

122

then,' he said to Shaw, 'go and burn them.' He climbed into his pickup next to Bomber and slammed the door shut.

'And how the hell am I supposed to get back?' Shaw said.

'Walk.' Quinn gunned the engine and pulled away with a spin of the tyres, followed closely by Michael, leaving Shaw in the middle of nowhere with five dead bodies.

Eighteen
'Distinctively Scarred'

Michael negotiated the heavy traffic, easily overtaking the other road users in his 3.8 litre sports car. Behind him he could see the spray off the tarmac, misting up into the air as he sped along the dual carriageway towards Gateshead. Melanie sat beside him, her gaze held on the passing scenery, occasionally releasing a sniff or a sob. Her face and clothing were still dirty from the basement floor and speckles of blood could still be seen dotting her face.

'Look, Melanie, are you okay?' he said, now regretting bringing her along.

She said nothing.

'Melanie.'

She turned her head towards him and nodded; every movement slow and sombre.

'Are you sure?'

She nodded again, her eyes red and puffy.

'Because no one saw that coming. I didn't see that coming.' He paused, recalling the incident himself. 'I had no idea Shaw was gonna do that, you know that.'

She turned her gaze back to the window, trying to understand why Shaw had killed those men. She had felt the deal was going bad and heard the man say something over the radio, but she just couldn't accept it. You can't just kill somebody. Shaw hadn't even flinched. It had come naturally to him. Right there and then, she decided she wanted out. She didn't care if Slater pressed his charges of prostitution against her. Anything Slater could do to her was better than what had occurred today.

Michael's iPhone rang in his pocket, breaking the silence between them. He pulled into the slow lane, steadying his speed, and answered the call. 'Hello,' he said.

'Hello, Mikey.'

The voice hit him like a wrecking ball. He swallowed then answered. 'What can I do for ya?'

Melanie recognised the sound of concern in Michael's voice and watched him closely.

'We need to have a little chat, me and you,' Paul Mallinson said. 'Where are you?'

'I'm in Gateshead at the moment. I should be back in Sunderland tonight. About half seven,' he said, still thinking about stashing the guns with Bomber and Quinn.

'Hmm, say half an hour at your club.'

'I told you, I'm in Gateshead.'

'I don't give a fuck what you've told me, thirty minutes is plenty of time. I'll be waiting at the club come quarter to five. Do not keep me waiting.' Paul Mallinson hung up.

Michael put his phone back in his inside pocket and hit the indicator. 'Change of plan, you're not going home yet.'

'What? Why not?' she said, her bottom lip wavering.

'Because I have to meet someone.'

'Well can't ya drop me off first?'

'I said no! We're going to the club. Then I'll take you home.' He exited the motorway at the next junction and headed back towards Sunderland, increasing his speed to over 100mph. He pulled out his phone and dialled Quinn.

Quinn answered.

'Something's come up, so I won't be at the house for a while.'

'Everything okay?'

'I'm not sure. It's Paul Mallinson.'

'What's he want?'

'No idea,' Michael said, hoping it had nothing to do with Jammin's death, 'but it shouldn't take too long. You know where the gears going?'

'Oh aye. We'll have it stashed under the stairs well before the girls are back.'

Michael killed the line to Quinn and dialled Kimberly. 'You still at the club?' he said once she'd picked up.

'Yes and probably will be for another hour or so, why?'

'Is Sherman with you?'

'No, he's with Will at that house. Why?'

'So who's with you at the club?'

'No one, Michael,' she said with a laugh. 'I'm on my own. I'm a big girl now, you know.'

Michael explained that Paul Mallinson was on his way to the club to see him and that it sounded serious. He instructed her to let him in and give him any drink he wanted. 'Just keep him entertained until I get there,' he said. 'I'll be about thirty minutes.'

Kimberly had been at the club most of the afternoon, checking stock, going through the paperwork and refilling cabinets for the night's business. She loved running the club for her cousin, helping him out, allowing him time to run all his side-lines, especially since he paid her so generously. She'd always felt well looked after since her brother had died a couple years back, growing closer to him since the funeral. Most of her time was spent at the club, making sure it was running properly, supervising staff, dealing with security, and mixing with clientele.

It wasn't long before there was a buzz on the intercom, distracting her from her work. She looked at the intercom's monitor, making sure it was Paul before allowing him and his hired muscle to enter.

'Michael won't be long,' she said, meeting the pair of them at the door. 'Can I get either of you a drink?'

Paul eyed her up like a piece of meat on a menu, starring at the tight denim that hugged her buttocks. 'Aye. I'll have a gin and tonic.'

'I'm fine, thanks,' his hired muscle added.

She turned about and headed back into the club, feeling Paul's eyes on her as he followed. 'He shouldn't be long,' she said. 'He wasn't that far away.'

'I don't mind. He can take as long as he likes.' Paul smiled, looking down her black blouse as she bent forward for a glass. 'Always a pleasure to see you, Kimberly, you know that.'

She poured him his large gin and popped the cap off the tonic bottle, adding it to the spirit. 'Ice?'

'Please.'

'What is it you need to see him about, anyway?' she said, adding the cubes. 'If you don't mind me asking.'

'Nothing too serious, you know how it is. Just need to get a few things straight.'

She handed him his drink and showed them to a table with four soft armchairs surrounding it.

'You still seeing that loser, what's his face? Or have you come to your senses and decided to let me take you out?' he said.

'Depends on where you're going to take me. I'm not cheap.' She looked across at Paul's hired muscle and smiled.

'Oh, I'd treat you good, Kimberly. Like a fucking princess.'

Kimberly took a mouthful of her sparkling water and placed the glass on the table in front, praying that Michael would walk through the door and save her from this moron. 'I'm no princess.' She looked again at the hired muscle, this time retrieving a smile back.

Paul opened his mouth to speak, but stopped when Michael walked in, whispering in Melanie's ear.

'Paul,' Michael said, reaching his hand out to him. 'Have you been waiting long?'

Melanie disappeared into Michael's office.

'Yes,' Paul said, accepting his offered hand. 'Luckily for you, your attractive cousin was here to keep me entertained.'

Kimberly picked up her glass and made her excuses before heading back over to the bar.

'You been raking through fucking skips again?' Paul said, looking at the filth on Michael's suit.

He looked down at his trousers seeing the ground in dirt. 'What was it that was so urgent?'

'Jebel Darbo.'

'Who?'

'Jammin.'

Michael's stomach knotted. 'What about him?'

Paul lowered his glass to his lap. 'A little birdie tells me you do a little business with him every now and again.'

Michael turned his eyes to his hired muscle before sitting. 'Aye, every now and again. But that's all, and only in small quantities, just enough for the VIP guests to feel that little bit more important. Why? You don't think I had anything to do with his death, do you?'

'I never said that,' he said, turning to face his hired muscle. 'I never said that did I, Levi?'

'No, Paul, you definitely didn't,' Levi replied back.

'But you do admit doing business with him?'

'Aye, it's no secret.' Michael's eyes darted between the pair of them, trying to read any signs they were giving.

'You met him on the day he was killed too, though, didn't ya? Was that a secret?'

Michael shifted in his seat, wishing he had a large Jack Daniels in front of him. 'Yeah, I bought some brown off him,' he said with a nod. 'And no, it was no secret. He was with some fat prick,' he added, knowing where Paul will have gotten his information from.

'Oh, I know all that, Mikey. I've been speaking with that fat prick. They call him Dooley. Good lad actually, just really fond of kebabs.

Although he won't be eating any for a little while due to his jaw being wired shut.'

'Do you have any idea of who killed him?'

'We've got a few leads,' he said, having a full description of the man who'd hit Dooley. 'Nothing concrete. You know how it is. Just got to follow your gut on these things.'

Michael nodded.

'So, Mikey-lad, who's supplying you with these cars?'

Michael rested back in his chair, feeling a little calmer now the subject had changed. 'Why, so you can muscle me out of my own deal?' he said with a mocking smile. 'I don't think so. Besides, come to think of it, I don't even need your uncle's money. So you can have it back.' He rose from his chair and turned towards his office, disappearing through a door.

Melanie stood with a fright as Michael entered and dropped her glass of gin, smashing it on the floor. She threw her hands up over her face and burst into tears. 'I'm sorry,' she sobbed through her fingers. 'I just wanna go home.'

'I know!' he said, his frustration getting the better of him. 'As soon as I'm done here, I'll take you.' He walked passed her and picked up the bag containing the twenty grand. He counted out ten and placed it in his desk, taking the remaining ten grand with him.

*

Shaw noted the black C class Mercedes with blacked out windows parked alongside Michael's GT-R and Kimberly's MR2. He walked up the stairs that lead to the strip club and pressed the buzzer, looking up into the CCTV camera positioned above the door. After he'd been left on his own at the church, Shaw had searched through the pockets of the dead bodies, finding a lighter, car keys, and the combined amount of £212. He'd then syphoned the fuel tank of the Vectra and set the basement ablaze before taking the vehicle and dumping it in a car park in town.

Kimberly opened the door. 'What do you want?' she said.

'Where is he?'

Kimberly curled up her nose, smelling the thick odour of petrol.

'Who?'

'You know who,' he said, pushing his way past her.

'Hey. You can't just barge your way in here.'

'Watch me. Is he down here?'

'Wait.'

Shaw stopped and turned to look at her.

'Wait here. I'll go get him.' She walked past him and back into the club.

Shaw followed.

Paul Mallinson watched the pair of them walk into the room, noting Shaw's distinctively scarred face. 'Who are you?' he said.

Kimberly turned and looked at Shaw. 'I told you to wait.'

Shaw looked at the young man and his obvious hired help and said nothing.

'Oi. Mr Mallinson asked you a fucking question,' Levi said.

'Did he?' Shaw said, his face deadpan.

Levi rose to his feet and stepped out from behind the table.

Paul placed his hand on Levi's forearm and shook his head, halting his advance. 'It's okay,' he said.

Michael appeared from the corridor leading to his office, interrupting the tensing atmosphere. 'Shaw,' he said, glancing at Kimberly and then to Paul Mallinson, who in turn returned the gaze. 'What the fuck are you doing here?'

'That's us finished,' Shaw said.

Michael approached him and ushered him back the way he'd come, stopping once they'd reached the bar. 'This isn't a good time, Shaw. You shouldn't be here,' he said, indicating the two men sat at the table.

'And that should bother me, why?'

Michael placed a hand on Shaw's shoulder, guiding him further away from prying ears. 'We'll talk about this later?' he said.

'No we won't. We'll talk about this now. Will's debt's paid, that's it. We're out.'

'Will's debt's paid? I don't think so. Not yet. Not by a long shot.'

Shaw grabbed hold of Michael's suit jacket and pulled his face close to his. 'You know I'm getting a little tired of your fucking shit.'

Michael looked down at Shaw's hands. 'I'd think very carefully about what you're gonna do next.'

A knot of muscle pulsed at the rear of Shaw's jaw. He released his hold and took a step back.

Michael straightened his jacket and looked back at Paul and Levi. 'Do something for me, and then we'll talk, okay?'

Shaw breathed out, defeated. 'Like what?'

'I need Melanie taking home. She's taken today badly.'

'What? And you think having her sat next to me will do her any favours?'

'To be honest, Shaw, I don't really care. She's doing my head in.' Michael handed him the keys to his GT-R. 'Bring it straight back.'

Shaw snatched the keys from him. 'Where is she?'

'Wait here.' Michael headed back to his office, a nervous smile on his face. Paul tapped his watch in response.

Shaw glanced at the two men, feeling their eyes on him. A second later, Michael re-appeared, holding Melanie by her arm.

'Ya actually want me te go with him? Is yar head cut?' She pulled her arm from Michael's grasp. 'After what he did teday?'

Michael grabbed hold of her arms and looked into her puffy eyes. 'Shut the fuck up, Mel, you're embarrassing me. You're going with him if you like it or not. Now do as you're fucking told.' He pushed her towards Shaw and watched them leave.

'Shaw,' Paul Mallinson yelled.

Shaw stopped and turned to face him, just in time to be momentarily blinded by the flash of his phone's camera.

'I'll be seeing you again,' Paul said.

Shaw glanced at Michael and turned his back on them and headed out of the club.

'Who was that?' Paul asked once the couple had left the room.

'That's Shaw.'

'And who's Shaw?'

'Ryan Shaw,' he said, wishing Shaw hadn't walked in on them. 'He's the guy I hired to check over the cars.'

'Right. Was that a bit of a lover's tiff?'

'That was nothing,' he said, concerned a photograph of Shaw had been taken. 'Some people just need to be reminded of who pays their cheques.' He smiled. 'Speaking of money. Here's your uncles' money back.' He reached over the leather holdall. 'Turns out I didn't need it after all.'

Paul ignored the gesture. 'Loans don't work like that, Mikey.'

Michael cringed inside every time he called him that.

'You made a deal with my uncles. That deal still stands.'

Michael's eyes flicked between the pair of them. 'Okay.'

'Is that Shaw a local lad, because he sounds a little Scottish?'

'Middlesbrough, I think. Why?'

'No reason. Just good to know someone who knows what their talking about when it comes to cars.' He finished the last of his gin and tonic and stood up. 'Oh, and one last thing.'

'Yes?' Michael said, seeing him to the front door.

'Your lads haven't been doing any work in the Washington area lately, have they?'

'My lads?'

'Yeah: Quinn and the other one.'

'No,' he said, feeling the knot grow even tighter in his gut. 'But then Quinn does his own thing, too, you know.'

'Thought as much. Say goodbye to Kimberly for me.' Michael closed the door behind him.

*

Once he was sat in his Mercedes Benz, Paul sent the picture of Shaw to Levi's phone. 'Show it to Dooley, confirm it's him. Then find out where he's staying and bring him to me. I want a word with this Ryan Shaw.'

Nineteen

'Honest work'

The soft red leather seats of Michael's sports car creaked and crunched under Shaw's buttocks. He waited for Melanie to sit next to him as he clipped in his seat belt and adjusted the seat and mirrors.

'Where am I heading?' he said, allowing the car to creep forward.

She said nothing.

'If you don't tell me where you want to go, how can I take you there?'

'Gateshead,' she said, her Northern Irish accent soft and quiet.

Shaw pulled forward. Ten minutes later he slipped onto the dual carriageway and followed the road signs for Gateshead.

'How?' Melanie asked out of the blue, breaking the long silence between them.

He looked at her pretty face, still stained with speckles of blood and dirt, but her eyes remained focused on the road ahead.

'How could ya just murder those men and feel nothing?' she added, refusing to return his gaze.

He eased off on the accelerator, allowing a lorry to pull out in front of him, spraying their windscreen with road moisture from its tyres. 'You think I murdered those men?' he said. 'Those men were going to kill us. You wouldn't be sat there crying now if I hadn't done what I did.'

She turned and stared at him, absorbing every creased scar that cut through the left side of his unshaven face. She knew he could feel her eyes on him, even though he never returned her gaze. 'Yar not worried I'll ring the peelers, tell them what happened, what ya did?'

'Why, you gonna?' he said, already feeling the worry churning in his gut.

She turned back to the passing scenery. 'Who are ya really, Shaw?' she said, knowing her digital audio device would still be recording.

'I'm nobody you need to worry about.'

She looked back to him. 'So who does need te worry?'

Shaw said nothing.

'Is it the people Michael's going te rob? Is that why he has ya hanging around still?'

'Is that why Michael's purchased those guns? He's going to rob someone?'

'Yar telling me ya didn't know?' she said, unconvinced.

'No, I didn't. The only reason I'm still here is because my brother can't keep his fucking hands out of other people's cookie jars.' Shaw changed down a gear, slowing the sports car to a manageable speed to take an upcoming bend. 'And as always, he leaves the mess for other people to clean up.'

'I don't believe ya,' she said.

'Sweetheart, you believing me is the least of my worries.' Shaw changed back up and floored the accelerator, overtaking a collection of slow moving cars. 'Now you answer me something,' he said. 'What the hell are you running around with the likes of him for, anyway? You just don't seem the type.'

'Why, because I'm a Norn Irish church going girl?'

'Something like that.'

Her mind instantly found the memory of Slater blackmailing her into it, threatening her with the fabricated charge of prostitution and drug possession. 'I have my reasons,' she said.

Feeling a need to change the subject, Shaw chose one he knew a little more about. 'So, whereabouts in Northern Ireland are you from?'

She looked at him. 'Ya actually wanna make small talk with me?' she said, firing air through her nasal cavity in disbelief.

'Fine, fuck ya.'

The pair sat in an uncomfortable silence for a few more moments before Melanie spoke. 'Are ya familiar with Norn Iron?' She couldn't remember the last time anyone had even asked her that question, wanting only to see her tits.

'I did a tour over there a few years back. Plus my wife liked to visit the place whenever she could.'

'Yer married?'

'Not for long, she wants to divorce me.'

'I'm not surprised.'

Her accent sounded tender on his ears, fuelling the memories of his wife, but Shaw could only laugh in agreement.

Melanie found herself smiling too. 'Do ya have any wein's?'

133

'One. A four year old called Douglas.'

'A Scottish name.'

'Yeah.' He paused, fearful that these last few days had drawn a distinctive line through a possible relationship with his son. 'So, whereabouts are you from?'

'Newry. It's on—'

'The borders of County Down and Armagh,' he said, finishing off her sentence.

'Aye.' She smiled, impressed with his knowledge of home.

'So why did you move here?'

'Sunderland?'

'England in general,' he said. 'Surely, Daddy didn't want his little catholic girl moving over here.'

'How did ya know I was catholic?'

'You're from Newry, the chances are you'd be catholic.'

She went quiet, an image of her father standing tall and proud at church entered her mind.

'So why did you move here?' he asked again.

'Education and opportunities, I guess.'

He looked at her filthy clothes and blood speckled face. 'So how's that going for you?'

'Not the best, sure.' She rested her head back against the red leather headrest. 'Ya know I came over here with such aspirations. There was so much I wanted te do: musicals, television, the West End, ballet.'

'So what happened?'

'Nothing. That was the problem. I couldn't find enough work te pay the bills.'

'So you started stripping?'

She reddened and nodded.

'No shame in that,' he said. 'It's honest work.'

She turned her head back to the window.

'Can I give you a piece of advice?' he said.

She looked back to him.

'Go home. Staying with Michael will only get you hurt, if not worse.'

She turned back to the window. *If only I could.*

Several minutes later, Shaw turned off the dual carriageway. 'Where do I go from here?'

134

Melanie directed him towards her neighbourhood of new builds and freshly laid lawns. 'Just here'll do,' she said, pointing to a bus stop.

'Where is it you live?'

She pointed to a cul-de-sac. 'Just in there. Well thanks for the lift home.' She popped the seat belt and climbed out, surprised at how much talking about home had calmed her nerves. She smiled and closed the car door.

Shaw watched her run into the cul-de-sac, burying her head into her shoulders to fight off the frosty chill, and approach her front door. Now, along with everything else that was going on, he had the possibility of her babbling to the police do deal with. He still couldn't get his head around the fact she'd been present at the deal in the first place. That act along showed just how much of an amateur Michael actually was. He gunned the engine and reached for the gearstick, noticing a mobile phone trapped in the recess between the centre column and the passenger seat. He dug it out and activated its screen, finding the key coded wallpaper of a black and grey tabby cat sprawled across a black leather sofa. He killed the engine, figuring it belonged to Melanie, and climbed out into the cold, taking the phone with him. Her front door was still unlocked and opened when pushed, opening up into a small warm passage with shoes lining the wall and coats hanging from hooks.

'Hello,' he said aloud, entering her flat, 'Melanie.'

*

Michael swallowed the remainder of his drink and poured himself another. 'I think we may have a problem.'

'In what sense?' Kimberly asked.

'He knows.'

'Knows what?'

'That we did Jammin.'

'How? He didn't say anything like that to me.'

'Shaw. Dooley had to have given Paul a description of him.'

'He told the police he didn't see anything?'

'Nobody grasses to the police, Kim. But he will have told Paul.'

'Then we need to do something,' Kimberly said, her hands resting on the bar. 'We can't have that little prick fucking it up now. Speak to Bomber, have him do something.'

'Don't be daft,' he said.

'Why?'

'You know why.'

'So get rid of them, too.'

'You can't just kill the two hardest hitters in Sunderland, Kimberly. It doesn't work like that.'

'Why not? Everyone knows they've got a list of enemies as long as the Wear. No one would ever know it was us. Nobody would even suspect us.' She could see the idea ticking over in his head. 'You know it makes sense.'

'It comes down to money, Kim. Money we don't have. I don't even have enough to refill the cellar or pay the girls, let alone pay someone to off the Mallinsons. Until this transaction goes down, we're broke.' He massaged his temples and cursed. 'But you're right. We need to do something.'

'Would Bomber not do it for a bigger cut of the take?'

He looked up at her. 'Possibly. I'll speak to him tomorrow after the meeting.'

'You know I don't care about the money,' she said. 'All I want is Shaw's last breath.'

'I know that, Kim, but I do. This money's everything. We need this money. Besides, Shaw won't just roll over, you know that, right? He won't be an easy man to put down. The Taliban put five rounds in him and he's still here.'

'Aye, and two of them hit his body armour,' she said, unimpressed.

'That's not the point.'

'Christ, you actually sound like you respect the man.'

'I do. And you'd be a fool not to, also.'

'What? Have you forgotten already?' Kim said, her voice wavering with anger. 'What he—'

'No, Kim, I have not forgotten!'

'He's just a man, Michael, nothing more.'

'You didn't see him in the church basement. He dropped four heavily armed men in under five seconds—'

'I don't care,' she interrupted, her bottom lip quivering. 'I want him dropped for what he did.'

Michael placed his hand on hers. 'And he will be, just as soon as this deal's done. Then it'll be just me, you and five-hundred grand

136

soaking our feet on a sunny beach in Thailand.'

'What about Bomber? I couldn't give a shit about Quinn or that slut you're fucking, but Bomber, I like Bomber.'

He downed his glass in one. 'Kim, we've discussed this. There isn't enough to go round. If we want to start again, we'll need it all.'

Kimberly took his empty glass.

'Speaking of Shaw.' He pulled out his iPhone and called his number, going straight to his answering service. He then dialled Melanie's, but that too went straight to her answering service. He hung up and dialled Quinn.

Quinn answered, stashing the last of the guns under the floorboards in the brothel.

'How's it going?' Michael asked him, knowing Bomber will have had more to do with the task than Quinn.

'They're sorted,' he said, standing to his feet.

'We have an issue.'

Quinn listened.

'Paul Mallinson knows you did Jammin.'

'What, the little nigga? So fuck.'

'Paul's uncles work for Weathers, Quinn. This is a problem. Especially for you.'

'How does he know?'

'I don't know,' Michael said, not wanting to have to explain everything in slow time to him. 'But he needs dealing with, and soon.'

Quinn ran his free hand through his hair. 'You want me to deal with the problem now?'

'Not this very minute, no,' he said, 'but what I do need you to do is head over to Melanie's and see if Shaw's there. He has my car and I want it back.'

'He's got your car?'

'I gave him it to drop Melanie off. Just go to hers and see if he's there. If he is, get him to bring it back here.'

'Okay. I'll leave the rest of this with Bomber.'

Michael hung up and leaned forward on the bar. 'Do you know where Shaw's staying?'

Kimberly shook her head. 'Why?'

'I wanna keep a closer eye on him until this is done. And I can't do that without knowing where he's staying.'

Kimberly wiped his empty glass dry and placed it back on the shelf. 'You want me to give Sherman a call? Get him to get Will to tell us.'

Michael smiled. 'Aye.'

*

Melanie's home had never felt more welcoming. Her tabby friend greeted her as she entered and purred at her feet. She reached down and picked him up before walking past the blinking Christmas tree and into the kitchen. She bent forward and opened the cupboard beneath the sink, retrieving the cat food that sat next to the spare sponges and cleaning products.

'There ya go, wee man,' she said, spooning it into his bowl. 'I can always count on ya.' Her stomach still churned with the thought of what may have happened earlier that day. If it hadn't been for Shaw, they would all be lying face down in a shallow grave somewhere, possibly in that graveyard next to the church. Without warning, she threw up, catching her vomit in the kitchen sink. Her left hand trembled as it turned the tap, washing the vomit down the drain. This was too much. She wanted out. She wanted to go home. She cupped her face in her hands and sobbed, feeling the strength in her legs disperse. She turned and slid to the kitchen floor, resting her back against the kitchen unit. She called out for her daddy and laid her head in her hands. Trigger appeared at her feet and purred, smearing his scent around her ankles. She sniffed back the tears and climbed back to her feet, determined to get through it. She made her way through to the bathroom and flicked on the light. The bulb flickered several times before staying on. She inhaled involuntarily, not ready for the reflection before her. Her skin was filthy and tired looking. Her eyes were red and puffy. Her makeup was diluted and smeared. But the biggest shock of all was the blood that stained her platinum hair, and the speckles of dark red that dotted her face like freckles on a school girl. She filled the sink and scrubbed her face, scrubbing until sore, unable to remove the horror that stained her skin. She pulled off her wet sweater and blouse together and used them to dry her face, hoping it would cleanse her. It didn't. She threw them on the floor beside the bathtub and peeled off her jeans, kicking them beside her sweater and boots. She stood in her black bra and pink stripy briefs, her skin goose-pimpling from the cold.

The sound of her phone ringing snatched her from her trance. She walked back through to the living room and answered it. 'Hello.'

Slater's voice erupted down the line. 'Where the hell have you been?'

She said nothing.

'Melanie?'

'I know,' she whimpered.

'What the hell happened, Mel? Where were you?' he said, his voice now calmer. 'What happened?'

'They changed the location. I had no way of contacting ya.' She could feel her voice breaking as she relived the moment.

'It's okay, Mel. It's not your fault,' he said, identifying her distress. 'Just as long as you're safe, that's what's important. Now, tell me what happened?'

Tears again filled her puffy eyes. 'He killed them.'

'What?' he said, not sure if he'd heard her correctly. 'Who killed them? Killed who?'

'Shaw, Shaw killed them.'

'Killed who, Melanie? Who?'

The lump in her throat finally gave way and she sobbed, sniffing back the tears as best she could. 'The dealers, Shaw killed the dealers.' Melanie's heart suddenly jumped a beat. That, almost, sixth sense feeling of a presence behind her.

'Who the fuck are you talking to?' a male voice said.

139

Twenty
'Stupid girl'

Melanie's breathing stopped, the hairs on her neck spiked and her heart rate increased. She turned to face the voice behind her, already knowing who it belonged to.

Shaw stood in the doorway, his eyes cold and empty. In the background he could hear a male voice speaking on her phone, repeating her name over and over again.

'Who are you talking to?' he said.

She stared back at him, unable to speak.

'I asked you a fucking question.'

'Please don't hurt me,' she said.

'Who are you talking to?' he asked again, but he already knew. Who else could it have been? His mind raced through a dozen questions, a dozen additions to this new situation. If she was a police informant, then that meant a wire and surveillance. But why hadn't they intervened when her life had been put at risk, and why hadn't there been any arrests? 'Who do you work for?'

'What?'

'I said who do you work for?'

Melanie swallowed, her saliva tasting as bitter as battery acid. 'The police,' she said, unmoving from her position. 'They made me do it. Honestly, Shaw. I didn't want te.'

Shaw leaned back against the magnolia wall and buried his face in his hands. He was screwed. There was no going back now. His future was gone, blinked away in a heartbeat.

'Yar not gonna hurt me are ya?' she said, her gentle Irish voice wavering.

He looked up. 'Hurt you? Why would I hurt you? You're the only one who's done nothing wrong.'

'It's Michael their after, ya know, not ya.'

He wanted to vomit, knowing he'd lost, knowing he'd never be allowed to see his little boy again. His heart laughed at the irony of his life. Both the Taliban and Al-Qaeda had failed in killing him. Even Irish paramilitaries had tried once or twice, yet all it was going to take to defeat Ryan Shaw was an attractive blonde stripper from Newry.

Melanie hung up on Slater. 'Run,' she said. 'Run now. Go.'

'How long?' he said, ignoring her silly suggestion. 'How long have you been working for the police?'

'Look, Shaw, they'll be on their way,' she told him, knowing Slater would have sent them the second he'd heard Shaw's voice. 'And once the police have lifted ya, they'll be going straight for Michael.'

The white door to the passage creaked opened. 'And why would they do that?' a second male voice said, deep and hostile.

Melanie's eyes grew wide. Shaw turned his head to see Quinn's imposing frame step into view.

Quinn entered the room and closed the short distance between him and Melanie in two large strides and grabbed her damp hair. 'Have you fucking called them?'

Shaw took a single step forward, prepared to intervene, but stopped, not wanting to make his situation any worse than it already was. 'No one's called them,' he said. 'We were just talking.'

He turned to Shaw. 'Was I talking to you?' Foaming spittle escaped the corners of Quinn's mouth as he spoke. He turned back to Melanie and tilted her head with the strength in his hand.

She gripped his wrist, desperate to relieve the pain. 'I'm sorry,' she whimpered, tears rolling down her cheeks. 'They made me.'

Because of those last three words she was as good as dead, and Shaw knew it. He watched Quinn's free hand clench into a fist and his grip almost lift her from the ground.

'They made you?' Quinn echoed through gritted teeth.

'I'm sorry,' she sobbed. Her fear-filled eyes bored into Shaw's. 'Please,' she mouthed, strands of saliva stretching between her lips. 'Please.'

It would take only minutes for the police to get here, but it would only take Quinn a second to break her neck. *Stupid girl.* Shaw hated her for putting him in this situation. He snatched a glass vase from the pine cabinet on his right and smashed it into Quinn's face. Flowers, water and glass exploded on impact. Quinn stumbled back against the white door, slamming it shut. His brown rimmed glasses, broken from the blow, fell from his nose as he raised his hands to his bleeding face.

Melanie fell back on her buttocks, landing painfully against the pine coffee table in the centre of the room.

Shaw went straight to work and landed a series of punches to his gut.

Quinn dropped his elbows to block and snatched out with both hands, seizing either side of Shaw's head. He crashed his thick bloodied

141

forehead down into his face, rocking him back a step. He then moved in and grabbed Shaw's zip-up hoody with his large hands and swung him to the right, lifting his feet from the ground.

Shaw crashed back into a pine cabinet, destroying the glass panels and knocking down ornaments, picture frames and Christmas cards. His right hand struck the TV remote, turning on Melanie's flat screen TV, filling the room with the sound of 'Winter Wonderland' by Michael Bublé. Before he could recover, Quinn was on him again, moving swiftly for a man of his stature, and returned the blow to his gut, following it with a powerful left hook to his jaw.

The impact shuddered through Shaw's skull. He instinctively brought his left arm up to defend his face, anticipating a follow-up right that connected hard against his forearm. He absorbed the punishment and landed a right jab of his own, continuing it with a sharp left hook to Quinn's right eye, giving him the room he urgently required. He reached back with his left hand and snatched a fallen ornament off the cabinet behind him and smashed it across Quinn's face, opening a deep wound along the top of his right eye. Quinn's legs buckled from the blow as Shaw lunged forward with both hands, hammer punching his chest. Quinn reactively reached out and grabbed Shaw by his top, pulling him down with him. The pair of them toppled across the pine coffee table, scattering the perfume dried flowers that lay in a glass bowl, and crashed onto the laminate flooring with Quinn's head pressed up tight against one of the two black leather sofas.

The pair of them could hear Melanie in the background, screaming for them to stop. But neither of them had any intention of stopping. They tussled on the floor like professional wrestlers, each of them wriggling to gain the upper hand.

Shaw felt Quinn beneath him, pulling his head into a headlock, pulling and twisting in the hope that his neck would break. He hooked his right foot over Quinn's waist and tucked it in tight, stabilising his platform, all the while pushing his left knee up against his neck, keeping hips low.

Spittle escaped Quinn's mouth as he increased the strength of his hold around Shaw's neck. He threw two desperate jabs with his left hand, bloodying his nose.

Shaw parried a third and slammed the palm of his left hand against Quinn's bloodied face. He pushed, using the strength in both his arms and legs, until his bodyweight broke the headlock. With Quinn's right arm now locked out behind his head, Shaw punched him repeatedly in the face, throwing two vicious rights and a left, then another right, breaking the

142

skin beneath Quinn's right eye.

'Enough!' Melanie screamed. 'For God's sake, enough!'

A large bubble of blood popped at Quinn's nostril as he exhaled through his mask of crimson. His right hand, still locked out behind Shaw's head, found its way to his hair and pulled, halting his attack.

Shaw grabbed Quinn's wrist and rolled back, choosing to abandon his position. He scrambled back to his feet and snatched the glass bowl from the floor.

Quinn climbed to his feet at equal speed and deflected the thrown bowl with his forearm, feeling the smashed glass shower his head and back. He looked up, just in time to feel Shaw spear into him with a powerful rugby tackle. He dug his heals in and caught Shaw's charge, using his own bodyweight and momentum against him, twisting one hundred and eighty degrees in order to get him airborne.

Shaw crashed through Melanie's flat screen TV, silencing the music, and thumped off the wall behind it.

Melanie jumped on Quinn's back and wrapped her arms around his neck, her legs around his waist. 'Stop!' she screamed, deafening his right ear. 'Stop it!'

Quinn clamped hold of her blood smeared forearms and prized loose her grip, relieving the pressure around his throat. Before him, he could see Shaw regaining poise. 'Get the fuck off me!' he growled through gritted teeth. He bucked her up and reached for her hair, gripping it in his right hand. He bent forward and threw her over him, slamming her down hard against the surface of the pine coffee table beside him. 'Fucking bitch!' he said. 'I'll deal with you in a minute.'

Shaw groaned as he rolled onto his hands and knees, feeling the broken TV crunch and crack beneath him.

Quinn advanced on him, effortlessly moving the heavy TV unit that sat between them. He kicked away Shaw's stabilising hand and kicked his size eleven shoe into his face, throwing up a spray of deep red, flipping him onto his back.

It felt like a dark hood had been pulled over Shaw's head. His vision darkened, his hearing dampened. He felt Quinn's boot stamp down on him, cracking his ribs. He felt him straddle his waist and grip his hair. He felt his fist club into his face. He fought back unconsciousness and frantically searched through the TV's debris, searching for anything that may help: a sharp edge, a thin point. But the only thing within his grasp was loose cabling.

Quinn placed his hands around Shaw's throat and squeezed, pressing his thumbs tight against his larynx. 'I hope she was worth it,' he said.

Shaw's eyes bulged. His mouth opened wide. His hands clawed at Quinn's arms and pulled at his fingers. But it was no good. He started to panic, realising his body was shutting down. He trailed the cabling beneath him back to a heavy-set plug mounted on the wall above his head and pulled it free. It took only seven seconds to fall unconscious from an effective strangulation, fourteen if you were lucky and taking less than a minute to die. His eyes rolled back as the darkness began to engulf him.

Melanie rolled off the coffee table, landing unstable on her hands and knees. She spent a moment collecting her breath, letting the pain in her back subside before thinking about what was happening. She looked towards them, seeing Quinn straddling Shaw, the pair of them positioned between the thick glass TV stand and the wall. The thought of running crossed her mind, to save herself and get to safety, but Shaw had already saved her twice today. She stood up, using the coffee table as support, and picked up the ornament that Shaw had already used to strike Quinn. It felt heavy in her hand. The thought of how Quinn had even survived Shaw's attack frightened her. She approached him from behind, seeing first-hand the damage he'd already inflicted on Shaw, and raised the ornament high above her head. Her body trembled as she crashed it down as hard as she could. The impact against Quinn's skull was sudden, shuddering up through her arm and into her shoulder.

Quinn's head rocked forward, blood spilling from the impact area. His large powerful hands fell either side of Shaw's face, stabilising his own large frame, allowing Shaw to cough and suck in air. The trauma to his skull quaked through his entire body, defusing the rage within him. Warm liquid cascaded down round his chin and down his back, soaking through his blue shirt.

She watched in horror as Quinn seemed to recover from the blow, regaining his state of mind.

He sat back up straight, ignoring Shaw's coughing and spurting, and turned to her, the whites of his eyes penetrating and prominent, surrounded by a thick sea of red claret. His eyes transfixed on hers. She was next.

Shaw's eyes opened. He gripped the heavy-set plug that lay just above his head and lunged forward. He aimed the three forks of the plug at the carotid pulse that rhythmically rose and fell in Quinn's neck, plunging

144

them deep behind his Adams apple. Bright red blood squirted down over him as he ripped out the giant's throat.

Quinn gurgled as the air rushed up through the new hole in his neck, his eyes wide with horror. His hand gripped the wound in a frantic attempt to stem the flow of blood. But it was futile. The oxygenated blood squirted out from between his fingers to the rhythmic beat of his heart. He rocked back on his knees, attempting to stand, blood pumping out of him as the strength in his legs failed him. He dropped to the floor, sprawling out in front of Melanie, his free hand reaching out to her, as if pleading for her help.

A wailing melody and blue flashing lights filled the sudden silence that followed Quinn's death. Melanie turned to her front window, seeing multiple figures, silhouetted by the flashing lights. 'Thank God.' She looked back to Shaw, who lay motionless on the ground, not knowing if he was alive or dead.

'Melanie,' a calm male voice said. 'Melanie. It's the police. We're coming in.'

*

The bedroom door opened and PC Clement walked in. Melanie sat on her bed, dressed in a T-shirt and leggings, her eyes red and puffy.

'Here you go,' the female officer said, handing her a steaming cup of sweet tea.

Melanie took the mug from her and held it in both hands, as if cuddling on its warmth. 'Thank ya.'

'Someone will be along shortly to speak to you.' The officer placed a hand on her shoulder. 'Is there anywhere where you can go tonight: a friend or family member? You really shouldn't be on your own.' Before she could answer, a knock came from the bedroom door.

'Can I come in?' a familiar male voice said. Slater peered around the door, seeing the two women sitting on the bed. 'Clement,' he said, acknowledging the officer who returned it with a smile.

'If you need anything, I'll be just outside,' Clement said, comforting Melanie with a gentle arm before standing to leave.

Slater smiled at the officer as she left. He closed the door behind her and crouched in front of Melanie. 'How are you doing?'

She returned his gaze. 'Not good,' she said in a quiet voice.

'This is going to be hard, but you need to brief me on what happened here, and earlier today. We can get the official statement from you later.'

In-between sobs and spurts of tears, Melanie told him the events of the day, explaining in brief detail on why the plan had been changed and where the deal had taken place. She also told him how Shaw had been forced to kill the four men in the church basement.

'And Quinn?' Slater said.

'He was protecting me,' she sobbed. 'Quinn was going te kill me.'

'Right.' He placed his warm hands on her knees. 'I need you to do something very difficult for me now. I need you to return Michael's car to him.'

'No way!' she said. 'Ya can't make me.'

'You're right, I can't. But what I can do is arrest you, and you don't want that, do you?'

'Arrest me, I don't care anymore. I've had enough of all this shite. For God's sake, Ian, I was nearly killed teday, twice.'

'I know, Mel, I know. But now I can charge you with accessory to murder.'

'No,' she said, anger replacing her tears. 'Ya can't do that.'

'I can, Mel, and I will,' he bluffed. 'You never informed me of the change in location and four men died as a result of it. And that's not including what's happened here with Quinn, in your home.'

'No. Ya can't, I wasn't. I fucken wasn't,' she said, tears now running down her cheeks. 'None of it was my fault.'

The door opened up behind Slater. 'Is everything okay, sir?' Clement asked.

'Yes, everything's fine,' he replied, not giving Melanie the chance to speak.

The room fell silent as it waited for Clement to withdraw. 'Okay,' she said, closing the door.

'You're going drive back to him after we've had our chat and pretend like there's nothing wrong. Shaw dropped you off and headed home, leaving you with the car. Quinn was never here.'

Melanie sniffed as the tears rolled down her cheeks.

'Okay?' he said, asserting his words.

'Yes!'

'Good girl. Now go tidy yourself up.' Slater stood up, keeping his eyes on hers. 'You need to find out where these guns are being stashed, Melanie. You don't want any more deaths on your conscience, do you?'

146

Twenty-One
'The King's Badge'

'Ryan, can you hear me?' a male voice said. 'I think he's coming around.'

Shaw opened his eyes to see a brunette wearing the indistinguishable uniform of the Northumbria Police force peering down at him.

'Ryan, can you hear me?' the male voice added from his immediate left.

Shaw's eyes, now swollen, turned to see a ginger haired man dressed in a green paramedic's uniform. The throbbing ache in his face and the reality of his cracked ribs suddenly became apparent.

'Well at least he's responsive now,' the Paramedic said.

'Where am I?' Shaw mumbled, attempting to sit upright.

'Just lay back, Ryan. You're in an ambulance. You've had a quite a beating. Nothing life threatening, so you'll live,' the Paramedic said, sharing a jolly smile that lifted the edges of his thick ginger moustache.

The memory of Quinn came rushing back to him, followed by a light tugging on his left hand and a clamping at his wrist.

'So he'll understand me now?' the brunette said in a strong Mackem accent.

'I should think so. Like I said, he's quite responsive now,' the Paramedic replied.

Shaw looked down at his hand and saw the glint of the metallic handcuffs clamping his left wrist to the bed pole.

'You don't have to say anything, but it may harm your defence if, when questioned, you fail to mention something you later rely on in court. Anything you do say may be given in evidence,' the female officer stated, as if reading the police caution straight from the text book. 'Do you understand?'

Shaw remained silent, staring at the ceiling of the ambulance. He understood. He'd been to prison before and was aware of his rights as a detainee. He also knew at some point his clothes would be removed from him and taken as evidence. He also knew he wouldn't be allowed to get washed until a full body mapping had been carried out on him by forensics and, until then, he'd spend the night in a dry cell.

The dirt under his fingernails, the blood on his clothes, the gunshot residue on his sleeves would all be collected and documented for evidence against him. Then the interrogation would begin. This was going to be a long night.

*

PC White wheeled Shaw's wheelchair through the automatic doors of Accident and Emergency. His female colleague for the evening, PC Galloway, walked on ahead, wanting to speak with the nurse behind the reception.

'This way,' Galloway called, waving them both over. 'They're going to see to him first.'

The three of them made their way through the waiting area of the ward, following the lead of the male nurse in front. The smell of antiseptic wash battled against the combined odour of BO and vomit, whilst the noise of screaming children filled the corridors. An elderly man caught Shaw's eye sitting on a chair in the corner of the waiting room, a blood soaked tea towel pressed tight against his head. A young red headed female nurse crouched in front of him, trying her hardest to comfort the man's trauma.

The short journey along the brightly lit corridor stopped at a curtain that the male nurse pulled to one side, revealing a firm looking hospital bed with blue sheeting and a side unit. The nurse looked at him with concerning eyes, taking in the state of his body and the two uniformed officers that accompanied him.

'Are the handcuffs really necessary?' he asked.

White nodded. 'I think so, yes.'

'Okay. Should I be worried?'

'You'll be fine,' Galloway said.

'Do you think you could manage getting up on here?' the nurse asked Shaw, padding the bed.

He stood out of the wheelchair and climbed onto the bed with a concerning groan. Over the course of the next two hours, Shaw had his body pulled, pressed and stitched, taking several stitches in his top lip, left eye, and back of his head. He'd also suffered a broken nose, two cracked ribs and severe bruising to his spine, ribs, throat and face, almost closing his left eye.

After having his clothes removed and taken for evidence, Shaw was supplied with an all-in-one navy-blue jumpsuit and black plimsolls for his journey to the station for his compulsory body mapping.

*

148

It wasn't the thought of driving Michael's £60,000 sports car in her high stiletto heels, or the concerning worry that she may be caught unaware by the sheer power of the engine that made her want to vomit; it was the thought of seeing Michael again that churned her stomach, the thought of having to pretend to enjoy his company. She'd phoned him before leaving, letting him know she's be returning it, which hadn't gone down well. Shortly after the forensic team had finished with her, Melanie had been allowed to get washed and dressed, choosing a tight, strapless pink mini-dress and black lacy heels.

She pulled into Michael's allocated space at the rear of the club and glanced at herself in the rear-view mirror, giving herself one last quick inspection before climbing out. Her hair was wild and unwashed, but surprisingly still stylish, and her makeup was as flawless as ever. The time on the dashboard read 20:32. She climbed out feeling scared. A fear that gripped her so tight she could have fainted. She walked towards the rear door to the club which, as always, was open at this time, allowing the bar staff access to the bins. The night club was empty of clientele with the bar staff still arriving to carry out their pre-nightly duties. She scaled the swirling staircase to the strip club above and opened the double doors, impersonating confidence. She walked across to where Michael was sitting, her hips swaying from side to side.

'Where the hell have you been?' he said. 'And where's my car?'

'It's downstairs,' she said, feeling a weaver in her voice.

'What you doing here anyway? Thought you wanted to be alone tonight?'

She forced a smile. 'I did, but now I don't.'

Michael's eyes lightened as he looked her up and down, admiring her choice of wardrobe. 'What do you wanna drink?'

Melanie sat down in the chair opposite him, purposely crossing her legs to reveal her toned smooth thigh. 'I'll have a vodka and lemonade.'

Michael stood up and walked over to the bar. He'd been washed and changed by the time Melanie had got back to the club, dressing in a dark crisp suit with matching waistcoat. He placed her drink in front of her and sat down.

'So Quinn didn't even bother to show?'

'No, like I said on the phone, I've not seen him since we left the church. The only person te come te the flat was Shaw, and even he only dropped me off with yar car before he left.'

'Just seems a little strange for Quinn to just disappear like that, don't you think?'

'I guess,' she said, taking a sip from her drink. 'But I don't really know him all that well, sure.'

'I'm sure he'll turn up,' he said, taking a handful of her thigh.

A shiver ran through her, feeling his touch. Not sure if it was fear or loathing that made her so nauseous.

*

Slater crashed through the double doors of the corridor leading into the interrogation wing of Newcastle police station. He was tired and pissed off after spending the last five hours trying to explain why his whole gun deal operation had been such a disaster. He knew it wasn't anyone's direct fault, things like this happened during operations, but he couldn't help but feel a brisk anger towards Melanie. He made his way down the corridor avoiding the two uniformed officers, each carrying a box of paperwork which reminded him of the truck load he still had to fill out. In his hand he carried his leather-bound briefcase, bought for him by his father twelve years ago. He opened the last of the double doors before arriving at the room he required. Waiting outside the room stood another uniformed officer, Sergeant Brady.

'Has he spoken to his lawyer yet?' Slater asked him, placing his briefcase on the floor beside him to re-adjust his suit jacket.

'Nap,' Brady said with a shake of his head. 'Hasn't even requested one. Hasn't said a fucking thing the whole time he's been here.' Brady was a thin looking man with curly black hair and a pencil moustache that wouldn't have looked out of place in an Errol Flynn movie.

'Has anyone spoken to him?'

'Sammy tried, but the bastard just sat there staring at the desk. Thought we'd just leave it for you's to deal with, seeing as that's what you boys do.'

'Has he had anything to drink?'

'No, like I said, he's not speaking. So he hasn't asked for anything.'

'Okay, go get me a cuppa tea or something, milk with two sugars.'

Brady walked away, mumbling under his breath.

*

The interview room walls were a bland grey with a thick wooden boarder along their centre. There were no windows in the room and the only exit was the door in which Shaw had entered. A small, dark brown desk was attached to the wall in front of him. On it was a dual CD recorder. He sat

150

supporting his ribs with his left hand, thinking about all the mistakes he'd made in his life, and how this one was going to take his son away from him forever, when the interview room door creaked open. He turned his head to see a man in his late thirties with dark hair cut short to his head and round cheeks. He wore a creased grey suit and white shirt that showed off the beginnings of a gut, and carried a black, leather bound briefcase and a steaming brew.

'Evening,' the suited man said, breaking the silence in the room. 'I'm DCI Slater. I take it you understand why you're here?'

Shaw remained silent and still.

'Cup of tea?' Slater placed the polystyrene cup in front of him. 'Wasn't sure if you took sugar or not, so I took the liberty of putting two in.'

Shaw took hold of the cup with both hands and placed it to his stinging lips, blowing on the steaming liquid. His DNA was already in the system, so a trap was fruitless.

Slater pulled out his chair and sat opposite him. 'I understand you've been here for some time now and haven't requested a lawyer. Would you like one present?'

Shaw took a sip of his tea.

'Okay, fine. I'll get straight to it then.' Slater placed his leather-bound briefcase on the floor beside him and pressed the buttons on the dual recorder, activating the microphones. He introduced everyone in the room and stated the time and date. He then reached down into his briefcase and pulled out a brown cardboard folder, A4 in size. He placed the folder on the desk between them and opened it, revealing a small black and white mug-shot of Shaw's scarred face paper clipped to the top left of the records. 'Ryan Phillip Shaw, thirty-four years of age, born in Armagh, Northern Ireland,' Slater stated, reading straight from the document in front of him. 'It says here you were released from prison only six weeks ago after serving two years of a five year stint. Multiple accounts of GBH, three of which were on civilian police officers,' he added, resting back in his grey polypropylene chair. 'Not much of a people person, are you.'

Shaw said nothing, his eyes focused on a circular tea stain on the table in front.

'I understand staying quiet comes naturally to you now. Trained to resist all forms of interrogation; to be able to hold out indefinitely.'

Shaw cringed inside. He hated it when people said that. No man alive could hold out indefinitely. No matter how much training they'd had.

'But what you've got to ask yourself this time is, is it really in your best interest?' He pulled out five, A5 size, colour photographs, each one showing a close up of a different, charred black, dead body and two A4 size photographs of Quinn and Jammin's dead bodies. 'You've been arrested on suspicion of murdering these five men, Jebel Darbo and Leroy Quinn. And believe me when I say this, you will be charged. That's life inside if found guilty. And let's be honest, it's not looking good.'

Shaw remained silent.

'Think about Douglas.'

Shaw's eyes locked on Slater's, making him anxious. Slater bent down and picked out another file from his briefcase, placing it on the table for Shaw to see. On its cover read the words 'Her Majesty's' Service, MOD'. It didn't surprise him that the police had gotten hold of his military file so quick. He was wanted for questioning in the involvement of multiple murders after all.

'I was in the military for a little while before I joined the force, you know. 4th Regiment Royal Artillery I was in,' Slater said, hoping it would bridge some sort of gap between them. 'Only managed four years of it mind, couldn't handle all that bullshit.'

Shaw remained silent.

'Which is probably why I find this folder such an interesting read.' Slater opened it and began to read aloud. 'Corporal Ryan Phillip Shaw: Joined four-five Commando aged nineteen where you were awarded the King's Badge on passing out. You were promoted to Lance Corporal within your first eighteen months, gaining your second a year later. You then went on to achieve your ML and carried out reconnaissance for the Brigade in Iraq.' He looked up at him, seeing Shaw had returned his gaze back to the table, looking less than impressed. 'I had to look up what a Mountain Leader was. Impressive. But that's not the best bit, is it?' His eyes returned to the file. 'Three years after that you were promoted to Sergeant and went through the selection process for the SBS, but failed the jungle phase due to a broken femur.' Slater closed the folder and looked up, quoting the rest from memory. 'You were awarded the Conspicuous Gallantry Cross in Afghanistan. Only to be demoted to Corporal a year later and then imprisoned four months after that.'

Shaw's gaze remained locked on the circular tea stain, his face a blank canvas.

Slater sat back in the chair and crossed his legs. 'Once a Bootneck, always a Bootneck.'

Again, Shaw's eyes fixed on Slater's, bruised and swollen.

'But I'm not here to pick a fight or mock you, Shaw, far from it. We all know what you're capable of. And, more importantly, we all know you were involved in killing those seven men. We have hard evidence and a reliable eye witness to swear to it. Not to mention the audio.' Slater shifted confidently in his seat. 'And that's a long time inside, especially for someone with a convicted history of violence like yourself.' He placed the folder back in his leather briefcase out of sight. 'What I'm interested in, Shaw, is not throwing you to the wolves, but obtaining your corroboration. Think of it as penance.'

Shaw couldn't help but laugh. 'Penance? For what, all my sins?'

'If you like.'

'My sins are beyond your penance.'

'Then if not for you, do it for your brother.'

'My brother has nothing to do with this.'

'That's where you're wrong. Will has everything to do with this. We have documented audio of him agreeing to participate in and help organise illegal activity. The activity you ended up being involved in. We also have logged chat over the Facebook website where he clearly talks about and volunteers his services.'

Shaw placed the steaming cup of tea on the desk, revealing his badly bruised and swollen knuckles. 'And if you'd done your job properly, you'd have found that Will doesn't have the knowledge nor the experience to do what he'd volunteered.'

'That may be true, but he served in the Para's for almost a year. So proving he lacks the experience in the trade will be verging on impossible. Look, we've checked through your records and we've spoken with your probation officer.' He paused to check through his notes. 'A Miss Victoria Lane. She gave you an outstanding reference. In fact, she said, and I quote, "If his Post Traumatic Stress had been identified earlier, I believe none of the events leading up to Shaw's imprisonment would have taken place, and that he'd still be at home with his family".' He smiled. 'D'ya know what I think? I think you've been participating in Michael's activities against your better judgment. I think Michael found out your brother wasn't what he claimed to be and that you had no choice but to get involved. There's no way you'd risk doing this with your wife's divorce looming over you, and the possibility of never seeing your son again.'

'So you want me to help you, is that it?'

'In a word, yes.'

'And what do I get out of it, apart from God's forgiveness?'

'What will you get out of it?' He laughed mockingly. 'I'll look into getting your sentence served with a little more comfort, and your brother pulled off with minor offences.'

Shaw looked at him, unsatisfied.

'What did you expect, Shaw, a pardon? You've killed seven people.' He knew Shaw had no other option. It was only a matter of time before he agreed. 'And this deal has a best before date on it too, running out the second I walk through that door.'

Shaw replied immediately, feeling a sting in his lip. 'If I'm going to help you, I want something in return; something other than soft toilet paper and a TV in my room.'

'You're in no position to make demands. From where I'm sitting, the offer already given is more than reasonable.'

'The way I see it is, the evidence you claim to have can't be what you need. Otherwise it would be Michael sat in front of you instead of me. And how long do you think Melanie can keep her front up? A fortnight? A week? A day?'

'Until I say otherwise.'

'Melanie's not even on the force though, is she? She's probably not even a registered informant.'

Slater shifted in his chair and looked at the disc recorder. 'Are you going to corroborate or am I going to charge you with the murder of seven men?'

'My watch, I want it back. It was a gift from my wife. And I need you to find my brother, put him somewhere safe out of harm's way. Do that and I'll do what you ask.'

'Okay, that shouldn't be a problem.'

'Then you've got a deal. Oh, and just for the record, I only killed four of those five burnt bodies. Quinn killed the fifth.'

'I'll take your word for it.' Slater stated the time and that the interview had stopped and stopped the recording device. 'Did Will ever tell you how him and Kimberly met?'

'On Facebook, as far as I know.'

Slater smiled, as if he knew something Shaw didn't, and stood up from his chair. 'Have you seen her Facebook profile?'

'What's your point?'

'Well, she's a very attractive woman, sexy even. Men would be messaging her every two seconds trying to finger their way into her, especially with the pictures she has uploaded. Christ, I don't even think they coincide with Facebook regulations.'

'And?' Shaw said, wanting him to get to the point.

'And she chose to speak with Will. Don't you find that just a little odd? After all, Will's not the coolest kid on the block, now, is he?' he said, closing the door behind him.

Twenty-Two

'Like a bullet out of a barrel'

The music was loud. The rhythmic thump of its bass pumped to the beat of the crowd's pulse. The strobing lights above them flashed in the smoky darkness, creating the illusion of slow motion on the dance floor.

Kimberly pushed her way through the bouncing crowd and headed for the peace and quiet of the office upstairs. The heavily built doorman, his name unknown to her, nodded in her direction, making eye contact as she passed him. She made her way up the winding staircase and entered the strip club where the music was less demanding on the ears. A flexible blonde dancer with tattooed arms danced around the pole, watched by a handful of male admirers. She entered the unoccupied manager's office and poured herself a vodka with ice and sat in Michael's brown leather chair, placing her feet up on the desk.

*

The air was thick and difficult to inhale, smelling of cigarette smoke, marijuana, urine and mould. The walls were yellow and heavy with dark fungus, large patches of damp filled the corners of the ceiling, and the carpet was threadbare with hundreds of tiny cigarette burns and random stains. Sherman was sat on the grubby ripped sofa in the front end of the room, watching a programme on a tablet. The metal bed-frame which Will was cable tied to was uncomfortable and cold. He'd been refused a mattress and told if he needed the toilet, then he had to do his business where he lay. His hands had been strapped up tight above his head now for nearly eighteen hours, and the throbbing in his limbs was beginning to grow unbearable. The lights were turned off and the curtains were pulled tight, meaning the rooms only source of light came from Sherman's tablet. By now his fear had subsided and replaced with worry. Questions repeated themselves over and over in his head, like why was this happening after Ryan had agreed to help them? And what did they have in store for him after he'd out lived his usefulness?

Sherman's mobile phone vibrated across the surface of the glass coffee table. 'Yeah,' he said, muting his programme.

'I need you to get something for me,' Kimberly said, admiring her footwear that rested on the desk in front of her.

Sherman looked at Will. 'Like what?'

'Michael needs…' She paused, changing her choice of words. 'I

156

need some information from Will, along the lines of where his brother's staying. Think you can manage that?'

'Shouldn't be too much of a problem,' he said. 'Is that it?'

'Yeah that's it. Let me know when you have it,' Kimberly said, ending the call.

Sherman placed the phone back on the coffee table and looked at Will. He stood up from the sofa and arched back his shoulders, stretching off his back.

Will lay silent, fear, once again, bubbling up inside him, unable to speak due the sock stuffed in his mouth. He watched Sherman approach, his eyes growing wider the closer he got.

Sherman stopped and looked down at him, his eyes dark in the shadow of the tablet light. 'I'm gonna ask you a question,' he said. 'Do not lie to me.'

Will nodded.

'What address is your brother staying at?' he said, pulling the sock from Will's mouth.

Will's heart sank. He couldn't tell him that. 'I don't know,' he said.

The punch came hard and fast. Thick clots of blood flowed from his nose, down over his mouth and onto his chest. Blood spilled back down his nasal cavity, filling his mouth, causing him to choke.

Sherman cracked his knuckles, more for intimidation than comfort. 'Where is your brother staying?'

The black mist that had clouded Will's vision dispersed, washed away by the tears that now filled his eyes. He thought about his brother, how he hadn't even questioned coming to help him. How he'd risked everything for him. There was no way he could tell them. 'Fuck you,' he said, spitting crimson liquid from his lips, relishing in his moment of pride.

This time the punch connected hard against Will's mouth, splitting his top lip and gum. Will felt his front teeth come loose under the force of the impact. Darkness engulfed him again, only this time it swallowed him whole.

Sherman left him unconscious on the bedsprings. He'd never tortured anyone before, so was by no means an expert in the psychology of it, but he had seen enough movies to know it involved copious amounts of pain. He walked through to the kitchen, which was equally as repulsive as the rest of the house, if not more so. Pots covered in green and black mould filled the sink and surface tops. Black bags of rubbish were piled high in the

157

corner of the room, decomposing and leaking maggots. He turned the tap and filled the kettle, flicking the switch to bring the water to the boil.

Consciousness was snapped back into Will like a bullet out of a barrel. Pain so unbearable, it ripped the breath from his lungs, almost stopping his heart. The cable ties, binding his wrists and ankles, bit into his flesh, drawing blood, refusing him any slack.

Sherman held the kettle at the base of the bed. Hot steam evaporated up from Will's blistering swelling flesh, creating large bubbles of plasma over his ankles and feet.

Will screamed. Tears rolled down his cheeks, not only from the pain, but also from the shame of what he was about to do next. He wasn't built like Shaw. He wasn't cut out for this. 'I'm sorry,' he cried. 'I'm sorry.'

Sherman made his way up to his head and held the steaming kettle above his face. 'Don't make me asked again.'

'A bed and breakfast,' he mumbled, feeling his tears mix with the blood on his face, 'in Hendon.'

'Which one?' Sherman said, tilting the kettle further.

Will glanced at his blistering feet. He could see and feel the tight cable ties biting deeper into his weeping, bloated flesh. Will revealed everything in-between breaths of pain, feeling the shame grow with every word spoken.

Sherman put down the kettle and picked up his phone. He dialled Kimberly and relayed the address of the B and B Shaw was staying at.

Kimberly smiled. 'Excellent. Didn't think you'd have too much trouble.'

'Anything else you want?'

'Just keep him alive,' she said, ending the call.

Sherman walked back into the kitchen and doused a filthy towel in cold water. He then cut the cable ties from Will's ankles and wrapped the towel around his blistered feet, before pouring more cold water on them.

Will slipped away, falling once again into unconsciousness.

*

Kimberly placed her empty glass amongst the other glasses on the cabinet and left the office. She loved pleasing Michael, and this information would do just that. She made her way back through the strip club, spanking one of the girls' buttocks as she passed, gaining a smile in response. Kimberly wasn't sure if it was a lovable smile that friends gave each other in acknowledgment, or if it was out of fear of her cousin's reputation. Either way, she didn't care.

The dance-floor down in the club was still bouncing with intoxicated people, either high on drugs or drunk on drink. A group of hen-nighters dressed as naughty nuns caught her eye, trying their hardest to embarrass as many young males as possible. She made her way through the crowds, sticking to the areas of the club that she knew would be empty of dancers and drinkers, making her way up to the VIP suite. The muscle bound doorman, who looked like he belonged in some US Marine movie, stood aside and allowed her access. Two young attractive girls, wearing clothes that left little to the imagination, danced against each other, locking their lips and filling each other's hands with their own soft flesh. Watching them was a man called Jonno, a short athletic Geordie with receding fair hair and tanned skin. Accompanying him in the same booth were both Michael and Melanie.

'Can I have a word?' she said, approaching Michael's booth.

Michael rubbed his face and looked up. His eyes were glazed over, reflecting the use of narcotics. 'Sure.' He pinched his nose and followed her over to a quieter area of the suite. 'What is it?'

'You wanted Shaw's address?' she said, looking over at Melanie who made no effort to hide her eyes on the pair of them.

'Did you get it?'

She nodded. 'Of course.'

'Good.' He smiled. 'Write it down for me and leave it in the office.'

'Okay. What the fuck's she staring at?'

'Christ, Kim. Nothing she's just high.' Michael turned and re-joined his party.

She stared at Melanie, cold and hard. Her hatred towards her grew with every breath taken. Was it jealousy that caused her repulsion or something else? Kimberly couldn't quite put her finger on it. Of course, Michael had always had his girls that he fed on when he was hungry; regular girls that he would use and abuse. But ultimately, for the last three years at least, it had been just the two of them, Kimberly and Michael, and now, all of a sudden, there was her, sucking her way into his life. Kimberly didn't trust her, didn't like her, and the first sign of her going, Kimberly would be there to see it. She jotted down the address and did as Michael had asked, leaving it on his desk until morning, or whenever he bothered to look.

*

The feeling of high wellbeing and euphoria was exhilarating, increasing her alertness, forcing sweat to bead through her skin, soaking her tight black mini-dress. The music had been loud in the Newcastle nightclub and her ears still rang from the sheer volume. The frosty air kissed her moist skin, sending an exaggerated shiver down her spine. Chloe Banks had been out drinking for most of the night, dancing, laughing, and snorting copious amounts of cocaine. The supermodel looking male that had his hand glued to her right buttock followed her out, whispering promises of everlasting passion and fulfilment. He'd had his hands all over her all night and his tongue firmly buried between her lips, and now he was on a promise of his own.

They made their way down a dark side street and stopped in an equally dark doorway. He pinned her against the door and wrapped his arms around her waist and kissed her. His left hand peeled her dress up above her hips and gripped her fleshy buttock whilst his right hand fished out her generous breast. She pushed him back to arm's length and squatted in front of him, unbuttoning the fly on his jeans. She reached her hand inside and gripped his swelling manhood. He looked down at her, resting his hands either side of the doorway, welcoming the pleasure that was about to be bestowed upon him. It wasn't long before he gripped her hair and pushed down on her head, ready for his climax.

So enveloped in his pleasure, the nameless male didn't notice the two police officers approaching them.

*

Chloe felt the heavy drag of the cocaine's comedown. Her feeling of ecstasy had quickly evaporated, leaving behind a dirty reminder of self-abuse. The understanding of what she'd been arrested for filled her with rotten shame. She passed a blacked-out window in the corridor of the police station after having her fingerprints taken and a strip-search enforced and saw her own disgusting reflection. She looked appalling: makeup smudged across her face, hair a wild mess, and to top it off, she didn't even know the guy's name. Up ahead, a man carrying a leather-bound briefcase crashed through the double doors, walking with purpose, as if he belonged in the station. She recognised him instantly as the man who had wanted Melanie to dance at the private function a couple of months back. She wouldn't have given him a second look if it hadn't been for Melanie making such a big deal about him, insisting that she remembered his face in case things didn't go the way she'd hoped at the hotel.

'This way,' a female officer said, guiding Chloe into the room on her right.

Twenty-Three
'Desperate People'

'Dinger.' Shaw sat bolt upright in the B and B, startled awake by the demons of his sleep. The nightmares he thought he'd left behind had once again found him. 'It wasn't my fault,' he said. He slowed his breathing and gripped the bed sheet that still covered his legs, focusing on the feel of the fabric against his skin. He wiggled his toes and clenched his fists, grounding his body, trying to bring his awareness back to the present. He'd used the same technique after every nightmare since learning it in prison. Shortly after his sentencing, Shaw had been diagnosed with Post Traumatic Stress Disorder and instructed to attend a specialist programme for ex-serving servicemen called The Warrior Programme. Over the following months his mental health had improved, and his sleeping pattern had regained stability. It had been almost a year since Dinger had invaded his dreams. But the technique wasn't working. The vision of his driver burning alive before him still filled his thoughts. He rubbed his face, feeling the several stitches that ran through his lip, the painful reminder of the events that had occurred the day before, and inhaled through his mouth. He imagined the air being drawn through his toes and into his abdomen and pelvis. He rubbed the smooth face of his silver watch, calming the intensity even further, until the negative thoughts had dispersed completely. He waited a few seconds more and groaned out of bed, sitting upright with his feet firmly on the floor, his left hand cradling his cracked ribs.

His mind spun. Thoughts about his brother, his wife and son, and now his freedom all occupied his mind. He didn't know what to do. He couldn't think straight. He didn't know where his brother was or why he wasn't answering his calls. And he still couldn't get his head around the fact that Melanie was Slater's informant.

He reached forward and picked up the bottle of water that sat on his bedside cabinet and swallowed the dregs, stinging his mouth. He checked his watch, 12:32.

After pulling on the black plimsolls the police had provided him, a pair of navy cargo pants and an old Eagles T-shirt, Shaw climbed into his brother's Saxo. He felt trapped between a rock and hard place, feeling like the monkey that had to perform for two people. What he had to decide now was which one was more important.

He pulled up at the rear of Michael's club, parking next to

Michael's GT-R, and scaled the wooden steps to the strip club above. He pressed the buzzer on the intercom and waited.

'What do you want?' a male voice said through the intercom.

'I need to see Michael.' The door buzzed and unlocked, allowing Shaw to push it open.

Bomber greeted him as he entered. 'He's at the bar.'

Without replying, Shaw made his way through to where Bomber had indicated.

'I'm glad you're here,' Michael said, not bothering to look up from his paperwork. 'I wanted a word.'

Bomber walked in behind Shaw and took up position behind the bar in front of Michael.

'Well I want to talk about Will,' Shaw said.

'Will?' Michael looked up at him. 'What happened to your face this time?'

'That's Will's debt paid. He now owes you nothing.'

'You want a drink, Ryan? You look like you could do with one.' Without waiting for an answer, he turned to Bomber. 'Pour the man an Irish, will ya.'

'I haven't come for a drink. I've come here to tell you that that's it. Will's done. Do you hear me?'

Michael smiled as Bomber placed Shaw's drink on the bar. 'You actually threatening me, Ryan?'

'Take it however you please. But Will's through.'

Michael's face turned from neutral to indifferent. 'People like you don't threaten people like me.'

'And what kinda people am I?'

'Desperate people.'

Shaw clenched his fists and took a step forward, stopping only to the sound of a Glock 19 clanging off the bar in Bomber's hand.

'You spoke to him lately?' Michael said.

'What's it to you?' Shaw said, taking his eyes off the polymer handgun he'd inspected only yesterday.

Michael smiled. 'Didn't think so.'

Shaw thought about the plausibility of Michael's implication. Will hadn't been seen or answered his phone for all most two days now. 'What you're implying better be a fucking joke.'

'Do I look like a jester? You see, what you did for me yesterday doesn't even come close to what Will owes me.'

'If you've taken Will, that was a mistake,' Shaw said, deadpan.

'Really? Because I don't think so. I see it as capitalisation. If you play the game, both you and your brother may get to go home.'

Shaw glanced back at the Glock in Bomber's hand then back to Michael. 'And what game will that be exactly?'

'Michael says.'

A knot of muscle flexed in Shaw's jaw. 'I'm not playing any games until I've spoken to him.'

'Don't be silly, Ryan. This isn't some farfetched film where you get to make demands. You do as I say or I'll kill him. If you want to believe that I haven't got him, then that's up to you. But I think we both know that I have.'

Shaw glanced again at Bomber and the Glock in his hand. 'What is it you want from me?' he said, returning his eyes to Michael.

'I'll call you tonight with the details. Bomber will show you out.'

He picked up the whiskey and swallowed it in one and turned to leave.

*

Shaw sat back in his brother's car. He had no choice but to take Michael seriously. He pulled out his phone and made a call, dialling a number he wished he didn't have to. The phone rang endlessly, ringing and ringing. He hung up and dialled again, thinking he may have entered the wrong number, but knowing deep down he hadn't. Again, the phone rang, the endless ringing now starting to annoy him. Suddenly it stopped.

'Wha do ye want, Ryan?' his wife said. 'In fact, don't bother, I'm not interested.'

'Amy, wait! I'm not ringing to argue with you, or to cause any trouble, honestly. In fact, it'll probably benefit you.'

'Has Boyd caught up with ye yet?'

'Yes. That's one of the reasons I'm calling.'

'I'm sorry, but I need te start thinking 'bout moving forward.' Amy's voice was sad, and Shaw knew her words still carried love for him.

He rubbed his swollen eyes. 'Yeah I know.' The few seconds of silence that fell between them seemed like an eternity. This was it. Shaw realised his marriage to the only woman he'd ever truly loved was finally over, and it was all his own doing. 'What's Boyd's phone number, Amy? I need it.'

'I don't think I should really give ye that.'

'Amy, please. Just give me it. What am I going to do with it apart

163

from call him?' Shaw tried his best not to sound frustrated or sarcastic. 'I just need to speak with him.'

Amy reeled off the number, her tender Scottish voice flooding his mind with loving memories, turning his stomach with a knot of guilt and regret.

'Thank you,' he said, unable to hide the break in his voice. 'How's Douglas? Can I speak to him?'

'Ryan, ye know ye can't.'

'I just…'

'I'm sorry. Goodbye. And, Ryan, please take care.'

'Amy,' he said, managing to squeeze the last word in before she hung up, leaving the line dead, as well as his heart broken.

*

Sunderland's shopping mall thrived with Christmas shoppers. Parents queued with their children at the Santa's grotto situated in an open space, left of the café. The elderly sat on benches relaxing in the free warmth of the shopping mall, and teenagers gathered in huddles blocking the walkways.

Ryan had been sitting at the same table now for over three quarters of an hour, nursing his third cup of coffee. He'd chosen the table as it provided him with the best view of the music store. Deep enough in the coffee shop to conceal his presence but angled enough as not to weaken his arcs of vision. He had purchased a pair of cheap black boots, a dark jacket and blue trucker cap to help camouflage his injuries. His mobile phone was set to silent and his newspaper was still on an article about the latest celebrity charged with rape. He'd phoned Boyd an hour ago and arranged to meet him outside the music store in the shopping Mall. He drank the final mouthful of his cold coffee and waited for Boyd to arrive. Seven minutes later, Boyd made an appearance dressed in dark jeans and a black coat. Shaw had instructed him to come alone, so it came as no surprise to witness tell-tale signs of a colleague.

Built like a super-heavyweight boxer with a shaved head, and dressed in a pair of button-up tracksuit bottoms and dark sports sweater, Boyd's acquaintance took a seat on one of the benches opposite the music store and pulled out his phone, trying unsuccessfully to blend in.

The blonde waitress arrived at Shaw's table and took his empty mug, giving his injuries a suspicious once over. Shaw smiled at her and turned back to his brother-in-law. He noticed two attractive shop workers decorated in tinsel walk past him towards Boyd and his colleague, and not only did he identify their approval between each other, but also the approval of a third heavily built male standing some twenty feet from Boyd. He was equally as menacing as the super-heavyweight, but not as muscular.

He checked his watch, 15:56, and made his way over to the counter, satisfied Boyd and his two friends would wait a further fifteen minutes. He ordered another white coffee and returned to his seat. Five minutes later, his phone vibrated in his pocket. He pulled it out and confirmed the caller was Boyd before ignoring it and putting it back in his pocket. Ten more minutes passed before Boyd called again, and again Shaw ignored it. He hoped Boyd wouldn't wait too much longer, as the urge to urinate was beginning to overwhelm him. One of the few disadvantages of using a café as an observation post was the necessity to consume liquid. Finally, twenty-four minutes after their arrival, Boyd nodded towards his two large friends and left, all leaving in different directions. Shaw bowed his head and allowed the super-heavyweight to pass him before standing to follow Boyd. He kept a safe distance at all times, making sure to keep just enough shoppers between him and his target whilst he tailed him out through the automatic doors and into the cold Christmas air.

Boyd crossed the main road, busy with buses and taxis, and stopped outside one of the many bars in the area, lighting up a cigarette. He cupped it in his hands, protecting it from the wind.

Shaw increased his pace, closing the gap between them whilst Boyd reached into his coat pocket and pulled out his mobile phone. As soon as he was in reach, Shaw grabbed him by his bicep.

'I told you to come alone,' he said, snatching the phone from his hand.

'Wha the fuck—'

'In there.' Shaw pushed him through the first set of doors of the closest pub, cutting his sentence short.

Boyd stumbled, startled by the ambush. 'Get yer fucken hands off me!'

'Shut it,' Shaw said. He handed him back his phone and opened the second set of doors to the pub. 'Go take a seat. I'll bring you a drink over.'

Boyd scowled at him and did as he was told. 'So what's this 'bout then, Ryan?' he said with a raised voice, taking a seat at the nearest table. 'And wha the fuck happened te your bake? Ye been sticking it where it doesn't belong again, have ye?'

Shaw placed two pints of lager on the table between them and sat down. 'I need a favour.'

Boyd laughed. 'Your asking me for a favour?'

'Yeah.' Shaw found the word bitter in his mouth. 'I need you to go to Middlesbrough for me.'

Boyd took a mouthful of his cold lager and nearly spat it back out. 'And why the fuck would I want to go to that shithole?'

'I need you to take my mam back to Glasgow with you.'

'This just keeps getting better. Ye expect me to take your fucken ma back home with me?' He laughed again. 'And just wha the fuck am I supposed to do with her when I get her there, take her for a Buckfest?'

'I don't know. Take her to see her grandson.'

'No.'

'You owe me, Boyd, remember?'

Boyd sat back in his chair and allowed his hands to drop onto his lap, listening to the sentence he'd waited over five years to hear. 'I wondered when I would hear those words leave yer lips.'

'I need this doing, Boyd. I looked after your family a little while ago, now it's time you looked after mine. And to be honest, I think you're getting off lightly, don't you?'

Boyd sat a moment, remembering his family wouldn't be alive today if it hadn't been for Shaw. 'That wasn't my fault.'

Shaw frowned. 'Then whose fault was it, because it wasn't fucking Janice's? You decided to get wrapped up in all that football shit, not her. All you've got to do is take our mam back to Glasgow with you and keep her there for no more than a week.' Shaw reached into his jacket pocket, pulling out a white envelope, and dropped it on the table between them. 'There's over two hundred quid in there. That should be plenty to get her to yours and back. Her address is on the envelope.'

'And Amy's papers?'

Shaw sighed. 'I'll sign them, too.' His marriage was finally over.

Boyd reached inside his coat and pulled out a pen and a rolled up, brown paper envelope. 'Good, cause I just so happen to have a spare set.'

Shaw took the pen and signed them, feeling what was left of his life finally disappear. 'How are they?' he said.

Boyd knew he was a good man. He knew Shaw never meant any harm to Amy or his nephew, and that he loved them with all his heart. But Shaw had been baptised by war and was now damaged goods. 'They're good,' he said. 'Douglas started school in September.'

Shaw's eyes glassed over at the thought of his little boy growing up without him and forced a smile.

166

'Let yer ma know I'm coming,' Boyd said, 'I don't want her shitting her kex when I come knocking.'

Shaw bit back the tears. 'She's already expecting you. I rang her earlier.'

'Well, Ryan, I can only imagine the shite that yer in to call in on this favour. Whatever the outcome, I really hope it ends up okay for ye.' Boyd gulped down the remaining three quarters of his pint and stood up, taking the papers with him. 'Look after yourself.'

Shaw remained seated, trying to take everything in, but all he could think about was his wife. She was finally gone, taking Douglas along with her. Without them none of this even seemed relevant. He finished the last of his pint and headed to the gents.

Twenty-Four

'Launderette'

Michael rested back against the wall of his balcony, reading the address of the bed and breakfast Shaw was staying at. He felt the night's chill on his back, wondering what had happened to Quinn, and if Paul had managed to connect him to Shaw and the hit on Jammin, seeing as no one had seen or heard from him since he'd left the brothel yesterday. His intention from the start was to have Shaw identified for the murder of Jammin, but what he hadn't banked on was Paul Mallinson connecting Shaw to him. That now proved a problem. Getting rid of Paul would solve his immediate concern but left him with the matter of his uncles. And that was only if Paul hadn't already passed on his suspicions, which he no doubt had. He folded the piece of paper and placed it in his back pocket as Melanie passed the balcony window, wearing nothing but one of his partially buttoned shirts. He'd contacted all the members of his crew earlier, informing them of the location of a scheduled meet he had planned for later that night: an empty rundown boat factory on the River Wear.

*

Bomber dipped down on the clutch and dropped two gears, causing the engine to brake hard and over rev, decreasing the speed of his Alfa Romeo rapidly. He turned the steering wheel, throwing the whole weight of the car on to driver's front wheel, forcing the tyres to screech as they fought for traction. Shaw's body went ridgid; he gripped the passenger hand bar above the passenger door turning his knuckles bright white. Bomber was an amateur driver at best, and every manoeuvre he performed reminded Shaw of that fact.

The dirty black sports car sped down into the moonlit compound, passing through a chain-linked fence topped with barbed-wire, before narrowly avoiding a series of external piping. Seagulls screeched high above them, soaring around the lifeless yellow cranes that had remained unmanned since the late nineteen eighties, before perching themselves on the roof tops of the now abandoned, empty warehouses. Bomber raced the car through the giant open doorway of an enormous empty warehouse, filling the inside with echoes of its screaming engine and heavy breaking.

Once Bomber had stopped, Shaw prized loose his fingers and

climbed out, feeling the ache in his ribs. He followed Bomber through the only set of double doors, passing three more high performance cars parked inside the hanger, one of which being Michael's silver GT-R, and made his way down the dark corridors of peeling paint and ripped up floorboards, entering a room, illuminated by a single lamp, with the word 'LAUNDRETTE' labelled above its door. Inside, he could hear the sound of male voices, high in spirit.

'Aboot fooking time!' a Geordie accent yelled.

'Fuck you, Fisher,' Bomber said, smiling.

The walls of the office were more window than wall, and all but one of them were smashed. Filthy damaged blinds, thick with dirt, concealed the inside. The room was approximately seven metres by ten with an eight foot ceiling. A long filthy counter covered with bird faeces and old feathers was positioned at the far end of the room. Behind it was the only other visible doorway that led into a much larger, darker room, containing several smashed industrial washing machines. There were seven people waiting in the room. The first person he noticed was Michael, not dressed in his usual suit attire, but in casual jeans, grey sweater and jacket. Surprisingly, sat on the counter to Michael's right, next to the battery powered lamp, was Melanie, also dressed in jeans and a jacket. Her eyes grew wide upon seeing him. Apart from Sherman, the only other person he recognised was Picco, the large man that had accompanied him and Quinn to Jammin's house.

'So this is Shaw?' the Geordie said, standing with his back against the wall.

Shaw remained silent.

'I was in the forces, too, ya know,' the Geordie said.

The room smelt musty and damp. Dust lingered in the air, attacking the back of Shaw's throat.

'Is that right?' he said, trying his hardest to keep his eyes from Melanie, not wanting to send any unwanted attention her way.

'Why-aye. The Light Infantry, teeth of the British Army.'

'So why didn't Michael get you to inspect his fucking guns?'

'What fucking guns?' the Geordie said, stepping forward as if challenged.

'Fisher,' Michael enforced, 'leave it.'

To Shaw's amusement, Fisher relaxed his composer and rested back against the wall, his eyes glued on his.

'We'll give Quinn another ten minutes and then I'll just crack on.' Michael's voice hid a shimmer of uncertainty, as if somehow knowing Quinn wasn't going to turn up.

Throughout the next ten minutes, Shaw picked up on the names of the extra faces. Michael hadn't introduced him, so names clearly weren't high on his list. The man they referred to as Fisher, the Geordie, was an averagely built man in his late thirties, standing approximately six foot tall. His blond hair was cut short and straight, and his eyes were a deep blue. The man perched on the counter, on Melanie's right, was another Geordie called Jonno, an athletically built man in his mid-thirties with a slender strong frame. Comparing him to Melanie in height, he didn't appear to be much taller. His hair was also fair coloured and receding, and his skin was almost perfectly tanned. Last of the new faces was Roach, a skinny man in his late twenties with sunken features, thick eye brows and brown hair that had been shaved short and allowed to grow out.

'So what's this about then, Michael?' Picco said, leaning forward on a yellow crate.

'A DNA test. Fisher wants to know who the real father of your kid is,' Bomber said with a laugh.

'Well it wouldn't be you, you limp-cocked-cunt,' Picco said, raising a laugh from the others.

Michael stood up straight. 'Right, let's get on with it. Quinn's obviously not coming. I've asked you's here because I've come across a job,' he said, looking each one of them in the eye.

'What job?' Jonno said.

'A job paying thirty grand… Each.'

Fisher laughed through his nasal cavity. 'Fuck aye,' he said. 'Thirty grand? Who've I gotta kill for that?'

Michael met his gaze, his eyes deadpan. 'Turks. Not sure how many until we get there.'

'What, seriously?' Jonno said, the smile leaving his face. 'And how's that gonna work?'

'I've arranged an exchange of two hundred and fifty grand for ten kilos of heroin. Obviously, I haven't got ten kilo of heroin, which is why we're gonna have to hit them hard. So I need trigger fingers I can trust.'

Fisher glanced at Shaw and back to Michael. 'That's what he was talking about; inspecting guns?'

Michael nodded.

The man they called Roach looked around nervously.

'What about the fallout?' Fisher said. 'Surely there'll be repercussions. You can't just wipe-out a gang of Turks and have nothing said.'

Michael lit up a cigarette and inhaled. 'Fallout's sorted. They're conducting this entire arrangement without Nolan's approval, so no one up here even knows about the deal, let alone authorised it. And they're not gonna tell anyone and risk fucking up their flow into the North East. We just need to make sure that none of them get home to blab about it.' He paused, allowing his words to sink in. 'I don't need to tell you that this will be fuckin' messy, so if you don't want in, I suggest you fuck off now.' He looked at them all individually, happy to see none of them move. 'Also, I don't need to remind any of you that this doesn't leave this room. And that includes Dirty Donna, Picco.'

Everyone except Shaw and Melanie nodded in agreement. He couldn't believe what he was hearing. Michael was getting this bunch of cowboys to carry out a complicated hit like that. A quarter of a million was a lot of money, and there was no way these Turks were going to just hand it over. 'Where's this job taking place?' he said. 'I assume that'll be your call, seeing as it's you doing the apparent selling.'

'Actually,' Michael said, unamused with Shaw's tone, 'they're deciding on the time and location.'

'What? You mean like the last exchange you were involved in?'

'You got something you want to say?'

'Would it make a difference if I did?'

'Not really.'

'Then what the fuck am I doing here?' Shaw said.

'Your job'll be to stick close to me. Where ever I go, you'll follow.'

'When's this deal taking place?' Jonno said.

'I'm not sure yet but were looking at Thursday.'

Shaw looked at each of the men individually: Michael, Picco, Sherman, Fisher, Jonno, Bomber and Roach. Every one of them appeared mean and menacing, more than capable of surviving the streets. With the exception to Roach who resembled the skinny wimp the big kids found funny to have around. But none of them came across as qualified to carry out such a hit. Even the ex-infantryman, Fisher, clearly wasn't as good as he obviously thought; otherwise Michael would have had him inspect the guns instead of risking a fresh face. Attacking drug dealing Turks with this rabble was suicide.

'As soon as I know more, I'll let you know,' Michael said. 'But until then, keep a low profile. I don't want any more of you's doing a Quinn.'

Michael stuck around once he'd finished, watching the men leave one by one. 'Bomber,' he called, stopping the man in his tracks. 'Can I have a word?'

'What is it?' Bomber said.

Michael waited until they were the only two left in the room before speaking. 'I need something doing.'

'Something or someone?'

'Someone.'

'Who?'

Michael lit up another cigarette. 'Tony and Billy Mallinson.'

'You wanna top the Mallinsons? Are you out of your mind? Do you know the shit-storm that will kick up?'

'I don't care about the shit-storm, Bomber. I want them gone. I think they may have had Quinn seen to.'

Bomber's eyes widened. 'I want an extra eight grand of the take.'

Michael smiled and exhaled a lungful of smoke from his nostrils. 'I'd expect nothing less.'

*

Shaw pulled the collars up on his jacket and dug his hands into his pockets, beginning the short walk back to the loneliness of the B and B. He'd been dropped off at the bus station by Bomber after another white-knuckle ride. His mind couldn't help but think about his brother. Was he okay? Had they hurt him? And more importantly, where was he? Slater also entered his mind, reminding him that at the end of all this he still had prison to look forward to. His only warming thought was that his mother was safely out of harm's way.

He reached the B and B only to find it swamped in darkness. Every curtain was closed, and all the lights were turned off. He searched through his pockets for the key and cursed, realising the only key he had was the one to his brother's car. He checked his watch, deciding it was too late to knock the old lady up, and climbed into the

Saxo. He gunned the ignition and drove aimlessly with no certainty of a destination. He prayed his brother was comfortable and uninjured, and hoped there was some way he could shake off some of the shit that had managed to stick to him these last few days.

Thirty minutes later, Shaw found himself parked outside Melanie's flat. Her metallic blue Yaris was parked on her drive and her curtains were pulled tight. He couldn't understand why he'd even arrived here in the first place, let alone why he was now climbing out and ringing her doorbell. He stood there for several moments wondering what the hell he was doing, when the sound of the door unlocking froze him solid.

Melanie peered through the gap in the door, the brass chain clearly visible. 'Hello?' she whispered, trying to get a better look at the man at her door. 'Who is it?'

'It's me.'

'Shaw? Wha' do ya want? It's nearly one in the morning.'

'We need to talk.'

'We have nothing te talk about.'

'I think we do. You wanna invite me in or do you wanna do this on your doorstep?'

The door closed, followed by the sound of chains being pulled off. The door then opened fully, inviting him in. 'Hurry up then, before Trigger gets out.'

Shaw entered her front room which had been scrubbed clean and tidied. 'Police finished already?'

'Aye, said they had everything they needed so it didn't take 'em long. What is it ya want?' She stood in front of him in what could only be described as an extra-large grey T-shirt, which hung off her left shoulder.

Shaw took off his jacket and sat on one of her leather sofas. 'Cup of tea would be nice,' he said. 'White. Two sugars.'

She looked at him in disbelief, her hair all stuck up on one side and flat to her head on the other. Her eyes were puffy from the broken sleep and thick red pillow lines stretched across her face. Maybe it was the cheek in the request, or maybe she just couldn't be bothered to argue, either way, Melanie headed towards the kitchen.

Shaw threw his jacket on her sofa and followed her in. 'So… are you going to tell me what's going on?'

Melanie reached up to the cupboard and pulled out two

mugs. 'I'm making ya a tea.'

'You know what I mean. Why are you still here?'

'I don't expect ya te understand,' she said, dropping a teabag into each of the mugs.

'There's nothing to understand. You're putting yourself in danger by being here. These people won't fuck about if they find out what you are, you do know that?'

'The police wouldn't allow that te happen,' she said, handing Shaw his drink. She walked past him back into the main room, which now looked bare without her TV, and sat on the sofa beside the Christmas tree, tucking her smooth bare legs underneath her.

'You really think that, after what happened in here? The police don't give a fuck about you.'

'Slater said—'

'You think Slater gives a shit?' Shaw interrupted. 'Melanie, think about it, he left you hanging at the church, and took almost ten minutes to react to me arriving, let alone Quinn.'

'Aye I know, and I'm extremely grateful for wha' ya did.'

'I don't want your gratitude, Melanie. I want you to go home. It's Christmas Eve tomorrow. Spend it at home with your family.'

'I can't.' She took a sip of her tea, halting the break in her voice.

'Why not?'

She remained silent, refusing to pull the mug from her lips in case she started to cry.

Shaw didn't need her to answer. Her body language said it all. 'What's he got on you?'

'It's not like that,' she said.

Shaw sat forward and placed his mug on the coffee table. 'Mel, you don't need to do it anymore. Slater's got me to squeeze now. There's nothing stopping you going back home.'

She forced a smile. 'I will, once I've seen Slater. I promise.'

He could see there was no getting through to her. 'Just be careful.'

'I will.' A genuine smile spread across her lips. 'How's yar face? It looks really painful.'

'My face? It's fucking killing me,' he said, returning the smile.

'Would ya prefer something a little stronger?' she said. 'I'm sure I have an old bottle of vodka somewhere. Don't think I have

174

anything te go with it, mind.'

He watched her head back into the kitchen. 'Vodka straight would be just fine, thanks.'

Moments later, Melanie returned carrying a frosted bottle of clear liquid and two empty glasses. 'Can I ask ya a question?'

'Depends on what it is, and if you're wearing a wire or not.'

She placed the items on the coffee table between them and returned to her position on her sofa. 'How did ya get those scars on yar face?'

Shaw recalled the incident that had ruined his life. 'I was in an accident,' he said. The answer he always gave.

'Ya don't have te tell me if ya don't want te.'

'There's nothing to tell, really.' He paused, somehow feeling he could tell her. 'The vehicle I was in in Afghanistan was hit by an IED.' He felt the guilt of his decisions that had led to his crew's death, the flames burning his forearm as he tried to pull Dinger free, the bullets that pierced his abdomen and arm, and the final bullet that ricocheted off the Jackal and punched through the left side of his face. The final bullet was never in his dream. His dream was never about his pain, it was always about Dinger's.

Melanie starred at him, unable to find the words that said she understood, because she didn't, how could she? Instead, she asked a different question. 'How is it ya and Will don't look alike? I mean, ya've got dark hair for starters and he's got light brown. Ya've got a swirly complexion whilst he's pale white.'

Shaw released an unintentional held breath and leaned forward. 'We've got different parents,' he said, pouring two generous helpings of vodka.

'Ya not blood related?' she said, taking one of the vodkas from the table.

He swallowed the glass' contents in one hit, feeling the welcomed burn in his throat. 'I like to think we're more than that. My dad married his mam when I was five.'

'Ya love him, eh.'

Shaw nodded. 'Regardless if we have the same blood or not, he's my brother.' He leaned forward and poured himself another. 'My turn to ask a question.'

'Go on then,' she said, sipping her vodka.

'How did you end up here?'

'Sunderland?'

175

He shook his head. 'Slater. How did you end up on his payroll?'

She sighed, as if dropping a heavy weight. 'He said if I didn't help, he would charge me with prostitution and drug dealing.'

'He said what? He can't do that.'

Melanie shrugged.

'He's bluffing.'

'Ya well, I can't risk it. The allegations alone would destroy my daddy.'

If there was one thing Shaw was familiar with, it was Irish culture, Northern or Southern, Catholic or Protestant, good or bad, the church was highly respected, and to shame your family's name was to destroy it. How could her father have faced anyone in his parish knowing they'd know his daughter had been arrested for prostitution? 'Seems like we both have our constraints.'

She smiled and emptied her glass in one, almost choking on its effects. 'Can I ask ye another question?'

Shaw swallowed his shot and looked up at her.

'What's it feel like te kill a man?'

He'd been waiting for this question. He was surprised it had taken this long to be asked. Deep down everybody wanted to know. 'It doesn't feel like anything.'

'It must feel like something. Yer literally robbing the world of that man's existence. Not te mention the people that loved him.'

'What do you want me to say? That killing a man strips away a part of you. That it fills you with remorse and starves you of sleep. Well it doesn't.'

'Do ya not see their faces every time ya close yar eyes?'

Shaw paused. 'I've fought the Taliban in compounds so tight, we had to engage them with our bare hands. I've held dead or dying children in Nicaragua, and I've said goodbye to more colleagues than I care to remember. Yet it's not the people I've killed that haunt me, it's the memory of one eighteen-year-old Bootneck that I let burn alive.'

Melanie listened, horrified, watching the man before her change before her very eyes. 'Surely ye didn't let him burn alive? I can't believe ya allowed that te happen.'

Shaw said nothing and cupped his face in his hands, running them up through his hair.

She could see the sorrow in his bruised eyes. The wrinkles around them, proof of the years of pain he'd carried around with him; guilt maybe, regret? 'Do ya want te stay 'ere tonight? On the sofa I mean.'

Shaw could already feel the vodka numbing his pain: physically and emotionally. 'Aye, cheers.'

'I'll get ya a wee blanket.' She wobbled to her feet and left the room.

He rested his head back against the sofa. Sleep wanted to take him, and for the first time since arriving back in the North East, it wanted him nightmare free.

By the time Melanie returned, Shaw was already snoring. She laid the thick, grey woollen blanket over him and turned out the lamp.

Twenty-Five
'Chocolate brown mini-dress'

Will had been bound to the bed frame now for more than twenty-four hours and was beginning to feel the effects of dehydration. His arms and shoulders ached to the point he could no longer move them, and the pain in his feet and ankles had become excruciating. The swelling had increased, splitting the skin, and several blisters had now burst, leaking serum. A pain in his bladder had also grown to the point of unbearable, telling him he was about to urinate if he wanted to or not. He moaned and groaned, trying to fight off the inevitable, but it was too much. Will released his bladder, soaking his jeans and the carpet beneath him. The warm feeling was like a heavy weight being lifted from him, freeing him from the torment of hours of agony. No sooner was agony replaced with relief, relief was replaced with discomfort. The thick smell of his dehydrated urine was overpowering. The warm liquid quickly turned cold, helping in the evaporation of his body heat. Tears filled his eyes and spilled down the sides of his blood stained cheeks. He'd never really thought about dying, and now it was all he could think about. He was going to die, strapped to a bed frame in a filthy drug user's home, and he had no one to blame but himself. He closed his eyes, hoping, praying, that when he opened them again, he'd be back home in Middlesbrough, sitting on his mother's couch, waiting for her to bring him his dinner of egg, chips and baked beans.

'Where is he?' a familiar female voice said.

Will opened his eyes.

'He's through here,' Sherman said, appearing through the passage door.

Kimberly followed him in. 'What is that smell?'

'The previous tenants. They were rotten.'

'Good God, it's fucking disgusting. Open a window or something.' She approached Will. 'There you are,' she said. 'Not so cocky now, are ya. Not so fucking amazing anymore.' She looked him up and down, her eyes lingering longer on his blistered feet.

Will tried to speak but couldn't find the energy.

She bent over him, placing her face close to his. 'I've come to say goodbye, Will,' she said. 'So goodbye.'

He lifted his head in an attempt to speak, but only a muffled

178

weak moan escaped the confines of his gag.

Without saying another word, she turned and left the room, leaving Will with the dreadful feeling that he'd never see her again; that he'd never see anyone again.

*

Melanie opened the kitchen door, wearing grey slouch pants and a white vest top to see Shaw sitting topless on the sofa, the blanket folded beside him.

'I was just about te wake ya,' she said, glancing at his naked torso. He was an attractive man. Even with the scars and bruised face. There was no question about it. Athletic and muscular with naturally sun kissed skin. She even found his tattoos engaging. 'Ya hungry?'

He smiled. 'Starving.'

She walked back into the kitchen and returned with a bacon sandwich and a mug of tea. 'Slept okay then, I take it?' she said, handing him his breakfast.

He looked up at her and took his tea and sandwich. 'I did actually, yeah,' he said, surprised.

'Thought so, sure, wee Trigger 'ere thought there was a grizzly bear on the sofa last night, bless him.' She smiled, a smile he found soothing, a smile that made him forget who and where he was.

'Was I snoring?'

She laughed and held up her forefinger and thumb, keeping them millimetres apart. 'Maybe a wee bit.'

'Sorry,' he said. 'I haven't been sleeping too well lately.' He took a mouthful of his tea and eagerly bit into his sandwich, filling his mouth with soft white bread and crispy bacon. 'What time you seeing Slater?'

'Half eight.'

'What time's it now?' he said, simultaneously reading the time off his own watch.

'It's around seven-thirty.'

He paused for a moment, taking in her natural beauty. She had combed her hair into a simple pixie style and applied a dash of mascara and bronzer, makeup she didn't actually need. 'I should get going.' He placed his breakfast on the coffee table and pulled on his T-shirt. 'Thanks again for the sofa and breakfast.'

'Yer welcome.'

He pulled on his jacket and picked up his sandwich, gulping

down another mouthful of his tea. 'Think about what I said, though, Mel. You don't need to be here anymore.'

'I know.' She escorted him to her front door. 'Thanks again, for everything ya've done.'

'I think we're evens,' he said with a mouthful of sandwich.

She watched him drive away and headed back inside to finish her coffee, her imagination running riot. She couldn't stop thinking about him. All night she'd tossed and turned, thinking about making love with the man, craving his touch and having him in her bed beside her. Maybe it had been the stress and danger that had attracted her to him, the excitement of his nature. But now he was gone, and all she had to do now was meet Slater and update him on what was happening. She had already informed him of her progress in a text last night, receiving a reply within seconds, stating a time and place to meet. She checked her watch again, 07:32. She had one hour to get ready and get to the prearranged location: the subterranean Metro platform in Gateshead. She could drive to the platform, park up, and be ready and waiting in less than fifteen minutes. The idea of meeting at eight-thirty was to, apparently, blend in with the crowds, so she was to dress as if heading to work. She scooped the last of a tin of cat food into Trigger's bowl and headed to the bedroom to get dressed.

*

The Central Station Metro in Newcastle was cold and busy. People dressed in highly pressed suits and polished shoes carried their expensive briefcases as they talked business on their smart phones. Each one of them wrapped up to fight off the cold morning air. And every one of them was looking at her. Her creased tight black mini-dress, flat messy hair and smudged makeup looked less than glamorous after her uncomfortable night in the Newcastle cells. Chloe felt like a tramp, like a common whore, standing there, freezing in her bare feet, holding her black heels in one hand and her tiny handbag in the other. The embarrassment of last night's arrest ate at her like a rabid dog, forcing her to relive it over and over again. Her head pounded, and her breath stank, and to top it off, the train was packed. Men stared at her, looking at her with eyes of crude lust, whilst the women looked her up and down with revulsion. She could hear the whispers along the carriage as she climbed aboard, managing to get herself into a position against one of the side windows, trying her best not to let all the attention bother her.

A middle-aged man dressed in casual jeans and a jumper positioned himself so close to her in the carriage that she thought he was going to kiss her. He looked her up and down, taking in every inch of her appearance, not wanting to leave anything to the imagination.

'You had a good fucking look?' she said.

The man looked her in her eyes. A smug smile spread across his face before he returned his gaze back to her cleavage.

Too tired to fight with the man, she looked up at the route planner mounted on the wall of the carriage above the doors. Without counting the stops, she estimated she was going to be on the train for at least forty minutes.

*

Slater parked his Volvo in one of the few parking bays that remained at the snow covered station. Gateshead was one of the few subterranean stations with major use. He'd chosen the location for its convenience, concealment, and high level of background noise, finding it easier to hide a conversation in a large crowd. Just two people chatting on a train. He looked up at the screen displaying all the times and destinations and read the time, happy he had plenty. Once on the train and in view of Melanie, Slater would take a mouthful of bottled water, indicating to her that he was happy the meeting could proceed. If for any reason he hadn't drunk from the bottle by the time the train reached Jarrow Station, she was to leave the train and contact would be rescheduled for a later date.

Just as he'd hoped, the station was buzzing with life: workers heading to work, student's heading to college or university, all busy going about their morning rituals of drinking coffee or reading the morning paper. He entered the relevant platform and found a good position where he had strong eyes on the platform's entrance. He pulled a local newspaper from his grey shoulder bag and leaned against the cream tiles, keeping one eye on the articles and the other on the entrance.

*

The air down in the tunnel was cold and stale, people pushed and barged their way past each other, attempting to reach the platform before the next man. Once at the chosen platform, Melanie approached its tracks and looked left and right, scanning the area for Slater. She looked at her watch, 08:27. She was definitely on time and sure this was the right platform. She began to doubt herself, repeating Slater's directions over and over in her head. She searched once again, trying her hardest not to stand out. Nothing, he was nowhere to be seen. A blast of cold air hit her from her left, followed by the dampened sound of the approaching train. The people around her started to collect themselves, standing up straight, folding away newspapers, replacing lids on their coffee cups, readying themselves for the short journey into work. Finally, the train arrived. The crowds around her dashed forward like horses out of the standing blocks, only to be stopped by the occupants on board climbing off.

'Look forward and get on the train,' Slater said, his hand gripping her left bicep.

She gasped and looked down to her arm.

'Look forward.' He released his grip and stepped onto the train, using the doors further along the carriage. Melanie did as she was told, standing in the only space left available. She looked up the centre of the carriage and into the next one along. The train was packed, almost brimming with people. And she was beginning to think her chocolate brown mini-dress may not have been the perfect attire for the occasion, attracting every male eye on the train, along with the occasional female one.

After a minute or two, she finally noticed Slater sitting in the next carriage along, his back to the window. A large balding male with a badly styled goatee beard sat to his left, listening to a set of head phones that were wired up to his mobile phone. She watched him look up and down the carriage, repeating the action several times in as many minutes, before pulling a bottle of water out from his shoulder bag. Her heart raced, anticipating his next move. A couple of stops later, after the carriage had emptied slightly, leaving the seat next to Slater free and a little more room to manoeuvre, Slater took a mouthful of water.

She gripped the strap of her handbag slung over her shoulder and headed towards him, squeezing past a begrudging male teenager wearing a baseball cap and a bad case of acne.

'Excuse me,' she said, feeling him press up against her. But before she could take the seat, a well-dressed man in his late thirty's stole it from under her.

Slater stared at her, disappointed.

The well-dressed man caught a glimpse of her tanned leather boots standing in front of him. He followed them up past her thick brown tights and held his gaze on the hem of her chocolate mini-dress before meeting her eyes with his. His face flushed instantly, turning his cheeks an innocent rose.

'Oh, I'm sorry,' he spluttered, standing to offer her the seat. 'Did I pinch your seat?'

Melanie returned his kindness with a smile. 'Thank ya,' she said, taking the seat, adjusting her dress as she did so. The pair of them sat in silence for the next few stops until the carriage was even less crowded.

'Well?' Slater said finally. 'What have you got for me?'

Melanie tried to relax as best she could, finding it almost impossible to think straight. 'As of now, the deals taking place on Thursday.'

'Time and location?'

'No one knows yet,' she said, 'Michael doesn't even know.'

Slater again looked up and down the carriage. 'You need to find out the location of this deal, Mel, and if it's really happening on Thursday. Approximations are no use to me. So you need to get back in there and find it out.'

She shook her head. 'It's not on me, though, is it? Not anymore. Ya have Shaw in there now. Ya don't need me anymore.'

'Melanie, you're in the best position to acquire the information. You, not Shaw.'

'I said no, I'm out. After teday I'm heading back home,' she said. 'If there's anything else ya need te know, ya can speak te Shaw, well. I've had just about all I can take.'

Slater looked forward, staring at their reflection in the dark window opposite. 'Okay. I guess you've done your part. I won't be asking anymore of you after tonight.'

'Tenight? Why? What's happening tonight?'

'I need you available in case Michael wants to see you. If he gets the slightest indication that something's wrong, he may pull out, and we can't chance that. So we need you around, at least for tonight.'

'I'd rather not. I just want te leave it all behind me and head back home.'

'Well that definitely won't be happening. We may need you in court to testify.'

'Are ya wise? Is yar fucken head gone? There's no way I'll be testifying against Michael. I thought that was why I was getting all those recordings.'

Slater studied the faces of the surrounding passengers in the carriage. 'Look, Mel, calm yourself. You wanna tell the whole fucking train?'

'Well, I mean. What a stupid place te have this meeting. On the fucken Metro? Was this in the top ten of places te meet in yar meeting manual.'

'Fine, Mel. Whatever. In the morning we'll look into getting you back home, back to whatever little village you crawled from. But tonight, you make yourself available. If Michael wants to kiss, fuck or even piss on you, you make sure you're available. Do you understand?' Before Melanie could object, Slater continued. 'Because if you don't, those fantasy charges will become very real.'

'Okay, I get it.'

'I hope so,' Slater said. 'Now if he does call you up, don't forget to let us know. We can't protect you if we don't know where you are. Come the morning, we'll have you lifted for something bogus and banged up, preventing you from attending the deal.'

'Banged up for what exactly?'

'Does it matter?' he said. 'It's not important.'

'It is te me.'

'Drug possession.' The tone in his voice told her he was growing tired of having to explain himself. 'It's nothing to worry about. No real charges will be made.'

Melanie chewed nervously at her bottom lip. It was getting so close to all this being over. 'There'll be no drug tests happening though, sure.'

'No. No tests will be carried out. The only thing you'll have to endure is the uncomfort of a cell.'

A prolonged silence followed whilst Melanie thought about her future and her freedom.

'So it's happening Thursday?' Slater said, breaking the silence.

Melanie nodded. 'That's what he's told everyone.' She stood to her feet, holding the hand rail above her for support. 'Ya make sure ya lift him, though, Ian. I don't want te be looking over my shoulder for the rest of my life.'

'We will,' he said. He watched her press the button on the doors and step off onto the platform outside.

*

The train pulled into the Gateshead station, stopping at another platform bursting with people. Chloe seized the opportunity and grabbed the first seat that became available, sitting carefully to hide her modesty in her tiny black dress. She caught her reflection in the darkness of the window opposite, reminding her of her appearance and the reason for it. Out the corner of her eye, she thought she recognised a man walk in amongst the crowd and sit in the next carriage along. She quickly sat back out of his line of sight and watched him through the crowds of people. It took her a few seconds, but she finally recalled where it was she knew him from. He had been carrying the leather-bound briefcase in the Newcastle police station last night and had also been the client of Melanie that evening in the hotel.

'Small world,' she whispered to herself, remaining hidden from his view.

Several minutes later, Chloe tilted her head forward, checking to see if the male officer was still sat in his seat. He was, and to Chloe's disbelieve, standing in the same carriage as her, was Melanie. She cursed under her breath and snapped her head back from view. Her face burned red with embarrassment. The last thing she needed was Melanie seeing her in this state. Plus she hadn't spoken to her since Sunday; since the pair had been intimate with each other and Michael.

After several more stops, the train became less crammed and breathing space was now available. To her relief, the irritating male who'd held his eyes on her tits his whole journey had finally disappeared. She rubbed her tongue along the front of her teeth, feeling the build-up of plaque and wished she'd bought some gum from the store. She felt disgusting, and she looked disgusting, and now to top it off, a work colleague was almost on top of her. She looked towards Melanie confirming she was still on the train, and to her surprise, Melanie had closed the small distance between herself and the police officer and sat next to him. But what made it more suspicious was neither of them had acknowledged each other. She continued to observe, glued by their apparent suspicion, a suspicion that may have gone unnoticed by any other eye. The pair sat silent, staring around the cabin as regular as regular people could. He glanced up and down the aisle, eyeing up every other passenger around him like a creep in the shadows, whilst she sat playing with her nails.

The train rocked to another gentle stop, allowing more passengers to pass between the sliding doors. Chloe read the name of the station on the wall: Pelaw. Her stop was next. She sat patiently, waiting for the doors to close and the train to move on. She planned to step through the sliding doors at the last minute, limiting the chance of her been seen by Melanie. Thankfully, she was in the cabin up from her and wouldn't see her when the train pulled forward.

Then she saw it, the police officer spoke to her. In fact, they appeared to be having a full blown conversation. Melanie looked him in the eyes, shaking her head and raising her voice, but not enough for her to hear. Chloe's stop came and went; too interested in this meet to leave now. She stayed glued to the pair of them, observing their body language, keeping her face hidden from view. Less than five minutes later, the train stopped again. Chloe read the station's name: Bede station. Melanie stood up and left. Chloe sat back and watched her through the window of the train as she disappeared up the stairs of the platform, before turning her gaze back to the officer, who was already standing upright, waiting for the next stop. Was Melanie a snitch or, worse yet, a copper? Either way, Chloe decided, Michael needed to know.

Twenty-Six
'High heels, low morals'

Chloe opened the front door to the house she shared with three other people, never feeling so relieved to be home, warm and out of sight. The house was empty of life and deadly silent, just the way she liked it. She threw her heels on the passage floor and scaled the stairs to her room. She opened her wardrobe and pulled on a pair of old, red joggy pants, lifting her dress up over head before pulling on a thick grey fleece and woolly socks. All the while she thought about what she'd seen on the train and asking Melanie about it. Maybe it was completely innocent. Maybe they were arranging another private dance. Maybe she was sleeping with him. Who knew? What she did know, though, was that Michael was involved with certain hard hitters of Sunderland, and occasionally indulged in activities of a less than legal nature. All the girls knew it. She also knew that Michael had a bit of a thing for her, giving her attention when it wasn't required, watching her every routine and, on occasion, fucking her when Melanie wasn't around. Sunday night hadn't been the first. Maybe, if she passed the information on to Michael, regardless of its possible innocence, it would get rid of Melanie and put her in his limelight. Something she'd secretly wanted for a while. But before she chose to do anything, a hot shower and a strong cup of tea were desperately required.

*

Light snow continued to spot Shaw's windscreen, freckling the glass with specks of water. Snow had fallen steady all night, laying a carpet of pure white, but turning to filthy slush on the roads and walkways. He'd spent the morning following Kimberly's MR2, hoping she would lead him to where they were holding his brother, but he hadn't got to her flat until after 08:00, and couldn't say for sure if she'd been out before then. Now he waited, watching the entrance to the alleyway that led to the club's compound. He didn't know what else to do. He had no allies in which he could rely on and no resources in which he could use. He'd thought about kicking Kimberly's front door in and taking her by force, forcing Michael to release his brother or he'd snap her neck. But there was no guarantee it would work, and he wasn't even too sure on how close Michael actually was to his cousin. Two hundred and fifty grand was a lot of money. His mind stewed over the past, filling it with memories he wished he never had and a future he knew would

187

no longer happen; asking questions he may never again know the answers to: What were his wife and son doing right now? Was Douglas sleeping okay? Did he still suck his thumb when he was tired? Would he still remember him in years to come? He reached up and tilted the rear-view mirror, looking at his own reflection. The swelling in his bruised unshaven face had surprisingly gone down since leaving the police station. An adhesive strip had been pulled across his broken nose, and the pain in his lip and eye had thankfully begun to subside. His ribs still ached when he breathed, and his face still hurt when he smiled. Thankfully, he had nothing to smile about.

His phone vibrated catching his attention before bursting into tune. 'What?' he said, answering Michael's call.

'I need you at the club, now.'

'I'm busy,' he said, keeping his eyes on the alleyway that lead to the club itself. 'What do you want?'

'Don't ask questions. Just make your way to the fucking club.' Michael hung up.

Shaw started the engine, swallowed his anger, and headed away from the club, not wanting to arrive too soon. If he'd summoned, there was a good chance he may have summoned all the others. So staying put, he thought, wasn't a good idea.

*

Chloe parked her car in-between Kimberly's MR2 and Michael's GT-R. She would have usually parked her car in the twenty-four-hour multi-story car park, less than a five-minute walk from the club, but today she had important news for Michael. She made her way up the wooden steps to the backdoor of the strip club, dressed in baggy jeans, a scarf and a jacket, and buzzed the intercom.

Kimberly answered the door. 'Chloe, there's no rehearsals until twelve.'

Kimberly had always intimidated her and she wasn't the only girl to say so. Her presence had always thickened the air and made some of the girls less than comfortable. And right now, she made her feel very uncomfortable.

'Yeah I know. I was hoping to speak with Michael. I've got something he may find interesting.' She paused. 'It's about Melanie.'

Kimberly looked at her, curious. 'He's in his office,' she said, allowing her to enter. 'What's this about?'

'Could be nothing,' she said, 'but I'm sure I saw Melanie talking to the police this morning. And I thought Michael may want to know about it.'

'She was talking to the police? Are you sure?'

Chloe nodded. 'Saw her this morning on the Metro.'

Kimberly led the way through the club to Michael's office. 'I knew there was something dodgy about that bitch.' No music played and only the back store lights were turned on, illuminating the bar and back room, casting dark shadows across the club floor. 'Wait here,' she said. She knocked on the office door and entered, leaving Chloe outside. A moment later she reappeared. 'He wants to see you,' she said. She pushed passed her and made her way back onto the club floor.

Michael sat behind his grand desk, dressed in a dark suit and shirt. 'What makes you think Melanie's being a grass?' he said, looking up from his computer screen.

Chloe froze. The implications of what she was about to do hadn't been apparent until the word grass had been said out loud.

'Well?'

'It may be nothing,' she said, starting to think she may have made a mistake, 'but Melanie danced for a private function about six weeks ago—'

'So,' he interrupted, 'that's hardly a reason to come in here making accusations about her.'

Chloe suddenly found her mouth had gone dry and her palms sweaty. 'Well the guy that she danced for was a copper.'

'And how do you know that?'

'The night that he asked her to do the job, I was working. She begged me to go along with her, probably because it sounded a little dodgy and would appreciate the support. She made me remember his face whilst he was in the club, so if I needed to, I could identify him.'

'That doesn't explain why you think he's a copper. And even if he was a copper, what makes you think Melanie's grassing to him?'

'I guess,' she said, now regretting the whole thing, 'but I saw him last night in Newcastle police station, and he wasn't there to get his prints taken.'

'What were you in the Newcastle nick for?' he said, leaning forward in his chair.

'I got arrested: drunk and disorderly.'

'And you're sure he was a copper?'

'One hundred percent. He was in plain clothes, carrying a leather case. The kind you carry papers in, just not a briefcase. Plus I saw him stop to chat with one of the coppers in uniform before I was lead into the questioning room. The guy's definitely a copper.'

'He could have been someone's lawyer,' he said.

'He didn't look like a lawyer.'

'And? So what if he is a copper? We get plenty of the filth in here.'

'I saw the pair of them talking this morning on the Metro.'

'Saw who talking?' Michael said, feeling a tingle of anger build up inside him. 'Melanie and this copper?'

Chloe nodded. 'I saw them chatting on the train on my way back from Newcastle, all inconspicuous like, trying to make out that they didn't know each other.'

'Let me get this straight.' Michael placed his elbows on the desk and massaged his temples with his fingers. 'You're saying you think you saw Melanie discussing something with a plain clothed police officer this morning on the train?'

She nodded. 'Yeah.'

A knot of muscle flexed in Michael's jaw. 'You're sure?'

Chloe nodded. 'Yes.'

'And what was it they were saying?'

'I'm not sure. I wasn't close enough to hear. But Melanie looked uncomfortable, almost paranoid.'

Michael rubbed his eyes. He didn't want to believe her, but deep down he knew she was right.

'Look, Michael, I like Mel. I think she's a great girl. I wouldn't have come and told you this if I wasn't sure of it myself.'

'Okay,' he said. 'Who else have you told apart from Kimberly?'

'No one, I came straight here.'

'Well don't tell anyone else. If anyone found out I had a grass working in my club, there'd be more people in church on a Friday night than there would be in here.' Michael sat back, deep in thought. 'Leave it with me,' he said. 'I'll deal with it.'

'Okay.'

'And I'll see you get something extra at the weekend.'

Chloe smiled at the thought. The extra bit of cash would come in handy. 'Thanks, I'm just glad I found out. Who knows what could have happened.' She smiled once again before turning to leave.

*

Michael's office door had only been closed a few seconds when he heard a sharp knock, followed by Kimberly entering.

190

'Well?' she said, eager to find out what had been said.

Michael stood up and weaved his way round to the front of the desk and sat back against it. 'She seems certain.'

'Chloe's all high heels, low morals, but she's no liar.'

'Yeah I know.'

Kimberly could see the knot of muscle flexing in her cousin's jaw. 'What are you going to do about it? If anyone found out—'

'I know,' he said, cutting her sentence mid-flow. 'I'll deal with it.' In the back of his mind he was glad he'd found out before any real damage could have been done. He'd known something wasn't right when Quinn hadn't checked in. 'After everything I've done for her.'

'I'll leave you to it,' she said, sensing his anger. 'If there's anything you need, you know where I am.'

'Aye,' he said, not really listening. He heard his office door close and looked up. He couldn't believe it had been Melanie who had betrayed him, after everything he'd done for her, after everything he'd given her. All the while she'd been laughing at him behind his back, reporting everything back to the police: The guns, the drugs, the murders, the deal. It all started to make sense, now understanding her occasional unease, how she would get nervous when certain topics were discussed, and how interested she'd been when he'd mentioned the Turkish deal. He picked up his iPhone and punched in her digits, listening as the line connected.

'Hello,' Melanie answered.

'What you doing now?' he asked her, his voice calm and caring.

'Nothing really, was just about te head te the gym. Why?'

'I wanna see you.'

'What? Now?' Her heart pounded. 'Wha' for?'

'Meet me at the place where we all met the other night.'

'Why?' Her heart pounded faster still.

'Why do you think? I wanna fuck you there.'

'Ya wanna have sex in that dirty building?'

'Yes. Be spontaneous, Mel. Live a little.'

Her hands trembled, and her gut churned. 'I don't think so, Michael. The place was filthy. And it's freezing.'

'I promise you, the only dirt you'll get on you will be mine. Plus I'll give you the night off.'

'That just makes it sound like yer paying me for sex, well.'

'Then you can still work. I don't care. But I still want to taste you in that office.'

191

She buried her concerns, remembering Slater's last instruction, and agreed. 'When?'

'Right now.'

She could sense something wasn't right, Michael had, on occasion, requested to meet in places for sex, but there was something different this time. She put it down to paranoia. 'Okay,' she said. 'I'm sure I can remember my way there.'

'Excellent.' Michael hung up and poured himself a measure of Jack Daniels, swallowing it in one.

*

Shaw checked the dashboard clock. Fifteen minutes had passed. That was long enough. He indicated, doing a full circle of the upcoming roundabout, and headed back towards the club. Five minutes later he pulled up beside Kimberly's red MR2 and walked to the shelter of the steps, taking them two at a time. He buzzed the intercom and was let in.

'I'm getting a little sick of being whistled for like some fucking dog,' he said, entering the club.

Kimberly grinned, amused at his tone. 'Michael's not here.'

'What do you mean, he's not here?'

'He's popped out.'

Shaw scowled. 'When's he coming back? I'm not waiting around here all day.'

'He'll be gone for a while,' she said. 'He's away dealing with someone.'

'Someone? As in Will?'

'No, not Will. He's dealing with a grass.'

Shaw's heart skipped a beat, hoping it wasn't Melanie she was talking about. 'What do you mean a grass?'

Kimberly grinned.

'Who's a grass, Kimberly?'

'Melanie.'

'When did he find this out?'

'Earlier.'

'When did he leave?'

'About ten minutes ago.' Her grin grew wider. 'Slut won't be speaking to the filth for much longer, that's for sure.'

'Well I'm not waiting around here all fucking day,' he said, making his way back towards the door.

'You not concerned about Melanie? She could get you into a lot

192

of trouble.'

'I thought you said Michael was dealing with her?'

'He is.'

'Then no, I'm not concerned.' He opened the door to find the light snow had turned into hard falling sleet and made his way down the steps, not wanting to attract the attention of the CCTV cameras. He jumped in the Saxo and slammed the door shut. He hammered the gearstick into reverse and reversed out into the alley with a bump, before speeding down into the heavy traffic. He had to warn her. He had to get to Melanie before Michael did.

Twenty-Seven

'Maximum grip'

Shaw attacked the junction, his wipers fighting the snow, his tyres fighting for traction. A silver Clio swerved to avoid a collision and mounted a traffic island in the centre of the road, crashing through its standing illuminated post. Several horns blasted as he sped through a red light, stopping more traffic in its tracks. He hammered through the gears, gaining speed gradually in the badly maintained, one litre Saxo, and ignored a second set of traffic lights, causing a luxurious white BMW to slam on its brakes. He screeched sharply to the left into the free-flowing traffic crossing the River Wear. Traffic was heavier and slower moving across the Wear Mouth Bridge, forcing Shaw to overtake, narrowly avoiding the oncoming traffic. He dropped a gear and pulled out to overtake a silver Audi. An oncoming single-decker bus swerved suddenly to its left and bumped up the curb, avoiding the head on collision, scrapping off a chunk of maroon paint and snapping off Shaw's wing mirror. Metal bent and crunched as he pushed his way back into the flow of traffic, pushing the Audi up against the opposite curb.

He pulled out his mobile phone and dialled Slater as he weaved in and out of the cars, listening impatiently to the dial tone ring off to the answering service.

'Answer your fucking phone!' he yelled, approaching another set of traffic lights.

He dropped another gear and pulled out into the oncoming traffic, swerving at the last minute to avoid a filthy skip-carrying truck, and crashed through a central illuminated post. His mobile phone slipped from his grasp and fell beneath the pedals as he struggled to control the collision, speeding into the required lane of the dual carriageway, heading west passed the city's famous football ground: The Stadium of Light. He climbed back up through the gears and stretched down with his left hand, his eyes transfixed on the traffic ahead, feeling the tips of his fingers brush against his phone. His mind raced through his options, cursing himself for not getting Melanie's phone number. The only thing he could think of doing now was to head to her flat in Gateshead.

He glanced at the dashboard's clock, 11:39. It would take him at least another ten minutes to get to her flat driving at this speed, and Michael had at least a fifteen-minute head start on him. Finally, his fingers gripped

194

the phone. He sat back up just in time to negotiate a small roundabout, dropping down two gears to help control the speeding Saxo. The engine screamed as its tyres skidded on the wet tarmac, sliding through it's under steer towards the metal structure of pedestrian railings. He pulled up hard on the handbrake, bringing the rear of the vehicle round before slamming on the accelerator. The wheels span frantically, fighting for traction as the rear passenger wheel slammed into the curb, almost causing the car to flip. He controlled the bump and continued up the dual carriageway, taking him straight into the heart of Gateshead.

He skidded round the final corner into Melanie's street, using up the whole road to control his speed, and slammed on the brakes. The front wheels locked up and bumped up onto the curb outside her flat. On her windowsill, Shaw could see her tabby cat lying silent, watching the day go by. Without switching off the engine or shutting his driver's door, he sprinted towards her flat and banged on her letterbox and window. Her car wasn't in the drive and no one answered.

'Shit!' He ran a hand through his wet hair and turned back towards his car, trying to think of his next option.

The door behind him opened. 'Get in here,' a male voice said.

Shaw turned to see Slater's face peering from within the flat's shadows. 'What are you doing here?' he said, entering the flat.

Slater closed the door behind him. 'Collecting up evidence. Not that it's any of your concern. Why are you here?'

'Where is she?'

Slater's brow creased into a frown of interest. 'She's gone out. Why?'

'Stop fucking about, Slater. Where is she?'

'She's gone to meet Michael,' he said, not appreciating his tone. 'To do the work you should be doing.'

'Has anyone gone with her?'

'Shaw, she'll be fine. Michael'll probably just want to fuck her, or something.'

Shaw couldn't believe what he was hearing. 'Slater, Michael knows. He knows about Mel.'

The smile on Slater's face crumbled. He reached inside his suit jacket and pulled out his mobile phone.

'Did she say where she was meeting him?'

'Not exactly.' Slater put his phone to his ear and turned his back on him.

Shaw pulled on his shoulder, spinning him to face him again.
'Slater, what did she say?'

'She said she was heading to some laundrette. She left about fifteen minutes ago.'

Shaw sprinted back to the waiting Saxo and jumped in the driver's seat. He knew exactly where it was. He looked over his left shoulder, punched it into reverse and floored the accelerator, dismounting the curb with a bump, spitting soggy green turf up in front of him. He manoeuvred the small maroon car into a wider part of the street, free of parked cars, and accelerated to approximately twenty miles per hour. Controlling the vehicle with trained professionalism, he pulled sharply on the steering wheel whilst taking his foot off the power, transferring the weight of the car to the back, snapping the front of the car round. The tyres screeched across the puddled tarmac as he simultaneously stabbed at the brakes and clutch, locking up on the front wheels. The momentum of the turn combined with the rear weight transfer pulled the front end of the car round until it had travelled almost one hundred and eighty degrees. He slammed the gearstick into first, at the same time turning on the steering wheel making sure the wheels were parallel with the curb. Once he was happy the car was facing the direction he wished to travel, Shaw released the clutch, keeping the engine revved enough for the front wheels to spin and fight for traction, speeding him forward. He approached the tight junction up ahead and released the pressure on the accelerator, creating a forward weight transfer, providing maximum grip to the front tyres. He pulled down hard on the steering wheel, dipped in the clutch, and slammed on the handbrake, holding down tightly on the release button, causing the rear wheels to lock up and induce a slide. The steering wheel spun freely in his hands, realigning the wheels as he stabbed the gearstick into second. Car horns blasted in fury as other road users swerved or broke.

He raced back to Sunderland, weaving in and out of the heavy traffic. He knew Melanie's car was only a one litre and that she would take her time getting to the old shipyards. He only hoped he could get there in time.

He sped towards the large roundabout leading him onto the Queen Alexandra Bridge, reducing his speed to allow him the control he needed. He remembered the roundabout was filled with traffic lights from when they'd carried out the hit on Jammin a few days earlier. So instead of going left around the roundabout, and tackling the traffic lights head on, Shaw turned right into the oncoming traffic, forcing slow moving vehicles to carryout emergency stops or swerve out of his way.

A learner driver failed to stop, smashing into the tail end of a green Vectra, pushing that forward into the line of traffic from a freshly turned green light. That in turn was smashed into by a four ton white lorry, throwing it more than three feet. A fancy black Jaguar swerved at the last minute to avoid another emergency stopped vehicle, only to crash into a standing black pole holding the button for the pedestrian lights.

He shot across the roundabout's three lanes and mounted the central island, digging up its grass. He counter-steered, controlling his outrageous manoeuvre as he dismounted the large grassy roundabout and re-joined the traffic on the correct side of the road, leaving the carnage behind him. The Saxo was pushed to its limits as he again pulled out onto the wrong side of the road, crossing back over the River Wear, overtaking other road users before finally pulling back in to attack an upcoming roundabout.

*

The Saxo bounced down into the compound, scraping its plastic black bumper on the ground, almost wrecking the car's suspension. He passed through the familiar chain-link fence and made his way to the empty hanger. A stray wheel trim finally gave in and broke loose from its holdings, spinning off in front of him. He stopped the car behind a small out building, just short of the abandoned hanger, and killed the engine.

He stepped out into the sleet, fighting back the urge to run in, guns blazing. Instead he chose his training. He entered through the large open doors, slowly but surely, not knowing the hanger's layout or who was inside or how many. The melted sleet dripped down his face and his soaked T-shirt clung to him like a second skin. The sound of the sleet beating off the roof high above him echoed throughout the hanger like a drum in a marching band. He crept passed Melanie's parked Yaris, his ears tuned to the slightest of sounds, listening to the startled birds above him, the rainwater splashing in a corner of the room, and the hanger doors banging in the wind. He bent forward and picked up a foot-long rusted pole and thumped it into the palm of his left hand. Even though it was daylight outside, the corridors seemed just as dark as they had been the night he'd last walked down them, making it near impossible to access them without making a noise. He hugged the left-hand wall, presenting himself as a smaller target, all the while keeping a mental note of every open doorway to his front, sides and rear. Finally, he arrived at the doors that led him into the office, its glassless windows still concealed by the hanging, filthy blinds.

Twenty-Eight

'An unseen hope'

Melanie tried to recall the route Michael had taken through the shipyard, her wipers battling the relentless weather obstructing her view. She remembered the large rusty pipework that protruded from the ground and disappeared into one of the large nearby hangers, and the numerous coloured shipping containers that had been left abandoned by their previous owners. So she knew she was on the right track. Above her, the seagulls screamed as if giving warning to all other seagulls of her approach.

Her imagination ran wild as the shipyard's lifelessness closed in on her. She wondered why Michael had wanted her to meet him here instead of picking her up like he had done every other time. Something was wrong, and she could feel it. She mentally slapped herself, fighting back the sickening feeling that was budding within her.

'Stop it ya silly cow. There's no reason he should suspect anything,' she said out loud, unable to shake the eerily empty feeling of the flooded shipyard.

She approached the empty hanger, sleet thundering of the ground, filling the surrounding area with deep, rust coloured puddles. Its gigantic sliding doors were open, allowing the windswept sleet to soak the ground inside. Michael's GT-R sat silent under the cover of the hanger roof, water still cascading down its silver bodywork. She stopped her car and climbed out. The noise of her car door closing echoed around the large empty space, startling the nesting birds above her.

'Hello,' she yelled, filling the cold void with her Ulster accent, her breath visible in the air in front of her. She made her way through the dark, cluttered corridors, her hands trembling. 'Hello. Michael?' The room she was after came into view, somehow calming her nerves. Inside she could make out Michael smoking a cigarette in the centre of the room, alone. 'Michael,' she said again.

'I'm in here,' he said.

A smile broke her lips, calming her nerves further. Michael's tone hadn't held anger or concealed rage, not from what she could tell, anyway. She opened the door to the badly lit room, smelling the dust, damp, and cigarette smoke that continued to hang heavy in the air, and entered.

'Hi,' she said, trying to expel her fear completely. But Michael didn't reply, instead he continued to rub his temples with his fore finger and thumb. 'Michael?' she said again, tilting her head in an attempt to meet his gaze.

Michael stood tall, smoke filtering down through his nostrils, his eyes fixed on hers, emotionless and vacant. 'I'm going to ask you a question, Mel,' he said, 'and I want the truth.'

Melanie's heart almost ripped through her chest, beating faster than her body could handle. He knew. Her legs started to shake, barely containing the strength to hold her bodyweight. Her pupils widened unable to hide the fear that had infected her face. 'What?' she gasped.

Michael flicked his cigarette butt and took a step towards her, forcing her to take a step back, pushing her up against the filthy door. He lashed out and gripped her cheeks, holding her face in front of his.

Tears welled in her eyes, her breathing short and sharp. 'Michael, yer hurting me,' she whimpered, petrified.

'Have you been speaking to the fucking police?' he said through clenched teeth, the lingering smell of whiskey and cigarette smoke heavy on his breath. He put his free hand in his trouser pocket and pulled out the black and chrome handle of a flick knife, activating it near her face.

The wind off the blade flicked at her cheek. 'No, Michael, I haven't, I swear.'

He pressed the blunt side of the cold metal into her face, smearing the mascara that had run down her cheek. 'Liar! You were seen talking to one. I bet you're wearing a fucking wire right now.' He gripped the neckline of her brown mini-dress and pulled, ripping the fabric to expose her chest.

She released a scream as her torso snapped forward. Her fear enhanced by the sound of fabric ripping. 'Please,' she cried. 'I haven't.'

He pressed his forehead against hers. 'You were fucking seen!' he said, spraying her face with foaming spittle. 'Chloe saw you on the Metro.'

Her heart almost stopped. 'She's lying,' she said, turning her head to relieve the pressure from Michael's forehead.

He gripped her by her throat and slammed her back against the door.

'I'm sorry,' she spluttered, the fear getting the better of her. 'They made me.'

'You're sorry?' He snapped his head forward, crashing it down into her nose. Blood spilled down over her chin. 'You're fucking sorry?' He took a step back, his fists clenched into tight balls.

Melanie cupped her face in her hands. 'Please,' she sobbed, blood seeping between her fingers. 'I'm sorry.'

Every muscle in his body flexed, craving an action that would release his anger. He lunged forward and drove the blade deep into her gut, plunging it effortlessly through her brown dress and smooth skin. The blade scraped between the lower portions of her left ribs, forcing a rush of pain-produced air to escape her lungs. He pulled it free and took several steps back, witnessing a dark stain appear and grow on her dress.

She clamped her hands to the wound and looked down at them, seeing the crimson that now oozed through her fingers.

Michael's chest heaved with every breath, his hands shaking with rage. The stabbing wasn't enough. She needed to be punished further. He rotated his body and swung his right fist, driving with his hip and shoulder. The punch smashed into her left eye, knocking her from her feet. She hit the ground hard, coating the front of her mini-dress and tights with thick, damp dirt. She whimpered up onto her elbows and knees, blood dripping from her nose.

'Where the fuck d'ya think you're going?' he said, watching her sob into the muck. He closed the blood coated flick knife and placed it back in his pocket. 'I actually defended you against Kim. And what do you do? You stab me in the fucking back.' He took a step back, not giving her the chance to touch him. 'I should have listened to her.'

Melanie released one final murmur before he smashed his hard black leather shoe into her mouth. Her head snapped back in a mist of blood and teeth. A flash of darkness blinded her. Everything around her went quiet. Her mouth filled with blood. He kicked her again, smashing the toes of his shoe into the back of her head, snapping her head forward. He stood back and looked down at her motionless body, listening to the air gurgle up through her bloodied mouth.

'Look at me when I'm fucking speaking to you!' He rolled her onto her back and straddled her waist. He gripped her hair and lifted her head from the ground. Her mouth was puddled with blood. Several of her teeth, top and bottom, were broken and jagged. 'Grassing little cunt!' He balled his fist and punched her, breaking her nose, throwing crimson up across the top of her face, turning her platinum fringe blood red. Again, he punched her, again and again, fast and violent, until her face was a bloody mess. Too tired to continue, Michael climbed off, gathering his breath. 'Fucking bitch.' He spat and stamped on her face.

She was done. Her left arm lay outstretched to her side, as if reaching out for an unseen hope.

Twenty-Nine

'The perfect snow angel'

Shaw pushed open the door to the launderette. Particles of dust floated in the air, illuminated by the shards of light piercing what they could of the grubby windows. He scanned the room, visually and audibly, before entering, paying particular attention to the shadowy corners. At first the room appeared empty, silent, cold and abandoned, but then he saw it. Sticking out from behind the long counter was a single tanned leather boot. He was too late. Behind the counter, partially concealed by a fallen sheet of corrugated iron, was Melanie, lying silent and motionless. She lay on her back, her face a beaten mess.

'Shit, Melanie,' he said, not expecting a reply. 'Melanie.' He picked up the corrugated sheet and threw it on the opposite side of the counter. 'Melanie,' he repeated, crouching down beside her, 'can you hear me, sweetheart? It's me, Ryan.' His hopes of a happy ending were diminished as the puncture wound in her abdomen became known. Her filthy dress was ripped at the neckline, exposing part of a blood covered dirty breast, and hitched up high above her waist, revealing tights ripped at the left knee. He pressed the thumb of his right hand against her forehead and watched in relief as the capillaries refilled the blanched tissue. He was amazed she was still alive. But before he could deal with the bleed, he had to establish her airway. He leant forward, placing his right ear low above her face and waited for the rise and fall of her exposed chest, hearing a gurgled wheeze. He knelt up straight and placed his hands beneath the base of her head, instantly recognising the distorted symmetry of her face; a tell-tale sign of a fractured skull and felt for any sign of a cervical injury. Happy there was no further damage, Shaw pressed his thumbs against her broken jaw and slid it open, taking care not to open her airway anymore than it already was. Inside, he saw that her once perfect white teeth were now jagged shards of bone, protruding from her split, swollen gums. Along with the blood and broken teeth, her tongue had also fallen to the rear of her mouth. He tilted her head to the side, taking care not to injure her further, and carried out a two finger sweep of her mouth, clearing what he could. Blood spilled down the side of her face as he dropped the broken fragments on the floor beside her. He straightened her head, now her mouth was free of obstruction, and opened her airway fully. Her chest rose a little higher and the gurgling in her throat dampened. Next was the puncture wound. He stuck his fingers into the hole

201

of the dress and ripped the fabric, allowing him to see the wound for what it was. The puncture appeared no more than an inch in width and less than five millimetres thick, positioned approximately four inches two o'clock of her naval. But it was the depth of the wound that concerned him.

The thought of calling for an ambulance left his mind as fast as it had entered. Trying to explain his location and the directions in how to find him would have eaten up precious time. Time Melanie didn't have.

'I'm going to pull off your boots and remove your tights now, Melanie,' he said, doing so as he said it, taking the opportunity to check for further injury. 'I need them to hold the dressing in place.' Even though Melanie was unresponsive, there was no evidence to say she couldn't feel and hear what was taking place.

Once he'd peeled off her tights, he pulled off his right boot and removed his sock. He slipped the tights beneath her and wrapped them around her torso, making sure to cover the entirety of the sock that was dressing the wound, and tied them on her uninjured side.

'You're going to be alright, sweetheart,' he whispered, scooping her up in his arms. 'I'm taking you to the hospital. They'll fix you up.' But he knew from experience there were just some wounds you couldn't fix.

A noise escaped her lips, too quiet and mumbled to comprehend if it had been an attempt at words, or a simple response to physical pain. He cursed himself for not getting to her quicker.

'It's alright, Mel,' he said, feeling she could hear his every word. 'I'm right here.' He cursed Slater for allowing it to happen, and he cursed Michael for thinking he had the right. He carried her back through the hanger, taking care not to jolt her or trip over one of the many foreign objects that littered the dark corridor floor. 'It's okay, Mel,' he repeated, not sure if it was Melanie he was attempting to reassure or himself. She was in a bad way. He wasn't even sure she would be able to speak properly again. That was if she even woke up.

He quickened his pace through the damp air and opened the passenger door of the Saxo, kicking it with the heel of his boot. He sat her inside, wound back the seat to keep her head from falling forward, and clipped in her seat belt. He draped his black jacket over her, hiding the rip in her dress and her exposed flesh, and closed the door. He jumped in next to her and pulled away, increasing his speed once he was on flat level ground.

Less than ten minutes later, Shaw stopped the Saxo under the canopy of the hospital's A and E entrance and killed the engine. He ran around the car to Melanie's door and threw it open. He unclipped her seat belt and slid his hands beneath her. As expected, Melanie had remained unconscious during the journey.

'It's alright, sweetheart. We're at the hospital now. They'll make everything better,' he said, scooping her up out of the car. 'I need a hand here!' he yelled, entering the reception.

A female nurse with red hair ran over. 'What's happened?' she asked him, assessing Melanie's injuries.

'She has a single puncture wound to her abdomen. A fractured skull and a broken jaw,' Shaw told her. 'She's been unresponsive since I found her, approximately fifteen minutes ago.'

'We need a bed here!' the nurse yelled.

'There's a good chance she has internal bleeding,' he said, laying her limp body on a squeaky wheeled bed that soon arrived. 'Her heart rate's above 100bpm and she has an increased respiratory rate.'

The nurse looked up at him, surprised by his knowledge of hypovolaemic shock, and handed him back his coat. 'Did you do this?' she said, referring to the makeshift field dressing.

Shaw nodded.

'Do you know her name?'

He shook his head whilst a skinny male nurse wheeled her away, the beds front left wheel spinning frantically. A rage flowed through his veins knowing that this could have been avoided if the right precautions had been put in place. Slater had some explaining to do.

'Well, if you'd just like to wait over there.' She pointed to the waiting area. 'A police officer will be along shortly to take a statement.'

'I need to be somewhere,' he said.

'They won't be long,' she persisted, paying close attention to his bruised face and distinctive scarring.

Not wanting to raise anymore suspicions than he already had, Shaw agreed. 'Just there?' he confirmed, pulling on his coat, his hands painted with Melanie's dry blood.

The nurse smiled and nodded. 'They won't be long.' she said again.

He approached the plastic seats of the waiting room and fumbled through his pockets, stalling until the female nurse had turned her back on him. He gave her and the receptionist one last glance and walked out through the automatic double doors.

Two uniformed police officers were all over the Saxo when Shaw stepped out through the doors, looking inside and inspecting the blood stains on the seat. He cursed and changed direction, abandoning the car. He couldn't risk getting wrapped up in some eager-to-please police officer's investigation about her attack. Melanie was safe now, and that's all that mattered. He had more important things to deal with now, like finding his brother and making sure Michael and Slater paid for their insubordinations.

*

Shaw's lips wrapped around the cheap whiskey bottle he'd purchased from a local off license, guzzling another generous mouthful. He'd needed a drink, a stiff one, to take the edge of everything that was happening. And a cold park bench was as good a place as any to drink it. He rubbed his swollen face, feeling the alcohol's desired effect. He tried to focus on what was important, finding Will, but all he could think about was Melanie, and what Michael had done to her. He watched a man play with two young boys in the snow; all three of them lying on their backs, looking up at the dark sky, their arms and legs combing through the white powder. The sight reminded him of when his father had shown him and Will how to make the perfect snow angel, the trick of standing up without ruining the print.

'Fuck it,' he said, deciding to do what he should have done at the beginning. Nobody had ever bullied him into doing anything, and now he'd allowed a man to do just that. His life with his son was no longer a concern. His future was already written. Prison awaited him no matter what. He stood up from the bench and threw what was left of the bottle in a bush. The time on his phone read 18:12. After several rings, the phone was answered.

'Slater,' the answering voice said.

'We need to talk.'

'Shaw? Yes we do.' Slater looked at his watch. 'Do you know where the Lion pub is?'

'I'll find it.'

'Be there in half an hour.' Slater disconnected.

Shaw didn't know what he was going to say, or guarantee that he would be civilised when they met. But he needed Michael's address, and the only way he could think of getting it was through Slater.

*

The pub was a quiet bar in dire need of a little care and a fresh coat of paint. Standing behind the bar was a tall thin man with dark receding hair. Shaw waited no more than fifteen minutes, staring at the same double whiskey in front of him, before Slater made an appearance.

204

'Gents. Now,' Slater demanded, approaching him at the bar.

*

After the barman had watched Shaw down his drink and enter the toilets, he turned and picked up the phone.

'Levi, it's Phil at the Lion. That guy you're after… Well he's just walked in here.'

*

Slater paced the short length of the room, his fingers interlocked above his head. 'What the fuck happened to Melanie?' he said. 'She's in a fucking coma, for fuck sake.'

Shaw approached the single washbasin and filled his hands with cold water, only now attempting to remove Melanie's dried in blood.

'I'm fucking talking to you.' Slater grabbed Shaw's shoulder and turned him to face him. Without warning, Shaw lost control. He punched Slater on the bridge of his nose, sharp and fast. Slater stumbled, his nose bleeding, eyes watering. Shaw followed through, driving him through one of the two cubical doors behind him, snapping it in two. Slater crashed into the toilet's cistern, firing a pain up through his ribs. Shaw landed on top, punching his forearm into his throat, almost rupturing his windpipe. The pair slipped down beside the toilet bowl, landing in a puddle and a mound of soggy yellow toilet paper. Shaw pushed his forearm deeper into his throat, digging his heels against the cubical wall behind him for added weight.

Slater pulled at Shaw's arm, straining to ease the pressure. He could feel himself slipping away, growing weaker. He gripped Shaw's face, gaping into his bloodshot eyes, seeing a man more than capable of killing him and, more frightening than that, a man who actually wanted to. His eyes burned with a fury, a rage he'd only read about in his file. Finally, Slater's eyes rolled back as the darkness began to swallow him.

Shaw increased the pressure now that Slater had given up the fight. He didn't deserve to live after what he had let happen. 'Cunt!' he spat through gritted teeth, wanting Slater to not only feel, but to hear his hatred. Then out of nowhere, he heard a woman's voice. A gentle Scottish voice telling him to look at himself; to look at what he'd become. 'Amy?' he said, releasing his hold on Slater. He climbed to his feet, using the toilet bowl for support.

Slater coughed, sucking in air as if his life depended on it. He wriggled up against the back wall and rolled onto his side to vomit.

Shaw left the confines of the cubical and saw his reflection in the mirror. Amy wasn't in the room. She was in his head, repeating the words she'd used the night he'd smashed up the house; the night he'd attacked the police and camp guards; the night he'd lost his family. He rested his hands on the wash basin and inhaled, filling his lungs. He hadn't changed. He was still the same drunk, angry man he was when he went to prison.

Slater lay coughing on the cubical floor, his shirt and trousers soaked to his skin and covered in a layer of wet toilet paper. 'Is this about Melanie?' he said between gasps of breath. He climbed to his knees, coughing, holding his throat. 'It wasn't my fault she got hurt. How was I supposed to know? Melanie never left any word on where this laundrette was.'

Slater's pitiful voice only fuelled Shaw's rage. All he'd wanted was Michael's address. He turned to face him. 'Where was your manpower? You should have had her covered at all times. She's not an undercover officer. She's not a copper. She's not even a fucking security guard. She's a fucking stripper in a club. A fucking stripper! And you fucked her over.' He stepped forward, fighting back the urge to stamp his size nine down on his face.

Slater flinched. 'Manpower. Christ, we have just enough men to patrol the streets at night. I know what happened to Melanie was awful, but it wasn't my fault. You can't blame me.'

'Well I am!' he said, his hands clenched into fists.

'I understand you're angry. I would be too if I'd failed to reach her in time. But you can't hold me responsible.'

Shaw stared long and hard into Slater's eyes, fighting back his rage. He chose to do the only thing he could think of that would prevent him from killing him and, abandoned his question and left, leaving him bleeding on the toilet floor in a puddle of urine.

The cold air outside hit his face, reminding him of how drunk he actually was.

'Kimberly,' he said, deciding if he couldn't get it from Slater, he would have to get it from her. As soon as he stepped foot on the pavement and turned left, a black saloon pulled up several yards ahead of him. Two heavily built men climbed out and stepped onto the path, their eyes focused solely on him.

Shaw stopped four metres from them, his adrenaline once again fighting off the alcohol's effects. He clenched his fists and found his footing. 'Is there a problem?' he said.

The two men said nothing.

'What? You're just gonna stand there?'

Shaw didn't even see it coming. The cosh struck the back of his head, rendering him unconscious before he hit the pavement.

Thirty

'Large sticky teddy'

The Range Rover Sport came to a gentle stop on the wet gravel of the car park. The infamous pub, The Hairy Tavern, was located down in the old dark industrial area of the River Wear, an old pub, once used largely by the old ship builders and foundry workers, now home to trouble causing clientele banned from every other venue. The driver of the Range Rover, an enormous man with shiny, curly, jet black hair, looked in the rear-view mirror, watching his boss talk on his mobile phone, showing increasing signs of frustration.

'When you see him, you make sure you keep him alive long enough for me to have a word,' Billy Mallinson said. 'I mean it, Paul. I wanna see the little cunt.' He hung up and locked his eyes on his driver's in the rearview mirror. 'I tell you what, Gary. I love my nephew to bits, but sometimes…' he said, allowing his sentence to trail off.

'I know what you mean, Mr. Mallinson. My younger brother's very similar.'

Billy returned the comment with an uneasy smile. 'I'll not be long, Gary. About ten minutes or so.'

'No problem, Mr. Mallinson.'

Billy climbed out the rear driver's door, dressed in his usual business attire: a grey fitted suit, white shirt and long dark grey coat, carrying his umbrella, more for show than use.

Every Wednesday night, after ten o'clock, The Hairy Tavern paid its debts to the Mallinson's, and Christmas Eve night was no different.

Through all the frustration with his nephew, neither Billy nor his driver noticed the blood-red superbike with its single rider dressed in black leathers crawl past them at a slow, steady speed.

*

Bomber pulled into The Hairy Tavern's car park, the stolen Kawasaki purring between his thighs. He had successfully followed the Range Rover all the way from Billy's family home, four miles north of Sunderland. He eased off on the throttle and peered through the Range Rover's tinted windows, seeing the hulking ginger male sitting in the back seat, his large curly haired driver sitting in front. He turned the superbike around and wheeled it back into a parking space at the rear of the Range Rover, his engine running. He unzipped the tank bag strapped to the tank in front of him and partially revealed an Ingram Mac-10 and cocked it. He pulled in his clutch and kicked it into first, his fingers twitching on the throttle. Apprehension filled his body as he watched Billy Mallinson's car door bounce open and his right foot step out into the cold damp air. He counted down from three and gunned the 1200cc engine, the sheer power lifting the front wheel from the ground.

Billy jumped at the sound of the screaming engine, pinning himself back against the door of his Range Rover. The blood-red superbike slammed to a halt two metres from him, pushing down on its front forks. Bomber raised the submachine-gun, holding it in both hands across his chest, and aimed it at the ginger male's centre mass. He emptied the magazine, spitting out thirty-two rounds at a rate faster than ten rounds per second. The 9mm rounds thundered through the air, accompanied by the terrifying flash that erupted from the weapon's muzzle. Dozens of holes were punched into Billy's torso and limbs, pushing his hulking body back against the Range Rover's door. Blood misted up in front of him, exploding out from his ravaged clothes. The windows behind him imploded as the rounds punched through his flailing body and into the stylish interior.

Gary dropped down into the passenger footwell, but took several to his right shoulder, back and head, killing him instantly.

Billy's lifeless body slid down the rear driver's door onto the wet gravel into a slumped, seated position.

Less than a second later, the bucking Mac-10 stopped, exhaling a trail of carbonized smoke from its barrel. He zipped the Mac-10 back into the tank bag and released the clutch, feeling the power of the superbike's engine rush to its wheels, spinning the back tyre on the gravel and throwing the Kawasaki forward, out of the car park.

*

'Any chance we could turn the music down a little?' Emma asked. She was tired and hungover. Partying until eight o'clock in the morning didn't do anyone any favours, especially when they were working in a bar that same night. A throbbing thumped behind her eyes. Her stomach constantly churned. She didn't know if she needed to vomit or defecate, and the unforgiving tiredness willed her to do as little as possible. Her long blonde extensions, still thick with hairspray from last night's partying, were held back from her face by a simple black hair band. The makeup on her face was thick and old, and her tight black leggings and long black vest were clean and un-ironed. But she didn't care. It wasn't as if Sunderland was flooded with hot rich men looking for regular sex, not like Newcastle. That's what Emma needed, a rich man, someone who would spoil her with trendy clothes and expensive holidays. She scanned the empty floor of the Voodoo Bar, watching the other staff tidy away bottles and collect empty glasses. The manager of the club, who was still sitting on one of the many brown leather sofas, was working on his laptop computer, consulting with a heavily overweight building contractor.

'Aye, turn that shit down!' Tony Mallinson yelled, twisting in his seat to face the DJ. Almost immediately, the volume dropped, allowing the small number of people within the bar to hear themselves think. 'It's too fucking late for all that shit now. Christmas Eve has finished. We're fucking closed. Twat!' He turned his attention back to the laptop in front of him. 'So you think this is all possible within my budget?' he asked the contractor.

Emma watched her boss and his colleague discuss the future renovations they were planning for the club, her gaze glassy and lifeless, her wanting to sleep almost overwhelming. The only words she could make out were *glass panelling* and *cheaper lighting*.

'I don't care if he's a good lad or not, Danny. Is he cheap?' Tony stressed.

Danny replied, but Emma didn't catch it.

Tony turned away from the fat contractor sitting opposite him and locked his cold, eternally angry eyes on two young males that were chatting up Katy, one of his favored bar staff. 'Oi, you two, get the fuck out. We're closed if you hadn't fucking noticed,' he yelled across the lounge. 'Cole, what the fuck do I pay you for? Get those two cunt's out, will ya.'

Emma looked to the main doors and saw the large, dark skinned doorman approach them.

'You two. Out,' Cole said.

*

Parked up in an alleyway near the Voodoo Lounge bar, Picco reached over into the passenger footwell and lifted out the AK47 with fixed wooden stock. He released its curved plastic magazine, filled with thirty 7.62mm rounds, and checked they were seated correctly. He then slammed the magazine back into its housing, happy with the state of the weapon, and made ready. This was it. His heart was racing and his palms were sweaty. He placed a strip of minty chewing gum in his mouth and pulled a plastic paintballing mask down over his face. He knew Tony was in the bar. He'd rang the place only two minutes earlier to confirm he was still there, asking to speak with him and hanging up before a conversation could be initiated. He interlocked his fingers, tightening the fit of his black leather gloves, and clicked the automatic gearstick into drive. Drunken pedestrians walked to and from the surrounding bars, oblivious to his presence. He pulled forward up to the main road, stopping to allow a bus filled with passengers to pass, and turned right towards the bar. He parked the stolen SUV outside the front door and looked in through the large glass window that lined its front wall. Tony Mallinson was clearly visible, sat at the far end of the lounge, talking to a fat bald male, his face illuminated by the glow of a laptop screen. He climbed out into the cold air, his AK47 in hand, and passed through the double glass doors into the bar.

A barmaid to his left screamed in terror, causing Tony to look up from his laptop. Tony and Picco's eyes met as he pulled the soviet assault rifle tight into his shoulder.

Tony opened his mouth to speak, but his words were cut short by the AK47's deafening roar. His body flailed in his seat as multiple rounds punched into his chest, neck, and face, opening up the back of his skull and painting the wall behind him with brain matter. In front of him, the laptop exploded, the half-filled glasses shattered, the table top splintered. The bald contractor beside him received just the same, throwing him back off his chair and tearing his jaw from his face.

Picco twisted to his left, estimating he'd discharged only half his magazine, and aimed the AK47 at the several remaining people in the bar. He tucked it tight into his shoulder, looked down through the sights, and exhaled. One of the two men flirting with the barmaid was already on the bar, ready to take cover. He leaned forward into the weapon and unleashed the remainder of the magazine. The large doorman took the first of the rounds, taking several to his legs, hip and torso. The young man to his left came second, taking one to the chest and two to the face. Thirdly was his colleague on the bar who took one to the gut and another to his neck, pushing him off the bar. The mirrors and glass behind them exploded, spilling liquid from the shattered bottles that hung from the optics. Leather and wood ripped and splintered as the rounds punched into the bar before finally devastating the chest of the attractive dark haired barmaid, throwing her back against the shattered glass.

Emma tucked her knees into her chest, her hands firmly over her ears, trying to block out the relentless noise of the AK47. She pushed herself up tight against the inside of the bar, glass and liquid raining down on her from the exploding bottles above. She opened her left eye to see her friend, Katy, thrown from her feet, her chest torn apart, spitting out blood and muscle like stuffing from a large sticky teddy. Then, as quick as it started, it stopped.

The AK47's working parts locked to the rear. Blue tinted smoke rose from the barrel and the empty chamber where the final spent case had been ejected. The sound of clumsy movement to Picco's front snatched his attention. He looked down the weapon's sights seeing the DJ looking back at him, his arms raised in a pose of surrender, his eyes wide with terror, his jeans wet with urine. Picco lowered the AK47, turned, and left.

*

Michael's phone vibrated on the glass surface of the coffee table before being answered.

'The Mallinson's are no longer a problem,' Bomber said.

'Excellent,' he said.

Thirty-One
'Nail-gun'

The stench of stale urine and faeces was overpowering, almost causing Shaw to vomit. His head thumped from where he'd been hit earlier, and he was convinced he could feel sticky, clotted blood on the back of his neck. He opened his eyes to the sound of dripping water coming from behind him, and light fixtures buzzing overhead. He shivered, naked and sore, his hands bound behind his back and anchored by heavy duty cable ties to the metal framed chair he was sat on. The cold from the wet floor tiles seeped into his feet and climbed up through his calves. Through the dark pillowcase pulled over his head, he was able to make out certain features of the room, lit only by the single buzzing strip bulb attached to the ceiling. In front of him he could see only shadows. To his left he could make out the shape of two urinals attached to the wall. To his right were two prominent large sinks. He twisted in his seat, left and right, as best he could, trying to identify the dripping behind him. He scanned the walls for a window, attempting to distinguish the colour of the sky, hoping to get a marginal idea of how long he'd been held for. But the chair was fixed solid to the tiles beneath him. His heart started to pound in his chest. His adrenalin worked overtime as he started to panic.

'Stay calm,' he whispered to himself.

Questions filtered through his mind. How long had he been out? Where was he? Who had him? And what for? He pulled at the cable ties, testing their strength, but he was too weak. His limbs were too numb. He shifted in his seat, transferring his weight from one buttock to the other. He clenched and flexed his fingers and toes, attempting to fight off the aching numbness that had crawled through his limbs.

Finally, after what felt like hours, the creaking sound of a door opening filled the room. Multiple silhouettes stepped into his field of vision, coughing and grunting as they placed items down on the sinks to his right. He estimated at least three males, going by their size and heavy handedness. His heart pounded faster still as his body tried to fight off hypothermia. He braced himself for the impending strike, flinching every time there was movement close to his face. But nothing came, just movement and the swelling sound of preparation.

'Stay calm,' he repeated over and over in his head. 'Stay calm.' He remained quiet, not wanting to be the first to break the silence.

Out of the blue, his body went rigid as icy cold liquid was poured down over his head and shoulders. It seeped through the pillowcase, stinging his eyes and burning his nostrils. He clamped his eyes shut as tight as they would go, blowing out through his nostrils to keep him from inhaling. At least four litres was spilt over him, burning into his cuts and scrapes, causing him to growl in pain. A salty taste crossed his lips and a pungent rancidness, similar to ammonia, overwhelmed his sense of smell. *Piss.*

The instant the urine stopped pouring, a fist smashed into his face, re-breaking his nose, spilling blood down over his mouth and chin. The punch caught him off guard, snapping his head back and throwing stars up in front of his eyes. The pillowcase was pulled sharply from his head, catching on the stitches in his lip.

'Wake him up,' a male voice in front said.

A painful slap followed. 'Open your fucking eyes!' a second, deeper voice said.

Shaw opened them. The lavatory's yellowing tiled walls were stained with mold and human excrement, and the cold broken tiled floor was filthy and puddled. The single strip light above flickered intermittently. Stood directly to his front, in front of two dark toilet cubicles, was the man he recognised from Michael's club. Standing to his right was the hired muscle who had accompanied him that same evening. But it was the male standing to the man's left that caught his eye. He stood over six feet tall with broad thick shoulders and long dangly arms. His head was shaved and his face unshaven. His jaw was thick, and his brow was heavy. But what worried him about the man wasn't the size of his frame or how heavy his jaw was, but the look of the dirty red leather apron he was wearing. The kind of apron a butcher would wear to prevent blood staining his clothes.

'Do you know who I am?' the man from Michael's club said.

Shaw fired air out through his broken nose, expelling clots of blood and urine. 'You're Michael's friend,' he said.

'Michael's friend?' He laughed. 'Hardly. Do you know who I am?'

Shaw looked between the man's hired muscle and the butcher, the realisation of just how much shit he was actually in written all over his face. 'No.'

'Well you fucking will,' the man said, his teeth clenched.

Shaw glanced at the butcher who was searching through a black nylon bag he'd placed on the sinks. 'Whatever Michael's told you, it's bullshit,' he said, looking back to the man in front.

214

'Is that right?' the man said, pulling out a packet of cigarettes. 'So it wasn't you who robbed and killed the black man?'

'I didn't fucking kill him,' Shaw said, blood spitting from his lips. 'You've got this all wrong.' He could feel the urine burning his eyes, pulsing waves of pain through his open wounds.

The man sucked on his newly lit cigarette. 'I know you weren't alone,' he said, exhaling smoke from his nostrils. 'You had two others with you, one of them no doubt being Michael's prize bull. We'll get them two as well, don't you worry.'

That was the news Shaw did not want to hear. Whatever they had in store, it didn't involve questioning. There was nothing he could do or say that would change what was about to happen.

The man leaned in towards him, blowing smoke in his face. 'My names Paul Mallinson,' he said. 'Say it. Paul Mallinson.'

Shaw repeated it. He'd never felt any shame in begging when his life had depended on it. God knows he'd done it before.

'Again.'

'Paul Mallinson.'

'Louder!'

Shaw yelled. 'Paul Mallinson!' A sharp pain suddenly drove though Shaw's right shoulder, accompanied by the sound of escaping gas. His muscles clenched and his teeth gritted seeing the protruding head of a ring shanked nail and the thin trail of blood that now trickled down his right arm.

Paul flicked what was left of his cigarette in one of the overflowing urinals on Shaw's left. 'I'll be back in a couple of hours with Uncle Billy.' He looked at Shaw. 'Make sure he lasts the night.' He turned and disappeared through a door, followed by his darkly tanned lapdog.

'Now that I've got you to myself,' the butcher said, holding a cordless yellow nail-gun, 'we can start having some real fun.'

The muscle in Shaw's right shoulder throbbed, sending a pounding ache down his arm and into his hand. Judging by the size of the nail-gun, he estimated the nails to be anywhere between two to three and half inches in length. 'You don't have to do this,' he said, fighting back the pain.

'What else am I gonna do with a fresh battery and a full box of nails?' The butcher fired a second nail into Shaw's right shoulder, lodging it less than an inch from the first, only a centimeter of its length left visible.

'Look,' Shaw said between struggled breaths. 'This is fucking crazy.'

The butcher weaved around the back of him, remaining silent. Shaw twisted in his seat but failed to keep him in view. 'I have a little boy,' he said, hoping it would touch on his softer side. 'You don't have to—'

A clear plastic bag was pulled tight across his face, smearing the blood from his broken nose down over his chin and across his cheeks. His body went ridgid with panic, pulling tight on the cable ties that bound him to the chair. He sucked the bag tight across his mouth, desperate to fill his lungs. The butcher tied off the bag and made his way back in front, standing back to admire his handy work. He counted to five and stepped forward, firing another ring shanked nail into Shaw's naked body. The nail plunged into his right thigh, burying itself an inch and a half into his flesh.

He placed the nail-gun on the sink top beside him and pulled a metal Stanley knife from his nylon bag. 'What's the matter, cat got your tongue?' He laughed, waiting a further ten seconds before slicing the plastic that was sucked tight across Shaw's mouth.

Shaw inhaled, long and hard, filling his lungs with required oxygen.

'Breathe,' the butcher said. 'Breathe. I can't have you die on me, just yet.' He placed the blade back in his nylon bag and slammed the open palm of his left hand across Shaw's face, halting his frantic intake.

Shaw's head snapped to the left, blood and saliva dripping from his face. He coughed into the remains of the bag, still attempting to fill his lungs. He knew it was going to be a long night, and if he was to get through it alive, he had to hold his composure and keep his wits about him. Surrendering to the cold and pain was a sure way of ending up in the ground. He opened his eyes and turned back to him, just in time to feel a second nail plunge through his thigh, painting a second line of blood down between his legs.

The butcher looked down his nose at him. 'You're not gonna faint on me are ya?' he said.

Shaw said nothing, taking the given time to breathe and absorb the pain.

'I'm fucking talking to you!' The butcher yelled, smashing the palm of his right hand across Shaw's face, snapping his head to the right.

Shaw locked his eyes on his, spitting blood from his lips.

The butcher gripped his cheeks. 'You better fucking not. Not yet anyway. I haven't even started to cut anything off yet,' he said, exposing his cigarette stained teeth. He pulled the ripped plastic bag down over his head,

216

leaving it wrapped around his neck like a plastic scarf.

*

Slater pulled on a clean pair of jeans and a warm grey hooded sweater, feeling much better to be out of his urine-soaked clothes. His pride stabbed at him, wounded and humiliated by Shaw. But his anger wasn't for Shaw, it was for Michael. He would pay for what he did to Melanie, and he would make sure of it.

'Me. Not Shaw,' he said out loud.

'Did you say something, babe?' his wife said in the bedroom next door.

'Nothing, sweetheart. Just thinking out loud.' He pulled on a pair of trainers and entered the master bedroom, looking at his wife who lay across the double bed in pink stripy pajamas. 'What you doing awake, anyway?' he said. 'I thought you were up early in the morning?'

'No, I told you. I'm on the back shift tomorrow.' She wasn't surprised he'd forgotten. She knew his mind was usually filled with work issues, so it never came as a surprise to hear he'd forgotten something as trivial as his wife's shifts.

'Oh aye, sorry. I could be out late tonight, hun. So don't be waiting up for me, okay? Got a lot of shit to sort out.' Before he could finish what he had to say, his mobile phone rang. He waved at his wife, telling her he was sorry, but he had to go and answered the call. 'What is it?'

The voice was confident and straight to the point. 'There's been two shootings, sir.' Williams was a junior police officer on his team. Young, confident and good at his job.

'What?' Slater said, knowing his failed operation may have been the initial cause. 'Where?' He grabbed his jacket and headed out the front door.

'You won't believe this, boss, but one was in the city centre. The other happened down in Deptford. The Mallinson brothers. Both of them.'

'Dead?'

'Very. You best get yourself to the Voodoo Lounge in town. It's a fucking right mess.'

'I'll be there in ten.'

*

Slater pulled up outside the bar. Police cars filled the street, closing off every entrance and exit. Forensics dressed in their white paper suits and face masks dotted the area looking for potential evidence. Erected lamps flooded the scene outside, filling the gutters and pavement with much needed light.

217

Williams appeared from the front door and approached Slater as he climbed out of his car. 'It's a blood bath, sir. We've got six dead bodies, including Tony Mallinson.'

'Caliber?' Slater asked, already knowing the answer.

'Seven six two.'

'Shit.' Slater sighed at the thought of having to explain why his failed gun operation had turned into a multiple homicide.

'Looks like they've already hit the streets,' Williams said, turning back into the bar with Slater close behind.

What Slater saw shocked him. There were blood and bullet holes everywhere. Pools of it soaked the carpet and wooden flooring, whilst speckles of it spitted the walls and ceiling. 'Jesus Christ… Please tell me we have a witness or CCTV at least.'

'We've got two witnesses and the CCTV's been viewed as we speak.'

'He left two witnesses? Why would someone go through all this and then leave two witnesses?'

'Probably ran out of ammo. The DJ,' Williams checked his notes, 'James Baxter, claims the gunman never reloaded. And once his firearm was empty, he just turned and left. The CCTV will hopefully confirm it.'

'And Billy's been gunned down, as well?'

Williams nodded. 'Him and his driver. They were filled with 9mm rounds. Probably by a drive-by shooter. But as always with things down there, no one saw anything.'

'A Mac-10?'

'It's looking that way.'

Slater rubbed the back of his head and scanned the murder scene, absorbing its brutality. 'Professional hit?'

'Too sloppy. The bad grouping of the shots fired tells us he's not familiar with firing this kind of weapon. A professional at this kind of range would have put almost every round into Tony, and he definitely wouldn't have wasted time firing at the remaining bar staff if he was a pro.'

Slater concurred. He looked out through the large windows and onto the street. 'Why didn't he just fire through the window?' He looked back to Tony's lifeless corpse. 'I mean, he could have killed Tony from the front seat of his car.'

'Exactly,' Williams said. 'Not a pro.'

'What's the DJ have to say?'

Williams rechecked his notes. 'Said he was a large man, six foot plus. Didn't get a good look at his face, due to a mask of some sorts. Thinks he was on his own, but couldn't say for sure, and that he was using a silver 4x4 type vehicle. Possibly a Nissan.

'Probably stolen. Have a check done on stolen trucks in the area just to make sure.' He looked back to the dead bodies. 'What a fucking waste. And on Christmas Eve, too.'

*

Paul Mallinson made his way back to his Mercedes that was parked next to the scrapyard's portakabin. Mud and general muck was sprayed up its sides from the wet drive to the filthy compound. Smashed old cars were stacked four or five high and strategically placed to allow forklifts and personnel room to access them all. He sucked the last from his second cigarette and flicked it towards the reflecting light of one of the many puddles that littered the potted ground. The ground's Rottweiler, Rusty, lay still under the shelter of the portakabin, watching their every move with a sniper like vigilance.

'Where to now?' Levi asked him.

'Drop me off at Kerry's and then the night's yours.'

'Kerry's? I thought she was history?'

'What can I say? I'm a sucker for a big ass.' His phone vibrated in his trouser pocket. 'What is it?' he said, answering the call.

Levi popped the central locking on Paul's Mercedes C Class and walked around to the driver's door. He stopped before climbing in, noticing Paul's distressed face.

'When did this happen?' Paul said, his eyes turning cold and glass like. 'Is this some kinda fucking wind-up?'

Levi could hear a male voice speaking on the line but was unable to make out what was being said.

'You're sorry?' Paul turned his back on Levi. 'What happened?' A few moments later, Paul hung up and rubbed his forehead and eyes. 'Change of plan, we're going to my uncle's bar.' He opened the rear passenger door and climbed inside.

'Everything okay?' Levi asked him.

'No it's not. Not by a fucking long shot.' Paul sat silent during the remainder of his drive to The Voodoo Lounge, his gaze transfixed on the miserable wet city. He had a good idea who was responsible for his uncle's deaths, and he'd make sure him and everyone he knew would pay dearly.

Levi turned left at the traffic lights leading him to the bar but was immediately stopped by a policeman telling him the road was closed. Police vans, cars and numerous forensic tents were all erected on the closed off road.

Mixed emotions filled Paul seeing the police treat his uncle's bar like a crime scene. 'Head to Michael's club.' Paul dialed a handful of contacts from his phone and rallied the kind of men nice people stayed away from.

*

Kimberly chopped the cocaine that was laid out in front of her, sliding her silver credit card through the fine white powder, drawing it into two straight lines. She glanced up at the flat screen CCTV monitors mounted on the wall in Michael's office and snorted one of the lines, using a rolled up ten-pound note.

'Where did you get this gear from?' she said, squeezing her nose and sniffing hard to ingest every last grain. 'This is shit-hot.'

'A mate of mine,' Stewy said, sitting back on the black leather sofa. 'Good stuff, isn't it?' Stewy was a short, chubby man who had held the position of week-night head doorman now for almost a year.

She snorted the second line, feeling her face go numb. 'Oh aye,' she said, pinching the tip of her nose. 'You'll have to hook us up.'

'I'll give him a ring. See if he has any going spare.' Stewy was cut short by a voice in his fitted ear piece. He pushed his finger against it and spoke into the hand piece attached to his shirt. 'What's up?'

Kimberly rubbed what was left of the cocaine on her top gum and looked up at him.

'Roger.' Stewy looked at Kimberly. 'Paul Mallinson's downstairs. And he's brought muscle with him.'

'What kind of muscle?' she said, feeling the high of her cocaine come crashing down.

'Four men.'

Kimberly pulled on the jacket to her two-piece grey trouser suit and adjusted herself in the mirror, making sure there was no white powder around her nostrils. 'What's this prick want?' The pair left the office and made their way into the main room of the strip club, where a group of five men sat chatting to three girls, attempting to negotiate the fixed price of a private performance. Kimberly approached the bar and asked for her usual, before turning to look at the entrance, awaiting Paul's arrival.

*

220

Paul entered and watched Kimberly approach him from the bar, swaying her hips as if parading on a catwalk. Once she was in reach, he gripped her bicep and squeezed. 'Where's your cousin?' he said.

Kimberly objected and looked down at her arm. 'You're hurting me.'

He squeezed her tighter, making sure his point got across. 'I haven't even started. Now where's your fucking cousin?'

'I don't know,' she said. 'I haven't seen him since this morning.'

He scanned the club floor and pushed her towards the bar. 'Office,' he said, 'now.'

Her ankle twisted in her heels and she stumbled forward, but somehow managed to stay upright. She made her way back across the club floor, feeling every eye in the room on her. 'What is it you want with him?' she said.

Paul said nothing.

She opened the office door, glad to be out of sight, and was pushed inside. She crashed against Michael's large oak desk, dropping her glass and bruising her forearm 'Fucking hell, Paul. What's your problem?'

'Where's your cousin?' he asked again, exaggerating the actions of his lips. 'And don't fucking lie to me.'

Kimberly stood up straight and looked back at him and his four large friends, her knees trembling with fear. 'Paul, I haven't seen him. Not since this morning. Maybe I can help.'

The office door suddenly crashed open and Stewy and another doorman rushed in. Simultaneously, two of Paul's hired muscle pulled out handguns, stopping Stewy and his colleague dead in their tracks.

Stewy had never backed down from a fight in his life, but the barrel of a loaded handgun was a league he wasn't willing to play in.

'Fuck off!' Paul said.

Stewy met Kimberly's gaze before slowly closing the door in retreat. He didn't get paid enough to take a bullet for someone, no matter how attractive he thought they were.

Paul closed the small gap between him and Kimberly. 'Okay, Kim, maybe you can help.'

Kimberly returned her eyes back to Paul.

'Who ordered the hit on my uncles?'

Kimberly's eyes widened. 'What?'

Paul sighed. 'You can see I'm growing impatient with this fucking conversation, yet you're still going to make me repeat myself.'

She knew Michael had mentioned it, but never thought he would actually go through with it. Not without mentioning it to her at least. 'I swear I know nothing about any of that.' Her voice wavered.

Paul clenched his fist and punched her in the gut, doubling her over onto her knees. 'Grab her,' he said.

Kimberly held up her hand in retaliation, gasping for air as one of his muscle grabbed her by her suit jacket and pulled her to her feet. 'I'll ring him,' she said, struggling for breath. 'I'll get him to come here.'

'You do that. Ring him,' he said, giving the nod for his hired muscle to release his grip.

She lifted the phone from the receiver and called Michael, not sure if she wanted him to answer or not. The call went through to his answering service. She looked at Paul, her eyes red and teary, and tensed up, dreading his reaction. 'His phone's turned off,' she said.

'What's his home address?'

'Why do you want that?'

Paul slapped her across the face, stinging her left cheek. 'What's his fucking address?'

Kimberly put her hand to her face and turned to the desk. She scribbled the address on a piece of paper and handed it to him.

'I really hope you had nothing to do with it, Kim. I'd hate to see a pretty thing like you get hurt.' He turned and left, leaving one of his minders to close the door behind them.

Kimberly broke down, her tears finally running mascara down her cheeks. She slid down the side of Michael's oak desk until her bottom touched the carpet, her knees tucked up to her chest, her face buried in her hands. She reached up for the landline telephone above her and pulled it down onto her lap. She dialed his number again, and again it was answered by his answering service.

'Where are you, Michael?' she said.

*

Chloe fell forward, exhausted and out of breath. 'Oh my God,' she panted. 'That was amazing.'

Michael pushed her back, lifting her off him, sweeping her long dark hair from his face. 'What time is it?'

222

She looked at the digital clock on the bedside cabinet to her right. 'It's just after eleven. Why? You got to be somewhere?'

He climbed out of her bed and walked naked across her room, picking up his clothes that were scattered around the bedroom floor. After dealing with Melanie earlier, Michael had rushed home and changed, washing himself down and dispensing of his clothes. Which had been a shame. The suit he'd worn had been one of his favourites. 'I've got things that need doing.' He searched through his jacket pockets for his iPhone.

'Why don't you stay the night here, spend Christmas with me?'

'I just told you, Chloe, I'm busy.' One of the main qualities he liked about Melanie, apart from her looks and the sex, was her attitude to when they'd finished. Melanie had never asked him to stay the night, nor had she asked why when he told her to leave. The way a trophy girlfriend should be. He pulled out his phone and turned it on.

'I was thinking about getting one of my friends to join us next time. You'll love her, she's a real kitten.'

Michael ignored her and listened to a voicemail left by Kimberly.

'What's up, babe?' she said, puffing the pillows up behind her back.

'What?' he said, turning to look at her. 'Nothing. Shit to do with the club.' He started picking up his clothes and pulled on his jeans and trainers.

'Take it you're going then?'

'I just fucking told you, I'm busy!' He pulled on his T-shirt and left, closing the door behind him.

*

Michael soon arrived at the club and made his way up to his office. 'What happened?' he asked Kimberly, who sat in his chair drinking a straight vodka.

'He wanted to know where you were and if you had anything to do with his uncles being fucking killed. Christ, Michael. A little warning would have been nice.'

He could see she was as high as a kite. 'And what did you tell him?'

'What could I tell him? That you'd paid someone to massacre his two favourite uncles?'

223

'Alright, Kim, calm down.' He looked at the cocaine residue on his desk. 'I didn't think he'd step up this quick,' he said. 'Quinn was supposed to sort him out.'

'Well you were wrong, weren't you? You're just gonna have to speak with whoever popped Billy and Tony and have them do him, as well.'

'I'll sort it,' he said. He poured himself a drink.

'And I'm fine, by the way,' she said in an unappreciated tone.

Michael rolled his eyes and turned back to face her. 'Think of the money, Kim, and the satisfaction in knowing Shaw would've had his comeuppance.'

'Shaw's comeuppance? That's another fucking joke. None of it has gone the way I wanted.' Her bottom lip started to quiver.

'I know,' he said, 'but things haven't exactly gone the way I wanted either.' Michael placed his hand on Kimberly's knee. 'Are you okay?' He could see she wasn't.

She nodded.

'Do you want me to get Stewy to take you home?'

She shook her head. 'No, the guy's a fucking nugget. I'll be fine, don't worry.'

'Okay,' he said, finishing his drink. 'I'll see you in the morning then? And don't worry about Paul Mallinson, I'll deal with him.'

She finished the remainder of her drink, ashamed of what she was going to tell him next. 'There's something else,' she said, halting Michael at the door.

'What?'

She paused. 'I gave him your address.'

'You did what?' He closed the door and turned back into the office. 'Why?'

'He asked for it.'

'He asked for it. So you just gave him it?'

'What else could I do, Michael? The guy had four guys with him, who by the way had fucking guns. I couldn't exactly say I didn't know now, could I?'

Michael cursed, realizing the stolen drugs were stashed in his flat. 'Right. Okay. It's not a problem. So what if he knows, I'll not be going back there tonight anyway.' He opened the office door, said his goodbyes and left. Once he was sat comfortably in his GT-R, Michael pulled out his iPhone.

'What's up?' Bomber answered.

'I need another favour.'

'When for?'

'Now.'

'Now? Are you out of your mind? It'll have to wait until after the party.'

'It can't. It needs doing now.'

'I'm sorry, Michael, but it's gonna have to wait. I can't risk it this close to the hour.'

'Fine, as soon as the party's finished, I need it sorting.'

Michael hung up after thanking him for his time and made another call.

'Hello,' Sherman said.

'Clean your shit up and pack it away.'

'What do you want me to do with Will?'

'Do whatever you want. Just make sure he stays quiet.'

Michael hung up and gunned the engine.

Thirty-Two

'Da ya think I'm sexy'

The butcher slapped him across the face. 'Wake up!'

The sting from the slap vanished as quickly as it was felt, drowned out by excruciating pain that burned through his legs and shoulders.

He slapped him again. 'Wake up!'

Shaw's head rocked with the momentum of the blow, but still didn't rise.

The butcher picked up the nail-gun and gripped Shaw's urine-soaked hair. 'Open those fucking eyes,' he growled through gritted teeth, aiming the nail-gun at his genitals.

Shaw dug deep, willing himself to obey the command. He saw the nail-gun pointing towards his manhood. 'What do you want from me?' he said through chattering teeth, drool dribbling from his bleeding lips, his voice slurred and weak.

'I want you to open your fucking eyes.' He released his grip on Shaw's hair, allowing his head to drop forward, and turned back to his nylon bag.

Shaw kept his eyes open, watching the butcher as he filtered through the bag, the anticipation of what he was going to pull out was almost as bad as the pain he'd already endured.

'I almost forgot,' the butcher said with a smile. He pulled a digital camcorder from his nylon bag and positioned it on the sinks beside him. 'Don't want to miss your last moments now, do we?' He looked at the digital screen and zoomed out to acquire the whole picture. 'Do ya have any last words?' he said.

Shaw remained silent, feeling almost defeated; almost.

The butcher's phone rang, filling the room with Rod Stewart's familiar song, *Da ya think I'm sexy?* 'Hello,' he said, placing the nail-gun on the sink top, next to the camcorder.

Shaw strained his ears, trying to listen to the voice on the other end.

'Is he still alive?' Paul Mallinson said.

'Just about. Why, do you want me to stop?'

'Just until I get there. I have a few things I want to ask him.'

'Okay.' The butcher hung up and looked back at Shaw,

slipping his phone back in his trouser pocket. 'Looks like it's your lucky day. Seems you'll be getting a little extra time with your uncle Mark 'ere.' He reached into the nylon bag and pulled out a cheap red lighter and a packet of cigarettes.

Shaw watched him lean back against the stained tiled wall and slip a cigarette between his lips. He needed to do something, and it needed to happen now. If it didn't, he was sure he wouldn't get to see the light of day again.

'What could I say that would change your mind?'

The butcher laughed, releasing smoke from his crooked mouth. 'What, apart from 'ere, Mark, here's a million quid? Fuck all.'

'What if I told you I could get you that kind of money?'

'Then I'd say shut the fuck up, I'm not letting you go. Do you think I'm some kind of fucking amateur or something? I've been chopping cunts like you up for years.'

In a weird kind of way Shaw was impressed. It took a certain kind of individual to inflict copious amounts of pain on another human being, and this man had shown no sign of regret or remorse. He actually seemed to enjoy it.

'Then can I at least have one of those cigarettes?'

The butcher stepped forward with a sigh and placed a cigarette between Shaw's bloodied lips, returning back to his position against the wall.

'I'll need a light,' Shaw said, trying not to drop the cigarette.

The butcher chuckled, amused with himself. He leaned in close and flicked the flame on his lighter. Shaw felt the heat from the flame and allowed the cigarette to fall from his mouth, letting it drop onto his groin. He cursed and looked down at it, now wet with blood and urine.

The butcher's eyes followed Shaw's. 'I'm not giving you another one,' he said.

Shaw lunged forward, sinking his teeth into the hard bridge of the butcher's nose. He clamped firm, filling his mouth with warm, irony liquid. The butcher screamed in pain and gripped hold of Shaw's head. But Shaw held tight, refusing to let go, until finally, his teeth met in the middle. The butcher fell back to the floor, screaming in agony, his face cupped in his hands, blood seeping between his fingers.

Shaw didn't wait to see how he took it. He spat out the mouthful of blood and the remainder of the butcher's nose and took a firm hold of his own left thumb. He filled his lungs and braced. After first dislocating his thumb in Afghanistan, Shaw had found the joint weaker and prone to dislocation, having dislocated it several times after his recovery. An audible snap sounded, followed immediately by a breath snatching pain that raged through his left hand. He looked up at the ceiling and focused on the flickering bulb, knowing from experience that dislocating it was the easy part, relocating it was where the true discomfort lay.

The butcher clambered onto his hands and knees, blood oozing from the fresh new hole in his face.

Shaw slipped the restraints from his left wrist, fighting back the throbbing pain in his limbs, and reached for the nail-gun that sat on the sink to his right.

'You fucking cunt!' the butcher spat, blood spraying from his lips with every word. He placed his right hand on Shaw's knee for support. 'You're a fucking dead man!'

A loud crack thundered around the room as the ring shanked nail smashed through the butcher's cheek bone, burying itself two inches into his skull. The butcher's left hand flashed up to his face, just in time to feel another nail punch into him, nailing his hand to his cheek. He fell back to the filthy, wet tiles and reeled in agony.

Shaw dropped the nail-gun and reached over to the nylon bag sitting on the sink. He pulled it and the camcorder to the floor and scattered its contents, looking for anything that would cut the cable ties that bound his ankles. Amongst the scattered tools was a pair of pliers, a Stanley knife, and a hammer and chisel. He glanced at the butcher who continued to squirm on the floor, attempting to free his hand from his face. He grabbed the pliers and snipped through the two remaining cable ties at his ankles. His heart raced, thumping so hard it deafened him. He stood naked, bent with cold, cramp and pain, looking down at the six foot butcher lying at his feet. He bent down and reached for the nail-gun, feeling the butcher's hand grab his ankle. Shaw fired another two nails into his skull, nailing his right hand to his forehead, killing him. The intensity of the dripping tap and buzzing light fixture overhead became more obtrusive, as if the man's death had somehow increased their volume.

He was cold, cramped, and hurting. He dropped the nail-gun and crouched down beside the butcher, groaning in pain from the nails still embedded in his shoulders and thigh. He undone the laces on the butcher's steel capped toed boots and pulled them off one at a time, measuring them against the soul of his foot. The boots were heavy with a thick tread, and a size or two too big. But they would have to do. He undid the butcher's belt and slid off his wet trousers, immediately pulling them up over his own thighs, moving his right leg as little as possible. He climbed back to his feet and pulled the trousers high above his waist, thanking God for the belt, as the butcher appeared to have had a few extra inches around the waist then he did. He slipped on the heavy footwear and fastened them as tight as he could, feeling the cold, hard insoles on his bare feet. He dug his hands in his trouser pockets and pulled out its contents: some loose change, a mobile phone and a car key. His heart then sank, realising his silver watch had gone, the only thing he had left from his previous life. He crouched down and removed the butcher's watch, knowing he didn't possess the time to reminisce about its loss. He read the time, 23:25, and picked up the Stanley knife, slicing a small cut in the thigh of the right trouser leg, allowing the nails room to protrude. He then pocketed the Stanley knife and pliers.

He unlatched the main door, composed himself, and opened it a fraction, feeling the cold night air on his wet skin. The immediate area, from what he could make out, was dark and wet. Snow fluttered from the sky in large flakes, showing signs of a white carpet forming on the limited dry surfaces in the yard. The heavy aroma of engine oil and fuel filled the air. Moonlight reflected off the shiny wet gravel, aiding him in identifying the crushed cars that were stacked on top of one another. A large collection of tyres sat off to the right, filled with rain water and growing weeds. He listened for any sign of movement or voices, any indication of flowing traffic, anything at all. Nothing. The place was silent.

He opened the door fully and limped outside, scanning the open space for the butcher's vehicle. Cars stacked as high as four and five surrounded him, bunched up to fill as much of the space as possible. The majority of their windows smashed, their doors and wheels removed. A collection of car bonnets leaned between the wall of the toilet block and two large rusting drums containing rusty coloured water. His body shivered, and his shoulders and thigh throbbed, but he knew Paul Mallinson was due back at any minute, so his wounds would have to wait. He crouched low, using the stacked cars as cover, and hobbled his way through the yard, constantly watching where his next step landed, and always landing heel first before rolling through to his toes, keeping his steps as quiet as possible.

He stopped ten metres into his journey, his breath frozen, his muscles ridged. Movement was heard: the scarping of gravel, the sniffing of a nose, the panting of an open mouth.

'Shit.'

The Rottweiler's bark erupted, filling the silence of the scrapyard with the angry sound of a big dog. Shaw turned and bolted back to the toilet block, slipping in the wet gravel as he fought to keep his footing. His heart thumped, pumping his weak, injured legs, one in front of the other. He could hear the dog's breath panting as its paws ripped up the gravel. He fell onto his hands and knees, bursting through the toilet door. He turned and kicked it closed as the 130lbs Rottweiler smashed into it, almost breaking the strength in his legs, its face and teeth snapping through the gap. He held the door with his right foot and stamped down with his left, kicking the canine repeatedly in the face.

The Rottweiler's foaming jaws snapped through the gap, its jowls held back by the door and doorframe exposing its forty-two teeth.

He panted and panicked, struggling to push the Rottweiler back. But he knew it was useless. The strength in his injured leg wasn't enough to hold the door, and the dog would be on top of him in no time. He looked around him and stretched back through the filthy water. The several nails that were still embedded in his flesh burned into his muscles with every stressed movement. The fingertips of his injured hand brushed the nail-gun's yellow casing, moving it a fraction. Millimeter by millimeter it slid into his reach until, finally, he gripped it. Without a second thought, Shaw emptied six nails into the dog's thick forehead and face. The Rottweiler yelped and pulled back from the door, disappearing from view. Shaw kicked it closed and took a moment on his back, absorbing the pain in his hand and body.

He dug deep and climbed back to his feet, his breathing sharp and fast, knowing his time was running out. He pressed up against the toilet door, nail-gun in hand, and opened it, bracing himself in case the Rottweiler hadn't had enough. Experience had taught him large dogs, similar to the one outside, could take ridiculous amounts of damage and still keep going.

He peered through the gap and listened. The sound of heavy panting, slow and steady, could be heard coming from the direction of the tyres. He opened the door fully. Several metres from him, in an oily puddle, the Rottweiler lay on its side, its face a mess of blood and nails, snow collecting on its fur. Even though he was relieved the imminent danger had passed, he still couldn't help but feel a little sympathy towards the animal. He stepped out passed it and crept through the scrapyard, the cold night air attacking his wet skin, until the scrapyard opened up, revealing a dirty green Portakabin and a rusty white Transit van. He dropped the nail-gun and hobbled with haste towards the vehicle, pulling out the butcher's car key. The single key slid into the driver's door and turned, unlocking it. The rotten cab of the van stank of cigarette smoke and stale farts. The dashboard was littered with old Daily Sport newspapers and the passenger footwell was filled with empty Macdonald wrappers. He climbed up behind the steering wheel and slammed the door shut. He slid the key into the ignition. Relief replaced Shaw's pain as the old diesel engine spluttered to life, shaking the cab. He stretched across with his right hand and selected first gear. In front of him was the dirty green portakabin, a stacked collection of alloy wheels, and two large metal gates, locked with a heavy-duty padlock. He sighed with defeat. The padlock was enormous, and the gates were thick and heavy.

He climbed out, leaving the engine running, and inspected the padlock and gate. There was no way he was crashing through those. He looked around him. The surrounding walls were at least twelve feet high and covered in more barbed wire than Guantanamo Bay. He limped back to the toilet block, paying caution to the Rottweiler that still whimpered in the oily puddle, and entered. Once inside, he pulled off the butcher's leather apron and returned to the van. He climbed back up into the cab and selected reverse and maneuvered it back through the stacked cars until he collided with the brickwork of the twelve-foot wall.

In the distance Shaw heard the faint sound of wailing sirens, decreasing in volume as they travelled away from him. He dropped down off the driver's seat, grunting in pain from the nails in his thigh, and scaled the front of the van, slipping and struggling with the pain in his left hand and limbs. He remained on his left knee, left elbow and right hand as he pulled himself across the slippery, wet roof.

The van had lifted him eight feet from the ground, leaving another three to four feet of wall. The barbed wire was fastened to V-shaped brackets in rows of three and topped with an extended coil running the walls length, raising the height of the obstacle by a further eighteen inches. Using the pliers and the leather apron for protection against the razor-sharp barbs, Shaw snipped at the coil, cutting away a portion big enough for him to fit through. He laid the butcher's leather apron across V-shaped rows of barbed wire and peered over the wall. Open ground with thigh high grass and mounds of unearthed soil was what welcomed him on the other side. To Shaw's relief, approximately a mile in the distance, he could make out a large source of light and the occasional set of headlights.

With the apron providing partial protection against the barbs, Shaw jumped up and reached forward, leaning all his weight on his left forearm on the top of the brickwork, and gripped the barbed wire beneath the apron with his right hand. He painfully and carefully pulled himself up and forward. He brought his left foot up to the wall, negotiating the barbed wire around him, and attempted to maneuver himself, allowing him to drop down onto his feet on the opposite side. Suddenly, his right hand slipped off the wet leather, forcing him to reach out with his left. Pain speared up through his left hand and into his arm. His body fell forward, weakened with hurt. His right foot snagged on the barbed wire and pulled it loose from its brackets as he fell the twelve feet to the ground, landing in a heap at the base of the wall.

He lay face down in the dirt, inhaling gulps of air, attempting to absorb the punishment his body was being put through. He stole a moment, a moment he knew he couldn't afford, and rolled onto his back. He knew the swelling in his dislocated thumb would soon become unbearable, and that if he didn't relocate it soon, his hand would be useless. He took several more deeps breaths, peering up at the snow-filled night sky, and cradled his left hand in his right. He focused on the brightest star he could find. He took one more deep breath… and relocated it.

Thirty-Three

'Perfect'

The door to Michael's flat crashed open, taking the dark wooden door frame along with it.

'So, this is his gaff.' Paul was impressed. It was a top floor apartment in a highly sort after block of flats, overlooking the harbour. All his walls were magnolia except for a large feature wall that had a dark wooden finish. Mounted on it was a large flat screen TV. The carpet was chocolate brown and the two large leather sofas were cream.

They'd managed to bypass the security guard downstairs by acquiring an invite from a colleague who, coincidently, also lived in the building. Paul and his crew of four had found Michael's apartment and knocked. After gaining no reply, Levi had kicked it in. A neighbour had popped her head out hearing the commotion, only to be told to get back inside.

The apartment was silent except for the sound of a ticking clock mounted on the living room wall.

'Search the place,' Paul said, making his way over to the balcony doors.

'Aye, nay-bother, boss,' said one of his crew. He wiped his feet on the door mat and entered. 'What is it we're supposed to be looking for again?' he said, not quite sure if they'd been told already.

Paul looked back over his shoulder. 'I don't know. Anything. Look for a large stash of drugs or something,' he said, shaking his head in disbelief. He focused his eyes past his reflection in the glass and looked outside. He then opened the door and see the view for what it was. He stepped out on to the dark wood decking, feeling the cold winter night's chill on his cheeks, and looked down at the lights of the harbour, all positioned in neat rows, illuminating the individual docked boats. The view was impressive. The mouth of the River Wear opening up into the North Sea alone was worth paying for, let alone the breathtaking view of Seaburn lights and the city centre. He turned his back on the view and closed the door behind him, blocking out the sound of seagulls. He lit a cigarette and walked over to a large piece of artwork hanging on the wall.

'Paul take a look at this,' Levi said.

233

'What is it?' Paul looked at him, seeing the retro suitcase in his hand.

Levi threw it on one of Michael's sofas and popped its clasps. 'Maloney's death warrant.' Inside were two transparent bags stuffed tight with heroin, a couple of bags of blue and pink pills, and an A4 brown paper envelope.

'Is that what I think it is?'

'It's Jammin's suitcase.'

Paul ground his teeth. 'Let's go and pay the princess a visit.'

Levi closed the suitcase containing Nolan's stolen drugs and followed Paul out the front door.

*

Kimberly could feel the un-ease in her chest, the apprehension in her gut. The night had been an emotional one, especially with Paul's visit and the amount of cocaine she'd put up her nose. She turned off the engine and climbed out, grabbing her handbag. The slam of her car door stabbed at the unnerving silence of the partially lit subterranean car park. She crossed the short distance to the lift, the heels of her suede shoes equally penetrating in the silence. She pressed the call button and waited, glancing around her as if checking the shadows for an unseen presence. She checked her watch, 23:15, and rummaged through her handbag, acquiring her phone. The lift doors slid open to an empty lift. She entered and selected her desired floor. The phones display lit up as she fingered through the phonebook, searching for a number that was necessary to release the held tension in her body. She pressed the call button and smiled. It didn't bother her that Spence maybe asleep at this time of night, or that he may have company of his own. She needed seeing too, and he was the man she wanted. The lift juddered as it started its ascent to the fourth floor.

'Hello?' Spence said.

'Spence I'm all alone tonight,' Kimberly said, checking herself out in the lift's mirrors.

'Kimberly? Christ it's almost midnight.'

'So?'

'So it's Christmas Eve. I help my sister put the gifts out on Christmas Eve.'

'You saying you don't want me?'

'That's not what I said. It's getting late, is all.'

'Are you going to come round and fuck me or do I need to

ring someone else?' She threaded a strand of hair behind her ear. 'I'll let you snort some snow off my tits.'

Spence paused. 'Give me an hour.'

'You have until midnight.' The lift doors opened, and Kimberly hung up, exiting the lift. She entered her flat and placed her car keys and handbag on the cabinet. The peaceful sound of silence welcomed her, not Will and his annoying music, not Will and his annoying voice, and not Will and his childish company. Just silence. She pulled off her suede heels and prepared another couple of lines, chopping the coke on her coffee table with one of her credit cards, snorting one the instant they were ready.

Less than thirty-five minutes later, Kimberly was showered, groomed and moisturised with her make up on and hair done. She walked naked from the bathroom to her master bedroom and dressed in her new lacy red lingerie set, pulling the thong up over the straps of her garter belt. She then sat down on her double bed and pulled on a pair of nude stockings with a thick red splurge and seam running down the back. Finally, she pulled on a pair of red six inch stiletto heels, and stood to admire herself in her six foot mirror.

'Perfect,' she said, complimenting her reflection. As if on cue, the intercom in the passage buzzed, alerting her of someone down at the front door. She finished adjusting her stockings and made her way through to the intercom's handset mounted on the wall. 'Come on up,' she said. She pressed the button allowing them entry and turned her attention to another mirror mounted on the wall beside the intercom, carrying out any unneeded adjustments to her appearance. She estimated it would take Spence around two to three minutes to get to her flat, depending on where the lift was waiting, giving her plenty of time to do one more line of cocaine. She chopped at the remaining white powder, fining it down and spreading it into a nice even line before stuffing a rolled ten pound note up her nose, and snorting it away. She sat back on her sofa, pinching and sniffing her nose, making sure she got every last grain. She could feel herself tingling down between her thighs, the arousal of the drug turning her nipples hard through excitement.

The knock on her front door snatched her from her moment. She sat up straight and pulled her hands from between her thighs. She readjusted her lacy bra and straightened her thong and garter belt and approached the door. She rested her left hand against the doorframe and inflated her chest, increasing the prominence of her breasts. She unlatched the front door and placed her right hand on her hip, tilting her hips to the right.

'You've just made it,' she said. 'I was just about to give someone else a call.'

'Lucky me then, eh,' Paul Mallinson said, pushing the door open fully.

'Paul!' She stepped back with surprise. 'What are you doing here?'

Paul looked her up and down and entered, followed by two hired muscle. 'Expecting someone else, Kim?' he said, not hiding the unpleasant tone in his voice.

Kimberly took another step back. 'I've told you already. I don't know where Michael is.'

'I know you did, Kim. I know you did. But because I actually like you, I'm gonna give you another chance. And from looking at you right now, it would be such a fucking waste if you lied to me again.'

Kimberly's bottom lip quivered. 'My answer's still the same. I don't know. I haven't heard from him,' she lied, sure she'd come to no harm. She'd always known Paul had had a soft spot for her and seeing her dressed like this was a sure guarantee she'd be safe. She closed the gap between them and took the collar of his suit jacket with her forefinger and thumb, her bright red nail varnish glistening under the lights.

Paul remained silent, staring at her with cold, unnerving eyes, her pleasant scent filling his nostrils.

'Look, Paul, why don't you send your two heavies home and we can open a lovely bottle of wine.' She smiled.

His gaze remained steely and lifeless. 'Not this time, Kim.' He turned and walked away from her, back into the corridor.

'What?'

The man on her right snatched out and gripped her arm, his fingers biting into her flesh.

'Paul, please,' she said, her voice high and pitched. 'Let's talk about this. I'm sure we can sort something.'

The same man that gripped her arm threw a devastating punch to her midriff, doubling her over. She dropped to her knees, stunned, the wind knocked from her. He pushed down on the back of her head and forced her forehead to the carpet, whilst the second man grabbed her wrists and pulled them behind her back, binding them with a thick white cable tie. Within seconds, Kimberly found herself gagged, bound, and on the shoulder of one of the men, heading towards the lift.

She felt the cold, damp air on her buttocks and thighs as the man that carried her stepped out into the underground car park. 'Please. Put me down,' she cried, her voice muffled by the gag tied around her mouth.

'Throw her in here,' a fourth man said waiting in the car park.

Kimberly lifted her head as best she could to see where he was suggesting, only to see Levi holding up the boot of a dirty red Astra saloon.

Pain fired up through her hip as she landed on the sharp corner of an object in the boot, before the boot slammed down above her, swallowing her in darkness.

*

After what felt like an aeon of engine lubricant odour, cold air biting at her skin, and the sound of the engine and ground beneath her, the vehicle came to a stop, skidding along a gravelly road. The boot opened, letting in the cold winter air and falling snow. The same two men reached in and grabbed her.

'Please,' she mumbled. 'I don't know anything.'

The wet mud splashed up her bare skin, seeping into her expensive thong and stockings. She looked around, shivering with cold, trembling with fear, trying to gather an idea of where she was. Thick dark trees, illuminated only by the Astra's headlights, surrounded her, dense shadows shifting throughout. The ground beneath her appeared to be a churned-up track, thick with cold waterlogged mud and long strands of grass.

The same man pulled the gag from her mouth and gripped her by her arm, pulling her to her feet. 'Get up,' he said, pushing her towards the edge of the forest.

'Please. Please. Don't do this.' She stumbled, finding it difficult to walk on the uneven ground in her stiletto heels. 'What are you going to do to me?' she said, her voice quavering with fear.

'That'll do,' Paul said behind her. 'Turn her around. I want to see her pretty face.'

Kimberly stopped and turned, her slender figure bathed in the headlights, the ground beneath her boggy and waterlogged. 'Please,

Paul. I didn't have anything to do with your uncles,' she sobbed, tears streaming down her mud spitted face.

Paul kept his stance, standing proud and merciless. 'It was Michael wasn't it?'

'Yes,' she said, sobbing every word.

Paul could see her shivering, enjoying the helpless fear in her eyes. 'He was responsible for Jammin, too, wasn't he?'

Kimberly nodded. 'He sent Shaw,' she whimpered. 'But that was him. Jammin had nothing to do with me.'

Her constant lies fueled his rage. 'I want to know who pulled the triggers on my uncles,' he said.

'I don't know, Paul, I swear to you. You'd have to ask Michael that.'

'Oh, I intend to.' He paused, watching the emotion running through her face. 'Fucking kill her,' he said with a wave of his hand.

'What? No, Paul please, I have more to tell you.'

He held up his hand. 'Go on then.' He looked at his watch. 'You have thirty seconds.'

Kimberly didn't care. All that mattered right now was her survival. 'Michael's got a drug deal going down tonight.'

Paul's eyes widened. 'Does he now? And where's this drug deal taking place?'

Kimberly told him everything, explaining the whole plan in as much detail as she could remember. Who he was doing the deal with, and how he was going to conduct it.

'Is that everything?'

Kimberly nodded, shivering violently.

'Are you sure?'

She nodded again. 'I'm sure.'

Paul looked at his hired muscle and nodded. The shot rang loud through the empty wood, echoing off the trees that surrounded them. The muzzle flashed, sending the 9mm round through her chest, throwing her back to the boggy ground beneath her. She splashed down hard, her wrists still bound behind her back. The overpowering taste of blood was strong and thick as she gazed up at the snow falling from the sky, seeing stars burning brighter than she'd ever seen. Then a figure was stood above her, blocking her view. She didn't even hear the second shot. The round smashed through her face, blowing her brains out the back of her head, mixing them with the boggy mud beneath.

Thirty-Four

'I was my world was as simple'

Crossing the open ground had proven harder than Shaw had originally thought. He'd estimated it to be around a mile to the lights when, in actuality, it had been more like two to three. Unseen in the darkness, hidden beneath the waist high grass, had been dead-ground. That adding to the lights being on higher ground than his own location had all been benefactors in his misjudgment of the distance. But it wasn't the distance that had been tough, it had been the combination of his injuries, clothing and the ground itself. Rough and muddy one minute, swamped and water logged the next. It had taken him almost forty minutes to cross the open ground to a chain-linked fence that surrounded a well-lit compound. The chain-link fence stood ten feet high and was topped with rows of angled barbed wire. Inside the compound, Shaw could see a dozen un-hitched trailers parked beside each other, their rear doors held open, displaying their emptiness. Across the compound were several red lorries parked alongside each other with stacked pallets and oil drums behind them. To their right, directly to Shaw's front, was the main building of the compound, a two storey grey build with dark glassed windows and a gradual slopping roof. He scanned the compound from the comfort of the shadows, looking for any tell-tale sign of a security presence: notices informing of dog patrols, footprints in the snow, mounted CCTV cameras, or just a basic sign of the security contract holder. Nothing. Not even a sign informing that trespassers would be prosecuted. He kept to the shadows and followed the fence along, looking for a position closer to the lorries where he could remain hidden from view, allowing him to cut through the fence. Finding an ideal spot under an un-lit spotlight, Shaw sat down, taking care with his right thigh, and pulled out the pliers he'd taken from the butcher. He swallowed the pain in his left hand and squeezed, managing to cut enough links to allow him to pull it open, giving him enough room to slip under. Once inside, he stopped and listened, scanning the compound for any sign of activity. The throbbing pain in his leg and shoulders, a constant reminder that the nails were still imbedded in him. Happy his presence had gone undetected, Shaw hobbled with haste to the rear of the lorries, choosing the second one in from the left, as it had both the best cover

239

and best view of the main building. He climbed up the lorry's passenger door and tried the handle, finding it locked. He cursed and dropped down, again taking a moment to listen for movement before making his way round to the next. This time the lorry's passenger door creaked opened. He slipped in and closed the door behind him. He lay motionless in the passenger footwell, praying the brief illumination of the interior light had gone unnoticed.

After several minutes and no sign of activity, Shaw climbed up onto the passenger seat and glanced over his injuries. His broken nose would require hospital attention, so dealing with that at this time was futile. The two nails in his right shoulder, the nail in his left shoulder, and the two nails in his right thigh would have to come out now. The first to have been fired into him had been in his shoulder now for more than four hours and was beginning to show signs of infection. He opened the cab's glove compartment, searching for anything that could be of use. Inside were numerous sheets of old paperwork and a half-eaten packet of extra strong mints. He stuffed a mint into his mouth and looked back into the sleeping cab behind him. On the plastic mattress lay a pair of grimy red coveralls, much like the ones he would have worn to work. But what Shaw was most pleased to see was a green first aid box fixed to the wall of the cab. He reached through and grabbed it, deciding to keep to the passenger seat so he could maintain good eyes on the compound and anyone approaching from the building. He opened the plastic box and looked inside, using the ambient light from the flood lights outside. It was a typical first aid kit, the minimum required for its purpose: adhesive dressings, sterile eye pads, triangular bandages, safety pins, sterile dressings of various sizes, and alcohol free cleansing wipes. He turned his torso to the light and ripped open one of the cleansing wipes with his teeth. The flesh surrounding the two nails in his right shoulder was swollen and tender, forcing him to grit his teeth as he cleaned the wound. Once he was happy he'd removed as much of the filth and clotted blood as possible, he reached for the pliers. He took a deep breath, held it, and gripped the head of the first ring shanked nail. His fist clenched from the pain, increasing the nails resistance. Once it was out, Shaw threw the bloodied nail into the footwell and gave himself a second or two to catch his breath, before going to work on the second.

It wasn't long before he had all five of the nails out and patched up. His wounds would still require looking at properly, along with a tetanus jab and some antibiotics, but they'd do for now. He emptied what was left of the first aid kit onto the driver's seat and reached back for the coveralls. He removed his boots and pulled off the wet trousers, dropping them in the driver's footwell. The coveralls were clearly designed for someone with a much bigger frame than his. The legs were too long, and the chest was enormous. He rolled up the trousers and fastened the pop studs, just grateful for the dry clothing. He pulled his boots back on and fastened them as tight as he could get them.

It was then he saw the security guard walking across the compound, his hi-visibility coat reflecting the light from the flood lamps. Shaw cursed and dropped low below the dashboard. He filled the pockets of the coveralls with the remaining medical supplies and stretched up to disable the interior light, preventing it from illuminating when he opened the passenger door. He climbed down onto the snow-covered gravel, closed the passenger door too, and crouched low beneath the lorry's cab. The beam from the guard's torch swayed to and fro around the trailers. Shaw glanced back to the chain-link fence and identified the hole he'd created earlier. He turned back to the guard, his beam of light still in and around the trailers, showing no enthusiastic sign of getting around the compound.

Shaw ran with a limp back to the fence, keeping his footing soft where possible. He could feel the hotspots on his feet and ankles turning into blisters. He crawled through the hole and gave the guard one last look. His torch swung idly from side to side amongst the trailers. Not a care in the world.

'I wish my world was as simple,' he said.

*

He glanced at his watch. The time was approaching 00:26. He had to think of something. Calculate a plan. He didn't know where Michael lived, but he did know where Kimberly lived.

To his right, on the other side of what appeared to be a newly built housing estate, Shaw could vaguely hear waves from the North Sea crashing against the Eastern coast, telling him he was heading north. Adding that information to a road sign he'd seen two miles back for Teesside, confirmed he was heading back into Sunderland.

Up a head, parked up in a bus stop, was a white taxi capable of carrying seven passengers safely. Its driver stood on the roadside, leaning in through the open side door.

241

'Any chance you could drop me off in the town?' Shaw said, approaching the driver.

The silver haired taxi driver turned to face him, looking a little taken back by Shaw's appearance. 'No, mate,' he said outright, looking him up and down. 'I'm finished for the night.'

Shaw was sore, tired, cold and hungry. Plus, he stank of dehydrated, stale urine. 'Right,' he said, sounding less than surprised with his answer. 'Well could you tell me which way it is into Sunderland?'

The driver stepped back from his taxi and pointed down the road. 'Keep on this road for about another half hour. It'll take you—'

Before the driver could finish his sentence, Shaw grabbed him from behind, throwing his right arm around him with the crook of his elbow positioned over the midline of the driver's neck. He pinched his arm together, using his free hand to clamp his hold in place and compress the carotid artery and jugular veins either side of driver's throat. The driver's arms and legs punched and kicked the air as he failed to fight off Shaw's sleeper hold. Within seconds, the driver felt the symptoms of a cerebral ischemia, causing his flailing arms to fall limp and unconsciousness to soon follow. He picked him up and hauled him into the back of the taxi, sliding the door closed behind them. He searched through his pockets, finding the taxi's car keys, a mobile phone and his cigarettes. He pulled off his black coat, his grubby white trainers, and his grey socks, stuffing one of them into his mouth. He then attacked the rear seat belts with the Stanley knife he'd taken from the butcher, cutting them free and tying them around the driver's wrist and ankles, using the hogtie method, making sure his hands were bound behind his back and coupled to the knot around his ankles.

A car passed by the taxi, its headlights illuminating the interior. Shaw cursed. He froze solid, half in the coat, half out, knowing sudden movements caught the eye more than stationary objects. The car drove on by. He climbed out and zipped the coat up. The road was empty and quiet. Only the sound of the crashing waves could be heard. He slammed the door shut and pulled up his collars, shielding him from the wet night's chill. He walked around to the driver's door and sized one of the trainers against the soul of his boot, estimating their fit. He stuffed them down the front of his coat and jumped in the driver's seat. Within ten minutes of meeting the taxi driver, Shaw had the heaters turned on full and was heading towards the City Centre.

Several minutes into the journey, he peered over his left shoulder, through the glass that separated him from the rear cab, and checked the driver was still bound. The silver haired male squirmed on the cab floor, moaning and slavering into the sock stuffed into his mouth. There hadn't been as much material as Shaw would have liked, but the seat belts appeared to be holding. He drove past the bus station, seeing a long row of taxis in a taxi rank. Not wanting to risk getting noticed in a taxi that didn't belong to him, Shaw made a quick detour and turned at the next available junction.

Chatter on the taxi's two-way radio erupted with a female voice asking for Kev. Shaw reached forward and flicked it off. He needed to dump it, and quick. Then Shaw saw what he was looking for, the twelve storey block of flats overlooking the River Wear. He found a side street and pulled in, looking for somewhere to dump it. He stopped the taxi outside a boarded up pub on a decline heading down towards the river. He gave the area one last check and jumped out, throwing the taxi's keys onto the roof of the abandoned pub. He wasn't stupid, he knew it wouldn't take the station long to locate the vehicle, not with the GPS's that were fitted to most modern taxis.

Once he'd turned a few corners and put a little distance between himself and the taxi, Shaw hobbled into the shadow of a dark side street and pulled out his trainers. He rested back against a skip and pulled off one of his boots, feeling the relief on his blistered heel. The trainer felt like wrapped silk around his foot compared to the hard leather of the boot. He pulled off the second and replaced it with the remaining trainer, throwing the boots into the skip.

With the flats now in view, Shaw sat on a low built wall opposite and dialed 999 from the mobile phone he'd taken from the butcher. He knew the pedestrian's communal door to the building would be magnetically locked and manned by a concierge security officer, so gaining unchallenged access would prove difficult. A female operator answered and asked all the questions Shaw expected: nature and address of the emergency, telephone number of the phone being used. He explained that the phone he was using wasn't his and that a young woman he'd met during the night had overdosed on cocaine and stopped breathing. He gave a random flat number and name of the building before hanging up. Less than five minutes later an ambulance screamed into view, blue lights flashing, sirens wailing. Two paramedics leapt out into the snow carrying equipment needed for the emergency, and immediately gained entry to the building. That was Shaw's cue. Amongst the chaos of professional paramedics and frantic, unaware security officers, Shaw slipped unchallenged into the building and entered the lift.

The lift stopped with a judder and the doors slid open. He stepped out and turned right, not really knowing what he was going to do when he got there. What he was sure about was, that tonight, he was getting his brother back, one way or another.

He approached Kimberly's front door. His driving determination to get her to talk quickly changed to that of caution, seeing the door ajar. He pushed the door open and waited. Nothing. No movement, no sound. He pulled the Stanley knife from his pocket and entered. He crept past the cabinet on his left and Kimberly's car keys that were sat on them, and peered into the main room, his back pressed tight against the wall. Apart from the obvious furniture, the room was empty. He waited a further moment, listening. He'd seen no sign of forced entry, so he figured somebody had to be home. He entered the main room, alert and vigilant, his eyes scanning from corner to corner. He cleared it and made his way over to the bedroom door, leading with his heel before rolling onto the ball of his foot. He crouched low and pressed his ear to the door. Nothing. He opened it. It was empty.

After checking under all the beds and in all the wardrobes in all the rooms, Shaw walked back through to the front door and closed it, happy the flat was unoccupied. His body begged for rest, to lie down on Kimberly's enormous soft bed and sleep. But his mind refused him that pleasure. Instead he headed for the kitchen and searched through the cupboards. He found half a packet of painkillers and a three-quarter bottle of vodka and took them into the bathroom. He placed the glass bottle on the toilet's cistern and emptied his pockets into the sink, filling the white basin with the remaining bandages and adhesive dressings he'd stolen from the lorry. He popped out four painkillers and swallowed them with a good guzzle of vodka. He pulled his arms from his coveralls and tied them around his waist, exposing his naked bruised chest and the blood stained patches on his shoulders. He removed the patches, using the mirror for guidance, and cleaned the wounds beneath, using the vodka for sterilisation.

Once the last wound in his leg was cleaned and dressed, Shaw

244

pulled the coveralls back up above his thighs and tied them around his waist. He walked through to the master bedroom and searched through Kimberly's wardrobes, looking for anything that belonged to Will: a T-shirt, a jumper, a pair of jeans. But all he could find were skimpy tops, short skirts and alluring lingerie. He dropped her clothes on the floor and made his way through to the spare room. On the bed were two teddies sitting upright on top of the pillow. One was a 'Help for Heroes' teddy and the other was dressed in military combats. He opened the cupboard, remembering from earlier that there were two stuffed black bags at the bottom. He ripped the top one open and pulled out its contents.

'Jackpot,' he said. He pulled what there was of his brother's clothes on to the bedroom floor and started sifting through them, looking for anything that would fit. Amongst the clothing, he found only one pair of denim jeans that were of any use. He pulled off the coveralls and slipped the jeans up over his naked buttocks. He then pulled the canvas white trainers onto his bare feet and fastened the laces. At least now he was combat ready. He ripped open the second bag and pulled its contents out onto the floor, recognising a grey T-shirt he'd worn once before.

Under the black bags in the wardrobe, a framed photograph in an open shoebox caught his eye. He bent down into the cupboard, the T-shirt still in his hand, and picked it up. The photograph was of a young blonde girl, possibly eight or nine years old, kneeling next to a new born baby lying on blue blanket. His memory worked overtime trying to remember where he'd seen the young girl's face before. It was a face he recognised, but not on her. Then he saw it. His heart stopped. In the shoebox was another framed photograph. This time the photograph was of Kimberly, but with blonde hair. Standing next to her, tall and proud, was a young man wearing No.2 service dress. Shaw stood frozen, looking down at the photograph, almost wanting to vomit. He suddenly felt dizzy and unsteady on his feet. His mouth and throat had gone dry. He gripped the top of the wardrobe and inhaled through his mouth, attempting to control his hunger for air.

'No,' he said, rubbing his eyes, 'it can't be.' Something about the whole experience had been reminding him of that awful day and, until now, he hadn't been able to understand why. He opened his eyes and looked down at the photograph. It was. There was no mistaking his child-like face. The face he'd last seen covered in oil and dust. The face he'd witness burn alive.

A sound at the front door froze his breathing solid. His hearing spiked. His senses tuned. He heard the sound of the tumblers turning within the lock, the creak of the door opening, and the sound of a male voice calling for Kimberly.

Thirty-Five

'Irreversible issues'

Through the gap, between the hinges and the doorframe, Shaw could see the man he recognised as Jonno walk into view, followed by the skinny male he knew as Roach.

'Kimberly. You in 'ere?' Jonno yelled, entering the lounge.

'I'll check the bedrooms,' Roach said.

Shaw pressed his back against the wall behind the door and pulled out the Stanley knife. He took a single deep breath and held it as Roach pushed the door open fully.

'Kimberly,' Roach said, briefly looking at the mess of clothing in the room. 'You in 'ere?'

Shaw remained still and silent, his heart thudding in his chest.

Roach closed the door slightly. 'I don't think she's 'ere, mate.'

Jonno returned from the master bedroom. 'Where the fuck is she then? Her clothes are all over the place.'

Shaw pulled on Will's T-shirt and opened the bedroom door, just enough for him to observe the two men talking in the lounge.

'You think Paul may have been already?' Roach said.

Jonno ran a hand over his receding hair. 'Fuck knows.' He pulled out his mobile phone and dialed her number.

Roach pulled a black revolver from the waist band of his skinny jeans and placed it on the cabinet beside the doorway. 'I'm going for a shit,' he said. 'Let me know if she answers.' He looked up and down the passage, as if unsure of where the toilet actually was. 'Knew I shouldn't have had that sauce on my kebab.'

'Well don't take all fucking night. We're supposed to be in Boro for two, don't forget.'

Once Roach had disappeared from view, Shaw turned back to Jonno, who was also out of his line of sight in the kitchen. Without any indecision, Shaw opened the bedroom door and stepped out, grabbing the firearm, and returned to the bedroom. He closed the door slightly again and re-positioned himself behind it. Before he'd even gripped its pistol grip, he knew the weapon. It was the black FN Barracuda he'd inspected in the church basement. He released the catch and swung open its cylinder, seeing the six brass rounds that were loaded. Quietly, he repositioned the cylinder and thumbed back the hammer.

Jonno filled a glass with tap water and stepped out of the kitchen. 'I've tried ringing…' Jonno allowed the sentence to trail off to a whisper, now that he was staring down the barrel of a .357 revolver. 'Shaw? What are you doing here?'

'Where's Michael?' Shaw said, his right arm locked out in front of him, the .357 heavy in his grasp.

Jonno swallowed, but otherwise remained silent.

'Fine, we'll do it your way. Put your gun on the bench and get over there.' Shaw swung the revolver towards the lounge. He knew Jonno would be carrying a firearm of some sorts. People like him couldn't bear the thought of someone like Roach carrying one and not him.

'I'm not carrying,' Jonno said, putting his hands on his head.

'Do I need to put a fucking bullet in you? Put your fucking gun on the bench and get over there.'

'Okay. Just stay calm.'

'Slowly.'

'Okay.' Jonno reached round his back and pulled out a stainless-steel handgun and placed it on the bench next to the kettle.

Shaw repositioned himself in the kitchen and awaited Roach's return, the sights of his revolver never leaving Jonno's chest.

'What have you done with Kimberly?' Jonno said.

Shaw picked up Jonno's handgun, recognising it as the Sig Sauer P226 he'd also inspected in the church basement. 'I haven't done anything with her,' he said, tucking it into the waist of his jeans. 'I was hoping she'd be here.'

'Someone's been here. The bathroom sink's full of used bandages.' Roach turned the corner into the lounge and froze when he saw Shaw.

Shaw swung the weapon towards Jonno. 'Get over there,' he said.

Like Jonno, Roach did as he was told. 'You're a fucking dead man.'

'Maybe, but not today,' Shaw said. 'Now get on your knees. Both of you. And keep your hands on your heads.' With his foot, Shaw moved the armchair that blocked his line of sight before kicking the coffee table to the side, increasing the space in the lounge. 'Get your arses off your ankles. Get your fucking arses up!'

The two men looked at him, eyes wide and unsure, kneeling

with their backs poker straight and hands on their heads, preventing any opportunity of a surprise attack. Jonno's large brown eyes held a wise weariness, whilst Roach's held only un-experienced anger.

'What now?' Jonno said.

'Now you tell me where my brother is.'

A confused look spread across Jonno's face. 'Should I know?'

'You telling me you don't?'

'I don't even know who your brother is.'

Shaw turned to Roach, aiming the revolver at his forehead.

Roach laughed. 'You think I'm afraid of you, army man?'

'You should be.'

'Well I'm not.'

Shaw switched the revolver back to Jonno. 'Call Michael. Tell him I want a word.'

Jonno stared down the weapon's dark barrel. 'Okay, just don't do anything stupid.' He reached into the inside pocket of his jacket and pulled out his mobile phone. Seconds later, the line was ringing.

'What is it?' Michael answered. 'Is Kimberly okay?'

'We've got a bit of a problem with that,' Jonno said.

Shaw could hear Michael speaking on the other end. 'What do you mean a problem? Is Kimberly okay or not?'

'Give it 'ere.' Shaw snatched the phone from him. 'No more sitting on the bench. Where's my fucking brother?'

'Shaw? I've been trying to get hold of you all night.'

'Tell me where my brother is or I'll kill these two.'

Jonno swallowed.

Michael paused a few moments. 'Why are you at Kimberly's?'

'No more questions, Michael. Just answers. Where's Will?'

'Put Jonno back on.'

'The game's changed. I know who you and Kimberly are. I want my brother and I want him back now. Whatever issue your family has with me, it has nothing to do with Will.'

Michael paused. 'I want to speak to Kimberly.'

'Fuck Kimberly! Where's Will?'

'Not until I speak to Kim.'

Shaw pulled the phone from his ear and stared at Roach. Another level had to be climbed, a level he wasn't sure he was willing to ascend to. 'Do you know where my brother is?' he said.

249

This time Roach's bravado failed, reading the stone-cold seriousness in Shaw's eyes. 'No. I—'

The gunshot echoed around the room and traveled down the line into Michael's ear. The recoil traveled up Shaw's arm and into his shoulder. Roach's head snapped back, crumpling him to the ground like a puppet with cut strings. Unable to speak, and partially deafened by the gunshot, Jonno twisted his torso and looked down at his colleague reeling on his side, cupping his left ear.

Shaw deadpanned Jonno as he spoke to Michael. 'I'll ask you again. Where's my brother?'

'Fuck you, Ryan. And fuck your dead brother.'

'What?' Shaw's world crumbled as the line went dead, his mind numb. He stared at Jonno, fighting back the surfacing tears and the urge to kill him and his friend. 'Give me a reason not to.'

Jonno said nothing.

Shaw pulled the trigger again, this time punching a round into Roach's thigh. Roach let go of his bleeding ear and grabbed his leg, screaming.

'Where's Michael?'

Jonno said nothing, his eyes wide.

'Have you ever been shot?' he asked him. 'Do you know what happens? It's not like in the movies where it just creates a simple hole you patch up later. Bullets can hit hard tissue like bone and bounce around inside. Bone chips can ricochet, causing even more injury. Nerves and ligaments can be severed, organs can be damaged, causing irreversible issues.' He looked at Roach who was turning a pasty white, blood oozing through his fingers. 'But that all depends on you not bleeding out. The next bullet I fire will be going in your fucking lung.'

Jonno looked at Roach and back to Shaw. 'Okay, okay. Shit.'

'Where is he?'

'He'll be in Middlesbrough in about half an hour.'

'What's he doing in Boro?'

Jonno kept his hands glued to his head as he spoke. 'The deal, he's there for the deal.'

'Whereabouts?'

Jonno glanced at the .357 in Shaw's hand. 'You watch that thing doesn't go off.'

Shaw raised the revolver, allowing Jonno to see down its smoking barrel. 'Whereabouts?'

Jonno swallowed. 'The old shunting yard. It's taking placing in the shunting yard.'

Shaw knew the place. He looked at his watch. 01:31. 'And that's all you've got?'

'That's all I know,' Jonno said. 'Honestly.'

'Okay. I believe you. Now take off your coat.'

Jonno pulled off his black leather jacket and handed it to him.

Shaw took it and struck him across the brow with the barrel of the revolver, stunning him. He then opened the cylinder and dropped the remaining four rounds and two empty cases onto the rug and threw the weapon onto the sofa. There was only one thing on his mind now, and that was to make sure Michael told him where his brother was. He grabbed Kimberly's car keys off the cabinet and left.

Thirty-Six

'Into the shadows'

Sanalp closed the passenger door on his silver Megane and placed the long black bag on the snow blanketed pavement beside him. He kept his profile low as he peered over the four-foot concrete wall and looked down into the huge shunting yard below. He looked east through his binoculars and scanned the yard, locating what would be his central axis: a black Mitsubishi Montero parked beside the two storey warehouse, where a fellow Turk, armed with a submachine-gun, could be seen waiting on its white rooftop. Parked between him and the Montero, at the Montero's rear, was a red Astra saloon. In the distance, beyond the warehouse, were hundreds of graffitied trailers, filling the far end of the yard. To his left of axis, he could see a collection of shipping containers, stacked as high as three, where another fellow Turk armed with a submachine-gun waited in the shadows. Sanalp's right of axis was large open ground, scarred with an intertwining collection of railway tracks and a small copse of trees.

Happy he had Abdullah's Montero in view, he took one last look around his immediate location and undone the straps on the carry bag. Inside was a stripped down 7.62 Dragunov SVD sniper rifle, along with enough rounds to drop a charging elephant. Within minutes, Sanalp had the Dragunov built and in position, watching the Northern entrance of the shunting yard. A distant pair of headlights, north of his location, caught his eye. He checked his watch. 01:54.

'Michael's cutting it fine,' he said in his native language, wiping away the moisture that had collected on the binocular's lenses. The car had stopped at the entrance to the yard, almost a kilometre away. He picked up the walkie-talkie. 'They're here.' He always preferred his native language. He found English so barbaric.

'Is Michael with them?' Abdullah asked.

'Can't say for certain. There's at least four of them, two are climbing out and entering on foot. Both are armed,' he said, seeing everything almost perfectly due to the interior light coming on as the car's doors were opened. 'Amateurs.'

'Track the foot soldiers and, when I give the word, take them out.'

'As you say.' He split the Dragunov's bipod and positioned it on the four-foot wall. He took a quick moment to observe the falling snow and

252

used it to calculate the wind's velocity and direction. Ten minutes later, the car set off again, continuing through the shunting yard towards Abdullah. 'The vehicle is now approaching your location,' he said, 'carrying three occupants. I repeat three occupants.'

'Confirmed,' Abdullah said.

*

Visibility in the shunting yard was almost perfect at this time of night, due to the snow covering the ground, reflecting the light from the erected lamps and headlights. Bomber drove the stolen Volvo saloon, courtesy of Picco, along the bumpy, potholed track, its wipers on minimum speed, wiping away the steady snow that fell from the half-mooned sky.

Michael looked at Picco and Bomber sitting in the front seats. 'As soon as we're handed the cash, we let them have it,' Michael said, stroking the Mossberg 590 shotgun that lay across his lap. 'No messing.'

'I still can't believe Jonno and Roach blew out,' Picco said.

'Me neither, but they did,' Michael said, figuring they were both now lying dead on Kimberly's carpet. 'We don't need them anyhow. We can still do it with five men.'

'And where's Shaw? I thought you wanted him here too?' Picco said, twisting round to face Michael.

'No idea. Cunt won't answer his phone. But like I said, we don't need them.'

Picco faced forward, not sure if he believed him or not.

The Volvo crossed over a collection of railway lines at the appropriate crossings and turned right towards the large two storey building.

'There they are,' Michael said, seeing the Montero's main beam dip repeatedly.

Bomber stopped the Volvo a dozen yards from the Montero, holding up a hand to shield his eyes from its blinding headlights. For several more moments, both parties remained motionless, waiting for the other to make the first move. Michael could feel his heart pounding, sweat drenching the shirt on his back.

Picco glanced at Bomber, the palm of his hand sweating around the Mac-10's pistol grip. 'What now?'

A door from the vehicle in front opened and closed. The silhouette of a figure stepped forward between the two vehicles, embracing the light.

Michael opened his door and climbed out into the falling

253

snow, leaving the shotgun on the rear seat. 'Kill the fucking headlights,' he said, shielding his eyes with his hands, trying to make out the silhouetted figure.

'Hello, Mikey,' the silhouette said.

Despite the blinding headlights, Michael's pupils grew wide with the realisation of whom he was addressing. 'Paul? What are you doing here?'

Picco swung the Volvo's passenger door open and stepped out, his Mac-10 in hand.

Abdullah reached forward in the Montero's passenger seat and picked the walkie-talkie up off the dashboard. 'Kill the foot soldiers,' he said in Turkish.

Two clicks of the pressel replied back to him.

He stepped out into the falling snow, accompanied by Latif who stepped out of the rear passenger door. 'You think you can fuck me over, leave me dead in this fuckin' shithole?'

Michael's plan fell apart within seconds. How did Abdullah know? And what was Paul doing here? He'd been betrayed. He glanced down at the Mossberg lying across the backseat.

'Kimberly tells me you're the man responsible for my uncles,' Paul said.

'Kimberly?' Michael echoed.

Paul nodded. 'Just before I blew her fucking slut brains out.'

A shot thundered throughout the yard, echoing off every surface, startling everyone but Abdullah.

*

Shaw raced Kimberly's MR2 down the A19 and onto the A66 into Teesside, following a minor road that paralleled the River Tees. The shunting yard was a familiar location from his youth, so finding it wasn't a problem. He'd spent many a night there drinking cheap cider and vandalising property in his teens after moving to Middlesbrough with his step-mother after his father's death.

He killed the MR2's headlights as soon as he knew he was on the final stretch of road, dropping the engine's revs to quieten his approach. He stopped a hundred metres plus of the large metal gate and reached up to disable the interior light.

From what he could remember of the shunting yard, there were at least a hundred and fifty yards of open grassland before he reached any possible cover. So speed would be of the essence. He glanced at his watch, 01:58, and pulled out the Sig, checking the firearm was made ready: nine in the magazine, one in the chamber. The steady snow and cold frosty air went unnoticed as he climbed out. He was focused, driven. He tucked the Sig into the waist of his jeans and attacked the eight-foot wooden fence that separated him from the yard. He gripped the top and held himself in position, peering over to get a look at the ground before committing himself. Except for the white snow and three large mounds of upturned earth, the open ground was pretty much how he remembered it. He dropped back down and repeated his run up, scaling the fence in one fluid movement. He landed on the other side with a squatted thump, groaning from the pain in his thigh and ribs, and snatched the Sig from his waistband. He held it out at arm's length and scanned the ground before him, listening for any sign of movement. In the distance, beyond several rows of trailers and a collection of high stacked shipping containers, Shaw saw the repeated dip of headlights.

He crossed the open ground fast, keeping his profile low, using the mounds of torn up earth as cover. The snow crunched beneath his trainers and stuck to the ankles of his jeans. Once he was in the shadow of the first row of trailers, Shaw dropped onto his hands and knees and crawled beneath the linking arms of two. The sound of a car door slamming travelled far in the still night, echoing off the large surfaces within the yard. He edged forward looking left and right, his breathing controlled, his adrenaline fine tuning his senses. Footsteps stopped him dead in his tracks. He ducked back beneath the linking arm to the safety of the shadows and focused his eyes in the direction of the approaching sound.

Stooped low in the moon's pale blue light appeared Fisher, dressed in a loaded assault vest and body armour. In his hands he noted the AKMS-F with folding stock he'd inspected a few days earlier.

He skulked back, deeper into the shadows and waited for him to pass, choosing to immobilise him silently. Fisher passed from left to right, close enough for him to hear the fear in his irregular breathing and see the terror in his untrained eyes.

Shaw edged forward out into the open, ready to strike the base of his skull with the Sig when the back of his dark woolly hat exploded, painting blood, brain and skull across the trailers and snow beside him. A delayed second later, the shot filled the yard. Shaw flinched and fell back onto his buttocks, stunned by the shot. He scrambled back into the shadows beneath the linking arms and scanned the area from where the shot could have come from. He figured it had to have come from his right, west of his location, where the viaduct bridged the shunting yard. He looked back to Fisher lying less than three feet from him, the back of his head wide open. His heart raced at the realisation of how close to death he'd actually been. If he'd shown himself only seconds earlier, it would have been his head resembling a crushed watermelon.

A burst of automatic gunfire, accompanied by the sound of men shouting, grabbed his attention. He cursed, knowing if Michael was to die, any chance of him locating his brother would die along with him. He looked up at the viaduct, giving it one quick scan before reaching out for Fisher's corpse. He dragged him back beneath the linking arms, his injured muscles burning under the strain of the dead man's weight. When he was sure he was safely out of the sniper's line of sight, Shaw pulled off his jacket and relieved Fisher of his AKMS-F, body armour, and two extra magazines.

*

Picco, charged on adrenalin, looked out at his elbows and filled the air with the noise of gunfire. 9mm rounds ripped into Paul Mallinson's chest, flailing his body and shredding his jacket. The converted mechanism of the submachine-gun allowed the complete discharge of the weapon's magazine. In the blink of an eye, all thirty of its rounds had peppered into Paul Mallinson and the Montero behind him, punching neat holes into its bodywork, windscreen, front grill and left headlight.

Simultaneously, Abdullah took cover in the driver's footwell, avoiding the hail of rounds, whilst Latif crouched low behind his passenger door, also evading death.

The Turk on the corrugated roof of the warehouse to Picco's left, rained down a barrage of automatic fire onto him and the Volvo, punching holes through the roof of the silver car and its windscreen. The 9mm rounds bit into his left shoulder, throat and body armour, spinning him to face the warehouse. Michael dropped low and took cover on the Volvo's rear seat, grabbing the Mossberg shotgun.

Latif took his cue and returned fire from the side of the Montero. His submachine-gun hammered its rounds through the passenger door window and into Picco's body armour, stray bullets hitting the windscreen and bonnet.

Bomber dropped low across the Volvo's gearstick and

watched Picco's body slump to the ground, blood flowing from the hole in his neck. He snatched the AK47 from the passenger footwell and jumped out, firing the assault rifle across the roof of the car. The heavy burst of 7.62 was more than enough to drop the Turk from the roof. As if choreographed, Bomber snapped to the right, unloading another brutal burst of fire, blowing large holes into Latif and the Montero. The remaining headlight exploded, killing its blinding glare, revealing the otherwise hidden Astra behind it.

Sensing the lull in fire, Michael opened the rear passenger door and leapt out, taking the Mossberg with him. He fell onto his hands and knees, feeling the wet gravel beneath the snow bite into his palms. Picco sat dead, slumped against the open doorway of the Volvo, blood spilling down the front of his chest. Past him, between the Volvo and the Montero, lay Paul Mallinson, his legs and arms spread wide, his chest a bloody mess. He scrambled to his feet and sprinted past the dead Turk that had fallen from the roof, taking cover down the side of the warehouse.

Bomber withdrew to the rear of the Volvo, flicking the magazine release catch and pulling off the empty magazine. He took cover just in time to feel rounds pound into the driver's side, puncturing the rear tyre. He flinched back, narrowly avoiding a bullet. Out the corner of his eye, the orange flash of a muzzle lit up the darkness that surrounded the shipping containers. With a fresh magazine loaded, Bomber returned fire.

*

Consumed in the shadows of the shipping containers, Musa fired his submachine-gun from the hip. The aimless rounds punched half-a-dozen holes into the side of the Volvo, puncturing its rear tyre, missing the man wielding an AK47 by only centimetres. As soon as the magazine was expended, he ducked back behind cover and pulled out a full one. Even though he was only seventeen years of age, Musa was no stranger to automatic weapons. Within seconds he had the empty replaced and the weapon cocked and ready. But just as he prepared to send another hail of fire into the English thieves, the sound of gunfire erupted from the other side of a container. He held his fire and chose to investigate. As far as he was aware, he should have been alone amongst the containers.

*

Shaw reached the first of the shipping containers and pressed his back against it. He snapped his head out and back in again, looking around its corner. Nothing. The route was clear. He jogged down the gap between the two stacked containers, the AKMS-F in hand. He followed what he thought to be the quickest route through the small container maze, stopping only when he reached its edge. Again, he snapped his head out and back in again, getting a quick look of the scene. Happy no one was aiming at him, he peered around the corner, melted snow cascading down into his beard. Approximately twenty-five yards to his front, across a set of railway tracks, was the two storey warehouse, its barred windows filthy with years of train pollution. In front of that was a silver Volvo, its windows and bodywork peppered with bullet holes, steam rising from its radiator. With the folding stock locked out in place and the AKMS-F in his shoulder, Shaw watched Bomber fire from behind the weak cover of the Volvo's driver's door, aiming his rage at the equally shot up Montero. Parked close to the rear of the Montero he saw an Astra, its three occupants now climbing out. He took a moment, taking in the battlefield, searching for any sign of Michael. Then he saw him, like a snail leaving a trail of slime. Michael exited the silver Volvo via the rear passenger door and sprinted away from him, taking cover down the side of the warehouse. To Shaw's right, the three men from the Astra, one of which he recognised as the hired muscle from the scrapyard toilets, now stood in the falling snow. He watched the one he recognised pull out a pump-action shotgun, whilst another fired a submachine-gun from the hip, spraying the area around the Volvo. The third man lit the raggy end of a Molotov cocktail.

Shaw couldn't believe what he was about to do next. He pulled the AKMS-F tight into his shoulder, ceased his breathing, and fired, giving Michael and Bomber the covering fire they required. His controlled burst of single fire came fast and accurate, hitting his intended targets with every shot. The first hit Mr Molotov in the chest, pushing him back against the side of the Astra, releasing the flaming bottle from his hand. Mr Submachine-gun took three rounds to the chest, dropping him to the white carpet at his feet. The flames from the smashed bottle raged free, engulfing the side of the car and the two dead bodies lying in its reach. The man he recognised fired two shots from his shotgun and took cover behind the boot of the now burning car.

From the rear of the Volvo, Bomber opened fire, striking the corner of the container with an aggressive killing burst. Shaw flinched back from the shots, losing his footing. The rounds pinged off the wall of the container, sparking as metal struck metal. He took a step back in an attempt to regain his balance, only to be struck in the left shoulder by a ricocheted round. Blood soaked into the sleeve of his T-shirt and ran down his arm, diluted by the melted snow. He fell back, landing in a puddle, his AKMS-F at his feet. The biting pain left his shoulder as quickly as it had arrived, snatched from him by the sound of approaching footsteps crunching through the snow. Before Shaw could reach for his rifle, a figure appeared from behind the corner of the container to his rear. The thin Turkish male, standing less than five feet from him, was young; almost half his age, with a thin dark moustache decorating his upper lip. In his hands he carried an MP5K submachine-gun.

Shaw rolled onto his hands and knees, knowing there was no time to reach for his weapon, and powered up into him, palming the muzzle of the submachine-gun to the left. The volley of automatic gunfire that flared from the weapon was deafening in the confines of the containers. He kept his head low and drove his shoulder into Musa's thighs, lifting him from the ground. He kept his momentum and charged forward, slamming the startled Turk into the metal wall of a blue container, forcing him to release his weapon. In one fluid movement, Shaw relaxed his grip on Musa's thighs, slid his palms down his legs, and pulled on his calves. Musa snapped down hard, slamming into the ground at Shaw's feet. As if on autopilot, Shaw reached for the Sig tucked in the back of his jeans and fired four shots at point blank range into Musa's heart.

*

Sanalp pressed his eye against the rubber of the telescopic sight and watched the Astra burst into flames. He was glad to be up on the viaduct, alone with his sniper rifle. It was chaos down in the yard with bullets being fired from all directions. At the far end of the containers, a man with distinctive ears caught his eye, the barrel of his automatic weapon flaring from his hip. Sanalp tracked him, his large frame dead in his sights. In the distance, and approaching fast, he could hear the light drone of an incoming helicopter. He continued to observe, regulating his breathing for the killing shot, watching as the man appeared to empty his entire magazine into a shotgun wielding male standing beside the burning vehicle. The snow was beginning to fall heavier now, reducing visibility, and as Sanalp adjusted his aim accordingly, the burning car exploded, sending a smoking fireball high into the air. He pulled back from the rubber cushion of his sight, blinded by the sudden increase in light. By the time he'd rebuilt his aim, the man had disappeared from view.

*

A loud explosion echoed throughout the shunting yard, followed by the sound of more gunfire. Shaw picked up the AKMS-F and hurried to the warehouse, choosing a different route through the containers, not wanting to risk more gunfire by breaking the same cover twice. He crouched low and peered round the final container. There he saw Bomber carry out a full reload and hammer another killing burst into the Montero, screaming insults and promises of death and pain. Then, like the snap of a twig, the back of his head exploded, throwing him back from the Volvo. A second later, the sound of the Dragunov filled the yard.

Shaw's eyes flashed up at the viaduct, identifying the sniper's lens as it caught the light from the burning vehicle. He fired a hail of rounds up at him, knowing he had twenty yards of open ground to cross before he reached the Volvo, and sprinted as fast as his injured legs would carry him. He came down hard and aggressive next to Bomber's lifeless corpse, pressing his back to the Volvo's rear bumper. He stole a moment and swapped his fitted magazine for a full one from Bomber's assault vest. Then he heard it, the low drone of a helicopter. He searched what he could see of the smoke and snow filled sky but saw nothing.

*

Within the same breath, Sanalp switched his target, turning from his last victim back to the man he'd been tracking earlier, who'd reappeared from behind the bellowing smoke of the burning vehicle. His cross hairs hovered over the man's head just as a barrage of rounds smashed into the concrete of the viaduct's wall. Shards of debris splashed up from the impact, forcing him to snatch his shot and miss his intended target. The Dragunov rocked back on its bipod, punching a 7.62mm round into Sherman's body armour.

*

Shaw took another deep breath and pumped his legs the final ten yards, following the same route Michael had taken. Once he was out of the sniper's line of fire, he slowed his pace, taking slow, deliberate steps. Large, plastic blue drums were stacked on pallets along the side of the building with empty pallets and scaffolding frames beside them. Up ahead were two loading bays, their platforms four feet from the ground. He pulled his AKMS-F tight into his shoulder as he passed

260

them, his eyes wide and alert. Blood trickled down his left arm and dripped from his bent elbow, occasionally landing on the thigh of his jeans. Past the roller shutters of the two loading bays stood an external metal staircase. Footprints in the step's snow lead up to the floor above and a fire exit door that had been left ajar. He crept up the wet staircase, his heart pounding a thousand beats per minute. The police helicopter whirled above him, its powerful search light lighting up the white ground as if it were midday. He crouched low on the steps and pinned his back to the railings.

A quick burst of gunfire came from the front of the warehouse, followed by screams in a language Shaw didn't understand, forcing the helicopter to bank away.

Not wanting to be caught in its searchlight the next time it came around, Shaw ran the remaining steps. He opened the door with his foot, noting the shotgun damaged handle and lock. He took a quick moment to compose himself before snapping his head out and back in again, grabbing a quick view of the room. The room was dark and cluttered with low walls separating individual work stations. He took another deep breath, knowing that this could be his last night of freedom, or even his last night full stop. He folded the stock on his AKMS-F and entered.

Thirty-Seven

'A bond of blood'

The room was dark, almost pitch black in places. At first glance it appeared to reach in as far as seventy yards with a twenty-yard width. Plasterboard walls standing four feet tall separated the numerous cubicles, notices and advertisements pinned to each one. Shaw noticed several family photographs in one booth, and an A4 picture of David Beckham in another. The long wall on his right consisted mainly of glass windows, except for two private offices situated in its centre.

The police helicopter's search light panned passed the large window on his right, its eerie white light momentarily illuminating the office.

He crouched low behind a cubical wall, more for concealment than cover. 'I know you're in here, Michael,' he said. 'All I want is Will.'

Blue and red lights flashed into the room, illuminating the walls and ceiling. The police had finally arrived, and Shaw knew it would only be a matter of time before the armed response team made an appearance.

'I don't believe for a second you've killed him. Not yet. Why would you? Where's the satisfaction in that?'

A volley of automatic gunfire filled the silence. Rounds hammered into and through the cubical wall beside his head and shoulders. Shredded paper and wood chipping rained down on him like thrown confetti. Shaw's belly hit the floor. The rounds whizzed above him as he scrambled out of the killing zone and behind the closest solid cover. The second the fire ceased, Shaw snapped his head out from behind the office photocopier and looked into the suspected area of fire. To his surprise, instead of Michael, he saw a Turkish male creeping in the darkness, a Mac-10 held out in front of him.

Their eyes met.

Shaw pulled back behind the photocopier as another burst of wildly aimed gunfire came his way. Rounds whizzed past him, snapping at the air, drilling through cubical walls and punching holes into the photocopier protecting him. He returned fire, firing an automatic burst from a kneeling position. Monitors, keyboards and cubical walls exploded as the rounds missed their intended target.

The helicopter droned above, filling the office with its search light. The Turk scanned the office floor for movement, his senses alive with the incredible high of cocaine. He laughed at the English man's futile attempts of killing him. There was no way he was going down tonight, by his hand or the police. He was invincible.

Shaw positioned himself under a desk and waited, listening to the Turk scream words in his native language, confident he would step into his line of fire at any second. He exhaled his breath and held it. Again, the search light filled the room, this time engulfing the creeping Turk. Shaw smiled as he squeezed the trigger, punching a single 7.62 round straight through the Turk's right temple.

He crept out from beneath the desk and scanned the room, the muzzle of the AKMS-F pointing everywhere his eyes did. From within the shadowy confines of an office on his right, Michael appeared, partially illuminated by the search light. Shaw turned to face him, snapping the AKMS-F up in his direction, but was too late. Michael's 12-gauge shotgun exploded, firing a nine pellet buckshot. The pellets, grouped together to form a deadly killing zone the size of a volleyball, ripped through the office blinds and window and hit Shaw with a glancing blow to the body armour of his right shoulder, carrying enough force to dislocate it and throw him back over a work desk, taking with him the desks utensils.

Startled by the sheer power of the weapons recoil, Michael missed the centre mass of his target. He shook away the throbbing ache in his right shoulder and pumped the weapon's action, loading another shell.

Shaw scrambled to his hands and feet, snatching the Sig that had fell from his jeans, as the cubicle wall exploded, splintered by another deafening blast of the Mossberg.

'Satisfaction?' Michael growled, pumping another round into the chamber. 'I won't be satisfied until I've ripped the lungs from your chest.' He scanned the shifting shadows of the room, red and blue lights splashing the walls and ceiling. He knew there was no way he was going to get out of this, the entire Cleveland police force must have been outside.

Shaw kept low as he crawled away from Michael, weaving through the cubicles. His right arm useless and painted with blood. Hidden from view, he rested his back against a cubicle wall and breathed, filling his lungs, attempting to dispel the throbbing in his right shoulder.

Michael fired again, splintering a cubical wall and pumped its action. 'Come on, Bootneck. Show me your face so I can blow it off.'

Shaw stood up, fully exposed, the Sig Sauer trained on the back of Michael's head. 'Where's my brother?'

Michael froze. 'But you're not even brothers. Not really.' He turned and faced Shaw who was now stood behind him, his pistol outstretched. 'You see we had a bond you could never understand: A bond of blood.'

'So all this was about revenge, revenge for something I had no power over?'

'No. This was about greed. Revenge just so happened to come into it.'

'Well it's over. The police are gonna burst in any second.' Shaw knew that when they did, Michael wouldn't go easy. He would be killed, taking Will's location along with him.

Michael said nothing.

The helicopter light panned the office once again, illuminating the dark corners of the room. Bathed in light, standing less than twenty yards from Michael, Shaw saw another Turk, his assault rifle aimed high.

'No!' Shaw snapped the Sig in Abdullah's direction and fired five rounds, dropping him with three.

Michael pulled his trigger, punching a nine-pellet buckshot into Shaw's left side.

Shaw dropped the pistol and crashed back against a cubical wall, cracking its plasterboard. He slumped to the floor, his left hand clasping the bleeding wound, his breathing sharp and fast.

Michael stepped towards him, the barrel of his Mossberg smoking. 'Over? It's not over until I've watched your brother burn alive. Just like you watched young Dinger.'

Blood seeped through Shaw's fingers as he applied pressure to the gunshot wound that had managed to slip beneath his body armour.

Michael pumped the action on the Mossberg and aimed it at Shaw's face. 'This isn't how Kimberly wanted it. She wanted you to witness Will's death. But somehow I don't think she'd disapprove.'

Shaw gazed into space, oblivious to the shotgun and his surroundings. The memory of Dinger burning alive before his very eyes flooded his mind, the dying rasps of his screams filling his ears. He knew the memory of that day would be his downfall, he just didn't think it would be like this. He closed his eyes, the comprehension that he was about to die surprisingly comforting. His only regret was that he didn't get to save his brother. *I'll apologise when I see him.* The pain drifted away, falling to the back of his mind. In the distance he could hear shouting, men screaming followed by a gunshot. But he didn't care, they sounded miles away.

Epilogue

'A silver watch'

DCI Slater ran from his car to the main entrance of the James Cook University Hospital, avoiding the rain as best he could. He made his way casually through the maze of corridors, knowing the route he was taking perfectly. He entered one of the several large lifts, sharing it with a male nurse dressed in scrubs and an elderly woman sitting in a wheelchair. The lift opened at his floor, allowing him to exit the lift first. He turned left, smiling at an attractive nurse as he made his way to the unit's reception desk.

The middle-aged female nurse looked up at him from behind her mountain of paperwork. 'Yes?'

'I'm here to see the patient in room seventy-six,' he said.

'If you could just sign the book then please.' She handed him a black biro and pointed at the area of the book he was to sign.

Slater signed. 'Where's the duty officer?'

The nurse looked back up at him, but before she could answer, the duty officer appeared, stirring the steaming contents of a plastic cup.

'Where did you get that?' Slater asked him.

The officer stopped and looked up at him, waiting for his telling off. 'The vending machine,' he said.

'Go get me one.'

The officer's eyes widened. 'Okay,' he said, turning back the way he'd come.

Slater gave the officer an unconcerned glare and entered the room. Apart from the beeps coming from the medical apparatus and the deafening ticks of the wall-mounted clock, the room was silent. The window blinds were pulled open, allowing the cloud filled sky to be seen from the hospital bed. There was no TV turned on and no music played. He stopped beside the bed, between the handcuffed patient and the window, and placed a silver watch on the bedside cabinet beside him.

'I thought you'd like this back,' he said. 'It was found on one of the dead bodies in the shunting yard. Figured it was yours.'

Shaw glanced at the watch and turned his gaze back to the window.

'Oh, and I thought you'd like to know, your brother's been found.'

265

For the first time since Slater entered the room, Shaw looked at him.

'One of Michael's boys was found alive, believe it or not. He's resting up in Sunderland's Royal at the moment. He's in a pretty bad way, but he'll live. Michael on the other hand is in intensive care with a punctured lung and looking at life, what with all the evidence Melanie acquired and Sherman's statement, not to mention everything Will can add.'

'How is Melanie?' Shaw groaned, struggling with the pain.

Slater turned from Shaw's eyes and gazed out the window. 'She's still in a coma.' He paused. 'I wanted you to know, I won't be looking at pressing you with any counts of murder.'

Shaw said nothing.

'I owe it to Melanie, if anything.'

'What about the evidence?'

Slater turned to face him. 'Evidence goes missing all the time. And it's not as if they can query Melanie's statements. Michael will get what's coming to him and that's all that matters to me.'

The news was good. Will was safe, and he was getting a free pass on murder charges, but it didn't change anything. He'd still lost his family. Melanie was still in a medically induced coma, and he was still heading back to prison. Just not for the rest of his life. 'What about you?' he said. 'Will you get what's coming to you?'

'Probably,' Slater said. 'One day.' He headed for the door and left.